Praise for *Hold Fast Through the Fire*

"Wagers's second NeoG novel serves up buffet-size portions of everything their fans have come to expect: dug-in friendships, action, impossible odds, and clever dialogue that always hits home. . . . Wagers's characterization plumbs incredible depths, particularly with street rat–turned–engineering chief Jenks, a brain with vicious fists. Wagers's fans should snap up this fun, thrilling latest."
—*Publishers Weekly* (starred review)

"Wagers's sharp prose highlights the fast action and dialogue they're known for, bringing to life this story of found family, talent, and hard punches."
—*Library Journal* (starred review)

"Although the storyline is powered by an impressively intricate plot that features mystery, intrigue, and nonstop action, it's the deeply developed characters and the dynamic relationships among them that fuel this narrative. Wagers creates a cast of characters that are not only authentic, but endearingly flawed. . . . Top-notch character-driven science fiction."
—*Kirkus Reviews* (starred review)

"This brilliant and entertaining installment in the NeoG universe is a great choice for readers looking for military drama, evocative writing, and espionage."
—*BookPage*

"*Hold Fast Through the Fire* is an ambitious, outstanding breath of fresh air in the military SF genre, and I would recommend it even to those who may not think of themselves as military SF fans."
—Chris Kluwe for *Lightspeed* magazine

"*Hold Fast Through the Fire* is an intense, exciting, and delightfully entertaining novel. I hope Wagers returns to this setting, and these characters, in the future, because I'd read many more books like this one."

—Liz Bourke for *Locus* magazine

Praise for *A Pale Light in the Black*

"Wagers kicks off the NeoG series with this fun, feel-good space opera. This effortlessly entertaining novel is sure to have readers coming back for the next installment."

—*Publishers Weekly*

"If Wagers didn't serve, they certainly got the skinny from somebody who lived it, and it shows. They spin a captivating sea story in space. As an ex–Coast Guardsman, I appreciate that what the crew lacks in gear, they make up for in heart. *Semper Paratus.*" —Nathan Lowell, creator of the Golden Age of the Solar Clipper series

"Wagers delivers a space adventure that's a found-family story that's an interstellar conspiracy story that's . . . it just keeps going! Fierce, rollicking, kind, intimate, and vast. If *The Long Way to a Small, Angry Planet* had more kickboxing matches and death-defying space rescues, this would be the book. Go NeoG!" —Max Gladstone, author of *Empress of Forever*

"Great characters and white-knuckle tension. Recommended."
—Gareth L. Powell, author of *Embers of War*

"Perfect for fans of Becky Chambers, *A Pale Light in the Black* is an energetic, unique military sci-fi with a found-family heart." —Emily Skrutskie, author of *Bonds of Brass*

HOLD

FAST

THROUGH

THE

FIRE

ALSO BY K. B. WAGERS

THE NeoG NOVELS
A Pale Light in the Black
Hold Fast Through the Fire

THE INDRANAN WAR TRILOGY
Behind the Throne
After the Crown
Beyond the Empire

THE FARIAN WAR TRILOGY
There Before the Chaos
Down Among the Dead
Out Past the Stars

HOLD FAST THROUGH THE
FIRE

A NeoG NOVEL

K. B. WAGERS

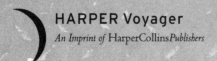
HARPER Voyager
An Imprint of HarperCollins Publishers

HOLD FAST THROUGH THE FIRE. Copyright © 2021 by Katy B. Wagers. Excerpt from A PALE LIGHT IN THE BLACK © 2021 by Katy B. Wagers. All rights reserved. Printed in the United States of America. No part of this book may be used or reproduced in any manner whatsoever without written permission except in the case of brief quotations embodied in critical articles and reviews. For information, address HarperCollins Publishers, 195 Broadway, New York, NY 10007.

HarperCollins books may be purchased for educational, business, or sales promotional use. For information, please email the Special Markets Department at SPsales@harpercollins.com.

Harper Voyager and design are trademarks of HarperCollins Publishers LLC.

A hardcover edition of this book was published in 2021 by Harper Voyager, an imprint of HarperCollins Publishers.

FIRST HARPER VOYAGER PAPERBACK EDITION PUBLISHED 2022.

Designed by Paula Russell Szafranski

Library of Congress Cataloging-in-Publication Data has been applied for.

ISBN 978-0-06-288782-5

22 23 24 25 26   LSC   10 9 8 7 6 5 4 3 2 1

To all those fighting for a better world

CAST OF CHARACTERS

ZUMA'S GHOST

Commander Nika Vagin (he/him)

Lieutenant Maxine Carmichael (she/her)

Ensign Nell "Sapphi" Zika (she/her)

Chief Petty Officer Altandai "Jenks" Khan
(she/her)

Petty Officer Third Class Uchida "Tamago" Tamashini
(they/them)

Spacer Chae Ho-ki (they/them)

Doge, ROVER (he/him)

DREAD TREASURE

Commander D'Arcy Montaglione (he/him)

Lieutenant Commander Steve Locke (he/him)

Warrant Officer Paul Huang (he/him)

Petty Officer First Class Ito Akane (she/her)

Petty Officer Second Class Aki Murphy (she/her)

Spacer Lupe Garcia (she/her)

FLUX CAPACITOR

Commander Vera Till (she/her)
Lieutenant Qiao Xin (she/her)
Ensign Saad Rahal (he/him)
Senior Chief Dao Mai Tien (she/her)
Petty Officer Third Class Atlas Nash (he/him)
Spacer Zavia Zolorist (she/her)

OTHER NeoG PERSONNEL

Commander Stephan Yevchenko (he/him)
Senior Chief Luis Armstrong (he/him)
Admiral Lee Hoboins (he/him)
Commander Lou Seve (she/her)
Commander Rosa Marie Martín Rivas (she/her)
Admiral Royko Chen (she/her)
Master Chief Ma Lěi (he/him)
Master Gunnery Sergeant Josh "Quickdraw" McGraw (he/him)* *CHN Marine joint duty tour*
Captain Kelly "Bliss" Evans (she/her)
Petty Officer Daly Hunter (he/him)
Captain Davi Kilini (she/her)
Commander Alice Trine (she/her)
Master Chief Paula Sox (she/her)
Commander Janelle Pham (she/her)
Ensign Inaya Gorelik (she/her)
Senior Chief Jen Davis (she/they)

SEAL TEAM ONE

Commodore Scott Carmichael (he/him)
Lieutenant Commander Ian Sebastian (they/them)
Lieutenant Tivo Parsikov (he/him)

Chief Petty Officer Adith Netra (she/her)
Petty Officer Second Class Diego Cano (he/they)
Spacer Emery Montauk (she/her)

OTHER CHN NAVY PERSONNEL

Captain Troika (she/her)
Commander Nebula Pach, MD (she/her)
Commander Laron Chau (he/him)

CIVILIANS

Pace McClellan (he/him)
Barnes Overton (they/them)
Monica Armstrong (she/her)
Gina Armstrong (she/her)
Elliot Armstrong (he/him)
Riz Armstrong (he/him)
Asabi Han (she/her)
Ernie "Sully" Sullivan (they/them)
Ria Carmichael (she/her)
Jeanie Bosco (she/her)
Senator Rubio Tieg (he/him)
Melanie Karenina (she/her)
Vincent Grant (he/him)
Julia Draven (she/her)
Chae Gun (he/him)
Michael Chae (he/him)
Abbott Bennington (she/her)
Blythe Hup (she/her)
Antilles Keba (she/her)
Jun Godfrey (they/them)
Dr. Trei Shaylan (she/her)
Senator Patricia Carmichael (she/they)

CONTENT WARNING

The following story contains moments of emotional manipulation in a relationship as well as discussion of suicidal ideation. Please proceed according to your comfort level.

HOLD

FAST

THROUGH

THE

FIRE

It is the mission of the Near-Earth Orbital Guard to ensure the safety and security of the Sol system and the space around any additional planets that human beings call home.

PREFACE

". . . and that, as they say, is that, folx. This is Pace McClellan and my faithful partner in crime, Barnes Overton, with TSN—The Sports Network. Thanks for tuning in with us over the last week. It was a wild one hundred and second Boarding Games that saw a whole lot of bloody noses and black eyes, near escapes and brilliant problem solving. There was heartache and triumph, not to mention a lot of really good fights! And in the end the Near-Earth Orbital Guard team, made up of *Zuma's Ghost* and *Honorable Intent*, decimated the competition for their second-ever win! It was a heck of a time, right, Barnes?"

"It was, Pace. Second win, and second in a row. The NeoG really went after it this year, while Navy went down hard, falling to a surprising third place behind the Marine contingent, who decided to come to play. Some of those black eyes were metaphorical, some not so much—I know the hit we're all thinking of was a hundred percent literal."

"It was, at that, Barnes. They're going to be talking about the black eye Carmichael gifted Parsikov during the semifinals for a good many years."

"Possibly because we'll keep showing the clip."

"True enough."

"Even though Carmichael lost this time around, that was payback for him knocking her out last year, Pace."

"And she wasn't the only one getting in her licks. Parsikov had to fight his way through nearly the entire contingent of NeoG fighters. After defeating Carmichael, he went up against Armstrong, and that was a hell of a fight."

"'Hell' being the operative word. We're lucky Parsikov is a good sport, because that's the kind of thing that normally causes deep-seated rivalries. But he seemed to take it all in stride."

"True enough, Barnes. I think he's resigned himself to the fact that he's not going to beat Jenks anytime soon."

"We're certainly happy to watch the attempts. Well, folx, if you're not ready to say goodbye to the Games just yet, stay tuned. We'll have plenty of wrap-up interviews and highlight reels in the next few days before we swing back to regular programming. For now, though, Pace and I are going to call it a day. We'll see you next year."

ONE

The music in the bar thumped up through the floor into the feet of Chief Petty Officer Altandai Khan. She danced, eyes closed and a smile on her mouth. The lower level of Drinking Games was packed with people celebrating the NeoG's victory.

Jenks was currently pleasantly buzzed and happily smashed between two handsome men. She didn't even care that she'd cried like a baby in front of everyone when Commander Rosa Martín had gotten on the fucking bar and announced her promotion to chief.

This was a perfect ending to a perfect day. She hummed and pulled Senior Chief Luis Armstrong in for a kiss.

"She's going to be this smug all night, isn't she?" Lieutenant Tivo Parsikov asked from behind her right shoulder, raising his voice to be heard over the music.

"That's Jenks," Luis replied to the Navy officer. "You get used to it."

"I kicked your ass." Jenks leaned her head back against Tivo's chest and grinned up at him. "He kicked your ass, even though he lost." She pointed her finger at Luis. "And my girl

Max kicked your ass even if she lost on points. So I get to be smug. If you ever manage to beat me and become the champion, *then* I will allow you to lord it over me for as long as it takes me to defeat you once again. Until then . . ."

"You're fucking insufferable." But Tivo smiled down at her when he said it, the humor carrying into his blue-gray eyes— one ringed with an impressive bruise, courtesy of Max. "I *am* going to beat you one of these days."

"It'll never happen, but you're cute when you try, so don't stop." She turned around and pressed against him, sighing when his hands tightened on her waist. "I want another drink and then I want you boys to take me to bed."

"That's the first sensible thing you've said in a while," Tivo murmured as he picked her up and kissed her.

"I am occasionally sensible. Don't tell anyone."

"THAT IS THE WEIRDEST TRIO."

Commander Nika Vagin blinked and looked away from the pair of women in the corner sitting with their heads close together. "Who is?"

"Your sister and her—" Commander Stephan Yevchenko gestured with a grin. "Whatever is going on there."

"I prefer not to think of my sister and her relationships, for obvious reasons." He slanted a glance in Jenks's direction, then sighed and glared at Stephan, ignoring the fact that the Intel officer's mouth was twitching into a rare full smile.

"You're enjoying giving me crap about my sister," Nika said.

"Well, that's now part of it, but I can also poke you about the fact that you've spent most of the night mooning over Carmichael if it makes you feel better."

That stung worse than the subject of his sister's relationships. Suspicious, he said, "Do you just enjoy seeing me miserable?"

"You know I don't. You also know you could fix this if you just went and talked to her," Stephan said.

"This is not a better topic than my sister." Nika took a drink of his beer.

He'd always been on good terms with Stephan, despite their rivalry in the sword ring, but the past year of working out of the Intelligence Division while he recovered had tipped things into a comfortable friendship. Enough that he could tease back in the hope it would deflect Stephan's laser focus away from the fact that Nika was, in fact, mooning over one Lieutenant Maxine Carmichael. "Let's try this one: How's *your* nonexistent love life going?"

"The same. Just how I like it." The handsome brunette picked up his own beer. "I enjoy my work, Nika, and I choose to devote my time to it. I haven't ever felt the need to be with someone, and if I did it wouldn't be fair to ask them to put up with my obsession."

"Don't you get lonely?" The question slipped out before Nika could stop it, and he only just managed not to glance Max's way again.

"I don't, but not every ace is like me, Nika. Remember that." Stephan chuckled. "For starters, I'm aromantic on top of it. I knew a long time ago I wasn't ever going to fall in love with someone. I have the NeoG. I have you all. That's enough for me. I like my quiet and I like having my own timetable without having to answer to anyone." Stephan drained his beer. "Speaking of, I've got a flight back to London to catch and an early morning meeting. Go talk to Max, Nik. Sitting here and staring at her is creepy."

"You're not my boss."

"I will be if you don't accept Hoboins's offer to go back to the Interceptors." Stephan patted Nika on the shoulder and tipped his head to the side. "But even without that, I'm also your friend. Go talk to her."

When he'd first met Max almost two years ago, Nika had

been on his way to Trappist and she'd been taking his place on *Zuma's Ghost*. Nika had left her a letter, mostly out of a sense of tradition, but also because he'd been intrigued by the quiet, uncertain lieutenant from the very first moment they'd met.

That one letter had turned into emails and then vid-coms, and when he'd been hurt in the explosion, Max's face had been the first thing he'd seen when he woke.

He'd been lost from that moment on. No, that was a lie. He'd been lost from the beginning. Nika had always picked his relationships with ease, knew himself well enough to know that he could fall hard and fast, but he loved the rush of it all. It was worth the pain of having to say goodbye when it was time to move on.

He glanced back at Jenks. By contrast, his little sister was so careful with her heart. She loved everyone, and in doing so loved no one. It was easier for it to be "fun and done," to steal her phrase.

There was something about Luis's quiet patience, though, and possibly Tivo's as well, that had slipped past her defenses. Even if the latter had come onto the scene only a year ago when Jenks had sparred—in the ring and out of it—with the Navy fighter, and Nika still wasn't sure if there was more to that part of the relationship beyond the sex.

He dragged that line of thought up short and sighed.

"You have issues, Vagin," he muttered. "Seriously." He looked to where Max sat with Rosa and sighed again. It seemed like Jenks's attitudes were changing. Maybe his should, too. Maybe it was time to put in the effort rather than walking away.

Everything had been going fine with Max, or so he'd thought, but a week before the Games she had stopped talking to him. Nika told himself it was because she was focused on winning and everything would be okay on the other side.

It wasn't.

He had a feeling if Maxine Carmichael was left to her own

devices, she'd let whatever was between them suffocate like a flame in a vacuum. Nika didn't want to live with himself if he let that happen before he found out whether she truly wanted this to be over or she was just unsure of what to do with her feelings.

Be honest, the voice in his brain whispered, *you don't want to lose her.*

He didn't. But he didn't want to lose her friendship more, and no matter what happened, he would walk away from the rest of it if that's what she wanted. So he made himself get up and move across the crowded bar.

"Hey."

Max's head snapped up at the sound of his voice and he recognized that familiar panicked look in her brown eyes.

"Nika! I was just leaving, you can have my seat." Rosa was up and out of her chair before Max could protest.

"Traitor," Max muttered at Rosa's back, and then she forced a smile onto her face. "Hey, Nika."

He considered making an excuse, letting her have her space—she was clearly uncomfortable with him around. However, something pushed him down into the space Rosa had abandoned. "I know this isn't the best time to do this, but maybe we should just get it all out in the air," he said, watching her. Max was looking down at the table instead of at him. "I need to give Admiral Hoboins an answer tomorrow and I would like your input on this, but if you won't talk to me, that's kind of difficult to do." It was part statement, part question.

"Nika. I don't want to tell you what to do with your life." She traced a finger over the tattoo of Pluto that now decorated her right forearm. Nika still couldn't believe his sister had been able to talk the reserved lieutenant into something so impulsive, but matching Pluto tattoos somehow seemed very like the two of them.

That friendship had shocked everyone—everyone but

Nika. Max and Jenks were as opposite as you could get, and yet it worked. Some of that had to be Jenks's gratitude for Max saving her life, but Nika was sure it was more than that.

Just like he was sure that what he and Max could have was more than . . . whatever they had right now. Which was why Max being on the defensive upset him so much.

I'm the one who should be afraid, he thought. *She's the smart one. The good officer. The better family. What have I got to offer her?*

"I'm not looking for you to tell me, but I do want to know how you feel about it all. It would change things for me to come back to *Zuma*." Now she lifted her head and the look of pain in her brown eyes sliced through him. "The NeoG doesn't have rules against relationships within the Interceptor teams, but I understand if that's too much for you."

Max rubbed a hand over her heart and took a deep breath before she spoke. "Nika, I value your friendship and I don't want to lose it. I have really enjoyed our time together. But with everything that's happening, I just thought it would be best—" She fumbled, the words failing her, and she squeezed her eyes shut. "I don't know what I'm doing. You know I'm terrible at this."

"Max, do you want to end this?"

The sob escaped before she slapped a hand to her mouth, and Nika pulled her into a hug when she leaned into him.

"I don't know. I don't know what to do. I'm sorry. I'm such a mess. This isn't fair to you at all." She was crying in public, which he knew she hated. Even more than his sister, if that was possible. Max couldn't get past the idea that had been hammered into her: Carmichaels did *not* cry in public.

"It's all right," he said, because he couldn't think of anything else to say.

"It's really not all right."

Nika pressed his cheek to the top of her head. "Max, I don't know what I want, either, as far as my career goes. I enjoyed working with Stephan, but the chance to be out there again is—"

"Nika! Did you make Max cry? We are supposed to be celebrating."

Great timing, Jenks.

Nika let go of Max and turned, surprised by the fury on his sister's face as Max covered her eyes with a hand.

"Jenks, not now," Nika pleaded.

"Damn right, now," she said.

He groaned and looked at Luis and Tivo standing behind his sister like a pair of hulking sentinels. "You two want to do something about this?" He was referring to his sister, but they didn't take it that way.

"Depends. Did you make Max cry?"

It was an interesting thing to see the frown on the Navy lieutenant's face and the slight narrowing of his eyes. Luis he could understand, but when had Parsikov become protective of Max?

When your sister did, idiot. Because Jenks has the gravitational pull of a black hole and everyone ends up in her orbit.

Maybe that's why he ended up with that shiner.

Nika could see it clear as daylight now. It was like Tivo to try to take it easy on Max in the cage—consciously or not—and end up with a fist in the face for his mistake.

Stephan's lessons have rubbed off on me.

Max peeked out from between her fingers. "Oh my god. He didn't, Tiv. I'm fine."

"All right." Tivo winked at Max, grabbed Jenks around the waist, and tossed her over his shoulder.

"But Max—"

"She's fine," Tivo said, and then her further shouts of protest were lost to the noise of the crowd. Luis gave Nika a nod and then followed the pair.

"Max." Nika brushed his fingers over the back of her hand and she reluctantly dropped it into her lap. "You want to go outside?" he asked. "Get some air?"

THEY SOMEHOW SLIPPED OUT OF DRINKING GAMES WITHOUT
being accosted by dozens of well-wishers, though Max found
herself caught between hoping and fearing someone would delay their path out into the cool night air. It had been bad enough
in public, but to discuss this in private . . . it might be too much.

And yet, she let him pull her along.

Nika had taken her right hand with his left—his real hand.
She hated that description, tried so hard not to use it, but she
also noticed that he didn't touch her much with his right.

She'd barely been able to tell the difference when he was
cupping her face. The skin on the prosthetic had been slightly
cooler, but it had flexed in time with the left.

*Be honest, Max, your thoughts weren't exactly focused on
assessing the differences anyway.*

That was the truth. She'd been too wound up, was still
wound up as they walked along the mostly deserted streets of
the Games village.

She'd fucked this up.

*You always do this. Try too hard and push people away.
When are you ever going to learn?* Her father's voice in her head
stung.

"Get out of your head, Max."

The order from Nika was gentle, accompanied by a tug of
her hand, and she looked at him. He was pointing across the
street, one blond eyebrow raised in question.

She nodded and followed him across to the park. "You're
good at this," she said as they settled onto a bench, picking up
a stray reddish leaf and spinning it between her fingers. "Dealing with me, that is."

"Max, I don't 'deal' with you. I—"

"Let me say this? Before I lose my nerve?" She could only
hold his gaze for a moment before looking back at the leaf. "I

spent the first part of my life being told what to do, what to think, how to act. My father, my mother, they—my input was not requested, and on the rare occasion I got up the courage to offer it, it was dismissed. That was the price of being a Car-michael."

It was surprisingly easy to say that now. To acknowledge who she was and where she'd come from. The Carmichaels were one of the most powerful families in existence, thanks in part to their control of LifeEx, the essential life-extending drug that provided humanity with protection as they explored the stars, but also because of their long-standing history of service to the Coalition of Human Nations government and the Navy.

A history Max had walked away from to go into the NeoG.

Nika nodded but stayed silent. She appreciated that from him. How he knew she was taking the long way around back to the conversation they'd left in the bar. He didn't push. Didn't tell her to get to the point.

Perhaps because of this, Max let herself lean into him, resting her head on his shoulder as she tried to untangle her own messy thoughts. "I don't trust easily, you know that."

"You seem to trust my sister well enough."

His tone was filled with humor and she laughed. "Jenks is pure. Oh god, do not tell her I said that."

It was Nika's turn to laugh, and Max buried her face into his chest for a moment.

"You know what I mean, though," she said. "Jenks doesn't pretend. She tells you if you fuck up. She tells you when you do things right. It's easy."

"I get that. You don't trust me?"

"I don't know you."

"Okay."

Max sat up and rubbed at her face. She was doing this wrong—again. The hurt Nika was trying to hide had bled through his words. "Emails and vid-coms aren't the same as real life, right? Rosa and I spent two years working together; I don't even think of her as Commander Martín, she's my friend. I am hoping it will be that way with you, too, even though—" She sighed. "I know that's not how this is supposed to work, and—"

"Max, is that you talking, or your parents?"

It was such a simple question, but it hit right at the heart of what she was feeling, like one of Jenks's side thrusts, and it stole Max's breath in much the same way. "I don't know," she said. Nika waited patiently for an answer while she floundered.

He'd been doing that—just listening to her—for over a year. Letting her find her feet, be herself. Always supportive and there for her. She was reasonably sure it wasn't the case with Nika, but in her old life, patience and kindness had always meant the other person was expecting something in return.

"I'm not being patient and kind because I'm expecting something from you. I do it because I care about you."

His slightly sharp reply made her realize she'd said that last thought out loud, and Max forced her eyes away from the leaf to look at him.

"I know. Or, at least, I know I *should* know that. I also know I've mangled this. I should have trusted you not to be the same as my parents and to actually be interested in my opinion. I don't know why I thought not talking to you at all would somehow make it easier. I'm sorry."

"Max." He smiled and slid his hand over her back, pulling her closer to his side. "I don't need an apology here. I just want to know what's going on in your head."

"I want to know what *you* want, Nika."

She could tell the response shocked him, and she continued before he could interrupt. "You have really enjoyed working with Intel. That's been clear enough from your letters and when you talk about it. I don't want you coming back to the

Interceptors just because you think it would make me happy. Does that make sense?"

"It does. And you're not wrong. I have enjoyed being attached to Intel, I just—as strange as it may sound, I miss being out there with all of you. I want to make this work. And I think we can, Max. If you want to try, I'm game. If you don't, I can either stay here or we can just be friends."

She felt her heart constrict, a quick beat of relief for a fear she hadn't even fully realized. This past year had meant a lot to her on so many levels, but the loss of this unexpected joy in her life would have hurt. It was, in the end, a surprisingly easy decision to make.

"Talk to Hoboins. You have a place with the Interceptors, Nika. You belong with us out in the black. I value you and I don't want to run just because that's what I've done in the past. I want to at least try," she said. That, she could say to him. "Just promise me we'll stay friends no matter what?"

"I promise." He leaned in, pressing his forehead to hers.

Max smiled back, hoping Nika didn't see the worry she couldn't quite seem to banish from the shadows. The worry that promises in her world were something so rarely kept, and all too often broken.

TLF DENIES RESPONSIBILITY FOR
ATTACK ON BLACKLAKE CIF

Trappist Associated Press

By Ittica Houston

The Trappist Liberation Front denied responsibility on Monday for an attack on the Near-Earth Orbital Guard Container Inspection Facility at BlackLake that occurred over the weekend. TLF leadership, speaking via an encrypted uplink, refuted any involvement in the attack, which injured four NeoG crewmembers and six civilians, and reiterated their position that they are committed to a peaceful settlement concerning the disputes over missing habitat supplies. Read More

NEOG TO DEPLOY NEW TASK FORCE
IN JOINT CHNN OPERATION

Press Release

Near-Earth Orbital Guard HQ

The Near-Earth Orbital Guard is deploying four Interceptor crews as part of a new joint task force to ensure safer trade routes around the Trappist and Jupiter Station junctions. Commander D'Arcy Montaglione will be in command of the NeoG force. Montaglione, a twenty-four-year veteran, will work with several Navy vessels in the area to combat the increase in smuggling activity over the last few years. Read More

TWO

Luis woke to the insistent ping of his DD chip and lay for a moment in the darkness of his bedroom in London before he carefully eased away from Jenks and out of the bed. She was, thankfully, curled up against Tivo, so it wasn't as difficult as it could have been.

He slipped from the room, snagging his stuff from the trail of clothes that littered the hall, finding his way by feel in the dim moonlight filtering through the curtains.

"Where are you going?" Tivo's quiet question slid out of the shadows and Luis glanced over his shoulder to see him carefully close the door to the bedroom.

"Someone tripped the dead drop."

"Were we expecting something?"

"No, and the signal is weird. I need to go check it."

Tivo frowned. "You need backup to do that."

"I'll be fine." Luis tipped his head at the doorway as he took a nondescript black hoodie from the hall closet. "If Dai wakes up and we're both gone, there will be a lot of questions we don't want to answer. Stay here and tell her I went for breakfast if she does wake up."

"She sleeps like a rock after the Games, you know that." Tivo crossed to him, his black hair disheveled from sleep. "If something happens to you, then I'm going to be the one left answering questions."

"Exactly."

"Asshole."

"Coward." Luis grinned. "Go back to bed. I won't be long."

"We're going to have to tell her about this soon." Tivo snorted a soft laugh at Luis's grimace, then grabbed him by the back of the head and kissed him. "Now who's a coward? Be careful."

"I will." Luis left the apartment, tugging the hood up over his hair, and headed down the stairs.

The London streets were empty save for a few scattered souls in the early morning hours. Luis ducked around the back of the corner grocery and climbed the fire escape, crossing the short distance to the drop over the network of green roofs dotted with gardens and chicken coops.

He stayed low as he reached the edge of the last rooftop, the grass muffling his footsteps, and spotted the body lying just a few meters away from the ransacked drop, partially obscured by the bushes in the park. A curse lodged itself in his throat.

He pulled up the encrypted Intel channel as he scanned the area for any sign that the assailants were hiding in the shadows.

LUIS: Stephan, we've got a body at drop 43.

STEPHAN: ID?

LUIS: Checking now.

STEPHAN: I'm on my way.

Luis lowered himself to the street and slid around the corner of the building. He didn't waste time castigating himself for not bringing a weapon—Stephan and Tivo would do it once they found out.

The streetlight between the building and the park was out and Luis used the same shadows the killers had to slip across the street and into the cover of the bushes.

He crouched, reaching a hand out to the man's neck. The weak pulse was a surprise, but even more so was the fact that the man managed to roll over. "Luis," he gasped.

"Fuck, Marty, just hang on." He pressed both hands to the dark sheen on the man's chest.

"They know about Carmichael. That she brought you information, that she's willing to testify."

"How?"

"No clue. You've got a leak in your op, man. Sort of like this hole in my chest." Marty coughed and spit blood onto the ground past Luis. "I'm—"

"Marty. Fuck." Luis started CPR, knowing it was a futile effort, but he didn't stop until Stephan showed up and pulled him off the dead man.

"MORNING, ADMIRAL."

Admiral Chen looked up from her desk with a smile. "Morning, Stephan, come in." The head of the NeoG waved him into her office. "You saw the news?"

"Yes." He nodded as he sat. "Hell of a way to wrap up the Boarding Games win."

"Do you think the TLF is lying?"

"I don't think it's that simple, ma'am," Stephan replied. "The TLF is more cohesive than the last few groups wanting Trappist independence, but that doesn't mean there aren't outliers who'd act on their own against their leadership's wishes. What I do know is I don't like the fact that Free Mars is making noises again and now we're also having to deal with this."

"I see. Do you think it's our target causing the problems?"

"On Mars and Trappist?" Stephan shook his head. "No, ma'am, no sign they've been operating back on Mars—Grant would get busted the second he landed there. And Trappist would be a bad idea, that's too much press for them. Shipments vanish before they hit the soil on Trappist, not out of our facilities. Not after the last incident. But if you're asking if I think this is a result of what they've been up to for the last several years? Then yes."

Admiral Chen heaved a sigh. "I was afraid you were going to say that, Commander. I spoke to Commander Montaglione this morning and he's not particularly happy about having to go public with his past. But he agrees it will help answer the questions flying around. You stick with the cover story of smugglers, though—if we do have a leak, I don't want Tieg to know we're closing in or how close we are to sorting out this Trappist situation into something everyone can live with. After that we'll deal with Mars."

"I hope you have a better plan for that than last time."

"We'll come up with something. The alternative is a war, and I won't have that."

"I understand. And Spacer Chae, their fathers?"

"Spacer Chae is going to *Zuma*. As is Nika Vagin, from what I hear. After what happened last night I'm admittedly relieved."

"Do you really think Tieg would allow Grant to go after a sitting senator?"

Chen made an uncertain noise. "Maybe not. But they may try to get her to recant her testimony. The family has the resources, so Senator Carmichael will have more protection than normal."

Stephan hated the sudden unease that gripped him. "But they might go after Max in retaliation instead?"

"Maybe. I think they're setting themselves up to do just that if need be. What I'm also thinking is between Chae and this new development, we're going to have to bring Nika in on the operation. I won't burden D'Arcy with this on top of what I've already asked of him, but I need eyes on the Interceptors, especially if things keep heating up with the habitats."

The admiral's dark green eyes unfocused for a moment as she mulled over the problem. "Let Tieg think he's got leverage in the NeoG and with the TLF—it will make that cocky bastard sloppy. I trust you to mitigate the potential damage, Stephan." She shook her head at his carefully blank look. "I know it's harsh, but short of putting all three of them into a safe house, there's little we can do; and if they're out of play, Tieg will just find someone we don't know about."

"The devil you know is still a devil, ma'am."

Admiral Chen smiled a second time. "Not in this case."

"No?"

"I think we've got one very scared kid with the bad luck to be in the wrong place at the wrong time and a pair of men who'll do anything to keep their child safe. But they came to us when they didn't have to, and I won't forget that gesture. I want to help Trappist if we can. They should be getting support from the CHN and we've dropped the ball hard on this. With all that in mind, I want you to tell Nika about Chae so he can keep an eye on them."

"How much do you want me to tell him?"

"Read him all the way in. He can't tell the others, but at least having him up to speed will help if things go sideways."

Stephan held in the curse, but judging from the raised eyebrow she knew he was thinking it. "All right," he said, because it was the only thing he could say. "I'll figure something out."

"You always do. Keep me in the loop, Commander."

"I always do that, too, ma'am."

"EVEN AFTER I SAY NO TO YOU," NIKA SAID TO STEPHAN LATER that day as he settled into a chair in Stephan's office, "you get your way after all."

The Intel commander grinned and spread his hands wide. "Working in Intelligence isn't just about getting info. It's about being smarter than everyone else. I feel like you should have realized that by now."

"I'll keep it in mind."

"Do that. In the meantime, we get the best of both worlds. You get to be an Interceptor and I get to keep you attached to Intel."

"You're excited about this."

"It's long past time we had a bigger presence in Trappist-1. The incident with LifeEx showed us that. The smuggling rings are more and more focused on the wild spaces. They have power out there we don't and that makes the higher-ups nervous. It's one of the big reasons Admiral Chen was able to get this task force greenlit."

Nika studied Stephan for a moment. He was nowhere close to getting in the man's head, but a year of working with him, plus many more of fighting with him in the ring, made it easier to notice the little things. "Is there something else going on?"

Stephan shrugged a shoulder. "Let's take a walk, I want to show you something."

Nika was intrigued. The commander was good at lying, had to be in his job, but would straight-up admit something sensitive in a way that surprised the hell out of Nika.

He'd learned early on that Stephan would do so to deflect attention from an even more important issue that he didn't want to talk about, and it worked about ninety-nine percent of the time.

This time Nika suspected that what he was about to hear was the important issue.

They headed down the hallway from Stephan's office and Nika's curiosity grew as he followed the man into a conference room. The faces around the table were all familiar, but it was the sight of Commodore Scott Carmichael and the rest of SEAL Team One that had him frowning. "What's this?"

"Take a seat," Stephan said. "You know everyone here, so I don't think introductions are in order." He leaned both hands on the table at the front of the room. "The task force is a cover, Nika. I'm about to tell you the reason behind it and you can't tell anyone else.

"Welcome to Project Tartarus."

THREE

"Jenks!"

The boys hit her the moment the door opened, and she scooped them both up. They were built like their father, tall and lanky, though at only nine years old neither had put on much muscle and she could lift them easily.

Plus it was fun to hear them laugh.

She'd been here five days and they were still greeting her like they hadn't seen her for a month when they came through the front door. It should have terrified her, how easy and comfortable it felt to be in Luis's apartment, to sleep in his bed, to have dinner with the kids every night.

But it doesn't.

"I have my first belt test next month! Can I show you my form?" That was from Riz, dark-haired and dark-eyed like his late mother; but all Jenks could see was Luis's face beaming back at her.

"I got a new book on twenty-first-century history," Elliot whispered. He was blond like his dad, but had the same dark eyes as his twin. "Do you want to see it?"

"All right, easy, both of you. You saw her this morning."

Luis laughed. "Go put your gear away and make sure your overnight bags are packed, your grandmas will be here soon."

There was a chorus of groans, but the boys trundled off to their room once Jenks set them down.

"They're going to miss you," Luis said, wrapping his arms around her and resting his cheek against the top of her head.

"Are you going to miss me?"

"Not in the slightest."

Jenks reached back and pinched him, laughing at his yelp of surprise and slipping out of his grip before he could retaliate. There was little room to maneuver in the tiny apartment and Jenks backed into the corner of the living room with her hands raised. "You're going to mess up my outfit."

"Should have thought about that, Dai."

"You started this," she said, and tried to scramble over the couch. He caught her by the ankle and she landed face-first in the cushions.

"Luis Oscar Armstrong, what are you doing?"

Jenks choked back her laughter as the grip on her ankle released. She rolled over, sliding off the couch onto the floor, and pouted up at Monica Armstrong. "He's being mean."

"I don't doubt it for a second," his mother replied with a smile on her full lips. "He's rumpled your gorgeous pants. Hello, darling. It's so lovely to see you and I'm sorry my hooligan of a son has no manners." She reached down and helped Jenks to her feet, wrapping her into a hug.

"It's fine. I'm used to it, and I know it wasn't through any fault of yours that he turned out this way." She hugged the woman back, still amazed more than a year later how easily Luis's family had welcomed her into the fold. How his mothers hugged and kissed her the same way they did Luis and the boys.

I am so fucked and I don't even care.

"It figures you'd take her side." Luis dodged his other mother's swing with a wicked grin.

Gina rolled her blue eyes and then leaned in to kiss Jenks on the cheek. "I'm so glad you got to stay a few days extra, it was lovely to catch up with you. Take care of yourself out there."

"I will, I promise."

"Riz! Elliot! Come say goodbye to Jenks," Gina called.

The boys spilled out of their room, faces glum, and Jenks was surprised by the answering twist of her heart.

"Do you have to go?"

She went down to a knee and hugged Elliot tight. "I do. I've got a job to do, just like your dad. We'll talk on the coms, though, okay?"

"Every day?"

"I can't promise that, especially when we're out on patrol, but we'll figure something out."

Riz hugged her tight and then stepped back. "Dad already thinks he's going to beat you in the prelims this time." Riz's announcement drew his father's attention and Jenks laughed.

"He always thinks that," she whispered. "We know he's wrong, though, don't we?"

"Do you see this, Mom? She's poisoned my own children against me."

Jenks grinned up at Luis. "Oh, hey there, Senior Chief, I didn't see you!"

He stared down at her, the laughter all too clear in his amber eyes even as he fought to keep his face straight. "Coming into my house and starting shit."

"Language!" Gina Armstrong thumped her son on the back of the head. "All right, boys. Grab your bags and let's get this show on the road."

"I'm not packed yet!" Riz yelped and ran for their room.

The adults all shared a look and Monica waved a hand. "You two go on. We'll lock up when we leave."

Luis snorted and called out. "Boys, I love you. Obey your grandmas or I'll tie you to the railing and let you hang there all night." He herded Jenks to the door as he spoke, grabbing his coat with one hand as he opened the door with the other.

"You in a hurry?" Jenks laughed, but it was lost as Luis backed her into the door he'd just closed and kissed her.

His mouth was hot against hers, the desperation barely in check as he lifted her onto her toes. It was always like this just before she left, both of them all too aware of the expanse of black that would be between them. Jenks fisted her hand in his shirt, tangling her tongue with his until her head spun. Then just as suddenly the kiss gentled and Luis pulled away.

"I lied," he murmured. "I am going to miss you."

"Of course you are." She sighed against his mouth, kissing him once more before she forced herself to stop, though with the door at her back there was nowhere to go and turning her head just gave him access to put his mouth on her throat, which he took full advantage of. "But we're in a rather public hallway and I was told there would be dinner."

"*Now* you care about public? You weren't complaining when we went out with Tivo the other day."

Tivo had spent two days with them before having to head back out with ST-1, and Jenks grinned at the memory. "Only because getting arrested with your family in the apartment behind us would be awkward, hooligan."

"Fair point."

He kissed her a third time until she was breathless and aching and seriously considering dragging him into the dark alley behind his building. "Dinner," she gasped, and managed to slip out of his arms, leaving him to follow her down the stairs.

The fall air was cool, the tang of ozone from the showers earlier landing heavy on her tongue as they walked hand in hand. It was clear now, though, and the streets of southwest London were moving in the late afternoon, filled with people going about their day.

It never failed to amaze her, just how fast humanity had

bounced back from the Collapse. Though the shadow of the greed and hatred that had caused it in the first place still clung in spots despite all the work humanity had done to fix it.

But it's getting better. You're helping it get better.

"We're not going to the bar?" she asked when Luis didn't slow to cross the street to his normal pub.

"No, I thought it'd be nice to have dinner somewhere we're not being interrupted every five minutes. I want you all to myself tonight." He smiled down at her and pointed. "Max put me on to a place up the street."

Jenks felt the first frisson of fear take hold as they continued walking. "This was a Max recommendation? Are you sure we can afford it?"

"Dai." Luis laughed. "First off, I'm paying, and yes, I can afford to buy you something more than a pint at the pub. Second, you're the one who's always after Max to take us to a fancy restaurant."

"Because *she* can afford it. And I don't really mean it anyway. I'm just giving her shit." Jenks swallowed when she spotted the crowd and the fancy sign ahead of them. "You should have warned me."

"I did."

"I'm not dressed up enough for this." There were glittering dresses and fancy suits lingering outside.

"You look amazing. Besides, you don't own a dress anyway." Luis squeezed her hand and slowed. "Hey, it really is okay."

Don't be a baby, Jenks.

She forced a smile that almost reached her eyes. "Okay. I promise not to start a bar fight."

"That's all I can ask," Luis said, leaning down and kissing her. Jenks quashed the sudden urge to beg him to just turn around and go back to the bar with all the familiar faces and tell her what on earth was going on. "I mean, at least wait until after dinner. Though Max might yell at both of us. The owner's a friend of the family."

"Of course they are."

Jenks smoothed a hand down her brightly colored pants, really the fanciest thing she owned. They'd been a silly impulse purchase on leave with Sapphi and Tamago. The blue thread shifted and changed in the light, making it look like the phoenixes were flying with every step she took, and she'd been a little mesmerized at the store.

But she'd never had an occasion to wear them before. Mostly she just pulled them out of her trunk and stared at them.

Which was why it had been a surprise for Max to hand them over, along with a soft cream-colored tank top that Jenks damn well knew she didn't own, when the LT had come to say goodbye before heading back to Jupiter with the rest of the crew after the Games.

She composed a message as Luis opened the door of the restaurant.

JENKS: You set me up.

MAX: Maybe. Stop messaging me and enjoy dinner. ;)

"I have a reservation for two, last name is Armstrong."

The man at the desk greeted them brightly. "Senior Chief Armstrong, it's a pleasure to have you." He looked at Jenks. "Chief Khan, congratulations on your promotion."

"I—"

"If you'll follow me."

Jenks wasn't sure if it was her nerves rubbing off on him, but Luis seemed equally tense as they followed the man to a quiet, secluded alcove, their table tucked behind an impressive barrier of live plants.

"I hope you enjoy your dinner. Francis will be with you shortly." The man gave them a little bow and left.

There was a fancy word for his job, Jenks knew, but she couldn't pull it up in her scrambled brain. The silence settled between them, broken only when they ordered food.

She tolerated it for as long as she could, then took a swig of her beer (served in a kind of glass she'd never seen beer served in before—so thin she thought she'd break it just by looking at it funny) and set it down. "Luis, what's going on?"

"I wanted to talk to you about something," he said. "I'm just not sure it's the right time for it."

"You're not going to ask me to marry you, are you?" Jenks grimaced. "Sorry, that sounded shitty. I—"

"Dai, stop talking." Luis laughed. "No, I think we've settled into something really good here. And maybe we'll want to change that later, yeah? But I love you and right now you promised me tomorrow. I don't need more than that."

"Okay." She took a deep breath. "Then what's going on?"

"I have been thinking a lot about the future. About me and the boys and what living on Earth has meant for us. But also what you said a while ago about getting off-planet and all the things you get to see. I want that for them."

Luis fell into silence and rubbed at his cheek. Jenks forced herself to keep her mouth shut as he obviously tried to think of the right words to say.

"You know about the new task force you're going to be on."

"I did pay attention to the briefing before we left for the Games," she replied.

"Good. Well, Intel is also going to open an office on Trappist-1d, where the main NeoG base is in Amanave. Admiral Chen has offered Stephan the opportunity to head it up and he can pick his team. I was at the top of his list." He smiled. "Not really a surprise, considering how long we've worked together."

"You're going to Trappist?" Her brain swung from the fear of commitment to the opposite direction and her chest felt like she'd just been expelled out into the black. "Oh god. Are you breaking up with me?"

Luis closed his eyes, visibly struggling to keep his composure. "Dai, breathe. No, I'm not breaking up with you. I love you—I just told you that. Can you focus on something that's not you for two seconds?"

It was so rare for him to call her out that Jenks blinked at Luis as she snapped her mouth shut. "I'm sorry. Go on."

"Stephan's up for the challenge and honestly, so am I. I talked it over with my moms and the boys and they're on board for an adventure."

"Okay, so it's a done deal." Jenks shoved down on the part of her brain that was screaming about distance and how the last time she'd sent someone she loved to Trappist they'd gotten hurt. She forced a smile. "That's awesome. I'm really happy for you."

He raised an eyebrow at her.

"I am," she repeated. "There's stuff in my head, but you just said it's not about me so it's my stuff to deal with and I'm really trying to get better at it so I'm not going to dump it all on you in the middle of this restaurant."

"Dai—"

God damn it, she was going to cry. Jenks slid off her seat with a curse. "I'm going to the bathroom."

Breathe in. Breathe out.

"Dai—"

She didn't wait to hear what he had to say.

The bathroom was as fancy as the rest of the fucking place and Jenks had to choke down the sob that tried to slip out.

"What am I freaking out about here?" she murmured to her reflection. "It's not like he's actually going to go to Trappist and die. You're going to be in Trappist just as much as at Jupiter Station, if the task force briefing was correct. What is your issue?"

You know what it is. You care about people and then they leave you. Every time. Without fail. Nika did it. Rosa and Ma are doing it.

Nobody actually wants to stick around for you. Luis won't, either.

Jenks couldn't stop the gasp as the words hit her like a well-placed kick and the tears slipped free.

"You okay, honey?"

Jenks jerked at the hand on hers and tears scattered as she blinked them away. "Fuck me. I'm sorry." She blinked again at the gorgeous trans woman in front of her, not quite sure she was seeing who she was seeing. "You're Asabi Han."

"I am. And at the risk of giving you a second heart attack, you're Jenks and I'm a big fan." Asabi extended her hand with a brilliant smile that glowed against her dark skin. "I did not think I would be telling you that in a bathroom, though."

Jenks laughed and took her hand. Asabi was, of course, taller than Jenks, with long limbs and a short halo of tight black curls on her head. Her gold dress draped in all the right places.

Down, girl. That's super inappropriate and this is really *not the time.*

"Now that that's out of the way . . ." Asabi pressed her other hand to the back of Jenks's rather than letting go; Jenks had to fight to keep her heart beating at a normal tempo. "Are you okay? You obviously don't need my somewhat inept help with kicking someone's ass, but I'm very good at causing a scene." She beamed.

"You probably don't want to listen to my issues."

"Nonsense." Asabi let go of Jenks and waved a hand in the air. "Bathrooms have been sacred spaces for telling strangers our troubles since time immemorial."

Jenks couldn't stop the laugh that bubbled up, and the tight feeling in her chest eased. "You're not wrong about that. I am not very good at change," she admitted, wiping the tears off her face. She blew out a breath. "And very good at imagining worst-case scenarios. I can't really go into specifics," she said with an apologetic shrug. Bathroom confessions were one thing, operational security was another.

"Oh, no worries. And tell me about it." The actress leaned against the counter. "You know those worst-case fears never come true, though, and sometimes the change leads to the best of things." She glanced at the door, a fond expression appearing on her face. "I met my girlfriend because I ended up in London through a series of unfortunate events."

"Is it creepy if I admit that I read about it?" Jenks asked. She was relieved when Asabi laughed.

"Not at all. My life is, mostly, an open book. You get used to it. Anyway, I just want to tell you this: it's going to work itself out, whatever it is."

"I'm slowly starting to believe that." Jenks looked in the mirror and wiped the remaining tearstains off her face. "I should probably get back out there before he thinks I ran off."

"At the risk of being weird, would you mind terribly taking a picture with me?" Asabi asked, and pointed at the cluster of plants in the corner. "I think if we do it over there it won't look quite so much like I waylaid you in a bathroom for a selfie."

"Only if I get a copy. Otherwise no one will believe me."

"Absolutely. I'll probably put it up on the SocMed, if that's okay."

Eight photos, a genuine compliment on her pants, and a flashing notification in the corner of her DD later, Jenks went back to the table in a bit of a daze. Their food was already served, but Luis wasn't eating and Jenks felt a twist of guilt as she slid back into her seat. "I'm sorry."

"Not gonna lie, I sort of thought you had taken off."

"I mean, I ran into Asabi Han in the bathroom and may have thought about it? Not to get away from you, but to be with her, obviously, though I suspect her girlfriend would have objected."

He whistled low and laughed. "Well, I'm relieved that didn't happen."

"You should be. She's apparently a big fan of mine." Jenks reached across the table for his hand. "I'm sorry I freaked a bit. It's just that thing about people leaving me and—well, you know." She sighed.

"It's okay," Luis said softly. "I know the timing is kind of shit. I think maybe I should have done this at the apartment."

"No, you're fine," she insisted. "It's not that much different than now, right? We'll still see each other. It's fine. I'll deal with it."

"You want to hear what else I was going to say before you ran off?" he asked.

Jenks knew he was teasing her, so she stepped hard on the panic that tried to surge back up and stuck her tongue out. "Go on."

"Stephan also gets to request a few Interceptor crews for permanent Trappist detail. A detail that would be specifically attached to Intel. We're kind of hoping that *Zuma* will be up for the move. This task force focused on smuggling is the first step."

"Wait, you—" The knot that had been slowly tightening itself again in her chest released with such force that Jenks couldn't stop her loud exhale. "You want me to move to Trappist?"

"*Zuma's Ghost,* but yeah. With Nika back—"

"Nika's back? Why the hell am I just hearing that now, from you?"

"Dai, you're adorable when you shift from panic to sadness to fury, but I need you to please—*please*—just listen. First, I didn't know you didn't know. But, to be fair, you've been here, and Stephan just got the official refusal from him about the job he'd offered. I don't know why he didn't tell you himself yet, but yes, Nika's taking Admiral Hoboins up on the request to come back to Jupiter and head up *Zuma* when Rosa leaves."

Luis tapped on the table with his free hand. "Anyway, Nika worked with us for a year and knows the ropes. And Max is smart as a whip and would have ended up in Intel if she hadn't been so focused on the Interceptors."

"And you need some muscle."

"Don't do that." Luis sobered.

"Do what?"

"Sell yourself short as just 'some muscle.' You're amazingly competent at everything you choose to do and I've never known anyone who's as good at piecing things together out of thin air as you when you really get focused on something. Rosa put together a hell of a crew, and the rest of the team is also well suited to the work we plan to do out there. We're hoping the other three teams will work out, but we want to see how you all mesh together on the task force first. The actual move to Trappist probably won't happen until after the prelims."

He paused, and her brain was scrambling to keep up. "Can I ask a question?"

"Yes," he said, laughing. "I'm done."

"So . . . we'd be working together?" She felt Luis's fingers tighten around hers.

"A good chunk of the time. Not every day, though. I promise you won't see my face so much that you get tired of it."

"I'm reasonably sure that's not something that will happen."

He grinned at her, a bright flash of a smile that lit up something inside her, and Jenks leaned over. "I love you," she murmured, and cupped his face, kissing him. "I'd say let's go back to your apartment and I'll show you how much, but Max will kill us both if we don't eat this dinner first."

"Fair enough." Luis wrapped his arm around her shoulder and pressed a kiss to her temple. "I love you, Dai. Today and tomorrow and always."

FOUR

". . . the banana in my split. Yoooooooou!" The off-key sing-ing turned into a piercing shriek and Max swallowed back the laughter that threatened when the man in front of her groaned. Jenks actually had a lovely singing voice, but when she chose to she could make it sound like someone scraping paint off a freighter hull.

"This is cruel and unusual punishment, Carmichael. Make her stop."

Max pushed the drunken prisoner ahead of her down the hallway toward Jupiter Station's brig. "She warned you, Riggs. I'd think the threat of Jenks serenading you would be an added reason not to drink and fly, but that's on you. Hey, Pablo, one for detox."

"Riggs again?"

"Yeah, D and F. He was piloting his shuttle outside the station." She leaned in, sniffed, and winced. "And as you can smell . . . he couldn't be bothered with an anti-inebriator."

"Those things will rot your brain," Riggs said. Or probably said; it was difficult to tell through his slurring.

"Drinking and flying rots your brain, you ass." Jenks

slipped around Max and for a moment the lieutenant thought Jenks's temper had gotten the better of her. But instead of slapping Riggs in the back of the head, she reached up and grabbed his face, tugging him down to her level. "I get it, man, you're hurting. But flying yourself into an asteroid or hurting someone else isn't going to bring your wife back, and I can't keep bailing you out of trouble. You promised, Riggs. You said you'd clean up your act. You lied to me. Do you know how *mad* I get when people lie to me?"

Max watched as Riggs's face crumpled. It was a tough call as to who was more surprised—her or Jenks—when he started crying.

"Ah, shit," Jenks muttered, catching the man when he fell into her. "Riggs, it's okay." She braced herself, somehow holding up all 120 kilos of sobbing man by herself until Max could get under an arm and take some of the weight. "Listen, buddy, go sleep it off and I'll see you in therapy next week, all right?"

"You're too good for this world, Jenks."

"Stop flying drunk, asshole."

Max handed Riggs off to Pablo and let the larger Neo maneuver the man toward the holding cell bunks. "Nice going, Chief."

"'Chief.'" Jenks laughed. "That still sounds fucking weird and I keep looking around for Ma when you say it."

"It's just as weird for us to say it, trust me." Max nodded to the guards at the hatch of the brig as she stepped through into the busy hallway. "Jenks—are you always going to deflect compliments? Or will you just say 'thank you' one of these days?"

"And now you *sound* like Ma." She paused for a second. "I miss him." Jenks's confession was almost too low to hear over the din of the crowd.

Max glanced at her friend. "Me too."

The retirement of Master Chief Ma Lěi hadn't been a surprise, but his absence spelled the beginning of the end for their two-time Boarding Games championship team. And, more important, it felt like the dissolution of their family. Rosa had left yesterday to take up her new post at the academy. Nika and their newbie spacer would be here in just a few days.

And in a few short months they'd be packing everything up and heading to Trappist-1d.

Change happens, Max. You can't fight it.

"We're gonna be fine," she said, as much to convince herself as Jenks.

Jenks predictably deflected again and Max resisted the urge to sigh out loud at her friend's next words. "I like winning, Max. I don't want to go back to losing."

Because she could hear the pitiful whine in Jenks's voice, Max let her shift the conversation to the Games. "You never know. Maybe we'll continue our streak."

"With a wet-behind-the-ears noob and my brother?" Jenks snapped her mouth shut and then muttered a curse. "That sounded shitty, even for me."

"I'm going to let it slide because I know what you meant," Max said. "But don't say it again, Jenks." She saw Jenks's lips twitch and the chief petty officer slanted a look in her direction. "What?"

"Calling me out on my shit twice in as many minutes. You've grown into this officer thing, LT. I'm proud of you."

Max laughed. "Well, thank god for that. I expect to see the same growth from you, being the senior NCO around here."

"You know expectations lead to disappointment." Jenks was grinning, but Max spotted the flash of worry in her eyes and stopped at the entrance to the zero-g tube with one hand on the rail.

"What is it?"

"What if I *do* fuck this up?" Jenks whispered. "You know I'm prickly and rude and shit. What if I keep violating rules or break our newbie, and do I really have to give up bar fights for good—"

"Chief Petty Officer Khan, you know how to do your job."

Max smiled as her words had the intended effect of shaking Jenks out of the spiral she'd started on, and her friend automatically stood straighter at the sound of her rank. "So I'm not worried about that. And you're not going to break our new spacer. For one, you have more sense than that. For two, I won't let you. As for the bar fights, can we keep them to a minimum?" She tapped her fist to her heart. "Got your back."

The worry vanished from Jenks's face as she tapped her own heart and swung her fist out, hitting it on the back of Max's before grabbing her by the forearm and pulling her down so she could press her forehead to Max's. "I've got yours."

JENKS LAY ON THE FLOOR AT THE EDGE OF THE SPARRING mats, her head pillowed on Tamago's stomach as she split her attention between the fight going on and the three-way chat with Luis and Tivo:

> *JENKS:* Why are both of you so far away? I need someone to save me from this slaughter I'm watching.

> *LUIS:* What's going on?

> *JENKS:* Trying to teach Sapphi how to fight.

> *TIVO:* *whistles* For the cage match? No offense, Jenks, but she's not going to last long if you're thinking of putting her in Ma's slot.

> *JENKS:* I know. But until I get a look at our new spacer this is the plan.

There was a thud, a curse, and Jenks sighed. "Sapphi, if you don't watch the captain's feet she's going to dump you on your ass again."

The ensign's grumble of protest mixed with Captain Evans's laughter. Jenks tipped her head back to look at Tamago.

"You knew this would be a challenge when you started it," Tamago said. "Sapphi's hell on the computers. Getting her to punch someone when her life isn't on the line is a lot harder."

"I know." Jenks rolled onto her side and got to her feet.

"This is not going to work," Sapphi said. The ensign's shoulders were slumped and Jenks reached out to slap her in the back of the head, but restrained herself. *Need to start working on my anger sometime—might as well be now.* She took a deep breath.

"Two years ago we thought it wasn't going to work, and look what happened. Stop feeling sorry for yourself." She pointed at the captain of *Burden of Proof*. "Bliss, stop going easy on her."

Kelly grinned and lifted her hands in surrender. "Whatever you say, Chief. Sorry about this, Sapphi."

"Fight or die, Saph," Jenks said, and headed back to Tamago with a grin.

"She's going to give you another virus," Tamago said, watching as Sapphi yelped and tried to defend herself against Captain Evans's renewed—and invigorated—assault.

Jenks laughed, thinking about the last time, when everything had looked blue for a week until Rosa had made Sapphi undo whatever weird filter she'd put on Jenks's DD. "It's worth it. She's been slacking anyway, too comfortable with her spot. She needs to step up some."

"Whew! Listen to you, Chief."

Jenks reached over and socked Tamago. *Okay—still a work in progress. This time it's warranted, though.* "Don't call me that."

"She's not the only one who has to step up."

Jenks groaned, rubbing a hand at her purple hair in frustration. "Whose bright idea was it to promote me anyway?"

"Pretty sure that was the NeoG, which means it was your fault to begin with. Stop being so good at your job."

"Punished for succeeding. Figures." Jenks winced as Sapphi got swept and hit the mat hard. "You should probably go make sure she's okay." Tamago walked over, and Jenks couldn't help muttering to herself, "God, I hope our new spacer is better at fighting, or the Games will be over before they start."

"HOW ARE YOU DOING?"

Nika looked away from the spread of faces and data on the wall as Scott Carmichael joined him. "It's a lot."

"It is."

"How long have you been involved?"

"A little over two years. When my sister—Patricia—contacted the NeoG with her concerns, Admiral Chen decided that Navy also needed to be involved to keep us from tripping over each other's feet." The quick grin reminded Nika of Max.

"But I haven't seen you around."

"You would have asked questions if you had. We went out of our way to not run into you." Scott leaned against the wall, arms crossed over his chest. "Comes with the territory."

Nika looked across the room to where Tivo and Luis were having a semiheated discussion, their heads pressed together as they examined something on one of the screens on the long wall of the conference center. "You've been involved since before the Games two years ago?"

Scott frowned at the seemingly random question, but then he saw who Nika was looking at and it clicked. "Ah. Yeah. They can't say anything to your sister without raising a lot of questions."

"There's going to be more when she finds out. Questions or, more likely, punches."

"It's Stephan's problem," Scott replied, tipping his head.

"She's not going to find out," the head of Intel said, joining them, "because no one is going to tell her. Right?"

Nika turned around to face Stephan. "You want me to lie to my sister."

"Of course. You're going to be lying to everyone who's not involved in this op, Nika," Stephan said. "If I'd thought it was an issue, I wouldn't have brought you in. But since we're on the subject, this is to keep your team—your sister and Max included—safe. The people we're after have killed plenty and they won't hesitate to kill more in service to their greed. You have a chance to do some good here."

Nika glanced back at the wall of information he'd only started to process, but what he'd seen showed him the rot went all the way to the Coalition of Human Nations government. A sitting senator was using his power and influence to steal supplies meant for the Trappist habitats and his people were bent on starting a war between the military and the separatists on Mars as a way to distract from their operation. It was a vicious and bloody plan, and the NeoG would be on the front lines of the conflict when it exploded.

He took a deep breath. "I'm in. What do you want me to do?"

The slight blond woman paced along the wide bank of windows, the stunning ocean view in front of her forgotten. She turned at the sound of footsteps. "We have a problem."

The burly man raised an eyebrow but didn't speak.

"Correction: we have *multiple* problems," she continued. "I can't get Tieg to listen to me. He seems to think that the NeoG didn't take Carmichael seriously simply because *he* doesn't take her seriously. But they've set up a fucking task force for the Trappist shipping lanes."

"Use your NeoG contact."

"They've gone dark." She pinned the man with a fierce look. "You were supposed to stop Marty from talking."

"I vented a lung. How was I supposed to know he'd stay alive long enough for someone to get to him?"

"It's your job to take care of these things."

"What do you want me to do? I can't go after the senator, she's too well protected."

"I know." She waved a hand in irritation. "But if my freighters get tagged, it'll expose my role in this whole mess, and I have gone to a great deal of trouble to keep us out of it."

"Do you want to run?"

Even without the bite of sarcasm in his voice she knew he'd asked the question to make her focus. Neither of them was willing to run until they'd seen this through to the end.

"No. Damned if I'll run now. This may have been Tieg's idea originally, but it's our hard work. It's our money. You get back to Trappist, tell those TLF bastards that if they won't cooperate with moving the shipments you're going to make sure their kid comes back to them in pieces. I'll talk to our contacts on Mars, have them hit the NeoG and make sure it hurts. If we cause enough trouble they'll have to turn their gaze away from Trappist."

"Mixing business with pleasure, my dear?"

Her smile was cold. "I want the NeoG bloody, Grant. I want them so tied up chasing shadows and licking their wounds that they don't have time to focus on us until we're out of here. Tieg can twist in the wind after, for all I care." The senator had been a useful cover with his dismissive hatred of the habitats and obsessive need to make them pay for every scrap of assistance they got from Earth, but she could see the writing on the wall and it was time to finish this.

After Grant left she cued up the call. "Julia, how's our Neo?"

"Clueless as usual. What do you need them to do?"

"I want you to tell them who you work for. Tell them we're watching and that you'll have instructions when they get to Jupiter Station."

"You want them scared?" Julia's vicious nature was part of the reason she'd been chosen for this job.

"Not so much that they'll run, but enough that they won't think to breathe a word of what we want to anyone. They're our second pair of eyes on what the task force will be up to and I want to be able to route ships around the NeoG in my sleep, understood?"

"No problem, boss."

"Good." She disconnected the call and stared back out at the storm growing over the ocean. Despite what she'd told Grant, it was almost time to cut and run, but not before Melanie Karenina paid the NeoG back for ruining her life.

FIVE

Spacer Chae Ho-ki muttered curses in as many languages as they could think of while they sprinted through the crowded bay.

One bad choice years ago, and a cascade failure of epic proportions followed. It felt like it was never ending. Even the bright spots of the last few years were now tarnished black like burned bones.

"Please don't let me miss this transport. That's all I ask. Throw a thousand more things at me after and I will take them on. But just give me this one thing."

As usual, the universe didn't listen. They crashed into a burly Navy spacer and went flying sideways.

"Watch where you're going!" The spacer's eyes narrowed further as they realized Chae was in a blue-gray NeoG uniform, but before they could do anything more than take a step forward Chae scrambled back to their feet.

"Sorry!" they called, and vanished into the crowd.

There were few benefits to being all of 154 centimeters tall, but one was that it was easy to get lost in a mass of people, and Chae took full advantage of that now. They dodged another near-collision and hit an open space as the crowd cleared.

"Please still be there. Please still be there . . ."

Their heart leaped in celebration when they spotted the NeoG transport still in the dock, but it was quickly followed by a crushing drop when the DD handshakes of the two men standing at the loading ramp resolved in their vision.

"Fuck," Chae muttered, and gripped the strap of their bag as they skidded to a stop a few meters away. They walked briskly the rest of the distance, trying to catch their breath.

"There they are." The smile on Commander Nika Vagin's face seemed genuine, but was that a tightness around his blue eyes? "Ho-ki, I was about to call Admiral Kwon at the Interceptor training facility and make sure something didn't happen to you."

"I'm sorry, Commander. I was—" Chae cut off the babbling explanation and snapped into a salute. "I'm sorry I'm late."

Your fucking new commander doesn't want to hear about how your ex-girlfriend hasn't really been your girlfriend for the last few years but just someone criminals paid to keep track of you, Chae, so shut your mouth.

"You're good," Nika said after a moment's pause and a glance at the NeoG captain standing next to him. "It gave Hiro and me a chance to catch up." Nika smiled again. "Let's get you settled so we can get moving." He grinned at the captain. "I know you're itching to try this ship out."

Hiro grinned back. "Not every day we get new equipment. I'm going to have to send Max a present."

"You know she'll kick your ass if you do."

"Tell her I wouldn't mind." Hiro's grin widened and Nika rolled his eyes. Chae was so shocked by the interaction they almost missed the commander reaching for the bag at their feet.

"I've got it, Commander." Chae snatched it up, spotted a flicker of something on their commander's face, and bit down hard on the inside of their cheek to keep from saying something stupid.

"Come on." Nika jerked his head toward the loading ramp. Chae hoisted their other bag higher onto their shoulder and followed.

"You were born on Mars," Nika said as he turned left down a pristine corridor. The *Gajabahu* was a brand-new transport ship, just off the line. Chae remembered hearing something at basic about the test ships that could open mini-wormholes allowing for in-system transport for the NeoG, but it hadn't been anything more than scuttlebutt. "Have you been out past the belt yet?"

"No, Commander." The lie came organically. They hated that it did, but there wasn't an easy way to say *Yes, I was born on Mars but I lived on Trappist until I got arrested.*

Nika stopped at the base of the stairs and laughed. "I get you're still kind of in basic mode, but Nika's fine unless it's an emergency or I'm chewing your ass for something, Ho-ki."

"Okay." Chae could feel the commander's first name stick in their throat and it took obvious effort to get it out. "Nika." Chae closed their eyes with a sigh. "And if it's all right, I prefer just Chae." They swallowed down the urge to explain that it made them feel closer to their fathers to use their family name.

Nika laughed again, but it was kind and reminded Chae of their fathers even more. He reached out and patted them on the shoulder. "It's perfectly fine. We're a team now. It gets easier, I promise. Come on, we're just up and on the right."

Chae followed, guilt and fear a twisting snake in their belly. *You made peace with this choice, Chae, just play it out,* they reminded themself. *Fix the problem, stop the cascade. Everyone will be safe.*

Nika stopped at an open door and gestured Chae in. "Home sweet home, at least for the next few hours." He followed them in, the door sliding shut behind him.

Chae put their bags down on the empty bed and turned

around to find Nika leaning against the door with his arms crossed over his chest.

"So, as my grandmother used to say, if you ignore the bear in the corner for too long it'll eat you. You want to tell me what it is a nineteen-year-old prodigy did to land themselves in a plea deal that involved joining the NeoG?"

Chae's heart dropped through the floor of the ship.

Missed point. Can't backtrack to former. Cascade failure imminent. One more step until full explosion.

"I was told they were going to seal the record," they said in a quiet voice.

"It was sealed." Nika's expression didn't change. "You can find out a lot working in Intel."

A lot, but not the reason. Or he wouldn't be asking me.

"I don't know what specifically, that's why I'm asking you. That part is sealed well enough we couldn't get the info," Nika said, as if he'd read Chae's mind.

"I'll tell you now that Lieutenant Carmichael probably does know what landed you in hot water," he continued. "She's got better connections and she's thorough. She's also polite and may let you wait to tell her. I won't. I want to know if you're going to be a danger to my crew. If I should com Hiro and tell him we're putting you back out in the bay."

"You can't," they said in a rush. "I have to be here."

It was the wrong thing to say and Chae knew it the moment Nika's expression went dark. They braced themself, expecting the worst.

It's all going to fall apart. My parents will end up dead or vanished and I'll have given up everything for nothing.

But Nika didn't move, didn't push away from the door, and his expression didn't change. He just issued a quiet order in a voice so calm it was terrifying. "I'm your commander, Spacer Chae. I can do whatever I want."

It was so hard not to flinch, and Chae knew they did anyway. The words left them in a rush. "You remember the Trappist Heist a couple of years ago? It was all over the news?"

"Yes."

"That was me."

NIKA STARED AT THE KID AS THE WORDS FILTERED INTO HIS head, crashing into memories he'd rather leave in the dust. Memories of Trappist and fire and the crush of a building collapsing. It took more work than he wanted to admit to himself to shake it loose and keep poking. The lie and the bluff he'd tossed at Chae had done the job of getting the spacer to admit why they were here without Nika having to reveal his source beyond the vague allusion to his time at Intel.

"You're the one who broke into a NeoG warehouse, stole a bunch of medical supplies. Military medical supplies."

Chae was twisting their fingers together until they realized what they were doing and shoved their hands into their pockets. "Yes, sir."

The muscles in Nika's back unclenched a little. He'd read the file from Stephan before leaving HQ—it had been big news just before the hundredth anniversary of Games, which they'd lost. And then not a peep on the newslines. He remembered Sapphi's offhand comment about someone being arrested, but the government wasn't talking about who.

Everyone had assumed it was the separatist group—the Trappist Liberation Force—but the TLF had denied involvement. Nika could see the thread clearly now that he had all the pieces. Stephan was fairly sure the kid had just been in the wrong place at the wrong time, trying to steal materials for the chronically undersupplied habitats, and circumstances spiraled out of control when Tieg got wind of the case— Chae became the perfect patsy to obfuscate *why* stealing supplies was necessary in the first place. The fact that their parents were involved with the TLF had been the lock on the door.

"That's a big job to pull off alone. Someone set you up?"

"No, sir. I planned it all and I was there on-site."

Nika immediately softened his expression. He was pushing too hard, scaring them when he needed them to trust him. "That a fact? I don't like it when people lie to me, Chae." He watched the kid's back straighten and they squared their shoulders to meet his gaze.

I'm a hypocritical son of a bitch two seconds into this. Saint Ivan help me.

"Officially it was me," Chae said.

"Then I'm asking you to tell me the unofficial version."

Chae took a deep breath, then said, "They were going to arrest my parents, too, and some others who helped. My fathers are doctors on Trappist-1d. We needed the supplies. I saw a way to get them. My parents do good work out there in the habitats, sir. I figured better me than them. So I took the deal the CHN offered."

Nika had questions, but he knew Chae couldn't answer most of them and filed them away to ask Stephan later.

The doctors on the habitats shouldn't need to steal medical supplies. They were sent enough to handle whatever might come up, and more as requested. But Nika had already seen the flow Tieg had managed to set up: the dissemination of habitat supplies to numerous warehouses on Earth and then a complex network of shuffled shipments, supposed pirate attacks, and paperwork errors had led to the disappearance of trillions of dollars' worth of supplies over the last two years alone.

He studied Chae. The kid was doing that look-past-the-commander's-shoulder thing Nika remembered all too vividly from Interceptor training. Nika switched on his com. "Hiro?"

"Right here."

"We're good to go."

"Roger that. Enjoy the ride."

Nika couldn't stop the audible snort and saw Chae flinch out of the corner of his eye.

"Commander, are you going to tell the others?"

God damn if the kid didn't sound terrified. They were in this deep. Nika shook his head. "No. It's your story to decide what to do with. Like I said, though, Max almost certainly knows already, but she probably won't push you to tell her right away." He felt the slight tremor in the floor as the ship lifted off and he pushed away from the door, hitting the panel to open it. "However, I'll say this: secrets don't last, Chae, and they're hell on the soul. Out in the black you need to be able to trust the people you work with."

Nika paused with his left hand on the doorframe. "Get settled. I hear this trip is a little rough. I'll be back in a bit."

"Yes, sir."

Nika didn't correct them for the "sir" instead of his name, and he waited until he was down the corridor to exhale. That had gone better than he expected, and yet he knew Chae hadn't told him the whole truth. But that was expected, too: There was no way the kid was going to just fess up that they'd been approached and threatened by Tieg's associates. That if they didn't cooperate and feed information about the new NeoG task force over, their family was at risk.

You didn't exactly set things up for the kid to trust you, either, Nika. Stephan's voice was in his head.

Hopefully Max would be better at getting the spacer to open up. And even if Nika couldn't tell her about the op, he knew once she talked to Chae for two minutes her instincts would kick in and she'd follow that thread all the way to the end. He made a note to mention to Stephan that it could be an issue if Max dug too deep, especially if she involved Sapphi in it. *Zuma's* hacker was a pro at finding out things no one else could.

I'll worry about what I can control, he thought. *Like not getting killed by Hiro or this new test ship.* Nika grabbed for the railing with his right hand as the ship took off with a jolt. The prosthetic worked as it should, and yet his arm still felt different, more than a year and a half later, even with everything synced perfectly. The doctors insisted that was in his head, but as far as Nika was concerned it didn't fucking matter.

His arm was gone.

This thing in its place was perfect in every conceivable way, but it wasn't *his*. He knew it every time he picked up a sword, though after a year of Stephan beating the absolute shit out of him in the practice ring he could at least trust that he could hold his own in a boarding action.

But he wasn't winning any tournaments with it, not anytime soon.

Nika blew out a breath and continued up the stairs, trying to ignore the voice in the back of his head telling him he'd made a mistake accepting this job and everyone would be better off if he'd officially stayed with Intel rather than hide in this lie about being an Interceptor commander again.

He'd thought he'd been good with the choice, but it seemed like all his insecurities, all his worries and fears had slammed down on him the moment he left Earth, and trying to ignore them was like trying to ignore a siren wailing in his ears twenty-four/seven. Despite what he'd promised Stephan, he knew he was in over his head.

I've got a new team member I'm not sure I can trust, and I'm going to be lying to people who trust me in the process.

What the hell am I doing?

CHAE SANK DOWN ONTO THE BED AS SOON AS THEY WERE alone in the room, gripping the back of their head with both hands and fighting to hold in the scream that wanted to tear through the air.

It was worse than they'd feared. Worse even than Julia's parting shot, delivered with a cool and unforgiving kiss.

We'll be watching, Chae, don't forget that. We own you now, and if you know what's good for you, you'll do as you're told. Keep your mouth shut, do what we tell you, and everything will be fine back home.

"I can't trust anyone except myself." They murmured the words like a mantra.

They wanted desperately to believe the kindness in Nika's eyes was real. That everything would be okay and they could just play out this punishment with the NeoG, keep their family safe, and maybe someday this nightmare would end.

Secrets don't last, Chae. Nika's words were ringing in their head.

These secrets have to last, though. Or everyone I love dies.

SIX

"What are we doing here again?"

Max rolled her eyes at the question. Jenks knew very well what they were doing, and the chief wasn't as annoyed about it as she was pretending to be.

"Starting a new tradition," she replied anyway. Max hoped she looked more relaxed than she felt, standing at the edge of the docking bay with her hands in her pants pockets as the transport pulled into its spot. "We're family and family makes the time to say hello and goodbye."

"Bye bye bye."

"Oh stop, Jenks," Sapphi said with a laugh when she started singing. "You're not fooling anyone. We know you're as hyped to see Nika as the rest of us. You're practically vibrating with excitement."

"Fine. I am excited to see him."

"And the newbie," Max reminded her.

"Of course the newbie." This time Sapphi's wicked grin was identical to Jenks's. "What was their name again?"

"Pretty sure their name is *not the master chief*." Jenks held her hands up with a laugh when Max leveled a look in her direction. "I kid. I'm sure Spacer Chae Ho-ki will fit right in with the rest of us."

"They prefer to be called Chae," Max said. She hoped they would fit in, knew how much Chae's nerves must be jumping. She'd been through it herself on her first day at Jupiter Station. And their new crewmember had even more reason to be nervous.

Sending us a nineteen-year-old kid caught up in something far bigger than themself, Admiral Chen. I hope you know what you're doing.

Max couldn't say how she knew, only that something in her gut told her the head of the NeoG had been the one to pull the strings behind Chae's assignment in much the same way she'd put Max with *Zuma* on the request of her older sister, Ria. She wondered if Nika knew about Chae's record. She'd debated sending him the information she'd gotten and eventually decided against it, wanting to tell him in person so she and Nika could talk about how best to handle it. It hadn't felt fair to tarnish his first meeting with Chae with "Hey, your newbie got busted stealing medical supplies on Trappist-1d and did a plea deal with the CHN."

Even worse, Max didn't know how Nika would react. That was a shocking realization. A man she'd been talking with for more than two years and she didn't have the first clue how he would handle this.

She hoped the compassion she'd seen when he talked about Jenks's early days living on the streets would extend to a stranger, but Max couldn't stop that voice in the back of her head from whispering that people could surprise you in the most unpleasant of ways.

Maybe it's better to just rip the bandage off, she thought. *If you're in the room when he finds out about Chae, there's less a chance that he'll go off on them.*

"Hey, LT, stop daydreaming!" Jenks elbowed her in the side, and Max shook her head.

Nika was hugging Sapphi and Tamago at the same time while Chae stood off to one side, gripping their bags and watching the welcome with a look Max knew all too well.

Yearning.

"Chae."

The kid dropped their bags and snapped into a picture-perfect salute. "Lieutenant Carmichael."

"Max," she corrected, unable to stop the smile at how much that motion reminded her of herself only two years ago. She crossed to them with open arms. "We're a rather huggy bunch around here, unless you have an objection."

Chae's startled look was followed by a nod of consent and they stepped forward into Max's hug.

"Welcome to *Zuma's Ghost*," Max said. She could have sworn the newbie Neo muffled a sob as they hugged her back.

NIKA WATCHED FROM BETWEEN SAPPHI'S AND TAMAGO'S heads as Max enveloped Chae in a hug before his sister hit all three of them like an asteroid.

"Welcome home!" Jenks kissed him noisily on the mouth. "We didn't miss you at all, but it's nice to see your face again."

"You're such a liar," he said, and grinned at her.

Tamago and Sapphi wriggled free, protests echoing into the air, and Nika laughed as he scooped his sister into a hug. "I did miss you, brat, for reasons unknown to all of humankind."

"Because I'm the most interesting woman in the universe, that's why." Jenks pressed her forehead to his and Nika realized there were tears in her mismatched eyes—one blue, one brown. "Doge missed the hell out of you."

"I'm sure he did." Nika squeezed Jenks once more, kissed her on the forehead, and then dropped her to the deck, bending over to pat the ROVER on the head. "Missed you, too, buddy."

"Welcome back, Commander Vagin." The AI's voice came

over the com, but it warmed Nika's heart just as much as any of the other greetings.

"Don't tell Max I said this," Jenks said, "but it was a good idea to come down and meet you."

"This was her idea?" Nika glanced over to where Sapphi and Tamago were introducing themselves to Chae, both of them pulling the somewhat shocked-looking spacer into welcoming hugs.

"She's taking the family thing pretty seriously." Jenks shot him a sly look. "I'm not calling you Mom and Dad, though—just FYI—because that's weird."

Nika reflexively cuffed his sister in the back of the head, wincing at her yelp of surprise. "Shit, sorry." He still forgot the metal of his prosthetic wasn't going to connect the same as his real hand.

"God damn! Reminder to me not to let you hit me with that. Can you punch through a door? We should put you in the cage matches."

Trust his little sister to make it into a joke. Jenks seemed to realize what had come out of her mouth and snapped it shut. Nika couldn't stop his laughter, though, and was thankful it erased the sudden uncertain look creeping over her face. He pulled her into a second quick hug and then released her.

"I missed you, brat. No, I'm not going to be in the cage matches, and you're fine. You don't need to apologize. Go say hello to your new Neo, Chief."

"Yes, sir, Commander, sir." Jenks skipped away, crossing paths with Max, the pair exchanging a quick, complex handshake as they passed each other.

"Thank God you're here," Max said, and though the smile on her face was genuine, Nika saw the tightness around her eyes and wondered at the cause. "Rosa left a week ago and I was starting to think these three would gang up and stuff me into an airlock before the real commander got here."

"I think 'real commander' is a bit of a stretch," Nika replied, suddenly unsure about his initial inclination to hug her. "You're as much in charge of this bunch as I am."

"I'm just the lieutenant." Max took a step forward, stopped, and sighed. "I was going to go straight in for a hug, then I second-guessed myself and now I feel like the window closed and this went awkward fast?"

"I'm still game for a hug." He spread his hands apart.

"Oh good."

Nika wrapped his arms around her, felt her return the hug, and even the sick feeling in his gut about what he was going to have to do receded somewhat. "It's really good to be back," he murmured. "Thank you for this."

"All I did was remind you where you belong. Welcome home." She pulled away and looked over her shoulder. "I was going to send Jenks and the others to get dinner so we could have a quick talk with Chae. There's something we need to address. I don't know a better way to put this than—"

"I know," Nika said. "We talked about it on the flight over." He glanced past her; the others were chattering away, Chae still looking more than a little stunned. "I'll be honest, I wasn't expecting you to want to talk about it right off the bat."

"I wasn't expecting you to know about it, so we're even." She laughed in obvious relief. "Stephan?"

Nika nodded. "Bosco?"

Now it was Max who nodded. "I asked her to do some digging after something Hoboins said piqued my curiosity. I can send you the files she got me."

"I'd appreciate it." Nika gestured subtly toward Chae and the rest of the crew. "And I'm up for doing this however you want to."

"I just thought it would be better to get it out in the open now." Max turned around and whistled. "Chae, you're with us. You three go get us dinner and meet us in quarters in twenty."

Sapphi, Tamago, and Jenks headed off with parting waves

and Nika waited with Max while Chae grabbed their bags and crossed the deck to them.

"Admiral Hoboins is in a meeting so we'll touch base with him tomorrow," Max said as she headed out of the docking bay and toward the zero-g tube. "Chae, have you used these before?"

"Just during training."

"They're easy, though Nika could tell you I made a fool of myself the first time I was in one with him and that was with plenty of experience." Max grinned and neatly stole one of Chae's bags from their hands, slinging it over her shoulder and grabbing for the bar. "We're going up, just push off a bit on your way out of the tube and stick close to the side. Nika will be right behind you."

Nika followed the pair, more than a little enthralled at how easily Max had handled things. She had been awkward and botched her first landing when they'd met, though not as badly as she seemed to remember. Now she soared upward effortlessly while keeping one eye on Chae and a hand ready to grab the spacer if they got too far away.

It was more than just navigating the station, though. It was how on top of the situation with Chae she was. How she had organized the welcome. How she had *been* so welcoming.

He'd known she would settle into her role, had seen hints of it over the last two years. But seeing it now in real time made something in his chest ache.

Max is a leader and you're just here to help Stephan out. Simple as that.

"You okay?" Max's question knocked him out of his daze and he saw the flicker of concern when he grabbed for the bar by the exit to the Interceptor quarters.

"Fine," he lied. "Just thinking about how things change."

She smiled, first at him and then at Chae, though the spacer was staring at their boots and missed it. "Some things. Quarters are the same. You get Rosa's room along with all those other commander perks. Speaking of, hot water's been iffy for a week. I recommend standing outside the spray when you're washing your face, ask me how I know." Max rolled her eyes and pressed her hand to the panel next to the door, unlocking it.

"CHAE, NO ONE WANTED MA'S BUNK, WHICH FRANKLY WAS kind of a surprise given it's a floor-level one. So you're good to put your stuff right there." Max pointed at the lower bunk, ignoring the way her heart hammered a bit at the prospect of this confrontation.

She'd read everything Jeanie Bosco, head of security for LifeEx, had sent her about the Trappist Heist and one Chae Ho-ki. Despite Jeanie's thoroughness, Max's gut was telling her that something was missing.

The now nineteen-year-old should have been on their way to medical school, following in the footsteps of their brilliant parents.

She could hear her own parents sneering judgment in her ear at the thought that someone would waste their medical expertise in the backwater of the habitats. What was the point of becoming a doctor if you weren't serving the greater good by joining the CHNN?

The irony of them thinking that someone's path was only good if it was with the Navy was still enough to leave a foul taste in her mouth. She hadn't spoken to her parents or her older sister Maggie in nearly two years. Instead, Ria, Pax, or Scott caught her up on the family situation in their weekly communications.

When Admiral Hoboins had told her and Rosa about the new spacer, he'd said they were from Trappist. But when Max had looked at the file, she'd found it as barren as one would expect for a brand-new recruit.

A brand-new recruit from *Mars*.

It wasn't like Hoboins to get that information wrong and so she'd gone digging, trusting her gut just like Rosa had encouraged her to for two years. On the surface it was little more than Chae joining the NeoG, passing through basic and then a year of Interceptor training to land on Jupiter Station's doorstep.

It had been a week later when Max had remembered the news reports. The Trappist Heist had been all over the newslines just before she'd left HQ for Interceptor training herself, and she remembered snippets of a conversation between Stephan and Admiral Chen about catching the people responsible—the name Chae had factored heavily in that conversation.

They said "people," but here Max was with a single kid who'd put their future on the chopping block for whoever else had been involved in the heist.

And not just any heist: a heist of medical supplies for an outlying habitat on Trappist-1d called West Ridge. A habitat that should have been well provisioned and taken care of, per CHN regulations.

Yet that was about all Max could find. That, and the results of Chae's plea deal, signed off on by Admiral Chen herself, for them to join the NeoG.

When her gut still didn't settle, Max had reached out to Jeanie Bosco. She'd never much gotten along with her older sister Ria's lifelong best friend, but they'd come to an understanding a year ago when Max and the rest of *Zuma's Ghost* had helped stop a plot to destroy LifeEx and the Carmichael family.

Amazing how saving someone from the figurative fire can do wonders for a professional relationship.

Two days later Max had a wealth of information that raised more questions than it answered, but it was enough for her to piece together that Chae had taken the fall for their parents and everyone else involved in the theft.

Again, on the surface it looked as though they'd done so willingly, and their scores at both NeoG basic and Interceptor training showed a spacer who was more than determined to prove themself on the job.

Yet there was still something scratching at the back of Max's intuition. How had Chae found out about the supplies? It was weird enough that a shipment of medical items would be languishing in a NeoG warehouse, but for a teenager from the habitats to know about them just didn't add up.

I wonder if Stephan told Nika anything else.

"How do you want to handle this?" she murmured to Nika as she walked with him to Rosa's old room.

"I'll follow your lead." He tossed his bag onto the neatly made bed. "Like I said, we had a conversation already."

"I'll get you Bosco's files after so you can look at them, and we should talk later to compare notes," Max replied. Nika hesitated for a moment, but then he nodded as they crossed the main room.

"Chae, come have a seat." She pulled out a chair at the table in the common area and sat, waiting for the spacer to take a seat before she continued. "I told Sapphi to dawdle for me, but we've still got a little less than twenty minutes. You want to use it to tell me the story of why a supersmart teenager decided it was a good idea to steal from the military?"

Chae's glance at Nika spoke volumes and Max had to swallow down a laugh when Nika murmured, "I told them you'd probably wait to ask."

"Old me, maybe." Max rested her elbows on the tabletop and then her chin on her folded hands. "New me would like to know who I'm working with from the beginning. I have a decent guess based on what I read in the CHN files, but guesses are messy and get people killed."

Chae visibly gathered themself. "Lieutenant, if you've read the files, you know the story. I stole things, got caught, the NeoG offered me a deal. I took it and ended up here."

"You've been practicing that one for a while, haven't you?" she asked, hearing Nika's poorly suppressed snort of laughter. "Chae, I'm not judging you on this. If anything I think you did the right thing. I looked at the requests from that habitat and you should have had the supplies months before you decided to break into that warehouse."

Max leaned back in her chair. "I'm honestly more curious about why you, a *sixteen-year-old at the time,* were the one who took the fall. Did your fathers make you because of their work with the TLF?"

"No!"

There. She'd cracked that stoic exterior and Max watched in satisfaction as a fierce loyalty flashed across Chae's face. Loyalty she could work with, as long as it didn't impact the team.

"Make a choice, Lieutenant: either the NeoG is your first and last or you find somewhere else to finish your stretch. I don't need split loyalties in my crews or on my station, am I clear?" Those had been Admiral Hoboins's words to Max when she'd made the mistake of trusting her sister instead of her crew, and they rang in her head.

Zuma's Ghost had Max's loyalty now, and more than anything she wanted to know if it was going to have Chae's also.

"Go on," she said, when Chae didn't continue. The spacer swallowed nervously.

"My parents do good work on Trappist-1d. They're only marked as part of the TLF because they don't ask questions about the habbies who come into their clinic and sometimes *they're* TLF. It was better for me to do this than for them to end up in a mining camp, Lieutenant."

"Max," she corrected. "You don't need to use my rank unless you're in trouble." She went quiet, waiting for Chae to look her in the eyes. When they did, she said, "And you're not, Chae. I just want answers."

Nika was watching them, she could see it out of the corner

of her eye, and the parade of emotions on his face was an interesting puzzle Max had to tear herself away from to focus on Chae. She told herself she'd follow up later when they were alone. She didn't buy Chae's explanation, though it was entirely possible that's what the kid's fathers wanted them to think.

"Feels like it." Chae dropped their head into their hands once more. "I've done everything that's been asked of me. I don't know what more you need."

Max pushed out of her chair and went to crouch at the kid's side. An amused voice in her head pointed out that she was only six years older than they were. But there was a lifetime of difference between their situations that she was deeply and painfully aware of in that moment.

"Chae, look at me. I want to know two things. First, even though you're not here strictly because of your own choices, are you committed to the NeoG? Can I trust you to look after this team with the same loyalty you're showing for your family? Can I trust you to let us do the same for you?"

They lifted their head and Max's gut twinged at the fear lurking around the edges of their dark brown gaze. A fear that shouldn't be there just from this conversation.

Damn it, I hate being right. There's something else going on here.

Chae took a deep breath and then nodded. "Yes. You can."

"Good." She shoved away her own worry as she put her hand on their shoulder. "I thought as much, but it's always better to hear someone say it out loud. Here's what we're going to do: you can tell the others in a time and manner of your choosing. Together or individually, whatever's easier for you. If you need me and Nika there with you we'll be more than happy to do that. But you have to tell them before we go out in the black and that means you've got two weeks. I don't want secrets on this team. It gets people killed."

Chae nodded as Max stood. "What's the second thing?"

"The second? Oh." Max laughed. "I realize that per the details of your plea deal you're not supposed to speak with your parents." Her smile was gentle. "However, that doesn't mean I can't talk to them. Would you like me to pass messages along for you?"

The shock on Chae's face was echoed on Nika's.

"You . . . you can't."

Max raised an eyebrow at Chae's choked protest. "I'm a Carmichael, and a lieutenant in the Near-Earth Orbital Guard. I realize it sounds a bit arrogant, but I do what I want." She gave them a level look. "Trust me to do it in such a way to keep all of you safe, if that's your concern. I'm just letting you know that if you have something you'd like your fathers to know, as your superior officer, it's my duty to pass that along."

There was the fear again, consuming their brown eyes whole before it was buried beneath an apologetic expression so quickly Max wondered if she'd imagined it.

But she was sure she hadn't.

"I'd rather stick to the terms of my plea agreement, Lieutenant, if it's all right with you," Chae replied.

She slipped her hands into the pockets of her pants and nodded. "Fair enough. Offer's on the table, though, anytime. Go stow your gear."

Chae, physically relieved, got up and went to their bunk to unpack.

"You got more out of them than I did," Nika murmured, standing and leaning against the table next to her. Max glanced away from Chae as the noise level in the rooms suddenly rose with the reappearance of the rest of the team.

"They're scared, Nik."

"Not a surprise," he agreed, but his next words made her realize they weren't on the same page. "I'd think any newbie Neo would be, and Chae's been through a bit more than most."

"No, something about this doesn't add up."

"The case is over and done, Max. Let's focus on helping Chae settle in here."

There was a bite of command in his voice that had her swallowing down her next words. "Sure. It's good to have you back."

"It's good to be back." His reply was absent, almost formulaic, and made her stomach clench.

Because unless Max missed her guess, Chae wasn't the only one holding something back. They were just the easier puzzle for her to figure out at the moment.

She pasted a smile on her face and crossed the room to help Tamago with the food, telling herself with every step that things would be fine.

In time she might even believe the lie.

Commander Nika Vagin/Nik—

I am sorry to have missed you. I was hoping for a day or two of (almost) the whole team back together, but the powers that be decided I needed to head for Earth before you got to Jupiter. Don't tell Max, but I suspect that was Hoboins's doing to see how she'd handle being in charge.

It has been a long time since I have written on paper. I don't know if you know, but my faith has us transcribe our own Bibles from the master copy in our home church as a reminder of how quickly technology can be taken from us.

I confess I will miss being out in the black, miss being with all of you and though—

Look at me, making this all about me when I should be talking about you.

This letter would have been different had I written it two years ago . . . such is the way of it, right? I want you to know you are the best Neo I have ever trained. I say this without hesitation or any equivocation, even as I know you will look at Max and think I am lying. Max still needs someone to look up to, someone with more experience leading, and you are that person.

You are meant to be there and you are meant to be doing the work. I know you doubt your ability in that regard—I can see you shaking your head, but I'm smarter than you, so just believe me on this—and I wish we'd had a bit more time to get you past that, but you have a good team and they will follow you. Just trust in yourself and in them.

Do not forget how hard you worked to be where you are.

Do not forget that you are an amazing human being who is both infinitely capable and so very kind, a combination that is often a rarity in this world.

Do not forget you are a commander in the NeoG and we are better than all the rest.

Go with God, Nika, and with all my love.

Commander Rosa Marie Martín Rivas/Rosa

SEVEN

Chae watched in silent amazement as Jenks and Max fought. They'd seen both women fight in the Games. It was hard to avoid, since Chae had been part of NeoG by the time *Zuma's Ghost* had their first historic victory and then, of course, the Interceptor training facility had been buzzing about win number two from the prelims onward.

They wouldn't even deny they'd gotten wrapped up in the whole thing, the passing acquaintance they'd had with the Games as a way to kill time on Trappist having evolved into something that sparked a yearning in Chae's heart.

Especially the piloting bit. They'd watched Master Chief Ma's flights over and over, amazed by the cool interaction between Max and Ma as they blew through course after course in the most recent Games.

That had fully ignited a fire in Chae's chest that they'd buried with all the preparation for medical school. And then the events that had landed them here on Jupiter Station had all but eliminated any dreams of flying in the Games. They knew Max would probably take over the piloting seat for the competition. She was so good.

Yet now, with the preliminaries thirteen weeks out, they dared to hope that maybe someone would suggest them for the navigator seat.

Chae already knew they'd probably have to fight in the cage, as that had been Ma's spot also, and it made their stomach twist into knots. Because watching fights on the screen and dreaming about what it would be like was a whole different matter from sitting within two meters of these incredible fighters they would never live up to.

Max was tall and slender, moving with a fluidity Chae couldn't ever hope to match. The announcers and her own fellow Neos said that Max made up the ghost portion of the Interceptor team with her ability to predict people's moves both in the cage and outside it.

Jenks, however, was neither tall nor slender. The CPO was, as Max had gleefully pointed out Chae's first night there, a centimeter shorter than Chae at 153 centimeters, and built like the bruiser she was.

Both of them were infinitely more impressive than Chae could ever hope to be.

They noted that as the whole team sat along one side of the sparring mat. Other Neos in the gym had started wandering over to watch the show.

"They've both gotten faster," Nika murmured, more to himself than anyone else. Chae didn't have much to base that on but they were inclined to agree when Max dodged out of the way of a spin kick from Jenks that would have knocked all the air out of her lungs if it had connected.

Instead she landed a blow between Jenks's shoulder blades with her palm that sent the chief flying into the mat. Curses blistered the air, mixing with the cheers and laughter of the crowd.

Jenks rolled to her feet, but she didn't rush at Max like Chae expected. Instead she braced her hands on her knees and took several deep breaths, keeping one wary eye on the lieutenant standing and waiting patiently in the center of the mat, her hands up and an amused look on her face.

"Do you need a break?" Max asked, sending the crowd into laughter once again.

Jenks grinned back, smoothing a hand over the strip of bright purple hair she had braided and tied into a ponytail at the base of her skull. "You haven't beaten me yet, Max. We're not starting today." She gestured. "Come on. Let's go."

The pair clashed again. Chae heard Nika's sharp indrawn breath as Max couldn't avoid Jenks's sweep and hit the mat hard.

But Max rolled, and the elbow that would have landed in her gut hit the mat instead.

"Putting on a welcome-back show for you?"

Chae looked away from the fight as a big man sat down next to Nika. His DD handshake read *Commander D'Arcy Montaglione, he/him*. Chae froze.

Nika laughed and held out his hand. "D'Arcy, good to see you."

"When did you get in?"

"A week ago."

"We've been out, just got back in last night." D'Arcy glanced past Nika at Chae and studied them for a moment before reaching across. "Commander D'Arcy Montaglione, *Dread Treasure*."

"Spacer Chae Ho-ki."

There was a flicker of what could have been recognition in D'Arcy's dark eyes, but he didn't say anything and Chae relaxed a fraction.

They knew the commander by reputation only, both in the NeoG and his previous life with Free Mars, the separatist group Chae's own fathers had been a part of before they moved to Trappist to start a new life.

The assembled crowd cheered and Chae looked back at the fight to see Max on the mat, Jenks with an arm pulled tight against her throat.

Max reached up and tapped Jenks's forearm and the pair rolled away from each other to their feet. They reached out and tapped fists twice, then Jenks turned on a heel and crossed to the bench with a pleased grin on her face. "Win for me. You're up, Chae."

"Don't break them, Jenks," Nika said.

"I would never."

Chae got to their feet, rubbing damp palms against their thighs.

"You'll be fine," Max said. "Just don't watch her hands too much. She'll use them to distract you."

"That and her mouth," Tamago said.

"Stop giving away my secrets," Jenks replied.

"Your mouth isn't a secret, Jenks," someone called from the crowd, and laughter filled the air.

"Ha, ha." Jenks waved her hand. "Master Gunnery Sergeant McGraw, I'm so glad you volunteered to be my punching bag for this demonstration. Come here so I can show my newbie how to make a big guy drop to his knees."

"GOOD FIGHT," NIKA SAID AS MAX SAT ON THE BENCH NEXT TO him.

"She gets me with that every time. Hey, D'Arcy, how was Trappist?"

"Messy as usual. We were out on One-d helping with a major cleanup from some summer floods," he said at Nika's curious look. "Swear to god I'd just read about a drainage project in the works for that same habitat around two years ago. I guess whatever they put together couldn't handle the water volume."

Nika knew exactly what the problem was, but he couldn't say anything. The drainage project had stalled due to lack of quality materials. Yet another casualty of Tieg's greed.

"Is there a problem, Petty Officer Hunter?" Max's question

shook Nika out of his thoughts and he looked up to see the lanky PO from *Avenging Heroes* glaring in their direction.

There was a beat and then the man shook his head. "No, Lieutenant."

"Then find somewhere else to be before I tell Jenks you've volunteered for a two-on-one demonstration."

Nika wasn't sure what surprised him more, the razor-sharp edge in Max's voice or the angry look Hunter shot at D'Arcy before walking away.

"Sorry, D'Arcy," Max murmured, still watching Hunter for a moment before she looked in Nika's direction. "We've managed most of it since Hoboins sent him to Trappist, but Hunter's uncle was killed in the Hellas fight. He might be a problem."

"What am I missing here?" Nika asked.

D'Arcy shrugged. "Consequence of having me take over the task force was telling everyone about my life before the NeoG. It was—" He stopped and looked at Nika. "You heard about that, I'm assuming? That I used to be Free Mars?"

"Oh." Nika nodded as pieces slipped into place. "Yeah, I heard."

"You have a knack, Vagin, for making my disloyalty to the CHN sound like no big deal," D'Arcy said.

"Because it's not a big deal to me," Nika replied. "I understand what you were fighting for then and I know who you are now. You've had my six in the black more times than I can count. That's all that matters."

"Thanks," D'Arcy said with genuine gratitude.

"Jenks, hold it there." Max came up off the bench.

His sister had let McGraw off the hook, it seemed, and now had Chae wrapped up in a choke hold, but she'd paused at Max's order and was nodding enthusiastically at whatever Max was saying to Chae.

"She knew from the moment she stepped on this station two years ago," D'Arcy said with a wave of his hand in Max's direction. "Little shit apparently used her family connections and looked up my file when she was assigned to Jupiter. Came asking me about explosives when that thing with the LifeEx went down and someone tried to blow Jenks's EMU pack."

"She never said anything." Granted, it wasn't like Max to gossip for the sake of it, and they'd probably never been in a position where she felt like she could tell him.

I guess I'm not the only person keeping secrets.

"Max knows when to talk and when to keep her mouth shut." D'Arcy settled back against the wall. "We'll have to work together, but I get it if you don't want to be—"

"I already told you: you're my friend, D'Arcy," Nika cut him off. He stuck his fist out. "I've got your back."

"Well, all right then." D'Arcy tapped his fist to Nika's, and though his smile was easy, Nika could see the relief in his eyes. "You going to be able to wrangle those two?" D'Arcy asked, and Nika turned his attention back to the mat. "They've gotten to be thick as thieves in the last year."

"Should be fine," Nika replied. Max had taken Chae's place in the hold and was demonstrating a way to get out of it that would work for the shorter Neo.

"Rumor is you were working with Stephan a lot in the sword ring back on Earth. Do I get to see that soon?"

"You asking me on a date, Montaglione?"

D'Arcy laughed. "Not without clearance from Carmichael. I'm looking at the Games, Nika. Curious if you're up for a run."

Nika blinked in surprise. "You know *Zuma*'s probably not a contender. We haven't talked about it, but I assumed we were just going to take the year off and focus on work. It's going to take a lot to get this team up to speed."

"You probably want to make sure those two are on the same page," D'Arcy said, tipping his head toward the mat. "Not to mention Sapphi and Tamago. They're all talking about a three-peat."

Mark that up as another thing you've missed, Vagin, he

thought. *Apparently the rest of the team was planning on making a run at the Boarding Games and here you are, content to hide in a corner.*

"Sounds like I'm outnumbered," he finally said, and forced a smile he hoped D'Arcy wouldn't pick out as fake.

"Excellent." D'Arcy tapped Nika on the knee and got to his feet. "I've got to go talk with Hoboins, but come find me at Corbin's tonight and I'll buy you a beer. We can talk about strategy and when I'm going to get to kick your ass in the sword ring."

Nika watched him go and blew out a breath. Most of the crowd had filtered away as Max and Jenks had settled into an intense training discussion with Chae.

"That's new," he murmured to himself as the two women went through the same complicated handshake routine he'd seen the day of his arrival.

"Lot of stuff new, Nik." Tamago's soft voice carried through the crowd noise. "You've been gone for a while."

He jumped and looked over. The petty officer had slid down the bench, silent as a ghost. They were good at that, slipping in and out of spaces without being noticed.

"You really thought we weren't going to do the Games?"

"It was more weighing the odds," he said. "Chae's brand-new and I'm not exactly at the top of my form here."

"You think Sapphi hasn't calculated for all of this?" Tamago's question was gentle, and as always their calm presence eased some of the worry coiling itself in Nika's chest. The petty officer was amazing. Rosa had once said they could talk the planets into new orbits if they chose, and Nika knew in this moment she was right.

"Can I see?" They held their hands out and Nika shifted so he could rest his right hand on their palms. "It feels really close, weight-wise. Skin texture is a little strange, but that's probably just me and my sensitive fingers. I miss the tattoo." They looked up at him and smiled. "You're not quite back yet, are you, Nika? I'm not expecting you to be the same, but you're still not sure who you are."

It shook him how easily they'd read him. But it didn't pay to deflect now, so he went with a half-truth. "Basically."

"Well, you're wrong. You're you. A little different, but that's life, right? It changes all of us whether we want it to or not."

He pulled Tamago into a hug so they couldn't see the tears in his eyes. "I missed you, Tama."

"I missed you, too. Max goes a long way to balancing Jenks out, but with Rosa and Ma gone the rest of it was falling on me and you know I love her, but it's also exhausting AF. I don't know how she lives in her own head."

"She'd say practice." Nika chuckled. "Here's hoping having a newbie to wrangle will divert some of that energy, but I'm happy to take the burden off your shoulders."

"Not really a burden. Just a lot of work. Jenks is going to do great," Tamago said, squeezing Nika once more before sitting up. "She doesn't think so, but she's really good at this."

Nika looked back at the sparring circle, surprised at Tamago's observation that Jenks was concerned about anything. His little sister was normally the self-assured one of this bunch.

She didn't seem concerned right now. Instead, Jenks was currently waving her arms in the air, and Max had an arm resting on Chae's shoulder, the pair laughing at whatever wild story she was telling them.

I'm doing this to keep them all safe.

He wasn't sure if he believed it was worth the lies, but there was nowhere to go now but forward. Nika looked back at Tamago.

"Yeah, she is."

SEVERAL DAYS LATER MAX DRAGGED IN A BREATH AND TRIED not to let her trepidation show as Chae banked the craft they were flying into a hard port-side turn and blew past the course marker with less than a meter to spare.

"Are you seeing this, LT?" Sapphi said on their direct com. "Sorry, you're in the passenger seat, of course you are."

"Actually, my eyes are shut tight—" Max choked on a laugh, mostly because Chae cut the engines for a second, dropping them thirty meters down. It was a trick that worked only because the simulator course they were on was in atmo with a decent gravity reading. But it *did* work.

As terrifying as this was, Max was also in awe. Ma had been an amazing pilot with over forty years of flight experience between his Navy and NeoG service. Max's help on navigation had improved upon what was already there.

Chae was something else entirely, though. She'd never seen anyone who could fly like this. It was indescribably gorgeous. And—as her grip on her armrests testified—a little scary.

An alarm blared and Chae swore. "Sorry, LT," they said, reaching over and slapping it off. "I usually turn those stress indicators off when I fly—their parameters are too sensitive."

"They're there to keep the ship from breaking apart around us, Chae."

"I know." They shot her a quick smile. "But if you're paying attention, a ship will give you plenty of warning before that happens. You just have to listen. Bit harder in a simulator, though."

They said this all without taking their eyes off the screen in front of them, and flew the craft through the big hologram sign that read FINISH LINE.

"Time: three oh-four." Sapphi's voice was on the main com and Chae made a face.

"What?" Max asked. "That's great."

"It's just . . . I could have done it in two fifty-nine. Should we go again?"

"God no, my stomach couldn't take it." Max patted Chae on the shoulder as she stood. "Good job, Chae."

"You okay?" Jenks asked as Max opened the simulator door. She grinned up at her. "You look a little green."

"They're a hell of a pilot, better than I will ever be. Honestly, I might make you navigator for the races, though."

"Can't do that, LT," Sapphi replied. "Has to be an officer."

"I'll make Nika do it, then. Chae certainly doesn't need my help and I'm not sure my nerves can take it." She leaned against the simulator bulkhead and rubbed her hands over her face. "That was wild, Sapphi. Put them into the pilot slot, and lock it in. I'll stay at navigation, for all the good I'll do. They're going to win every single race by a landslide on that talent alone."

"I'm not that good, LT," Chae protested, and Max spun on them with a raised finger.

"You *are* that good."

"Don't argue with her, kid," Jenks said with a laugh. "Once LT decides something, that's what's going to happen." She clapped Chae on the shoulder. "Come on, we've got some maintenance work to do on *Zuma* before we head out tomorrow."

Max watched them go, concealing the frown that wanted to escape because she knew Sapphi was watching her. Chae's deadline to tell the others about their secret was up and Max was reasonably sure she'd have heard about it from Jenks if the spacer had fessed up.

But they hadn't, which meant she was going to have to talk to Nika and see what he wanted to do.

"I'll have to run all the projections, but we may actually have a chance at winning the prelims," Sapphi said, breaking through Max's thoughts. "I still need to see how we can work as a team for the Boarding Action and the Big Game, but Chae flying like that will give us a huge boost in the numbers I've compiled."

"I wouldn't count Nika out just yet, either," Max murmured.

"I'm not. It's just, have you seen him fight?"

Max shook her head and Sapphi sighed.

"I haven't, either. Can I say something, Lieutenant?"

The fact that the ensign used her rank made Max look away from Jenks and Chae and at Sapphi instead. "You sure you want to, Ensign?"

"No." Sapphi sighed. "But I feel like I should. Is it just me, or is Nika avoiding us?"

"How do you mean?"

Sapphi waved a hand. "He wasn't here to watch this and I kind of assumed he would be. He seems distant in quarters and is on private coms more than usual, especially back to Earth. I know it's different for you and for Chae. Tamago, Jenks, and I, though? It's not the Nika who left us and I feel like we were all expecting it to be."

"It's barely been two weeks since he got back."

"I know, but—" Sapphi's shoulders slumped and she looked down at her hands for a moment before looking back up at Max. "I guess I'm wondering if I'm doing something wrong by behaving like everything is back to normal?"

Max chewed on the inside of her cheek as she tried to come up with an answer. The problem was, Sapphi wasn't wrong. Nika had been reserved, more so than even she'd expected. However, expecting things to be back to normal wasn't the least bit realistic. There was no normal.

Everything had changed in the last two years. Not just Nika. And with all the work they were doing for the task force, it just kept changing.

"You're not doing anything wrong," she finally said. "This is going to be an adjustment for all of us. I'll admit part of me sort of wishes we weren't doing a run at the prelims this year."

"Really? Why?"

"It's pressure we don't need?" Max rubbed at the back of her neck and made a face. "On the one hand it's good for us, gives us all something to focus on in the chaos of picking up and moving to Trappist. On the other, what if we win? Are we a good enough team to take on the other branches? Or would letting *Dread Treasure* and *Honorable Intent* take the lead on this be a better plan? We have an important job to do; right now the Games feel secondary to that."

"I hadn't really thought about it," Sapphi admitted. "I know I get too wrapped up in the Games sometimes, and you're right. This task force is essential. I wasn't born until after the Free Mars riots, but I've read about them and I don't want to see that happen on Trappist. I don't want to be a part of it."

"I know. I'd like to think the CHN learned from their mistakes and that's why we're getting involved now rather than waiting until after it's too late to make a difference."

"I hope you're right." Sapphi's sigh was soft. "My projections for the preliminaries were actually good even factoring Nika at a baseline, but I can't make accurate predictions unless I see him fighting."

Max didn't chide her for the subject change and instead checked her DD. "The team calendar says Nika's supposed to be in the gym with D'Arcy," she said. "Do you want to go down and take a look?"

"Please? It's not like I can order him to let me watch." Sapphi grinned, but it faded quickly. "I feel guilty for focusing on this sometimes, LT."

Max slipped an arm around Sapphi's shoulders and hugged the slender, brown-haired ensign to her side as they headed for the low-g tube that led to the gym. "I get what you mean. But the Games are as much a part of us as the mission is, and lying to ourselves that they're not isn't very productive. You enjoy doing it and we all appreciate the work you put into this, but I also have never once thought you would put this above what we do day in and day out. We've all seen the good that came from us winning the first Games—the budget increases, the bump in recruiting, the new ships, the way the press talks about us. It's why we show up."

"Kicking Navy's ass three years in a row would be pretty sweet, too."

Max chuckled. "Some things never change. But some things do, and the only thing we can do is take each day as it comes. I have faith that our team can overcome anything headed our way—both in the Games and in the black—as long as we remember to trust each other."

But even as she said the words, Max's thoughts wandered to Chae and the unshakable feeling that there was something her new Neo wasn't telling her.

I just wish I knew how to get them to trust me.

EIGHT

"You know Stephan sent me a message the other day."

"Did he?" Nika gave D'Arcy a look as he slipped his practice sword out of its sheath. They were in the back corner of the mostly deserted gym, and he was appreciative of the man's awareness in picking a time to spar when most folx were on duty, even if Nika should have been watching Chae's piloting test with Max and the others. Instead he was here precisely because he knew they were otherwise occupied.

Similarly, his own uncomfortable feelings about his arm had pushed him to hit the gym to practice in the early morning hours when the space was also quiet and sparsely populated. He was determined to do better if the rest of the team was set on a Games run, and the extra practice was always a good thing.

You're going to have to get over people watching you fight, Vagin, unless you make a command decision here and pull Zuma from the running for the Games entirely.

"So what did Stephan have to say?" he finally asked D'Arcy, his tone as noncommittal as he could make it.

D'Arcy grinned. "He wanted to go over this task force plan

for Trappist before we head out. However, he also asked me to talk with you."

"Is he going to mother-hen me behind my back from five hundred and eighty-eight million kilometers away?" Nika asked with a laugh.

"No, I think he wants *me* to do it while in your face."

"You can tell him I'm fine."

"He said you'd say that." D'Arcy rolled his left shoulder as he stepped into the ring. "We all know you're a terrible liar, Nik. And no matter what Stephan wants, I'm not your babysitter—"

Nika snorted. "Too fucking right."

"I am your friend," D'Arcy finished, his voice cool. He leveled Nika with a look that sucked the humor out of the space like air rushing out of an airlock. "So is Stephan, and friends look out for each other." He spun his sword. "Anyhow, when you're ready."

Nika wasn't entirely sure whether D'Arcy meant ready to talk or ready to fight, but it seemed the easier solution was to start sparring rather than admit everything going on in his head right this second.

I'm apparently a better liar than you realize.

D'Arcy obliged, meeting him in the center of the ring, blocking Nika's opening strike. Nika shook off the impact and spun to the side, a move that announcers had called "impossibly graceful" more than once in his NeoG career.

It wasn't impossible, though. It was genetics and years of training. Nika's mother had been a dancer. His grandmother also. And before that a line of family stretching back before the Collapse who'd been part of the once great Bolshoi company.

Nika could still remember the early days, before his father's drinking ruined everything. The lessons, his mother's endless grace and poise, learning to mimic her walk. They'd been a family then, young and hopeful with the whole world in front of them.

Now he had the captain of *Dread Treasure* in front of him.

The dulled swords rang against each other. Nika relaxed into the fight, ducked under a wild swing D'Arcy tossed his way and easily avoided the follow-up strike he knew was coming. For the first time in two years Nika felt some joy well up inside him.

Rehab had been six dark months of pain and misery. He'd been angry at the world, trying to hide it from everyone. Trying not to take it out on everyone.

Even after the prosthetic had been fitted and calibrated and the doctors cleared him for activity, Nika had spent another two months ignoring his sword. The simple tasks came as easily as the doctors had promised. It was strange to pick up a coffee mug; however, he could do it and drink from the damn thing without spilling all over himself. But coffee was just something he consumed. His sword . . . that was supposed to be a part of him, an extension of him. He couldn't stand the idea of it not feeling natural.

D'Arcy swore as Nika slipped past his guard and scored a touch on him. "You haven't gotten any slower, that's for sure."

Nika grinned and saluted with his sword as he stepped back. "You have, apparently."

"Oh, I see how it is." D'Arcy saluted back and they clashed again.

The rhythmic ringing of practice swords was a sound that had always eased Nika's nerves. He hadn't even considered how good he'd been at sword fighting until the academy. His mother had been long dead by that point and some part of him still grieved at how she'd never gotten to see him compete.

Never saw him dance.

Baba did at least. I hope she told Mom all about it in the afterlife.

The sword almost felt right in his hand now. That had been Stephan's doing, the Intel commander showing up day after day to drag Nika—sometimes forcibly—out the door to the gym. Stephan had drilled him for hours, an unrelenting taskmaster who refused to give up.

Or let Nika do the same.

Nika narrowly avoided D'Arcy's attack, but missed the follow-up. D'Arcy used the hook on the end of his sword to send Nika's sword spinning across the floor of the ring.

"YOU HAVE TO USE IT, VAGIN. IT'S THE ONLY WAY YOU'LL GET *used to it being a part of you."*

"What if I don't want it?"

Stephan had stopped, lowering his sword and studying Nika with those intense blue eyes of his. "Do you really not? You didn't have to take the prosthetic, Nika. Plenty of people choose not to."

"I did—I thought—I don't know." Nika dropped his own sword and followed it to the mat, grateful that they were alone in the gym so no one else could see his tears. "I don't fucking know, Stephan."

"Hey." Stephan went to a knee next to him; the warmth of his hand on Nika's back grounded him some. "Look at me. It's okay. You're okay."

"No, I'm not. I'm a fucking mess." Nika couldn't help the laugh that escaped him.

"Given everything that's happened in the last few months I figure you're entitled to be a mess," Stephan replied. He reached a hand out, laying it on Nika's right forearm.

"I'll say it again," Stephan continued, "you don't have to have this to be a whole person. Choosing it doesn't diminish what you've lost. It would be bullshit for me to tell you what to do as someone who's never had to go through this, so what I will tell you is I'm your friend and I'm here to help you however I can."

NIKA SPOTTED MAX AND SAPPHI AS HE BENT TO PICK UP HIS sword. The pair was standing off to the side—Sapphi with that slightly faraway look that indicated she was checking something on her DD chip, Max with her arms crossed over her chest and those brown eyes of hers coolly assessing.

Remember when I said you were going to have to get used to performing for a crowd? Looks like the time is now.

"You want to quit?" D'Arcy asked after a glance at the pair.

"Nah, I'm good. Let's go."

"I GOT ARRESTED."

Jenks sat up faster than she should have and bashed her head on the piping above her. "Motherfucker. No, I'm fine." She locked a hand on Chae's arm before the spacer could wriggle away. "Unless I'm bleeding. Am I bleeding?"

"No."

"Okay, you want to run that by me again? Because it sounded like you just said you got arrested." It wasn't often Jenks could use her size as an intimidation tactic, but in this small space of *Zuma*'s underbelly, with Chae on their back, it seemed to work wonders.

"I did."

"When?" Jenks frowned. "I mean, obviously previous to getting here. I feel like I would have heard about it if it had happened in the last two weeks. What the actual fuck, Chae—why is this the first I'm hearing about it?"

"I was . . ." Chae swallowed and the story spilled out, a little disjointed, but enough to make perfect sense.

Jenks rubbed at the bump on her forehead and sighed. "Do Max and Nika know?"

Chae nodded. "The lieutenant said I could tell everyone else however I wanted to, but that I had two weeks. Which is up when we go out into the black. I'm sorry I waited so long, I just didn't know how to do it."

"I mean, just coming right out and saying it is fine, even if you tried to run like Prince Harry after."

"Like *who*?"

Jenks waved her hand. "Not the point. Next time, can I ask that you not tell me important shit while I'm under something that's going to put a dent in my skull?" Jenks blew out a breath as the relief flooded her. At least she didn't have to figure out how to tell the others. "Cuttin' it close to the wire there. You ashamed of it, Chae?"

"No." The kid seemed surprised by the question. "No, I chose this. We needed the supplies. I planned it. I was fine with taking the responsibility. And it put me here."

There was something more there, Jenks could see it buried in the back of Chae's nervous expression, but she didn't push. Instead she lay down on the deck next to them and went back to work.

"You know I grew up on the streets, yeah? Hand me that eight-five-mil wrench, will you?"

"Yes, Chief."

Jenks took the wrench, resisting the urge to tap Chae with it in frustration at their formality. "This conduit likes to get gummed up, so you have to take it apart every so often and clean it out. It feeds into the secondary power supply that runs from the tanks to the nonessentials. In a pinch you can pull it and attach to the main line there so it loops back to essential systems." She reached out and tapped the line above her head. "Real useful if you need to boost your com signal or make your life support last longer. It keeps the bleed-off lower, and out in the black those extra five hours can save your life and the lives of your crew. What you don't want to do is attach the green feed to that blue line up there." She pointed. "It's complicated, but it'll send a live charge up to the bridge that will short out everything in the ship.

"Anyway, I grew up on the streets," Jenks repeated without missing a beat. "Never worried about anyone but myself, never trusted anyone but myself. The couple of times I tried, it ended badly. It's kind of a shitty way to live, but it kept me alive. Of course, when I got out of it?" She sucked air in between her teeth and turned her head to look at the Neo.

"It took me a really long time to realize I wasn't going to lose

Nika and all this if I fucked up. I've done some shit, Chae. Most of it was to survive, so if you think I'm going to judge you for what you did to keep your family and your people alive? Think again. I'm good with it. Tamago and Sapphi will be fine with this, too. We'll find them as soon as we're done here so you can tell them. Understood?"

"Yes, Ch—"

"I swear to god, kid, if you call me Chief one more time I'm going to brain you with this wrench and tell Nika you tripped over your own feet and fell down the stairs."

"I won't believe you," a voice said from above them.

Jenks glanced over and saw Nika's boots. She threw a wink at Chae as she snorted loud enough for her brother to hear. "Hand me that bucket, Commander, before I open this and get goo all over your shiny boots."

Nika laughed and dropped into a crouch, handing the bucket over. Jenks held it and tipped her chin at Chae. "It's loose enough, just twist it open and immediately put the line in here."

Chae reached up and grabbed the link, twisting and shoving the ends into the bucket.

"Remember when you told Tamago to do that and they didn't wait for the second part of the instructions?" Nika asked with a laugh, and Jenks joined him, rolling her eyes.

"I do. It sprayed everywhere. We were covered in goo. I was still finding dried bits a month out. Thank you for waiting for me to say the whole sentence." She reached out and patted Chae on the shoulder. "Hey, Nik, do you know where Sapphi is?"

"She came up with me from the gym; she's on the bridge with Tamago."

"I thought I smelled something." She winked at him. "Tell them both to come back here a moment, will you? We need to have a quick talk."

Encrypted Message

NEOG TASK FORCE AT TRAPPIST JUNCTURE–JUPITER STATION SIDE AS FOLLOWS:

Zuma's Ghost running from 6233/9983 to 8466/9983 and 107.7
Flux Capacitor in the main belt lane, closer to Jupiter Station
Wandering Hunter in the Saturn patrol area
Dread Treasure in the main belt lane, closer to junction

OTHER SHIPS OF NOTE:

Burden of Proof patrolling between Jupiter and Saturn
Keppler's Folly at transport point

Teams 1–6 advised to fly no cargo, no raising suspicions. Task Force has list of possible ships to watch for and board as necessary. Recommend swapping decoy ships for those on list and run usual spoiled cargo as a distraction. The Belt run is still a go.

NINE

Max stretched in her seat. *Zuma's Ghost* was quiet, the gentle hum of the ship less a noise in her ears than a vibration in her bones.

God, she loved this ship. She smoothed a hand over the console with a fondness she'd never expected to feel for a vessel. Two years had gone by in the blink of an eye. She remembered how unsure she'd been, how out of place she'd felt, and now she couldn't imagine being anywhere else.

Laughter wafted onto the bridge from the galley. Sapphi and Chae were making breakfast.

They'd been out in the Kuiper Belt for the better part of a week, patrolling the high-traffic lanes around the junction that fed from Jupiter to Trappist. It was quiet work, a few stops to check on freighters' paperwork, but other than that nothing major, and she was glad for the post-Games downtime.

Plus it gave Nika and Chae a chance to settle into the crew. Which Chae seemed to be doing. *Seemed*—the spacer was a little hard to read at times. They were watchful and careful, giving almost nothing away with words or gestures. Max had thought for a moment she'd run into yet another Jenks, but after a few days she knew that was wrong.

Chae was as predictable as most people, but so careful in their actions it almost had the opposite effect of telegraphing what they were going to do once they'd decided to do it. It was like they thought everything through in triplicate and then did it again before committing.

Except for flying. Chae let go when they were flying and moved on instinct.

Max also knew Chae was still hiding something, which worried her more than she wanted to admit. She'd tried to tell herself that everyone had secrets, but whatever this was had worked its way into the fabric of Chae's being. *And if the seams fray at the wrong time . . .*

She'd continue to keep an eye on them.

And Nika.

Max suppressed a sigh.

You're making that into more than it should be, Carmichael.

She'd tried to talk to Nika twice now about Chae, and each time he'd brushed off her concerns, insisting they had been dealt with. She'd known Nika would be a different leader from Rosa, but she'd also thought maybe he'd be more willing to listen to her—not less.

Maybe he's just busy, or you really are making something out of nothing, or he doesn't trust your gut the same way Rosa did . . . because he's not as good a commander as she was.

It was an uncharitable thought and she felt immediately guilty.

"Morning, LT."

She looked up at Tamago, putting a hand on theirs where they'd rested it on her shoulder. "Morning. How'd you sleep?"

"Good." Tamago slid into the empty seat next to Max. "Hey, do you have a minute? I wanted to—"

"*Zuma's Ghost*, this is *Flux Capacitor*, do you copy?" The ship's coms crackled to life, interrupting Tamago. Max held up a finger as she toggled the coms.

"Copy you, *Flux*. Lieutenant Carmichael here."

"Hey, Max, it's Tien. We've got a positive return on the list headed down the lane for the wormhole point. You want to back us up on a boarding?" *Flux*'s senior chief petty officer, Dao Mai Tien, had a sweet voice that didn't so much as hint at her absolute brutality in the sword ring.

"We'd love to. Send me coordinates and I'll wake the others."

Tamago was already out of her seat and down the bridge stairs before Max finished speaking.

"What's up?" Nika asked a few moments later. He rested a hand on her shoulder in the same spot Tamago had just left and Max reached up, tangling her fingers with his.

"*Flux* called. They've pinged a suspect ship from the list and asked if we wanted to back them up on the boarding."

"*Honor's Fury*?"

"Good guess."

He grinned. "I can read briefings, Carmichael."

"She's not big—a D-class freighter from Trappist Express waiting for a ride across to Trappist. Four of us would do it in addition to *Flux* putting four of theirs in."

"I don't know if we need four. I could take Jenks and Chae. It'll be an easy board, most likely."

"Four's the standard for a ship that size." She frowned as he slipped away from her, physically and mentally, his mind so obviously somewhere else that she called out as he headed for the stairs. "Nika, if the ship was on the briefing, it might not be easy."

"Fine, I'll take Tamago, too."

"Be careful," she whispered, but he was already gone.

NIKA LEFT MAX ON THE BRIDGE AND HEADED FOR THE BACK, stopping when he heard the laughter wafting in his direction from the galley.

He'd slipped, and of course Max had noticed. The first one had been easy enough to cover with humor, and it wasn't a huge stretch that *Honor's Fury* would be one of the ships they tagged. But he should have paid better attention and acted like this boarding could be dangerous, even though he knew *Honor's Fury* was likely nothing more than a decoy ship because of the information Chae had passed along . . . and Intel had intercepted. There would be little more than maybe a carton of rotten food, or broken equipment. All easily explainable as poor quality control in the warehouse.

And yet you should be careful, Vagin. Any boarding could turn nasty in the blink of an eye. Intel is not the same as surety, and a good commander isn't cocky.

A good commander . . .

He sucked in a deep breath, letting it out slowly.

"Commander, Commander Till is reporting the ship has heaved to and is agreeing to an inspection. You still want to board with them, or hold back?" Max asked over their private com. Her voice was stiff, the use of his rank hitting like a punch.

"Let's board," he replied. "Strange that they would agree so readily, and you were right that we should go in standard force."

"Thank you for that. I agree that it's strange. They might actually be clean this time, though. Or thinking they've got shit hidden well enough. I looked over the manifests in the registry, and everything seems in order, but—well, you know."

He did. He also knew he'd been discounting her gut feelings about Chae and that it had to hurt Max. Yet he was going to have to figure out a way to shut her down on that before too much longer. Nika rubbed a hand over his face. "I guess we'll find out, won't we?"

"Good luck. Be careful."

"You said that already."

"I didn't think you heard me."

Nika didn't know what to say to that, so he stuck his head in the galley instead. "Jenks, Chae, Tamago—get your boots and swords on. Sapphi, you're staying here with Max. Doge, you know the drill."

The ROVER dropped back into the corner of the galley in what Nika would almost call a sulk if he'd thought the robot were capable of such emotion.

"No suits?" Jenks asked.

Nika tried to ignore his uncertainty and shook his head. "They heaved to. I think we're good without them."

They moved without hesitation, Jenks cursing as she tried to drink the last of her hot coffee faster than a human should and Chae moving with a look of wide-eyed wonder that only a brand-new spacer could have.

"Hey, you'll be fine," Nika said as the kid passed, and they nodded. "Stick with Jenks, follow her orders, and keep your eyes open."

"Yes, Commander."

Nika grabbed his boots from the locker just off the airlock and laced them up, his heart still thumping an odd tattoo that was a confusing mess of preboarding nerves and every lie he was telling his crew.

"Hey, space ranger." Jenks snapped her fingers in front of his face. "You in charge here or what?"

He took the sword she was holding and attached it to his belt. His little sister was grinning at him, bouncing on the balls of her feet in that familiar way, and for a moment everything slid into place just like he'd never left. "That's the rumor."

"Good. Let's get our asses on that ship before Vera gets to have all the fun."

Nika heard Commander Vera Till chuckle over the live coms. "Don't start none, Jenks. If this goes smoothly, we get to go home early."

"Roger, we are in ancient Tibetan mode: don't start none, won't be none—"

"Let's focus, folx," Nika said over the top of Jenks's singsong.

Max's cool voice came over the main com. "Airlock secure on the port side. Commander Vagin, Commander Till, whenever you're ready."

"We're on starboard side, locked and ready to board."

Nika hit the panel to cycle the airlock, glancing down out of habit, and did a double take at Jenks's neatly laced boot.

"You fixed your boot?"

Jenks looked at him and then rolled her eyes. "Yeah. LT kept fucking stepping on the lace. For someone so smart she couldn't seem to figure out how to not do it and I got tired of almost landing on my face over and over."

Nika was reasonably sure Max hadn't done that accidentally at all. They'd all spent years learning how to avoid Jenks's bootlaces, knowing she wouldn't tie them correctly. The only time she made sure they were tucked in was during boarding actions and at the Games, but she'd refused to fix them completely no matter how many times he or Rosa or even Hoboins had threatened her.

In under two years Max had gotten Jenks to fix the damn things without even asking. A glance in Tamago's direction netted him a slow smile, as if they knew exactly what he was thinking. Gravely, Nika winked back.

"Well," he said, and had to clear his throat, earning a suspicious look from Jenks. "Let's go see what *Honor's Fury* is up to, shall we?"

CHAE FOLLOWED JENKS LIKE A SHADOW THROUGH THE boarding. The spacer was good at being quiet and watchful, and asked questions at just the right moments. It had all gone very smoothly.

Too smoothly.

Now Jenks leaned against the bulkhead, watching *Honor's Fury*'s captain and first officer as they talked with Vera and

Nika. There was no hostility in their stance, but just enough of something to make her nerves stay on high alert.

Even though the Neos hadn't found shit so far.

"Nothing," Tamago said. "Everything on this manifest matches."

"It happens." Jenks shrugged. "Maybe the intel was wrong. Maybe they went straight and narrow for this run." She scanned through the manifest on her DD chip, keeping one eye on Chae and the crewman who was leading them through the mass of pods. "It's all headed for Trappist-1d. Building materials, foodstuffs, the usual."

"Intel's not typically this far off with their leads." Tamago leaned against the bulkhead next to her, a frown on their face. "I expected to see something that would explain this itch."

"Maybe you just need to see the doc." Jenks grinned and dodged Tamago's shove. "Hold up." She noticed Chae's posture, the Neo hunched over a container, and pushed away from the wall, crossing the cargo bay. "Problem, Chae?"

They looked away from the container at her and shook their head. "Busted seal. It happens, but if they don't seal it back up these cabbages will all rot out before they get to where they're going." They shrugged at Jenks's curious look. "We saw it a lot in the habitats."

Jenks looked at the crewman, whose handshake read *Crewman Penor Crie, he/him*. "You got stuff to fix it?" she asked.

"Yes."

"Well, go get it. We'll give you a hand." She dropped into a crouch as the crewman ran off, running her fingers over the seal. It was loose on the bottom edge. "Pressure differential," she murmured. "You know, internals on the ships were supposed to fix this issue."

"Chief?"

She looked up at Chae. "We see it off and on, but sounds like it happens a lot more than just the occasional case." The seal was curled inward like it had never stuck to the container and Jenks took a few photos, out of habit more than anything. "You open this to make sure it was produce?" She rolled her eyes at Chae's sudden embarrassed expression. "You always gotta look, kid. Hey, Tamago, come give me a hand."

On the team com, she said, "Nika, we've got a broken seal on a container. Could be nothing but we're gonna open it up."

"Roger that, proceed."

"Take a corner," Jenks said, pointing at the other side. Chae and Tamago lined up and Jenks nodded. "On three, lift and slide toward that empty spot. One, two, three."

The smell was immediate and awful. The lid of the container clattered to the floor of the cargo bay. Tamago started retching. Chae looked horrified, but unbothered by the smell.

"If that doesn't smell like my childhood," Jenks muttered, breathing as shallowly as she could and peeking into the container. "Too late to fix the seal on that."

"Holy fuck, Jenks, what is that smell?" Commander Till demanded over the com.

"Rotten cabbages." Jenks skirted the container, grabbing both Tamago and Chae and dragging them away. "Breathe through your mouth, as shallowly as you can, Tama," she said gently. "Nika, we're not going to want to hang around here. Trust me when I say you don't want that smell getting in the Interceptors."

"We're done here anyway," Till replied. "Let's wrap it up and go, people."

The exclamations and protests of the freighter captain filled the air along with the stench as the Neos abandoned them to their rotten cargo.

"Do not puke on my boots." Jenks shoved Tamago toward the head as soon as they were through the airlock. "Strip your clothes and bag them. They're not so bad we can't save 'em, but we don't want them out in the air."

"Rotten cabbages?" Max asked, recoiling as she caught a whiff of the smell. "Good lord."

"Those things were black as space. Long gone. That seal failed well before the pod made it on board *Honor's Fury*." Jenks muttered a curse as she bent to unlace her boots. "Was easier to get these off before, you know." She pulled her shirt over her head as she went up the stairs.

"You're the one who decided to start tying them properly." Max leaned against the doorframe of the room the other four members of *Zuma's Ghost* shared.

"Vera should tell the captain of *Honor's Fury* to file a complaint with Trappist Express. Those things were probably rotten before they even made it on her ship." Jenks glanced over at where Chae was dutifully putting their clothes into a sealed bag, after folding them neatly.

"You can tell her. We're going to hook up with *Flux* and have breakfast."

Jenks grinned.

Tamago's groan echoed from the head. "Don't talk about food."

CHAE SEALED THE BAG AND SLID IT INTO THE STORAGE locker near the door, moving back to their bunk and getting dressed in fresh clothes as they listened with half an ear to Max and Jenks. They wondered if the fact that they hadn't found anything but rotten food was because of the message they'd passed to Julia before leaving on patrol, but the thought made their chest ache so they tried their best to shove it away and peeked in on Tamago. "You okay?"

Tamago looked up from the sink and spit out the mouthful of water they'd been rinsing with. "Yeah, that was foul. How did you not throw up?"

Chae shrugged. "Not my first bin of rotten food, honestly. Like I told the chief, we saw it a lot in the habitats."

"You shouldn't have." Tamago rinsed their mouth out and

spit into the sink again. "I thought that was part of the agreement for folx who moved to Trappist?"

"It is. Reality is usually pretty different from what's on paper, though." Chae held their hand out. "You want me to bag those for you?"

"You're a blessing, yes please." Tamago nudged the clothes over with a bare foot. "There's nothing left in my stomach, but that won't stop it from trying to expel something if I smell that again."

Chae scooped up Tamago's uniform, carrying it out of the bathroom. The rotten stench had dissipated for the most part, but they could still smell the faintest trace and a memory rushed up to meet it.

"SEVEN OF THE FIFTEEN CONTAINERS ARE USELESS. SEVEN, *Gun. And none of the medicine we requested. How are we supposed to survive this winter?"*

Chae pressed themself closer to the wall in the hallway as they listened to their fathers.

"We'll figure something out, Michael. Daki's got a new batch of protein in the mix, and the kale is already growing. It might be tight, but we'll make it."

"Not if they don't deliver those medical supplies. I keep getting the runaround on it. They say it's been here since the ninth, but I told them they were welcome to come down and look at our fucking empty stores if they thought I was lying."

"I know you're frustrated. I am, too."

"This is beyond frustrating, Gun. This is wrong and you know it. Things were supposed to be different after Mars. That's why we agreed to the deal."

"Your naivety is one of the things I've always loved about you."

"Oh, shut up." Their father's laughter faded as quickly as it had arrived. "We really are going to have to do something."

Chae took a deep breath and walked into the kitchen. "Hey, Dad, I have an idea. Julia told me about . . ."

"CHAE."

They jerked when Jenks snapped her fingers in their face. "Sorry."

"It's fine. *Flux* just hooked up. Come down and meet everyone for real. Tama, come down when your stomach has settled."

The Interceptors were designed to be able to connect the rear airlocks together, giving the crews a chance to meet up out in the black and exchange supplies, assistance, or even a meal.

The ship always felt large with just the six of them on board, but now with the added crew of *Flux* in the galley and the hallway outside, it seemed cozy for the first time since Chae's arrival.

"ZZ, you are officially no longer the fucking newbie. Chae, meet Spacer Zavia Zolorist, aka ZZ. This is Spacer Chae Ho-ki, but call them Chae." Jenks gestured grandly.

"Chae it is, then." The woman offered up a bright smile. "I hope the chief here isn't giving you too hard a time."

"She's great." Chae choked back a laugh at the raised white eyebrow ZZ offered in response just before stage-whispering, "If you need rescuing, just wink your left eye."

"ZZ likes to think she's a comedian, but truth is Nash is funnier."

The trans man behind Jenks shook his head with a roll of his eyes. "Hi, Chae, Atlas Nash. Welcome to the NeoG. I hear you get used to Jenks. I don't see how, but don't sweat it."

Chae rubbed their hands down the front of their pants in an effort to smooth out their nerves. "It's really nice to meet you."

"Don't put them on the spot, you two."

Chae looked behind and spotted the commander of *Flux*

Capacitor, Vera Till, standing with Nika. "Welcome to the NeoG, Chae," she said.

"Thank you, Commander."

Vera grinned and Nika shook his head as he said, "We're still trying to break them of that habit."

"ZZ did it for six months," she replied. "It's like the sergeants at boot haven't been out in the black in forever, and insist on this nonsense during basic." She shook her head, lavender curls bouncing. "They'll settle in when they're ready, yeah, Chae?" The commander didn't wait for an answer before shouting over Chae's head, "You want to unblock the hallway there so we can get to the food?"

Jenks was in an embrace with a taller woman with a shaved head whose handshake read *Senior Chief Dao Mai Tien, she/her,* and Chae choked back a startled gasp as both women lifted a middle finger to Commander Till without looking back.

Nika laughed and patted Chae on the shoulder. "Your first official ship meeting, kid. Move your ass, Jenks, before the food gets cold."

Jenks's reply was lost to laughter and Chae found themself swept up in the group of people headed for the galley, all thoughts of the past and worries of the future forgotten for the time being.

TEN

It all came crashing back down on Chae when they stepped off the last rung of the Interceptor back on Jupiter Station and spotted Julia chatting with a lime-vested deckhand.

The memory rushed in, carrying with it the awful certainty that they had been set up for this whole thing. That Julia had found them on Trappist-1d, and dropped the information about the medical supplies. All just to get Chae here.

But why?

They almost bolted, but Max was right behind them and she put a hand on their shoulder. "Good job out there, Chae."

"Chae!"

Chae froze and felt Max's hand tighten, her fingers digging into their shoulder for a moment before she relaxed and let them go.

Julia was crossing the open space with a practiced smile on her face, and for a desperate moment Chae wished they'd taken one of the hundred opportunities Max had offered to tell her the truth.

It's too late for that; you're in too deep and they'll kill your fathers if you don't cooperate.

"Hi! I'm Julia Draven, Chae's girlfriend. They've told me all about you, Lieutenant."

"Girlfriend." The smile on Max's face was polite but lacking any of her normal warmth, and it was all Chae could do to stay relaxed. "What brings you to Jupiter? Besides Chae, obviously."

"I work for Off-Earth as a consultant and we're running a few prototypes for the NeoG. Testing keeps me flying back and forth between here and Earth, but the nice bonus is I get to see Chae when they're here."

"You should have dinner with us."

"No!" Chae scrambled at Max's look. They hadn't meant to say it quite so forcefully. "I'm sorry, LT, is it okay if Julia and I go to dinner alone? I haven't seen her since graduation."

Max's suspicion disappeared and she smiled. "That's totally fine, Chae. I'm sorry. I didn't even think you might want some privacy." She lifted her bag. "Have a good evening. It was nice to meet you, Julia."

"Likewise." Julia's bright expression didn't fade, but it turned calculating as she slipped her arm around Chae's shoulders. "It's so good to see you."

"I did what you told me."

"Oh." Julia laughed as she walked them out of the Interceptor bay. "You're not in trouble, Chae! You did brilliantly. Everyone was right where you said they'd be."

"So what do you want?"

"Watch the hostility," Julia said. "You're supposed to be happy to see me." She patted their cheek. "I'm here to tell you that you did a good job and to let you know that we've got some freighters coming through in a few weeks with important cargo. I want you to put these in your quarters and on the ship. The bridge and as close to Commander Vagin's room here on station as you can get should be fine."

"What are they?" Chae's stomach was a ball of frozen fear as Julia dropped two button-like devices into their hand.

"Does it matter?" Julia folded Chae's hand closed. "Relax—they're only listening devices. You're ours, Chae; we wouldn't do anything to put you in danger."

Chae wrestled with the desire to wipe the smirk off Julia's face, the sudden and stunning fury resulting in them just nodding as they fought to keep their hands where they were. Julia didn't notice and patted their cheek again.

"Also: I'm not actually going to dinner with you, Chae—I don't think I'd want to have my meal ruined by being near you too long. I hope you weren't looking forward to that." Her laugh was sharp, savage, and lingered in the air as she left them alone in the hallway.

Chae turned on their heel and headed back to the Interceptor bay before they could stop to think about it.

Cascade failure imminent. Reset this switch and keep moving.

"Hey, Chae, I thought you headed out to dinner. Max said your girlfriend was here."

They froze at the sound of Jenks's voice from the galley. "I forgot something in my bunk. She's going to meet me."

"All right. Just make sure you lock the ship up when you leave."

"Yes, Chief."

There was a pause and then a resigned sigh. "I swear, Chae, one of these days . . ." Jenks's muttered threat trailed off as she left the ship.

Chae felt the hot sting of tears start and for a heartbeat all they wanted to do was drop to the floor and sob over the unfairness of it all.

Just get this done and forget about it. You have to keep your dads safe. They're all that matters. You can't afford to care about anyone else.

Chae looked around the bridge and moved toward the far wall. They slipped one of the devices out of their pocket and reached as far as they could behind the main coms panel. The button stuck with a metallic click and Chae pressed their head against the metal for a moment, letting the tears fall.

I'm so sorry.

"I STILL CAN'T BELIEVE YOU GOT JENKS TO LACE HER BOOTS properly."

Max chuckled at the disbelief in Nika's voice and looked up at him. She was curled against his side in his room, the door closed, though the others were down at Corbin's and unlikely to be back anytime soon.

There was a movie playing on the tablet propped up on the desk, but neither of them had been paying it much attention in favor of the conversation.

"It was easy once I figured out what the issue was."

"You finally able to predict my sister?"

"Not in the slightest," she replied with another laugh. "As Hoboins told me, 'Even Jenks doesn't know what she's going to do until she's done it.' And he wasn't wrong about that. No, the bootlace thing was her making sure the team knew she was part of it." Max propped herself up on one arm and smiled down at Nika's obvious confusion.

"I don't get it. She's the heart and soul of this team most days. So why would she think she needed that?"

"Think about how she grew up, Nik. My parents may have treated me poorly, but I knew they wanted me. And even without affection, I was well cared for. With Jenks, she didn't even get that assurance until much too late. That kind of abandonment leaves scars."

"You're saying she deliberately left her lace untied so we'd step on it?"

"Sort of." Max smiled again and rolled the next words around in her mouth before she said them. "I'm not saying that you all did the wrong thing by avoiding it, but what she needed was someone to acknowledge that she was there. So I did." She grinned. "Once she realized that I was recognizing her presence, it annoyed her enough to fix it. More important, she didn't need it anymore."

"I don't think I've ever told you, but I'm glad you two are friends."

"I love her," Max said, and laid her head back on Nika's shoulder before he could see the gleam of tears in her eyes. "She's an amazing human being."

"You are, too. All this time and I thought she was just doing it to be annoying. It never occurred to me it might be more than that."

"I mean, it *was* annoying. But it was also more. It's okay, though—sometimes we don't see these things when we're really close to a person." Max took a deep breath, bracing herself for the potential fallout. "Can I ask you something?"

"Anything. What's up?" Nika frowned at the look on her face as he sat up with her.

"Did you know Chae had a girlfriend?"

"What?"

"Julia Draven. She met us at the Interceptor bay, probably has clearance because she works for Off-Earth. I know they've been here testing a few new things—apparently we're supposed to be on the list for the new helmets at some point. It's just odd that Chae hadn't mentioned her at all."

"Chae's not going to tell either of us about their love life."

"No, I mean *at all*, Nika. I asked everyone and they didn't know, either."

"Max, what's your point?" Nika's voice held enough of a snap that she blinked at him in shock. "It's just a girlfriend."

"My point is the same as it's always been. That something is off here. It's fucking weird for them not to mention her a single time." She slid off the bed, suddenly furious at his dismissal. "Why won't you listen to me about this? This is more than Chae just getting busted for stealing. My gut—"

"Saint Ivan, Max. Your gut is not always going to be right.

Stop looking for problems where there are none and deal with the fact that not everyone talks to you about everything going on in their lives. This is supposed to be our downtime and you're wasting it trying to push something that's not there. I know you don't have much experience with relationships, but can you give it a rest and actually focus on us when we're together?"

She stared at him, the sick dread in her chest spreading like a shipboard fire at the echo of her father's words: that she was always too pushy, imagining things, not thinking of others but only of herself. Max tried to shake the encroaching pain away. This was Nika; he hadn't meant it the way it sounded. "I am trying to do my job." It came out in a whisper.

"No, you're trying to do *my* job and I'd appreciate it if you'd stop second-guessing every decision I make." His reply hit like a slap and Max couldn't stop herself from retreating in shock. "Nika, I—"

"Look." Nika shoved a hand into his blond hair with a frustrated sigh. "We're not going to get anywhere with this and I just remembered Stephan wanted to have a call this evening with the task force commanders. I need to go and sort through what he might need for that." He somehow backed her up through the doorway of his room and Max stood in shock as he closed the door in her face.

She fisted a hand, tempted for a second to pound on the door and demand he open it again. But too many years of being told to respect the demands on other people's time kicked in and Max turned away.

Just because he's being a jerk doesn't mean I have to be one back. I haven't been second-guessing him. I was just pointing out the regs about the boarding, and it was his fault for only wanting to take Jenks and Chae. I didn't do anything wrong.

"Damn it." She grabbed her workout gear from her trunk and headed out the door, composing an email to Jeanie Bosco as she went.

Jeanie—

At the risk of owing you, I have another favor to ask.
This one isn't really a rush. Can you do some digging
for me on an Off-Earth employee by the name of Julia
Draven? Whatever you can find.

Thanks,

Max

Thankfully, she didn't run into anyone she knew on her
way to the gym. Max settled into the back corner by the punching bags. She'd debated a run to clear her head, but she really
needed to hit something.

Before I punch my commander in his thick head.

She wrapped her hands with smooth, practiced move-
ments and started in a routine Jenks had set up for her months
ago. The clock in the corner of her vision ticked away and Max
let the impact of the bag pummel all the worry and tension out
of her shoulders.

"Carmichael, did that bag do something unforgivable to
you?"

Max jerked out of her zone at the sound of D'Arcy's voice
and backed up a step, breathing hard. "Sorry, what?"

"You look like you're trying to kill it." He tilted his head to
the side, studying her with dark eyes. "Everything okay?"

Two simple words and it all came crashing back. Max
pressed her fist to her mouth, cutting off the sob that tried to
escape as she turned away.

"Shit, I was mostly teasing." D'Arcy circled with his hands
up. "Max, what's going on?"

"It's nothing." She fumbled with her wraps, unable to come
up with a better response, knowing D'Arcy wouldn't let it go.
Her hands were throbbing in time with her heart, the same
wounded pain echoing from both spots. The replay of Nika
slamming the door in her face came to life in her head. He'd

shut down right in front of her eyes, the blank look on his face turning him into a stranger. Max knew she hadn't been in the wrong, but too many years of conditioning were surging up to cut off her air and make her question all her decisions.

It was everything she'd feared about them being on a team together and it felt like taking a sword to the gut.

"You're full of shit, Carmichael. Sit down."

Max didn't protest when D'Arcy pointed to the bench. She held her hands out so he could finish unwrapping them. He was a strange study in contrasts. A big man with a violent past who'd never so much as raised his voice in her hearing and seemed to possess a bottomless well of compassion.

"D'Arcy, what do you think of Chae?"

He paused in the act of rolling up a wrap; the hesitation was so slight anyone else might have missed it, but Max didn't. "Seems like a nice enough kid. Why?"

"I'm not sure they're settling into the crew all that well." It was the best she could come up with, but D'Arcy didn't seem to be buying it.

He didn't question her about that, though, instead asking, "You talk to Nika about it?" He sucked air between his teeth when Max looked pointedly at the bag, not trusting herself to speak. "Gotcha. Well, do you need advice, or just someone to listen?" He pointed at her bruised knuckles. "Because you're done hitting things for today."

"I need Nika to trust my gut the way Rosa did." Max squeezed her eyes shut after the words slipped out in a rush. "Everything is off, D'Arcy. I know I don't have anything concrete—just a lot of weird pieces and my intuition screaming. Chae's afraid of something, but no matter how many times I try to coax it out of them they won't talk to me." She swung a hand through the air. "And then Nika tells me I'm imagining things and should drop it. He accused me of trying to do his job, of not caring about our relationship, and I don't know what to do." The story of the fight and what had happened before the boarding action spilled out of her. Max knew she should have felt guilty talking about her commanding officer like this, but all she really felt was relief at having someone else listen to her.

D'Arcy stayed silent well after Max had wound down. She clenched her fingers, wincing as her knuckles protested, and waited.

"Rosa did a good job with you, Max. I knew she would. You've gone from an uncertain lieutenant to a leader right in front of my face. Listen, every commander you serve under is going to be different. That's the way of it. You'll learn something from each of them, and sometimes it'll be how not to lead.

"I'm not saying Nika's in the wrong here, except that how he handled it obviously hurt you. I like you, you're a good officer, and you should know by now I don't say shit like that lightly. More, I trust you out there to cover my ass. I trust Nika to do the same, though. Do you?"

Max opened her mouth, but the automatic yes didn't come like she expected it to and she floundered. Was she just mad he wouldn't listen to her the same way Rosa had? Was D'Arcy right that it was just a case of different leadership styles? Did she have any cause to be upset when she knew damn well that even Rosa would have wanted proof of something before taking action?

"I don't know," Max finally whispered. "I'm sorry."

"Don't be, it's an honest answer. Think about it some more," D'Arcy said. "If you still don't know in the morning, you might want to talk to Hoboins. We have to trust the people we're going out into the black with, Max, or what's the point?" He looked around to see if they were alone before he spoke again. "On that note, I knew Chae's fathers. A long time ago."

"Oh . . . *oh*," she repeated as the realization hit. "On Mars?"

He nodded. "And I'll say this, it continues to be relatively terrifying how you figure shit out. If you were on my crew, I would trust your gut. At the very least I'd tell you to keep digging until you were satisfied one way or the other. But you're technically not my crew, so all I can really do for you is offer to talk to Nika."

"No." Max shook her head. "I appreciate it, but I don't think it would go over all that well. I'll handle it. I—maybe I was over-reacting."

"Hey, do you need a hug?" D'Arcy wrapped an arm around Max's shoulders at her nod. "I haven't known you all that long, Max, but you're not exactly the type to overreact about any-thing. I know how Chae feels, I've been there. I didn't trust that anyone was going to watch out for me when I first got here, either. Give them some time and maybe they'll come around." D'Arcy offered up a half smile. "Sometimes you can't do any-thing but step back and hope they figure it out."

"Okay."

D'Arcy got to his feet. "I'm going to get a drink. You wanna come?"

"No, I think I'll shower and turn in." Max picked up her wraps. "Thanks, though. For everything."

"Anytime, kiddo."

"I am not a kid," she muttered at his retreating back, and he chuckled. Max frowned. "Hey, D'Arcy? Why weren't you in the meeting?"

D'Arcy turned. "What meeting?"

"Nika said—oh."

He lied to me. Just to get out of the conversation. And I fell for it.

Max shook her head as the realization slammed down on her.

"Max?"

"Nothing, never mind. I misheard."

D'Arcy hesitated a moment, but then walked away. Max squeezed her wraps in her fists until her hands screamed with pain. Then, sure her eyes would stay dry, she headed out of the gym and back to quarters. She'd cry in the showers, where no one could see.

ELEVEN

Nika pressed his head to the other side of his door with a muttered "Fuck."

How had that spiraled out of control so quickly? His brain insisted on replaying the shock and hurt on Max's face just before he'd closed his door and Nika suddenly wanted nothing more than to open it again and tell her everything.

It's probably too late for that, never mind that Stephan would kill you; but you just accused her of wasting your time together and of trying to steal your job all in the same moment. You got what you wanted, she'll drop it.

He just hadn't thought about what it would cost him.

"Get your shit together, Vagin," he snapped, and grabbed for the tablet, shutting off the movie and calling Coms. "Hey, Sully."

"Nika, what can I do for you?"

"Can you put a high-security call through to Commander Yevchenko for me?"

"Sure thing."

Nika rubbed a hand over his face as he dropped back onto the bed.

"Welcome back," Stephan said when the vid came up. "You weren't going to call me until tomorrow. What's up?"

"The run went well. As we expected, they only had the decoy ships in the transit area. Jenks spotted a carton of rotten cabbages. Easily played off as a warehouse issue. I recommended to the captain that they file a complaint."

"I'll bet that smell lingered." Stephan's grin vanished as quickly as it appeared. "So Chae is passing along the task force routes as expected."

"Yes. I was thinking: we could tell the kid their fathers are working with us and we'll keep them out of danger. Something tells me they'd still play along."

"Maybe, but it wouldn't be as authentic. I want these bastards to believe Chae's scared. The best way to do it is to have them actually *be* scared."

Nika dragged in a breath. "I don't think we have to worry about it. They're terrified."

"Oh?"

"Chae's handler is on station."

"Julia?"

"Yeah. Max said she called herself Julia Draven and claimed to be working for Off-Earth. That gives her a lot of access, Stephan."

"Max talked to her?"

"She walked right up to her in the Interceptor bay and introduced herself as Chae's girlfriend. I was already gone. Max is suspicious, Stephan. She wanted to know why Chae hadn't talked about having a girlfriend to anyone." Nika rubbed at his face again. "And her gut is apparently still screaming at her that Chae's hiding something else."

"Huh, figures Max would pick up on it. It makes sense they'd have someone watching Chae, feeding them instructions beyond what we've seen in the emails. If they're still using Chae's girlfriend it means Tieg's people may not realize we know they've got Chae under their thumb." Stephan thought for a moment and then seemed to come to a decision. "I want a visual on Julia to match with what we have from the graduation—to verify it's the same person. Talk to Hoboins about getting footage of the Interceptor bay; he knows the basics of what's going on. You have clearance to tell him anything else you think he needs to know. Send the files my way, I'll do the rest."

"Okay. What should I do about Max?" Even as Nika asked, he realized he was hoping Stephan would order him to tell her the truth.

"You need to get her to drop this. However you can. If she keeps digging, it puts a target on her head, and her family is already in the crosshairs. And more, it could compromise the whole operation. We need everything to go smoothly on your next task force run. It's dangerous enough with the weapon that freighter will be carrying, and the *Laika* will have to stay back far enough not to get picked up by anyone's sensors. Do what you need to do to get her to drop it."

I've probably already done that. And made her hate me in the process.

"I will," Nika said out loud. "I should go catch Hoboins before he turns in for the night."

"Nika, I know this is difficult. You're doing a good job."

"Thanks." It was all Nika could muster up as a reply before he disconnected and dropped his head into his hands.

I'm doing a good job lying to my crew. I'm not sure what that says about me.

"JESUS CHRIST, THIS IS A CLUSTERFUCK," JENKS MUTTERED into the early morning stillness of the bay. She'd thought things were bad when Max had joined. Then, *Zuma's Ghost* only had to get used to having one new teammate, and it had been more than a little painful.

Jokes about Max's awkwardness aside, the LT had actually settled into her role without too much difficulty.

The same was not going to be said for Nika and Chae.

"I was expecting an adjustment period, but this—" Warrant Officer Paul Huang of *Dread Treasure* broke off with a whistle.

"I decided you all could have a little win, as a treat."

"I am not even going to ask," he said.

"This is a slaughter and I hate you." Jenks bumped her shoulder into his with a smile to soften the words and turned her eyes back to the carnage on the screen in front of them.

She'd gotten accidentally taken out by Chae early in the fight. The spacer had crashed into her while Jenks was trying to fend off Paul, and then he'd fallen to Nika about five minutes after that. Now they were watching the rest of the teams work through the deconstructed hull of a freighter she'd talked Admiral Hoboins into letting them keep in the far corner of the Interceptor bay last year. The argument that it would be good to run drills in had been surprisingly effective.

It also meant they could do practice boarding actions to train for the Games. Or, as was the case right now, let *Dread Treasure* utterly wipe the floor with *Zuma*.

"Stabbed in the back by my own fucking teammate. Come on, Max." Jenks sighed and then muttered a curse as the lieutenant took a blow from D'Arcy that rendered her left arm useless. She somehow dodged the follow-up strike that would have tagged her suit with a mortal blow and ducked back behind the cover of a stack of cargo.

"She falls apart a bit when you're not around," Paul noted. Jenks glanced in his direction with a raised eyebrow. "You two realize that, right? You've jelled so well in such a short amount of time that you've got big targets on your backs as far as the Games go. Why do you think I came after you?"

"Should you be sharing your secrets?" Even as she teased him, Jenks was doing the math in her head and knew he was right on both counts. She and Max did work well together, so well in fact, it hadn't really registered to her that it had only been two years.

Feels like she's been here forever.

There was something else there, though. Max and Nika had been snappish and short with each other even as they spoke to the rest of the crew like normal, and Jenks didn't know what to make of it.

She wasn't sure she wanted to make anything of it, but if it continued she was probably going to have to get involved.

I hate being the chief.

"You were bound to figure it out eventually anyway, and if we end up on the team together I'd rather you have a half-dozen months to mull it over." Paul shrugged and looked back at the screen.

"That's a big 'if' at this point, but fair enough." Jenks chewed on her lip as she watched Nika. His initial hesitation when they'd started this run was gone, but it had fed into this shit show in the first place and she didn't see a way out of it now.

Except, there was Chae, slipping between a broken gap in the wall just behind D'Arcy, as quiet as a mouse. He was so focused on hunting Max that he didn't see the spacer.

"You warn him, Paul, and I will break all your fingers," she said.

"I couldn't even if I wanted to," Paul replied, and whistled again as Chae hit D'Arcy in the back with a wound that immediately registered as fatal. "Looks like your newbie is something of an assassin, Chief."

"They are, at that," Jenks murmured with pride. Then she punched Paul in the shoulder. "Don't call me Chief."

MAX SAT IN THE PILOT SEAT OF THE EMPTY INTERCEPTOR, ONE knee pulled to her chest. She frowned at the blank screen in front of her as it fuzzed to life.

"Hey, Max." The head of LifeEx's security dipped her head in greeting. "Sorry for the short notice."

"It's fine. Admiral Hoboins said I didn't need to be at the debrief." Max quashed the feeling of guilt. It hadn't entirely been a lie to the admiral that she needed to make an important personal call. This was both personal *and* important.

You're getting to be a little too much like Jenks, following the letter of the rules rather than the intent, Carmichael.

For some reason, that thought made her feel more pride than guilt.

"You okay?" Jeanie asked. "You look a little tired, and I'm not saying that to be a shit, Max."

"I'm fine. I didn't sleep all that well."

Zuma's quarters had been deserted when Max had returned from the gym, and she'd retreated into the second of two private rooms that were normally empty so she could once more comb through all the files Jeanie had sent her about Chae.

She'd fallen asleep at some point, only to wake with a pain in her neck and more questions than when she'd started. There was video of Chae's graduation and Julia was there—plain as day—but there had been nothing to indicate her existence prior to last night. No incoming coms for Chae. No requests for a few hours of leave.

Chae hadn't even seemed happy to see her. If anything, Max was sure the spacer had been even more tense than usual.

"Max?"

"Sorry, my mind wandered." She shook herself, attempting a reassuring smile at the frown on Jeanie's face. "Did you find something?"

"Just that Julia Draven is contracted to Off-Earth and should be on and off the station for the next few months while they test a number of new systems."

Max's heart sank.

"Thanks, Jeanie. Sorry to waste your time."

"What is it, Max?"

"It's nothing. My gut. Never mind." She shook her head.

"Far be it from me to tell you how to do your job, but my gut's saved my ass a few times. Sometimes it's good to listen to it, even if everything else is telling you not to."

"You sound like Rosa."

"Hey, your former commander knew a thing or eighty." Jeanie rubbed a hand over her short hair and made a face. "I feel like I'm missing part of this story, so feel free to discard this advice if it's off-base. You're good at your job, Carmichael. Don't let anyone—even people you trust—tell you otherwise."

"Thanks. I appreciate it."

"No problem. And tell you what, I've got contacts at Off-Earth. I'll do a little more digging. If anything turns up I'll let you know. Take care of yourself."

"You too. Tell Ria hi for me." Max disconnected the call and rested her head in her hand.

Maybe Nika was right and Chae's just not ready to talk to any of us about their personal life. God, did I just mess up things between us for no reason?

Max sighed and pushed to her feet. She headed for the stairs and was halfway down them when she spotted Jenks with Doge.

"Didn't want to interrupt your call," Jenks said, her mismatched eyes full of questions. "Everything good back on Earth?"

"Yeah."

"You are sad," Doge said over the channel, and both women froze at the declaration.

"Sorry. He's really into telling people how they feel lately." Jenks patted her dog on his metal head. "You can't just bust it out, though, buddy. It's rude."

"It's fine," Max replied. She made it down the stairs before Jenks spoke again.

"Since Doge started it anyway, you seemed kinda off this

morning in practice. If you need to talk about anything, you know I'm here, right?"

The fierce longing that Jenks's quiet offer woke in Max stole her breath. "I appreciate it. I just . . . I probably shouldn't talk to you about it."

"You mean because Nika's my brother or because he's our commander?" Jenks snorted at Max's surprised look. "I'm not oblivious, Max. I just act like it sometimes because it's easier than caring."

"You always care, even when you're pretending otherwise."

"Maybe." Jenks shrugged and winked. "But I'm not only your . . ." She paused and rolled the word around in her mouth, finally sighing. "Chief. I'm also your friend if you need it."

"I wish I could compartmentalize things as well as you."

"I'll be honest, I'm not sure I recommend it," Jenks replied, and Max couldn't stop the pained laugh that slipped out. "Every time we have a crew change things are a little jerky. It's okay. We're not just going to fall into a rhythm without some work. But it's on all of us to do the work, not just you. I figure if I'm supposed to step up around here it involves things like calling our commander out when he's wrong. Okay?"

"Okay." Max nodded.

"I'm going to tear apart the water system and see if I can't figure out where that recycler's failing. You want to help?"

Max thought of the pile of reports in her inbox, but going back to quarters and chancing a second run-in with Nika was enough to make her nod before she even realized she'd moved her head. "Sure."

Jenks's brilliant smile slid over her nerves, easing them even more, and Max followed her aft, thoughts of Chae and Nika fading into the background of tangible work on this ship she'd come to love.

"Grant, we have a problem."

The burly man's expression didn't change. "Tell me."

"Carmichael is poking around about Julia. The last thing we need is someone figuring out that the real Julia Draven is dead. I covered our tracks there as well as I could, but I wasn't able to hack all the way into Off-Earth's database."

"You want to be more specific about which Carmichael?"

Melanie bared her teeth at him over the com, but Grant just grinned. "Maxine. She talked to her sister's security chief about Julia—thankfully on the bridge of the Interceptor, or we'd have heard about it too late."

"Gotcha. What do you want me to do?" Grant didn't hold any illusions about who the brains of this outfit was. His job was to hurt people and he was good at it. Melanie could figure out the details.

"We can't touch Maxine—I suspect if we tried to get Chae to do it right now they'd balk, and hard. So let's cut off her intel—stop Jeanie Bosco from digging, however you need to. Just make sure it looks like an accident."

"Consider it done." Grant disconnected the call without waiting for a response.

TWELVE

Jenks kicked her feet up on the empty chair and sighed. She was restless, and not just because of the fiasco this morning or her brief conversation with Max on *Zuma*. They hadn't touched on it again while they wrestled with the bio-recycler, and in some ways Jenks felt like she'd let her friend down by not pushing her a little harder to open up.

Something she couldn't pinpoint was eating at the edges of her nerves. The not-good kind of restless that used to land her in a bar fight before the end of the night . . . and the brig, after.

"Now I'm supposed to set a good example," she muttered into her beer. "Why did I agree to a promotion again?"

"Stop, you're scaring the newbie with your grumbling." Tamago tapped her on the knee and pointed at Chae.

"Ignore me," Jenks said, mustering a smile.

"It's almost the midpoint," Sapphi interjected. "Jenks gets itchy when it's been too long since she's punched someone in the cage."

"You fought that big guy yesterday, didn't you?" Chae asked.

Jenks grinned and rubbed at the bruise on her thigh that

was already a wicked purple. "Master Gunnery Sergeant Mc-Graw, yeah. He's a Marine, but we don't hold that against him. He's on a joint duty tour with *Wandering Hunter*. But that's not the same. That's just sparring."

"She means fighting in the cage at the Boarding Games," Tamago replied. "Or the prelims at least, which are still nine weeks away."

"Why is it different from sparring?"

"Because our chief needs an audience to tell her how good—ow!" Tamago rubbed their shoulder where Jenks had punched them.

"Of course, it's possible she's just snarly because she hasn't seen Luis for too long."

"Sapphi, I just hit Tama, and I'm not above doing the same to you. I might not get in trouble if I fight one of you instead of one of these grabtastic pieces of amphibian shit, right?" Jenks grinned as a table of Navy officers near them heard her, but they all shook their heads when they realized who was talking and went back to their conversation. "The real problem is I can't get anyone to fight me anymore. Not for real."

Tamago chuckled into their own beer. "Oh, poor Jenks, the trials of being undefeated."

"Careful. I'll get in a fight just to spite you."

"LT's not around to help you, and you just alienated every-one at this table." Tamago sniffed. "You'd be on your own." The sparkle in their brown eyes would've told Jenks they were lying even if she hadn't known better. Yet Tama had a wicked sense of humor, and Jenks couldn't put it past them to sit it out as she fought a table of spacers.

"Did Lieutenant Carmichael really tackle some Navy guy in a bar?" Chae asked, breaking Jenks's train of thought. "She just seems so . . . proper."

Jenks choked on her drink, nearly snorting beer out her nose, and folded over, coughing. "Oh, she is, Chae, but she'll drop you faster than a high-g planet if you fuck up."

It was supposed to be a joke, but the real fear that flashed on Chae's face wasn't the least bit funny and Jenks wondered what in the hell would cause them to be afraid of Max.

Sapphi lifted her glass before Jenks could say anything. "And one of the ways to fuck up is to put a hand on her team. Which now includes you, Chae. Welcome to the family!"

Jenks lifted her own beer. "Family buys the next round." She drained her glass and stood. "Come on, Chae, I'll help you carry."

A second terrified look crossed Chae's face and Jenks raised an eyebrow. She gestured and Chae scrambled to their feet, following her away from the table.

"What's up? If you have an objection to buying beer that's all good, and I'm sorry for putting you on the spot."

"It's not that, Chief." Chae shifted, looking at the floor and then the wall, everywhere but at Jenks. "Well . . . it kind of is."

"What are you talking about?"

"I don't have enough feds."

"We just got our basic and you're tapped?" Jenks desperately wanted to ask the kid where their income had gone—something made her wonder if it went to their "girlfriend." Julia had vanished pretty quickly rather than hanging around, and while Chae's explanation that she had work to do was reasonable, it still seemed odd they wouldn't want to spend more time together.

Jenks shook her head. The middle of the bar wasn't the place to have this conversation. "All right, I've got you. We're gonna talk about this later, though. You can't be spending all that right after payday."

Chae followed her to the bar. "I sent it home." The whisper was almost too soft for Jenks to hear over the growing volume of the crowd, and she pretended she hadn't for a moment as she ordered drinks from Abbott. The sweet-faced bartender fluttered eyelashes at her from beneath a fringe of bright blue bangs and Jenks grinned back.

"You want to tell me why?" she asked, turning to Chae.

"Why what?"

"Why you sent it all home, kid. Your fathers are established doctors with basics of their own, plus whatever their practice brings in. Have you been sending them every single fed since you got here?"

"Yes, Chief."

"I swear I'm going to give you a beatdown the next time we spar if you don't stop calling me that." Jenks closed her eyes for a moment. "So why?"

"I'm just used to it from training—"

"Not how you address me. Your pay."

"Oh. The habitat needs it more than I do."

There were eight million questions clamoring for priority in Jenks's head. None of which were appropriate, again, for a conversation in the middle of Corbin's.

"Jenks, beer for your team."

She passed them to Chae, frowned at the count. "That one mine?" She nodded at the beer Abbott was still holding in her hand.

"It'll cost you."

The Navy spacer next to her at the bar protested loudly as Jenks used him for leverage to boost herself up on the bar and leaned toward Abbott.

She slipped her free hand into the woman's blue hair and kissed her until she whimpered.

"Don't be horning in on my action, Jenks!" There was laughter in the spacer's voice, and Jenks was in a good enough mood, all things considered, to not want to start a fight now.

"Oh, honey. Been there, made her scream." She blew another kiss at Abbott and the woman blushed. Jenks climbed back down with the beer in her hand and patted the spacer on the cheek before saluting with it. "Let me know if you need any pointers."

Laughter echoed through the bar as she herded a shocked-looking Chae back toward their table.

"Drink up, kiddo. We're going to have a long conversation about this tomorrow."

TOMORROW CAME SOONER THAN IT SHOULD HAVE, AND CHAE was reasonably sure that the chief had gotten them drunk so they'd be hungover on top of the misery already rolling around in their stomach.

"Here," Jenks said. She slapped a med patch onto their bare shoulder and handed over a metal container. "Drink all that water." She lay down on the weight bench and started her warm-up.

By the time she'd finished and had swapped out the weights, Chae was done with the water. They took Jenks's place on the bench.

"Okay, you've gotten enough of the hang of this that you can talk and bench press at the same time," Jenks said, grinning down at them. "So talk."

The way Jenks said it meant not talking wasn't an option.

"Life in the habitats sucks. I should clarify that: life in the outer edges of the habitats sucks. The cities seem to do pretty well now." Chae wasn't sure why they chose that to lead off with, but there it was. They were surprised to realize Jenks was right; the lifting was easier. Between basic and Interceptor training, they weren't soft by any means, but the schedule Jenks had both Chae and Max on for training was more brutal than anything the NeoG could come up with, and it was paying off.

"Okay, but the CHN is supposed to be on top of that." Jenks raised an eyebrow when Chae just sat up and stared at her.

"When was the last time you got a full requisition for parts, Chief?"

Jenks blinked and then her laughter echoed through the mostly empty weight room. "Reprimand duly noted. Okay. Help me load this bar for some actual work."

The silence wasn't as heavy as they swapped plates and Chae took their spot at the top of the bench, Jenks lying down and settling herself into position.

"Do your fathers know you're sending them all your feds?"

"Not all," Chae protested, earning a flat look from Jenks.

The chief took a deep breath and did her seven reps before racking the bar. "What's frustrating is you're going to make me drag this out of you piecemeal, Chae." She shoved a hand into the shock of purple hair at the crown of her head and scrubbed with a hissing exhale as she got up. "It's punishment, I assume, for all the times I didn't trust my team enough to help me deal with shit."

"I'm not—"

"Don't lie to me." Jenks poked them in the sternum and Chae swallowed. "Refuse to answer, tell me to mind my own fucking business, withhold the information if you really have to. But don't *fucking* lie, Chae. I can't stand it."

"The habitat needs it more than I do." That wasn't a lie, but Chae was surprised how desperately they wanted to spill everything. They dared a look in Jenks's direction as they swapped plates again.

Please don't ask me why. I don't want to lie to you, but I will to keep them safe.

The lieutenant, and everyone else, joked that the chief was unpredictable. And they were right, but she also showed a great deal on her face. Right now there was calculation, presumably as she tried to figure out what to say next. But there was also concern, genuine concern for Chae.

It made them feel even worse.

"Maybe they do. But not at the cost of neglecting yourself. So here's the deal: you keep a hundred of it from now on. No arguments," she said, leaning on the bar and looking down at

Chae when they lay on the bench. "If you need some feds to get you through to next payday, you let me know. But from here on out you'd better take care of yourself also. That's an order."

"Yes, Chief."

"I should drop this bar on your throat," Jenks replied. "Then you couldn't call me that anymore." She winked when she said it and Chae found themself smiling back as they grabbed the bar to start their set. They were starting to suspect the threats of violence were nothing but threats.

At least until she finds out you're lying to her.

"We've got something else to talk about," Jenks said, leaning on the bar before Chae could unrack it, and the dread nearly stopped Chae's heart.

"You want to tell me what that shit was in the boarding action yesterday?"

"I—" It wasn't the question Chae was expecting and they scrambled.

Jenks didn't say anything as she stared down at Chae, content to wait as they looked away and chewed at their lower lip.

"I fucked up," they finally said.

"You did. You're not the only one, but you did," Jenks agreed without any heat. "Tell me what went wrong."

"I wasn't—" Chae dropped their hands from the bar and sat up, dragging them through their short hair. "At the beginning? I got distracted watching you and Max and forgot where I was. You stopped and I crashed into you and, well, you know the rest." They made a half-hearted stabbing gesture.

"Ah." Jenks tapped her hands on the bar, the rhythmic sound oddly soothing as Chae waited for the mockery. They'd tried so hard not to let their hero worship get in the way, but apparently it was dug in for the duration.

"I wondered if this would come up." There was no humor in Jenks's voice. It was even, patient, and made Chae want to cry. "You know we can't walk outside without a suit, right?"

"Chief?"

"Max and I aren't superheroes, Chae, no matter what the sports announcers and those jokers on the SocMed say. We get up, we do the job, we go to bed. Same as everyone else. I've fucked up." She inhaled and looked at the ceiling. "Man, have I fucked up. Thankfully, I haven't gotten anyone killed in the process. I really hope I never do."

"But you're so good at what you do."

Jenks wiggled her hand. "I'm good in the cage, yeah, but the Games aren't just the cage. And out there *really* isn't about what I can do alone. We're a team." She smiled. "Which is why I bring this up in the first place. We are so painfully not a team right now. Whatever the issue is between the commander and the lieutenant, they'll get it sorted."

"You noticed that?" Chae hadn't known what to make of Nika and Max's stiff interactions over the last few days.

"The whole station is gonna notice before it's done. Whatever." Jenks waved a hand. "That's not my point. Why didn't you tell anyone what you were going to do with D'Arcy from the beginning? We could have formed a whole plan around it."

"I—" Chae turned around. Something told them it would be better to face the chief when they said the words. "I didn't think it would work."

"Why on earth not? You smoked him. No one, and I mean *no one*, expected that from you." Jenks rubbed both hands over her face and muttered something that sounded a lot like "Fucking LT all over again."

"I'm sorry."

"Don't be sorry," Jenks said, dropping her hands, "just don't do it again. At least, not without filling me in first. You *tell* me when you have ideas. I do not care how wild they sound. I will listen to anything, consider anything. I won't always agree or approve it, but you have to speak up. You're part of this team or you're not. But if you're not, then that's something we need to figure out now."

"I'm part of the team."

Jenks leaned down, tapping her ear as if she hadn't heard. "What did you say?"

"I'm part of the team," Chae said with a conviction they almost felt.

"Good."

"We're not going to win the prelims." Chae couldn't stop the words from slipping out.

"Not with an attitude like that we're not," Jenks replied, then sighed. "Yeah, I know. Look, I've got a lot of experience at losing, and it sucks, but I'll tell you what Commander Martín told me. We don't lose *out there*." She pointed at the bulkhead. "What you did during the exercise might be training for the Games, but the Games is training for our *job*. That's what's important, and that's where I need you to be my teammate, more than anything. There's a whole lot of nothing beyond that wall, Chae. Empty space. It's overwhelming if you think too much about how alone we are in the universe." She held her hand out and squeezed when Chae took it.

"That's why this is crucial. Us, right here. We know we've got each other's backs. We know the job matters so much more than a fucking trophy."

"Yes, Chief."

Jenks leaned across the bar and pulled Chae into a hug. Then she tapped the spacer lightly on the side of the head. "From now on, when you're doing boarding actions you keep that sword point down and away from your teammates, got it? You get me killed in real life and I'll haunt your ass forever." She smiled as she pulled away. "You keep calling me Chief, and I might haunt you while we're both alive. And I'm going to train you on boarding actions until you hate me, because I do not want you stabbing me in the back for real."

Maybe I can trust her. If I told her what they wanted me to do, what I've already done, maybe she could help?

They were about to say something when another thought came into their head.

You thought Julia was trustworthy, too.

It was like a cold wind on the back of their neck, chilling them all the way to their core. There wasn't anyone they could trust here, not when the lives of everyone at the habitat depended on it.

Still, the weight of the new instructions they'd received was lying heavily in their stomach and Chae wished for all the world there was some way to keep both the crew and the habitat safe.

Even though they knew there wasn't.

THIRTEEN

"According to Stephan it's just the two devices. One on the bridge of *Zuma* and one by my doorway here on the station." Nika counted himself lucky that the conversation he'd had with Stephan in his room had happened before Chae planted the listening device.

"He's recommending we leave them for now," Admiral Hoboins said, steepling his fingers on his desk in front of him. "Thoughts?"

"The one in quarters is easy enough to manage. There's too much echo when everyone is in the main room and I can watch what I say otherwise." Nika rubbed a hand through his hair. "The bridge is trickier, but thankfully we haven't been back out since Chae planted it, so all they've likely gotten was Jenks grumbling about the lack of parts for the main console tune-up."

Hoboins grinned. "She's been in the requisition office three times since you got back. I'm working on getting those parts, Commander, I promise. If only so Captain Rells can get a good night's sleep."

Nika laughed, then sobered. "It will be harder to keep classified information secret when we head back out."

"The good news is you *want* them to overhear your next mission plans. It makes springing this trap easier." Hoboins paused and studied him for a long moment. "How are you holding up?"

"Fine." Nika resisted the urge to shift under the admiral's steely gaze.

"Excellent." Hoboins leaned his elbows on his desk. "Now you want to give me the truth?"

Awful. Horrible. I've made a huge mistake and Stephan should have tapped someone else for this position. Even Max could do a better job than I have.

All the words fought for prominence in his mouth, but none came out the clear winner before Hoboins sighed. "I know that look, Nika, even if you can't find the words for it. Rosa used to wear it a lot early on, before she realized just how good she was at the job. And she wasn't the only one. You get to be my age with this much time in the black, you see it a lot. What's on your mind, son?"

"Too much."

"Fair enough." Hoboins nodded, then considered his next words. "Let me ask you a better question: What are you most afraid of right now?"

"Getting people killed." The words brought with them a rush of memory. The warehouse on Trappist-1e and the sick realization that he'd walked his team into a trap. The heat of the flames as the lab caught fire. The desperation in his throat as he'd shoved his teammates in front of him toward the door. The shockwave of the explosion hitting him in the back and then the crushing blackness of the building falling.

"It's a hard thing to live with," Hoboins said, the quiet gravel of his voice breaking into Nika's thoughts. "I won't lie to you and say it'll never happen. You hope it won't, you train to keep it from happening, but sometimes things are outside of our control. Aren't they?"

Nika followed the admiral's pointed gaze down to his right hand. "Yes, sir."

"Is the issue that you've got your sister and Max to watch over?" As gentle as the question was, it was also unexpected and Nika stared at Hoboins in confusion until the man lifted a shoulder. "I didn't think it was, but it's worth eliminating the obvious."

"It's not them." Nika shook his head. "If anything, they're more competent at this than I am in every way."

"That's pure-grade horseshit." Hoboins waved a hand in the air. "Is that fear what's keeping you from doing your job?"

"No, sir." The words were out before Nika even thought of them and something he was sure was relief flashed across Hoboins's face.

"I didn't think so. You are the opposite of your sister in so many ways, Nika."

"You know we're not actually related, Admiral, right?"

Hoboins snorted and waved his hand. "We don't all get the privilege you two did, of choosing your family, but you're family all the same. And you are the thinker, sometimes to the point that you tie yourself up in knots over it, son.

"Now, if you ever tell Jenks I told you that it would benefit you to be a little more like her on occasion, I will not only deny it but I will bust your ass back down to ensign." Hoboins didn't crack a smile as he slid a tablet over his desk. "You're going back out into the black tomorrow with the task force. *Flux* and *Hunter* will stay on this side of the wormhole. *Zuma* and *Dread* will be on the Trappist side. I'm telling you this before the briefing so that if you need me to argue for keeping you on this side I can."

"I appreciate it, Admiral, but I'll be fine."

"Okay." Hoboins nodded. "You talking to your therapist?"

"Yes, sir."

"Good. It helps, trust me."

Nika wasn't sure how to decipher the admiral's comment, but rather than ask, he allowed the thing he really wanted to say out into the air. "This would be easier if I could just tell them what we were doing."

"Maybe," Hoboins replied. "But maybe not. I'm not going to overrule Stephan on his own operation, Nika. Moreover, I agree with him that the less they know here, the safer they are. These people aren't ones to underestimate. And you know your crew—what do you think would happen if Max and Jenks knew someone was blackmailing their Neo?"

Nika let out the breath he'd been holding and thought about how determined Jenks had been when Max had been kidnapped by the woman wanting to destroy LifeEx Industries. "They'd stop at nothing to get the bastards."

"Right. I'm not saying it's a bad thing, Nika, but they are dedicated to the idea that this is a family and right now they can both afford to treat it that way. You're in a unique position here and a difficult one, but you need the clarity that seeing the bigger picture brings." Hoboins touched the panel on his desk at the chime and the door slid open.

"Josa's here to see you, Lee," Commander Lou Seve said, poking her head into his office.

"I look forward to your report when you get back, Commander," Admiral Hoboins said to Nika.

"Thank you, sir. We'll see you in a few weeks."

He headed out of the office with an absent wave in Lou's direction, his thoughts already spinning as he walked down the corridor toward the zero-g tube.

Maybe I need to keep the space between me and Max. It would make it easier on all of us.

Max was waiting at the door of *Zuma*'s quarters. "Do you have a minute?" she asked, following him toward his room.

"Not really." It came out sharper than he wanted and he saw the flinch she couldn't quite hide.

"I'd like to apologize." Her words stopped him cold and Nika looked around the main room. The others were suddenly very busily not paying attention. "You were right and I overreacted. I'm sorry."

"I appreciate it." The words were cold and didn't feel like his. "We're headed back out tomorrow, briefing is this afternoon."

The soft smile on Max's face died. "Nika—"

"Was there anything else, Lieutenant?"

"No. Nothing at all." Max turned around and walked out of their quarters.

Jenks slipped off her bunk almost as soon as Max was gone. "Permission to say something as your sister, Commander?"

Nika knew he was going to regret it, but he nodded anyway. "Granted."

"I don't know what's going on, but you're being a fucking asshole."

He clenched his jaw against the urge to tell her everything. "Noted. Have the others get their gear prepped."

"Nika, what is your deal?" The frustrated love on her face cut him, but he ignored it and gave her a level look.

"That's an order, Chief."

"Fine, *Commander.*" She turned on her heel and walked away, her back ramrod straight.

Nika rubbed a hand over his eyes with a muttered curse and headed for his room.

MAX TAPPED HER FINGERS ON THE CONSOLE AS SHE STUDIED the traffic patterns of the ships on the Trappist side of the wormhole; the real-time data gave her something to do as they waited out in the empty space. Things had been quiet so far, but the same restless, anxious feeling she'd had just refused to abate.

And it seems like I'm not the only one.

"Sapphi, what is it?" she finally asked. The ensign had been fidgeting in her seat on the bridge for the first twenty minutes of their shift and Max couldn't take it anymore.

"Nothing, LT. I was just thinking about this time my fathers took us camping along the Haliacmon, but they didn't listen to Mom about how much food we kids could eat and . . ."

Before Max could tell Sapphi to hush, the message came through on her DD. Not on the team chat but in private mode.

SAPPHI: I don't know how good you are at talking and chatting at the same time, LT, but I really need you to not interrupt me or say anything out loud right now.

MAX: What is going on?

SAPPHI: I was doing diagnostics before we left and kept getting a weird pingback but I couldn't isolate it.

MAX: Can you give me more than "weird pingback" to go on?

SAPPHI: There's something interfering with my coms, but not enough to really be an issue. It's not supposed to be there. I tried to talk to Nika about it, but he said it was nothing.

Max had to swallow back the urge to snort at that. Apparently she wasn't the only one Nika was blowing off. She hated that he'd pushed her to this, but Max knew she was going to have to talk to Hoboins when they got back to Jupiter Station. Something had to change, and judging from the tension between Nika and everyone else it was going to have to be him.

MAX: I'm sorry he did that. What did you find?

SAPPHI: There's definitely something, LT. I finally got the signal sorted. I think there's a listening device on the bridge.

"A what?"

Sapphi didn't even pause, but she did make a face. "A fish, LT, keep up. They tried to make us eat fish from the river and we all rebelled. Mom laughed for days."

Sorry, Max mouthed. "I like your parents quite a bit."

"They like you, too, LT. They keep asking me when we're going to visit again."

MAX: Do you know where it is?

SAPPHI: No, which means either it's not hardwired into my systems, or it's just so damn good I can't find it. But if I were hiding a bug on my bridge I'd put it over there somewhere on the far wall.

MAX: Just audio or do you think it's recording video?

SAPPHI: My guess from the data is just audio. It records in four-hour chunks and then fires off the package. I'm pretty sure it's not in our network and just piggybacking off the coms to send out the transmission. At least I really hope it isn't smart enough to avoid my security on that front. What a nightmare.

MAX: Can you trace where it's getting sent?

SAPPHI: Maybe? I'd need to look at the actual device.

Max held up a hand as she got out of her seat and crossed to the far wall. She ran her hand across the sides of the com panel, reaching around the back and finding nothing . . .

Until she dropped her hand lower and felt a round disc under her fingertips. Max gestured with her other hand for Sapphi to join her.

MAX: Can I take it off?

SAPPHI: Let me see it first, LT.

MAX: You won't be able to get a visual.

SAPPHI: Trust me. ;)

Max held her breath as Sapphi reached around the main console and put her fingers in the same spot. When the ensign nodded, Max pulled away. She kept an eye on the door to the bridge as Sapphi examined the device.

SAPPHI: Definitely a bug, LT, sophisticated, too. I want to know who dirtied up my ship. Should I take it down?

MAX: Let's leave it for now. I don't know what it will do and we're a little too far out from Trappist if something goes wrong. I'll talk to Nika.

SAPPHI: You think he'll actually listen?

MAX: . . .

SAPPHI: Sorry, LT, that was unkind.

MAX: I don't blame you.

The scanner chimed and Max stepped away from the panel, returning to the pilot seat to check the main console. "Odd. What would a C-class freighter be doing out here alone?"

"What?" Sapphi joined her. "They're not getting through the wormhole without a ride."

"Unless they've got the ability to make a wormhole on their own? Then they could avoid traffic control."

"I thought that was restricted tech."

Max shook her head. "It is. And expensive. But the tech's evolving. Look at that newest transport we scored—it's about the size of a C-class freighter."

"True." Sapphi sighed and sank into her chair, throwing a look toward the com panel before speaking softly. "Sometimes it feels like we're making all the same mistakes over again, LT. Always pushing to make things better, and where does it lead us?" She pointed at the screen. "People using it for shit reasons."

Max didn't know how to reply to that, so she hit the com instead. *"Dread Treasure,* this is Lieutenant Carmichael. You reading that freighter?"

"Roger that, Lieutenant," D'Arcy replied. "We were about to order them to heave to for an inspection and accounting on why they're so far out of the regular shipping lanes. I'll put it on the main com."

"Appreciate it."

"Freighter *McConel's Pride,* this is NeoG Interceptor *Dread Treasure.* You're a bit outside your normal route."

"Hello, *Dread Treasure.* Special assignment from the higher-ups at Trappist Express. We were delivering some supplies to Trappist and are supposed to meet our return pickup, but there's been no sign of them."

Max shared a look with Sapphi, alarms screaming in her mind. "They're headed the wrong direction for a pickup to the wormhole," she murmured.

"I'm not showing any record of that in our files, *McConel.* Please heave to so we can hook up and do an inspection."

D'Arcy had barely finished the order when Max saw the thrusters on the freighter light up. She swore. "Sapphi, hang on." She slapped the general quarters alarm on the console and the klaxon blared through the ship.

"This captain is not smart," D'Arcy said over the com.

"Or they're too smart. D'Arcy, I have a bad feeling about

this." Max froze at the sudden press of Nika's hand on her shoulder.

"Hey, D'Arcy. It's Nika. Fire a warning shot."

"Can do, Nika."

Max was surprised by the edge in D'Arcy's voice and tried to push aside the sudden uneasy rolling of her gut as she glanced up at Nika and saw his mouth was drawn into a thin line.

What do you know that I don't, Nika?

"Freighter *McConel's Pride*, this is your warning shot. The next one will put your ship out of commission. Heave to and prepare to be boarded."

The freighter did not answer, nor did it slow its desperate flight away from the two NeoG ships. The first shot from *Dread Treasure* streaked just past the nose of the ship and Max started the count in her head for the required two-minute delay between the warning shot and the next one. She shifted *Zuma's Ghost*'s course without saying anything so they were slightly farther away from *Dread* than standard.

"Freighter *McConel's Pride*, this is your last warning. Heave to now. You—" D'Arcy's transmission cut off.

"Max, *Dread*'s gone dark," Sapphi's voice was steady, but the announcement froze everyone—except Max.

Reflexively, she threw *Zuma* into a downward angle, hitting the thrusters hard.

"What are you doing?" Nika demanded.

"Keeping us out of their blast range," she snapped. "I've got the helm, Nika. Tamago, is *Dread* still there?" The question was like the sharp edge of a sword in her throat.

"Yes," Tamago replied. "Intact, just no energy output. EMP maybe? But that freighter shouldn't have any weapons on it."

Being stranded out this far was basically a death sentence. While someone from Jupiter Station would come looking when they didn't report back, with no beacon or coms to guide them it would be like trying to find an eyelash on the ocean floor.

"Everyone hang on to something." Having issued a warning

this time, Max pulled the ship straight up. They were practically underneath the freighter, just off the stern. "Sapphi, when I say now, I want you to fire the rail gun at them."

"Max, you can't fire on an unarmed freighter," Nika said.

"We did a warning shot," she snapped, unsurprised by his protest but disappointed nonetheless.

"We don't know what's going on with *Dread*. They could have just had a coms malfunction."

"Are you kidding me? I'm not waiting around for them to figure out they missed us and take a second shot. Now, Sapphi."

The ensign fired the rail gun before Nika could protest a second time. The superheated projectile streaked through the black and slammed into the back end of the freighter, a fountain of fire appearing as the oxygen in the breached ship caught ablaze.

"Freighter *McConel's Pride*, this is Lieutenant Carmichael of the Interceptor *Zuma's Ghost*. Your engine is damaged. Heave to now or I'm going to put another shot right through the middle of your ship."

"Max, crew manifest says fourteen people." Jenks's voice was loud in the sudden silence on the bridge.

"Everyone suit up. Sapphi, not you. You get on the com and tell Trappist we need a tow for *Dread* and something bigger here as fast as they can make it." Max pushed out of her seat as the others started moving.

But Nika hadn't and she looked down at the hand wrapped around her upper arm. "We're not boarding them. They outnumber us more than two to one."

"The hell we're not," she replied, managing to keep her voice low at the last second. "I'm not sitting around waiting to see if they get the engine working again or, even worse, that weapon."

"Max—"

"What is *wrong* with you?" she hissed. "This is our lives and *Dread*'s on the line here and you're just standing there." A sudden, sick certainty flooded her. "Like you expected this to happen."

"Max—"

She pulled out of his grip and crossed to the coms panel, ripping the listening device free and holding it up for a moment before she dropped it and crushed it beneath her boot heel. She got right in Nika's face. "I don't know what you are up to, Nika Vagin, and I hope to hell it's not anything that's going to require me to relieve you of command. But we've had a fucking listening device on this bridge for who knows how long and that freighter was sent here to take both our ships out. I want to know what's going on."

He said nothing.

He'd known.

She watched the truth of it echo in his blue eyes and her heart broke into pieces.

Nika, what have you done?

"Lieutenant, I'm getting a com from a Navy vessel," Sapphi said. "It's the *Laika*. They are less than five minutes out."

Max stared at Nika. She didn't want to believe he was somehow working for the smugglers, but how else had he known about the freighter? Known they might come upon this ship and this level of danger and hadn't breathed a word of it to her. The surprise and betrayal coiling in her gut made her next words cruel. "You are not fit for command. Sapphi, tell the *Laika* we're boarding. I'm assuming my brother is on board and I'd appreciate the backup."

"Max." Nika's voice was hoarse. "I can explain, just not here."

Tamago and Sapphi were watching her. She could see Jenks and Chae by the stairs, the pair of them wearing identical horrified expressions. Max dragged in a breath as she wrapped the armor of her job around her and shoved everything else to the side.

"You stay by my side, and I swear, if you even think about stabbing me in the back I won't hesitate to take you down."

She didn't wait for his reply as she turned and headed for the airlock.

FOURTEEN

Nika stood off to the side of the freighter's cargo bay with Scott. Eleven of the crew had surrendered immediately, apparently moved to do so by Max's implacable warning message before they had boarded.

After a hard look at her brother, Max had left Nika and Chae to watch over the surrendered crew while she, Tamago, and Jenks went after the three who were loose on the ship.

"She was like that as a kid, too," Scott murmured. "Impossible to divert or refuse when she put her mind to something."

"Yeah." Nika kept his eyes on Chae and the crew. The spacer had a death grip on their sword, but Nika suspected the haunted look in their eyes wasn't from the boarding. "She found the listening device."

"Ah, is that why this didn't go down the way it was supposed to?"

"Pretty much. Also her damn intuition, I suspect. She pushed *Zuma* just far enough out of the blast range of the EMP and then had Sapphi fire on them before I could stop her." Nika glanced over as the sound of shouting echoed from a door on the far side, but Tivo and Chief Petty Officer Netra were already headed in that direction. "She knows, Scott. Or at least suspects."

"About the operation?"

"Well, at the moment I think she's convinced I'm involved with the smugglers."

That hurt more than he wanted to admit, but Nika couldn't get the look of abject betrayal on Max's face out of his head.

"If she thought that, you'd be in the brig," Scott replied. "I already sent Stephan a message. He and Luis are on Trappist-1d. Once we finish up here he said to bring *Zuma* and *Dread* over."

"I'm assuming he'll tell them?"

"Don't assume anything with Stephan. More likely he'll come up with a cover story that's got enough truth in it to mollify Max without completely exposing this op. We had a backup plan if this plan didn't work anyway, so my money is on him using it. He doesn't like opening his operations up to too many people; it reduces his ability to control the situation. I'd recommend you avoid her until we get on the ground, though, so you don't have to answer any questions."

Nika rubbed his free hand over his face. D'Arcy's Interceptor was going to need work before it could fly again, so it made sense to load it onto the *Laika*. *Zuma* was undamaged, thanks to Max, but it meant there wasn't anywhere he could hide on the long flight back to Trappist-1d. "You may as well plan on loading *Zuma* onto the ship, too, then."

"I was. It's easy enough to explain that the trip will be faster, and also safer."

Max and one of the freighter crew stumbled through the far door, their swords tangled together, and Nika barely had time to draw a painful breath when Max's sword clattered to the deck. She dropped into a spin below the crewmember's wild swing, kicking their feet out from underneath them.

They hit the deck and Max rolled to her feet, but Lieutenant Commander Ian Sebastian was already there, turning the crewmember onto their stomach and wrestling their hands into cuffs.

Nika winced when Max bent to pick up her sword and he saw the blood dripping down her right arm.

"Jenks and Tivo have the other two. Ship is secure," she said as she approached them.

"Sit down," Scott replied. Max glared at her older brother but dropped onto a nearby cargo crate, setting her sword next to her. "Captain Troika said they've got *Dread Treasure* on board. All the crew is fine. There's a second ship inbound to take care of this wreck. You did good, Max. Can you get out of that sleeve?"

Max undid the buttons of her ODU, shrugging out of the right side with a wince, revealing the black T-shirt underneath the operational duty uniform. "Happy coincidence that you showed up." She was talking to Scott, but her gaze was locked on Nika when she said it.

"Not much of one. We were headed for the transit juncture and you all were right in the middle of the lane."

Nika kept his face impassive, but he was thankful Max looked away from him. Scott's lie had been easy, practiced, and Nika didn't know how he could live with it.

Tamago showed up with a med kit and Nika dragged his attention away from them with a sigh.

"You want to tell me what's going on? Without any bullshit, if you please," Jenks said from his side.

JENKS WATCHED NIKA JERK AT HER SUDDEN QUESTION AND felt a little bit guilty for sneaking up on him the way she had, but the memory of the tense interaction on the bridge and her own concerns about whatever was going on between Max and him over the last few weeks quashed it pretty quickly.

"Was Max right? Did you know that freighter would be there with that EMP?"

"I can't talk about it, Jenks." His reply was low, with enough pain in his voice to make her even more concerned.

Jenks took a deep breath. "Look, you're my brother and I love you, so just tell me this: Are you in trouble that I need to bail you out of? Or is this actual NeoG shit and I'll let you suffer whatever wrath Max subjects you to?"

Nika's soft laugh was bitter. "I don't even know how to process that the two most important people in my life apparently think I'm involved in something illegal. That I would ever do something like that."

"I'm not judging, I'm *trying* to help. This is my fucking crew t—"

"It's actual NeoG shit, Jenks," he cut her off. "And I can't talk about it."

Jenks shoved both hands in her hair and blew out a breath as she watched him walk away. "Fucker."

"You maybe want to cut him some slack. It's tough being in a position where you can't tell the people you work with everything."

She managed to suppress her own surprise and turned her head as Tivo came into view. "What do you know about it?"

"SEAL team," he replied with a shrug. "Pretty used to not being able to talk about ops with anyone."

"Not even your own team?" Jenks scanned the cargo bay. Reasonably sure everything was under control now, she allowed herself a moment and slipped around to a shadowed corner. "You move pretty quietly for a big fucker, you know that?"

He flashed her a grin that had her heart thumping a little harder. "Demolition experts who stomp tend to get blown up, Pocket."

"Pocket?"

His grin widened and he held two fingers a few centimeters apart. "You know, because you're pocket-sized."

Jenks crossed her arms over her chest and stared up at him, willing herself not to smile back. She still wasn't quite sure what to make of the Navy lieutenant who'd been brought in to compete in the Games two years ago in a failed attempt to kick her ass.

She wouldn't admit it out loud, but it had been a close fight. And now . . . well, she wasn't in love with him the same way she was with Luis, but she liked his face.

Among other things.

"I'll deny it if anyone else asks, but I don't hate it."

"Good." Tivo grabbed her around the waist and boosted her up onto the supply crate. He leaned in, his lips not quite touching hers and laughter dancing in his blue-gray eyes. "Hi. I've missed you."

It was strange enough when Luis said it and even stranger to settle into the idea that there were two people out in this wild universe who missed her when she wasn't around.

More than that, really, Jenks; you should start getting used to it.

Jenks combed her fingers through Tivo's black hair. "I missed you, too."

THE TENSION AMONG THE CREW OF ZUMA'S GHOST PERMEated every bolt and bulkhead of the ship as they sped toward Trappist-1d on board the CHNS *Laika*.

With no need for urgency, Captain Troika had declined to burn the fuel needed for a second wormhole, so once the tow for the freighter had arrived they'd started the trip.

Chae hated that the bug they'd planted appeared to be at least part of the cause of the fight between Max and Nika. Hated that their lies had resulted in Nika's disappearance onto the Navy vessel and this uneasy silence on the ship, and now the conversations between crewmembers were stilted and the laughter that had filled the air on their trip out was absent.

The tension had been there before. Everyone had just pretended it wasn't.

Mostly, they hated that as much as they hated the situation they'd put everyone in, they'd do it again if it meant keeping their fathers safe.

Because they had their own problems. The message they'd gotten on their DD chip when they'd connected to the *Laika*'s com systems was a heavy stone in their gut.

We warned you what would happen if you didn't keep your mouth shut.

Chae had sent a frantic message back that they hadn't said anything about this latest mission and that they'd passed everything along just like they were supposed to. Silence had been the only reply.

"You doing okay, Chae?" Sapphi's question wasn't loud, but its sudden echo on the otherwise quiet bridge was enough to make the spacer jump.

"Sure." They busied themself with the console even though there was nothing to do, and Sapphi sighed.

"Well, I'm not and I really wish someone else would admit it." The ensign leaned back in her seat and then rubbed her hands over her face. "Shit's weird. This feels like when my parents fought and the aftermath where everyone was walking around the house pretending the others didn't exist."

"I remember that feeling," Chae offered. "My fathers don't fight much, but when they did?" They whistled. "It was uncomfortable to be in the house for like a day after. It never lasted much longer than that, though."

"My mom could hold a grudge at my dads for ages." Sapphi dragged the last word out and Chae couldn't stop the laugh.

"She always forgave them, of course, but me and my siblings would vacate the premises as fast as humanly possible."

"Can't do that here."

"True enough." Sapphi sighed again. "I mean, we could venture out into the *Laika*, but I wouldn't recommend it. I'm sorry. I know this probably isn't at all what you expected when you joined." She glanced over her shoulder toward the galley. Max was back there somewhere, working on reports.

"To be honest, I didn't have a lot of expectations." Chae swallowed down the urge to confess their fears that this tension between the commander and the lieutenant was all their fault. They'd almost bolted when Max had pulled the listening device out and destroyed it. The LT had thought Nika was responsible and somewhere, through their own horror, Chae had realized that the commander had *known* it was there. "Okay, maybe less frozen silences."

"I think it's going to get loud and heated pretty soon."

"Oh?"

"Yeah. Jenks is going to lose her shit on one or both of them," Sapphi replied. "I'm going to go get lunch started and maybe poke at the LT a bit until she spills the beans more about what happened. I hate trying to piece together incomplete data. You want to come along?"

A second incoming message notification pinged into their vision.

"Sure, give me a minute to finish running this diagnostic." Chae smiled as Sapphi got up, but the expression vanished as soon as they were alone on the bridge again.

Outside. Now. Second cargo area on the right.

Chae's throat closed up. There was no way Julia was on board the *Laika*.

Cascade failure prevention. Block and redirect.

They sent a reply back. Julia couldn't possibly know they were lying.

I'm under orders not to leave the ship.

A heartbeat later the reply came.

I don't care. Get there or things are going to be so much worse than they are right now.

The message was accompanied by a news flash from Trappist Associated Press: FOUR KILLED IN BUILDING COLLAPSE AT WEST RIDGE, TRAPPIST-1D.

They didn't recognize the three other names in the article, but Bean's name struck them with enough force to knock all the air out of Chae's lungs. Their best friend was dead. How had they moved so fast?

Chae pushed out of their seat, panic moving their feet through the frozen fear. They slipped down the stairs to the deck and paused a moment as they tried to orient themself.

"Hey, Chae."

Jenks was on her back less than a meter away, working on *Zuma's* underbelly with Lieutenant Parsikov. Doge lay nearby.

"I'm just going for a walk, Chief, stretch my legs a little."

"That's fine. Just watch out for Navy pukes." She was grinning at Parsikov's flat stare.

Chae nodded and walked away. The corridor between where the Interceptors had docked and the nearby cargo area was deserted and Chae's worry grew as they turned a corner.

Two burly spacers in maintenance uniforms emerged from behind a stack of supply crates. Their handshakes were off. Chae almost turned and ran.

Your fathers will end up like Bean if you do.

"Got a message for you, Neo. Actions have consequences."

"I didn't do anything but what I was supposed to."

Chae saw the slap coming and reacted without thinking, just like Jenks had been teaching them, knocking it out of the way and punching them in the jaw.

It had little effect. Both of them moved faster than Chae could avoid and the blows rained down, knocking them to the floor. They tasted blood, pain sparking as a boot landed in their ribs.

"Enough. That's enough." One of the attackers grabbed Chae by the hair and hauled them upright. "Someone's being unrealistic about their options here."

There was at least a bruise spreading across their pale skin. *Chief would be proud of me.*

They were oddly proud of themself.

"I didn't know what was going on when we went out on patrol—all I was told was patrol. But I swear, I didn't tell anyone about the listening device. I'm just a fucking spacer. You're going to have to find someone with more authority to get you the information you want."

"This isn't personal, kid." There was an odd flicker of sympathy in the person's eyes. "We do what we're told. You do what you're told. The message is this: make sure your ship gets grounded—or there'll be worse things than this beating down the line."

Chae watched as the other person flipped open a knife and sawed partway through the strap holding down the crates along the back wall of the room. Before they realized what was happening they were flying through the air. Chae crashed into the crates; pain surged as the boxes came loose, driving them toward the floor, and just before the blackness took them they were able to gasp a cry for help on the team channel.

"Jenks!"

FIFTEEN

"Navy pukes, huh?"

Jenks grinned at Tivo and then stuck her head back up into *Zuma*'s guts. "I make a case-by-case exception."

"Chae will be fine. No one is going to pick a fight with them."

"You'd better hope so." She dropped back down so she could meet his eyes. "I will straight up pull a Sea Hawk on your ass if someone hurts my crew."

"What?"

"I will set your boat on fire."

Tivo laughed. "I'm still having to ask Luis for translations, you know."

"Keep up or take a seat, Parsikov. And hand me the sixteen-mil socket."

"What are you doing again?"

"Keeping myself out of the brig through the wonder of calibrations," she murmured, and went back to work. It was mostly to hear him laugh again, but also not far from the truth. Being on a Navy ship was traditionally bad news for her, and it was even worse with everything else that was happening. "May as well do maintenance during the downtime instead of just sitting around on my ass."

"I can think of half a dozen things better than maintenance. Did I mention I have a room of my own?"

She slid out from under the ship. "You did not mention this."

Tivo leaned in. "You seemed pretty excited about getting to do work on the ship. I wasn't sure if I should interfere."

Doge whined.

"Jenks!"

She jerked from the volume of Chae's voice in her head, nearly catching Tivo with an unintentional headbutt he managed to avoid, if only barely. "Chae? Chae!"

"Jenks, what is it?" Tivo asked.

"I don't know. Max!"

"I'm right here. They were on the team channel. Where are they?"

"I don't know, they went for a walk." The map suddenly overlaid itself on Jenks's vision.

"Spacer Chae is in Storage Three," Doge said.

Jenks sprinted in the direction she'd seen Chae go, following the map. She could hear Max catching Tivo up as they ran behind her. "Oh no." She scrambled through the door and around the jumbled equipment boxes before anyone could stop her.

Chae was on the floor, partially obscured by the crates piled on top of them.

Jenks's heart stuttered in pain.

"This is Lieutenant Parsikov, we have a medical emergency in Storage Three, repeat, medical emergency in Storage Three. Jenks, be careful."

But all she was thinking about was her Neo.

She slipped below the precariously balanced cargo bin and her breath caught when she saw Chae's bloody face. "Chae, please no—" She reached out to rest two fingers on their throat. She exhaled, all too aware it was almost a sob, when a weak pulse beat against the tips. "I've got a pulse, Max. Chae, wake up for me." She squirmed farther under the stack and patted the spacer's face gently.

"Chief?"

"Hey, come on, you called me Jenks earlier."

Chae smiled weakly.

"Sorry, bad joke. Listen—don't move just yet." Jenks took in the edge of the box that was jammed against Chae's chest. It was braced on another box above, but not by much and if it slipped . . . "Tivo, get over here. *Carefully.*"

"Wasn't that what I told you?"

"You want to argue, or you want to help?"

"We've got people coming," he said.

"Tell them all to stop outside," she snapped. "We need to get Chae out from under this before people start tromping around and vibrate the fucking floor. If any of these boxes shift it's coming down on our heads. Now get over here—I can lift this, but I need you to brace the box from here and Max can pull Chae free."

"Chief, what about you?" Chae's voice was weak and Jenks reached over to squeeze their hand.

"Let me worry about me. These two won't let me get crushed. Besides, I know how much I can leg press and it's a lot more than you." She also knew that with Chae free, if anything went wrong she'd have enough time to push the box to the side and roll away before it smashed down on her.

And if not, better me than my crew, she thought. "Chae, you feel okay? Wiggle your fingers and toes for me?"

"Yes."

Jenks saw Max's boots as she rolled onto her back. "Reasonably sure Chae doesn't have a spine injury, Max, but it's a risk we need to take no matter what. Okay, you're good to grab them by the boots and when I say go, you pull them free. Tivo, just keep it all from crashing sideways."

"Jenks—"

She snorted at the warning in his voice. "Trust me, I'm a professional." She braced her hands and feet on the underside of the box and took a deep breath. "Go!"

The box was heavier than she'd thought and Jenks gritted her teeth as her legs protested. "Fuck." She was not going to be able to push it over and roll out of the way like she'd planned. *Worry about that later.*

Chae slid free and half a second later Tivo put a shoulder into the edge of the box between Jenks's feet, taking the weight off her legs. "Chae's clear. I got it, Pocket, get out of there."

Jenks wriggled free. "Clear." She hopped to her feet and between the two of them she and Tivo were able to lower the crate safely to the floor. Several others shifted behind it with a deadly rattle, but Max had dragged Chae toward the far door, well out of range.

Jenks knelt by Max, who was cupping the back of Chae's head. Jenks frowned. "How the fuck did you get a black eye? If any of these bins had hit you in the head we'd be scraping your brains off the deck."

The thought made her shudder.

"I'm sorry," the spacer murmured, but then they passed out.

"Jenks!" Nika's voice echoed from the corridor and Jenks shared a look with Max.

"I'll stay with them," Max said, and Jenks nodded, getting to her feet as the medical team rushed into the room.

"What happened?"

"I don't know, Commander." It was easier to slip into the formality. Jenks could pack all her worries and fears into the box and focus on what she was supposed to do rather than what she was feeling. "About ten minutes ago Spacer Chae told me they were going for a walk to stretch their legs. I approved it. Told them to be careful. About five minutes ago Spacer Chae shouted my name on the team channel and then went quiet. Doge had a location. We found them here and extracted them."

Jenks could hear Tivo talking to someone in the background and tried to keep her focus on Nika, but it was difficult.

"I want to see the security footage for Storage Three," Tivo was saying. "What do you mean out of commission? There was no maintenance scheduled for today. No, Commodore Carmichael is on his way, you can tell him—"

"Jenks," Nika said.

"What?"

"I asked if you were hurt?"

"Sorry. No, I'm fine. I'm going to go with them to medical, okay?"

Nika's eyes slid past her to where Max was talking with the orderly as they lifted Chae's stretcher into the air. "That's fine."

Jenks met the medics at the door, stepping into the hallway so they could pass. She fell into step with her lieutenant, the seething rage in her chest drowning under the weight of her worry for her crew.

"It's not just me, right, Max? Something's going on here. I don't believe for one second that was an accident. Someone hurt Chae deliberately."

"It's not just you," Max murmured back, her face grim.

"I'm not gonna lie, for once in my life I wish you'd said I was imagining things."

"MIRACULOUSLY, SPACER CHAE DOESN'T HAVE A CONCUSsion or any internal injuries beyond some bruised ribs." Commander Nebula Pach pointed out the areas on Chae's scan to Max and Jenks as she spoke. "I'm going to let them sleep, but you're welcome to stay. I'd recommend keeping them here until we get to Trappist. Unless the scans change, they'll be fit for duty once you get on the ground."

"That's less than twenty-four hours. You sure, Doc?" Jenks asked the question before Max could.

"I'm sure, Chief." Commander Pach's expression was even, but Max could see the amused annoyance in her blue eyes. "It could have been a lot worse. They got lucky."

Max shared a look with Jenks as the doctor turned away. "Do you want to stay here?" she asked.

"Yeah, but I was right in the middle of tuning up the stabilizers when this happened. I should finish it." Jenks scrubbed at her head in frustration. "I'll go back to the ship, fill Tamago and Sapphi in on everything."

"Do it outside the ship," Max said.

"I will, though knowing Sapphi she's been obsessively going over every system and running every scan she's got in her arsenal to make sure *Zuma* is clean."

"Good." Max nodded. "I trust her."

"Max, about Nika . . ."

Max could see the hesitation in Jenks's eyes and she shook her head before the chief could start in. "You don't need to get involved."

"The hell I don't, this is my crew, too. I asked him straight up if this was above board or not and he said it was. I'd like to think my own brother wouldn't lie to me."

It hurt that what she had to say might ruin the friendship between them, but Max knew she couldn't let the words keep rolling around in her head or she might end up screaming. "I thought he wouldn't lie to me, either, Jenks, but I was apparently wrong."

Jenks was silent for a long moment, then she nodded as if coming to a decision. "Whatever this is, I got your back, LT." She tapped her fist to her heart.

Max was so stunned she almost missed the handshake, but recovered and connected with the back of Jenks's fist. Blinking away the tears, she leaned in and touched her forehead to her friend's. "I've got yours."

When Jenks was gone, Max sank into the chair by Chae's bed and tried to go back to the report she'd been composing before the accident.

A message notification pinged on her DD.

Carmichael, R: **Max, do you have time to talk?**

Carmichael, M: **Give me a moment.**

"Commander, do you have a com panel I can borrow?"

Nebula looked away from the orderly she was speaking with. "Absolutely. You can use the one in my office."

"Thank you." Max followed the direction the woman was pointing to the open door and sat down at the desk. It seemed safer to route the call through *Zuma* now that the ship was hooked into the *Laika*'s coms and had a longer range. She trusted the ensign's encryptions more than anyone else's right now. "Sapphi, are we clean?"

"We are."

"Can you route a call to Ria for me?"

"Putting it through now."

"Max." Ria's eyes were red-rimmed and swollen and the sick feeling that had been steadily building rose up to choke Max. "Jeanie was in an accident. Her air car—I—" She dragged in a breath, composed herself. "They don't know if she's going to make it. I know you two weren't on the best of terms but I didn't know who else to call—"

"Hey, it's okay." Max caught herself reaching for the screen and dropped her hand back to the desk. "Breathe for me, Ria. Where are you?"

"Home. Jonah made me come back here. He thought it would be safer, until they're sure it was an accident."

Max issued a silent prayer of gratitude for her sister's bodyguard. "It's a good idea. Jeanie would want you safe just in case. What hospital?"

"She's at Sayreville General. I'm listed as her next of kin." Ria's eyes filled with tears. "Max, I don't know what I'm going to do if I lose her."

Max looked up at the knock and the door slid open to reveal her brother. She waved him in. "Ria, Scott's here."

"You're talking to Ria?"

"Why are you with Scott?"

Max ignored both questions. "Bosco was hurt in an accident." She couldn't stop the slight hesitation before she said the word and hoped neither of them noticed.

"Ria, are you all right?" Scott came around the desk and leaned into the com frame.

"I wasn't with her. For once I didn't work late but she did."

"It's okay." Scott's voice was soothing and Max shifted out of the chair so he could slide into it. The conversation faded into the background and Max wrapped her arms around her waist.

This was my fault. I asked Jeanie to look into Julia from the bridge. The listening device was probably already there. They heard it all.

This wasn't *an accident.*

The conflicting emotions of guilt and growing certainty that all of this was connected tangled themselves into a hot ball in her stomach.

"Max."

She turned around, almost running into Scott. "Sorry, what?"

"Ria said she'd talk to you later and thank you." He studied her for a moment. "You want to tell me what's going on?"

"I asked Jeanie to look into Chae's girlfriend for me." The story spilled out of her in a rush.

Scott listened. He listened to the whole thing without interrupting her or second-guessing her and it was a shock how badly Max needed that right now.

"Let me put a call in to Jonah. Bosco likely kept him up to

date on things, and even though this didn't have anything to do with LifeEx she might have mentioned it." He rubbed at his face. "I think you should go get some sleep. When we get on the ground at Trappist, you can hash this out with Nika and get everything sorted."

"You're right." Max would have laughed at the surprised look on her brother's face if she hadn't suddenly been tired all the way to her bones. "I'll see if the doc has a bed I can borrow. I don't want to leave Chae alone."

"Go on back to your ship," Scott said. "I'll stay with them."

Max hugged him tight. "Thanks. I'm glad you're here." She headed back to the Interceptor, surprised by the polite greetings from the spacers as she passed. News of Chae's injuries had spread through the ship.

"The only thing faster than light is gossip," she murmured to herself as she crossed the bay. Jenks wasn't under the ship, which meant she'd likely finished up what she'd been working on. Max climbed the ladder. "Hey, Sapphi," she called up the stairs to the bridge.

"LT. Ship's clean. I triple-checked and then rechecked everything. If there is another bug on *Zuma* it is way out of my league."

"Good. Can you put another call in for me? To Rosa. I'll take it in my room."

"Can do." Sapphi nodded once and turned back to the console.

Max settled onto her bunk with her tablet, and held in the sob when the com connected.

"Max, how are you?"

"Rosa, do you have a minute to talk?"

The smile on Commander Rosa Martín's face faded into motherly concern. "Of course I do. What's going on?"

Stephan stopped pacing the length of the makeshift office on Trappist-1d and rubbed a hand over his face with
a sigh as he stood next to Luis. "How did this entire thing
turn into such a clusterfuck in the span of a few hours?"

"You can't blame Max for being good at her job,
Stephan. Of course she went to Bosco for information,"
Scott replied. "I told you we should have read all four
crews in from the beginning. They could have kept Chae
in the dark, or better yet coached them on how to handle the whole thing."

"Which would have left us with Chae either further
isolated or worse, overconfident, Scott. We've talked
about this. I don't want the kid feeling like they have nowhere to turn, but we need them to be scared."

"Better scared than crushed by boxes. They already
feel like that, Stephan, and it's only going to get worse
from here. I say when we land on Trappist we lay the
whole thing out."

"I second that," Tivo said from Scott's side. "Jenks is
suspicious as hell. I had to lean on her a bit to keep her
from reporting to the COB that she suspected someone
of beating up her Neo."

"Then you keep leaning if you have to," Stephan replied. "I've already said no to reading *Zuma* fully into
this, never mind the other three Interceptor teams. We
had a backup plan in case you lost the freighter, so we'll
use it." Stephan met Scott's glare with a patient look.
"Do I need to remind you this is a NeoG operation, Commodore, and you're only here as a courtesy?"

"You don't."

The screen went black as Scott disconnected the feed from the *Laika*. Stephan turned and studied the opposite wall. Tieg's image shimmered in the projection. On his right was the image of another man with hard eyes. On the left was a blank silhouette.

Stephan followed the trail. He still didn't know who was pulling the strings on the shipping side. Whoever it was had been careful to avoid all his sources. There was nothing in writing, no video he could scrape an ID from.

From the intel he'd pieced together there was cargo on this freighter that would potentially break that mystery by flushing whoever was in charge of the shipping out into the open. If he dangled it as bait he knew they would do their best to keep the cargo from reaching the NeoG warehouse. Hurting Chae was the least of it—if anything, it was just a message to everyone that Tieg had even more people on the inside.

What a clusterfuck.

"Okay," Stephan said. "After we lay out the cover story, I'll mention that we're moving the confiscated goods from the impounded freighter to the warehouse."

"Why?" Luis asked.

"Chae will pass the info along. After what happened to their friend, they can't risk not cooperating."

"Why don't we just bring Chae in again?"

"Did I not just explain all that? Because we can't risk whoever's behind this getting suspicious. They've somehow got someone to send a message to Chae while on the *Laika*. That's a hell of a reach. Until I figure out how, I can't risk it, and this may be our one shot to find out who Tieg's got running this operation."

"If we at least read the rest of *Zuma* in, they could watch Chae," Luis protested. "And maybe have some other ideas."

"I am not having this discussion with you, too, Senior Chief."

"Yes, you are. I want it on the record that I don't agree with this. Chae could have been killed. Are you done trying to use that kid as bait, or are you going to push this until someone from the NeoG dies, too?"

Stephan raised an eyebrow at the set of Luis's jaw. "Your objection is noted, Senior Chief," he replied. "But the more people we let in, the more dangerous this gets for everyone. We will proceed as planned. If we catch them, this will be wrapped up and we can bring Tieg down for good."

"And if we don't, more people are going to get hurt."

"People are already getting hurt. Dismissed."

SIXTEEN

Nika pretended the stiff silence on *Zuma*'s bridge wasn't because of him as Max piloted the Interceptor down to the landing pad at NeoG Trappist headquarters just outside the city of Amanave . . . but he knew it was.

"Many thanks, Landing Control," Max said as she powered the ship down. "Your orders, Commander?"

Her cold formality stung.

"Stephan's got a temporary office in HQ. The others will meet us there."

The crew of *Dread* was headed back to Jupiter with their ship on the *Laika*. The EMP shot from that freighter had fried nearly every circuit in the Interceptor and it was going to take weeks—and the full resources of Jupiter Station—to get it sorted. However, D'Arcy had decided that as head of the task force he would stay behind and ride back with *Zuma* rather than going with his crew.

Nika was agonized that he would have to face down D'Arcy also, but he couldn't argue with the man. Stephan had seemed to agree that keeping the task force leader in the loop was a good way to make whatever story he was going to spin tie back to the original mission. Though he'd insisted that the other two teams on the task force didn't need to know, especially since they were close to wrapping everything up. So *Flux* and *Hunter* had stayed on the Jupiter side of the juncture to continue their patrols.

Stephan seemed certain they could play off ST-1's presence on Trappist-1d as necessary since they were down a ship, and Nika hoped he was right.

He headed off the Interceptor. Chae looked haunted, with bruises decorating their face. They were moving a little stiffly, but otherwise had been cleared by the *Laika*'s doctor to come back to duty.

The others wouldn't even look at him, though Jenks did spare a quick glance and a hopeful smile on her way by.

Is it going to get worse or better when they find out the truth?

Like Luis and Scott, he wished Stephan wouldn't go with the backup plan they'd had in place and instead decide to tell everyone the whole truth. As much as it would hurt, at least it would be over with and Nika could figure out where to go from there.

But the instructions from Stephan before they arrived at Trappist had been clear—even if the reasoning wasn't—and Nika had little choice but to obey. He knew what was at stake here. If Tieg's people packed up his operation and vanished, they'd never have enough evidence to arrest the senator.

In the meantime, though, I have a crew that hates me.

Jenks peeled off from the group as soon as they cleared the threshold of the conference room and she spotted Luis. She stepped into his embrace without the slightest hesitation and the ache in Nika's chest grew.

"I take it that whatever's had you acting strangely has to do with Intel," D'Arcy murmured.

Nika closed his eyes for a moment, swallowing back the curse that tried to slip free. "I really need people to stop sneaking up on me."

"I hear Trappist is good for relaxing, at least the tourist spots."

"You're very calm about this."

"No, I'm pissed. My ship got trashed. There better be an exceptionally good reason for it."

"Does the safety of the habitats count?" The question slipped out before Nika could stop himself and he was grateful that not only were they alone in this corner of the room, but Stephan was out of earshot.

D'Arcy smothered a curse. "You know how to get right to what matters, don't you?" He sighed. "I want to hear the rest of it, but fine, I'm not mad at you for trying to do the right thing. Not going to help you with Max, but at least I won't kick you while she's got you down."

"Gee, thanks."

"All right, people, gather around." Stephan's voice cut through the conversations and the room fell silent. "Intel has been on the trail of a decent-sized smuggling operation. What happened today was—" He sighed. "I'm sorry, things didn't quite go as planned."

"By that you mean I wasn't supposed to avoid the EMP and take out the ship?" Max's question wasn't laced with any particular heat, but Nika was all too familiar with that tone now.

It was the same one she'd used on him in the Interceptor.

"Yes," Stephan said. "We were hoping the smugglers would lead the *Laika* to their warehouses, or at the very least give us an opportunity to grab one of the crew when they got on the ground."

"Now you've got the whole crew."

"They won't talk, not with the story that they were boarded and arrested all over the news."

"They weren't headed away from Trappist, were they?" Max asked.

"No, they were headed for One-d. We think that's where their base of operations is."

"You used us as bait." Jenks's voice was low.

"Controlled bait," Stephan replied. "All they had was the EMP and the *Laika* was right there."

"What if they hadn't been right there?" Max asked. "If there had been other ships. If they had been armed. Any number of things could have gone wrong, Stephan. You sent us in there without a clue of what we were up against and I don't see a single reason for it. Why the f—" She stopped and took a breath, seeming to suddenly remember she was speaking to a superior officer. "Why didn't you just tell us all this when you assembled the task force?"

"It was on a need-to-know basis," Stephan said. "The smugglers are getting their information from a lot of different sources. It's hard to know what's been compromised."

Nika saw Chae's almost imperceptible flinch. He didn't think anyone else noticed, though it was probably only because Max and Stephan were currently in a staring contest.

"Then why tell Nika and not D'Arcy?" she said finally. "He's the commander of the task force."

"I'm also a man with past connections to Free Mars, Max," D'Arcy replied. "And that's an issue, isn't it? Especially if you think the TLF is involved in the smuggling."

"That doesn't make any sense," Chae blurted. "They wouldn't steal from their own people."

"The world's a bit more complex than we may like, Chae," Stephan replied. "What happened today was regrettable, but we've still got a good chance to hit the smugglers on their next run. As for the cargo we got off the ship, we'll be moving the supplies from Trappist Control's impound to the NeoG warehouse tonight so that we can get them where they need to go before they spoil. *Zuma*, we'll put you on air coverage for the trucks with SEAL Team One. Major Carmichael, you're fine with Commander Montaglione riding with you?"

It was impressive how easily Stephan had deflected D'Arcy's concern without actually confirming or denying it and how he ushered the conversation along to the more mundane planning aspects of the cargo movement, and the meeting broke up. No one left the room, instead breaking into smaller groups, and Nika suddenly felt very alone.

"Nika?" Max put out a hand before he could head for the door. "Can you wait a moment?"

He looked up at her and his heart twisted. "Max, I—"

"I'm sorry."

"What?" He stared at her in confusion. "Why are you apologizing?"

"I'm sorry for thinking the worst of you—for basically accusing you of being a smuggler. It was unfair of me."

Oh, Saint Ivan . . .

"It's fine. I get it. You don't have to apologize."

"I do, though. I was wrong. You are fit for command. I don't like the decision Stephan made, but I get it and I get what you were struggling with." She offered up a hesitant smile that cut him in two. "You were in a difficult position."

"I appreciate the apology." He forced out the words.

Max glanced over her shoulder and lowered her voice. "Will you talk to Stephan about Chae? I don't know if the smuggling is connected to what happened to them in the cargo bay, but it wasn't an accident."

"Do you have proof?" He hated the words, and hated the wince she couldn't hide.

"I still have a lot of pieces that don't make sense. I asked Jeanie Bosco to look into Julia, Nika. I was on *Zuma* when I talked to her. I didn't know about the bug. Ria messaged me while we were on the *Laika*. Jeanie's air car crashed. She's in critical condition." Max struggled for composure. "It was my fault."

"Max, I'm so sorry."

She cleared her throat and straightened her shoulders. "Scott was there when I talked to Ria. Stephan could ask him if he has questions."

"I'll talk to him," Nika promised. "Are you sure you don't want to do it yourself?"

"No, I think I'm going to go lie down for a little bit. I didn't sleep well and I should get some rest before the mission tonight." She offered up another smile, this one even more wan, and then walked away.

It was all Nika could do not to follow and tell her everything.

JENKS WATCHED MAX WALK AWAY FROM NIKA. NEITHER OF them looked happy and she scrubbed at her cheek with the back of her hand in frustration. "I don't get paid enough to be a relationship counselor." She elbowed Luis. "I should make you do it. It's your fault."

"Do what? And how is it my fault?" he protested.

"Smooth things over between Max and Nika. They've been at each other's throats for the better part of a month thanks to this shit—your Intel shit—which is why it's your fault, Luis."

"They'll be fine," Tivo said. "Let them work it out on their own."

"You have no idea how hard it's been to keep this team headed in the same direction with those two at odds. Should have just told us," Jenks muttered, glaring at Luis again. "You Intel goons act like we can't keep secrets."

"Dai, you're terrible at keeping secrets."

"Birthday surprises and operational security aren't the same thing and you know it." She poked him, then sighed. "I'm worried about Chae."

"Chae's fine."

Jenks tamped down her annoyance. Luis's upbringing sometimes made him completely miss how hard other people's lives had been and the reactions that came out of those challenges. It was obvious this was one of those times, but she didn't have the energy to dig into it so she let it go.

"Anyhow, I didn't get to do a postflight check on the ship when we landed, so I'm taking Chae and doing that now."

Luis caught her by the wrist and tugged her into his embrace again. "Who are you and what have you done with my Dai?"

She laughed, annoyance fading, and leaned into him for a long moment, enjoying the feel of him and the way the familiar smell of coffee and spice wound around her head. "Didn't you hear? I got promoted and now I have to be responsible."

Luis's laughter mixed with Tivo's and Jenks heaved a sigh of regret as she stepped away. "Maybe I'll get to see you both before we wrap this mess up tonight. I really do need to go tend to the ship, though."

"Go on, Jenks," Tivo said. "Come find us when you finish."

"Chae, you're with me."

The spacer snapped upright at her call and Jenks muffled a second sigh at their bruised face. For a moment she almost went back to Luis to demand he look into whatever was going on with her Neo, but she'd promised Max on the ride over she'd let her LT handle it. So she just waited a beat for Chae to catch up and led them across the base to the hangar.

"I want you to do the interior inspection. You've done it enough on your own it should be easy, yeah?"

"Yes, Chief."

The interior inspection didn't really need to be done. Even though Sapphi had said they were clean, Jenks had spent the time headed to Trappist tearing apart the inside of *Zuma* to make sure there weren't any more bugs, or worse, that someone hadn't tampered with the ship itself.

By "someone," you mean Chae, right?

Jenks muffled her sigh as they reached the ship and she climbed the ladder to grab her tool bag. She didn't want to think about the fact that it was likely Chae who'd planted the bug. That this kid was working for the smugglers—either willingly or not. She had zero proof of this extremely coincidental suspicion and so had kept her mouth shut during the meeting.

But it lingered nevertheless.

"Get to work, Chae. I'll come check on you in a bit."

As Chae walked away, Jenks hoped that they passed this test. It would be easy enough for her to double check their work and Sapphi was going to do another sweep before the mission. Whatever the deal with Chae was, she didn't think they were a willing participant, not if the bruises had come from fists like she thought, rather than the cargo bins. Jenks had been on the receiving end of a beatdown or two in her time. She'd also been in positions where she'd had to do horrible shit for other people in order to survive.

All of that made it hard for her to be angry at Chae. What she really wanted was for the kid to just fucking trust her.

"You are conflicted."

She looked down at Doge as her feet hit the ground again. "A little, yeah, buddy."

"Do you want to talk about it?"

She patted his head. "I appreciate that, but no. I can't do anything about it right now."

"Chae is scared."

Jenks put her bag down next to Doge and went to a knee. "How scared?"

"More than when they first arrived. They are also conflicted. Everyone has been upset. I don't like it."

"Me either." Jenks pressed her head against Doge's. "I wish I knew what to do about it, but I don't. So we'll focus on the stuff we can fix." She patted him and got to her feet, then started her walk around the outside of *Zuma*.

She noted a few new dings in her DD file for the exterior integrity. Damage from debris was to be expected, but she didn't see anything that would tip them over into the red zone.

"You're still in good shape, aren't you, baby?" she asked, grabbing for a handrail and pulling herself up onto the tail section. She continued along the top of the ship, taking notes as she went.

Panels 227–247 need cleaning and rotation.

Rail gun will need to be cleaned and ammo replenished.

Crack in panel 399 just hit yellow zone, check with requisitions about getting a replacement. Again.

Check bridge seal during interior, outside looks good.

Jenks let the soothing routine ease everything else out of her mind. She'd worry about Chae and all this mess later. Right now her ship was her only concern.

CHAE SWALLOWED DOWN THE BILE THAT KEPT RISING IN their throat. The sound of Jenks's contented humming was wafting in through the open door as she did her walkaround, and it was like the soundtrack to their own guilt. Jenks hadn't acted like anything was wrong; in fact no one had. They'd all been concerned about the supposed accident and visited Chae in the med bay on the trip to Trappist. If anything, everyone was united in being mad at Nika—and Stephan—*for* them.

They were treating Chae like one of the team and it only made them feel even worse.

It didn't stop them from sending the email, though. Not with thoughts of Bean filling their head.

We're moving cargo from the impound lot to a NeoG warehouse tonight. Coordinates to follow.

There was no answer. Chae didn't need one—they already had their instructions.

"Make sure your ship gets grounded—or there'll be worse things than this beating down the line."

They moved methodically through their inspection, the words pounding in their head to the beat of their heart. They already knew whatever they did had to be enough to keep the Interceptor from taking off. They didn't want to hurt anyone—not to mention they'd be on the ship, too.

They headed for the back, checking off each item on the list. The system was spotless. Jenks had apparently done a lot of work while Chae had been in the med bay.

Because she cleans when she's worried. Not to mention that bug I planted probably had them all checking the systems over and over.

Chae stopped in their tracks as the memory of Jenks showing them how to clean the power conduit flashed into their head.

"It'll send a live charge up to the bridge that will short out everything in the ship."

They were on their back and had popped the panel before they even really comprehended they were moving. "The blue one," Chae whispered, fingers finding the cable they needed. "And the green one." They connected them with shaking fingers and scrambled back out from the space, fitting the panel in place as Jenks's voice wafted from the doorway.

"All done, Chae?"

"Just finishing up."

"Good. I'll be outside." There was a pause. "Hey, Chae, I'm not trying to be pushy, but we've got downtime until the pre-mission brief and I haven't seen Luis in a couple of months, so if you could get a move on . . ."

Chae laughed, then clapped a hand over their mouth when it unexpectedly turned into a sob. "I'll hurry, Chief."

The heavy sigh from Jenks was their only answer, but the familiar banter sank like a body weighted with a stone. It dragged Chae down with it into the depths of misery.

SEVENTEEN

Max had tried to sleep, but after she'd emailed Ria to check on Jeanie's condition and tried to convince herself that all her unease was just a result of an adrenaline dump from the freighter incident, sleep refused to come.

She finally dozed off for an hour, waking with the same sick feeling in her gut. "I am so tired of this," she muttered, rubbing at her eyes as she sat up. The narrow bed of the officers' quarters on base was even less comfortable than her bunk on *Zuma*, and she stretched, trying to work the kinks out of her back.

She headed for the conference room where they'd met earlier in the day. Tamago and Sapphi were in the corner with Chae, and Max waved to them as she crossed the room and joined Stephan in front of the shifting wall of data. The others filtered in after her.

"You feel better?" he murmured as a greeting.

"Still angry with you."

He nodded. "You should have heard D'Arcy after you left. He warned me the next time we get in the sword ring it would be painful."

"Generous of him to give you a warning."

"Foolish. I am sorry, Max. This is not always easy. That's an explanation, not an excuse, by the way." Stephan reached a hand out and touched the screen, which froze the movement and brought an image to the foreground. "What do you see?"

"A building project." She leaned in, frowning at the screen. "Resolution isn't good enough to pick out faces, but—"

"No, big picture, Max. You're right—it's a building project; more specifically it's a drainage project that was supposed to help one of the outlying habitats with the massive rains that hit their area in the late summer."

"D'Arcy mentioned working on a project. The area that had been flooded out. Is it the same place?" Max looked back at the photo. There were two women in the front of the shot, one partially hidden by the other. A memory chased itself around her brain, colliding with another. "There were issues with the project. Supply issues. Thanks to our smugglers?"

"Very good, Lieutenant."

"How long has this been going on?"

"Too long. We dropped the ball on this one and I've been playing catch-up. If your sister hadn't contacted us, we'd probably still be in the dark."

"Ria?"

"Senator Carmichael." His smile was quick as he reached out and tapped the photo, sending it back into the shifting data. "She's on the Habitat Committee, noticed some concerning patterns, and came to talk to me about it one day. If I'd snagged you for Intel before you ran off to join the Interceptors—"

"I get it, I'd be on your side of this instead of where I am." Max shrugged. "But that's not what happened. I'm here, and since you chose to bring Nika into this, the least you could have done for us and for him was to let him tell me. I could have backed him, helped him out like I'm supposed to do anyway."

"I have my reasons for doing it this way, and I can't change my decision. Honestly, I'm not sure I would. You've probably figured out by now I like keeping my ops small and under my control."

"That's one way to phrase it."

Stephan laughed. "I suppose I earned that," he conceded. "Let's focus on what we can all do together: get these supplies moved so that the people of Trappist have what they need."

The pre-mission briefing was quick and to the point. The supplies had already been transferred to a pair of trucks at the Trappist Control facility forty-five kilometers outside of Amanave. *Zuma* and SEAL Team One would provide air support for the convoy as it circled around the habitat to the warehouses on the NeoG base.

"Any questions?" Stephan gestured to the door. "Let's roll out."

"Okay, Optimus." Jenks pushed away from the wall and Max choked back a laugh at his confused frown.

"Go on, you." Max shoved Jenks playfully in the back and followed her out the door.

Max was halfway to the ship when the memory from earlier slapped her full force. Blurry photo aside, there'd been enough detail to pick out the faces. The woman in the foreground had been Julia.

Are you sure?

She hung there as her uncertainty rose up with a scream. Rosa's recent pep talk about trusting herself slid away like sand under the onslaught of a lifetime of conditioning. It was far too easy to swallow down her concern and catch up with the rest of the crew.

She told herself that she would mention it to Stephan after.

NIKA TURNED AS MAX CAUGHT UP WITH HIM. "WHAT'S wrong?"

"Nothing," she said.

Nika knew he deserved this lack of trust. Deserved even more than that, really, for lying to her all over again. He hoped Stephan was right and they'd get the information they needed to wrap up this operation once and for all.

Then I can go back to being an Interceptor.

And I'd stop feeling like a piece of shit around my crew.

The familiar sound of Sapphi and Chae doing the preflight checklist filled the bridge as he climbed the stairs.

"Everything's green, Commander," Sapphi said. "Just waiting on the tower."

Chae jumped when Nika put a hand on their shoulder. "Stephan, we're good to go."

"Copy that. ST-One, what's your status?"

"Ready when you are."

"We have clearance from the tower, Nika. Hangar bay overheads are open."

He nodded at Sapphi's announcement. "Take us up, Chae."

Chae hesitated. "Sir, I'm getting some odd readings."

"Define *odd,* Chae."

"I don't know, sir. I'm sorry."

Nika looked to Sapphi. "You said everything was good?"

"On my end, yes."

"Jenks, can I get a confirmation we're good for takeoff?"

"She's being the normal amount of squirrely, Nik," she replied. "You're green."

Nika patted Chae. "Let's go."

Zuma lifted off. Nika glanced over his shoulder as the other three members of the crew came onto the bridge. They weren't often all up here at once, though there was still plenty of room. Max and Tamago moved to the bank of screens by the stairs, heads together as they watched the trucks head for the gate of the Trappist Control facility.

"Intercept in two minutes," Max said.

"I've got ST-One on the radar, port side. Everything else is quiet," Tamago replied.

"*Zuma*, ST-One, the trucks are at the gate and proceeding to the base."

"Copy that, Stephan. Chae, bring us around. You want to keep an eye on where ST-One is when you do."

"Copy that, Commander."

Nika didn't give Chae any grief for falling back into formality. The kid was nervous enough as it was; he didn't want to make it worse by distracting them.

Tamago thumped the screen. "Damn thing, do not fuzz out on me in the middle of this. Jenks, why is this—"

"*Zuma*, we've got contacts on the ground." Tivo's voice came over the coms. "Heat signature, three o'clock low!"

The lead truck exploded almost instantaneously with his warning.

Nika heard Jenks mutter, "Well, shit," from behind him.

"*Zuma*—" The com cut off and this time Sapphi swore.

"What the actual shit are you doing, girl?" she demanded of the ship. "I don't know why everything is screwed up. Jenks, shut the coms down and then turn them back on. We'll see if a hard start will help get her to stop being so fussy."

"We did a whole damn diagnostic on this piece of shit," Jenks muttered. She slapped at the coms panel. The bright blue spark that erupted from it flung her across the bridge and into the far wall as it streaked through the main console.

Nika jerked Chae out of the pilot seat, but he couldn't get to Sapphi in time and watched helplessly as the electricity ripped through his ensign.

MAX LUNGED FORWARD, KICKING SAPPHI FROM HER SEAT. The bottoms of her boots did their job and insulated her from the shock, but she swore she could taste the lightning on her tongue.

"No, damn it." Tamago jumped over a dazed Jenks and

landed on their knees next to Sapphi's still body. It was a sight Max would never be able to wipe from her mind, but somehow she pushed her fear and grief away and jerked the med kit off the wall.

The only light on the bridge was the dying sunlight filtering in through the main window. Max slammed a hand down on the emergency power switch, flooding the space with an ominous wash of red. The engines kicked on for a second, lifting them . . . and then died.

Chae jumped for the pilot's chair, starting the procedure for a loss of power. The manual emergency controls popped free from their storage and Max dragged her attention back to the rest of her crew.

Whatever her concerns about Chae, they vanished under the pressing need to help Tamago.

Nika was crouched by Jenks, checking for a pulse, and Max's own heart gave a painful thump when the chief protested groggily, waving her arms at him.

"Sapphi, you do not get to die on me." Tamago was doing chest compressions as Max set the kit down next to them. "Get the breather."

Max complied, not needing any more direction as her own training kicked in. She affixed the breather to Sapphi's face, trying to shove aside the thousand memories of animated expressions that might never cross it again.

"Come on, Sapphi. Can't call yourself a hacker if you're letting a little electricity bring you down." Tamago stopped compressions and checked for a pulse. "LT, I need—"

Sapphi convulsed, trying to drag in a breath against the breather's rhythm, and Max scrambled to get it off her face. "Easy, easy, Sapphi. We've got you."

The ship lurched again and Max grabbed for both Sapphi and Tamago as *Zuma* dropped into a nosedive, Chae's desperate call filling the bridge.

"Mayday, mayday, mayday. This is Interceptor *Zuma's Ghost*. Repeat, Interceptor *Zuma's Ghost*, Zz5. We have lost power. We are going down."

"NONONO." CHAE KNEW BEGGING WITH GRAVITY WAS USE-less. It was a miracle they'd coasted for as long as they had without gravity noticing.

Cascade failure of ultimate proportions. What's your solution?

They shoved both feet against the console and hauled on the manual controls, but the ship slid easily into a nosedive.

They'd done this before, but with shuttles. Smaller, easier to control than the massive Interceptors. But they had what they had, and if they could get it to level out, the crash wouldn't be nearly as bad.

You mean not deadly for you? You're going to call it a win that you've only *killed Sapphi?*

Guilt and panic went to war in their head, even as the training drummed into them by their Interceptor instructors took control.

"Mayday, mayday, mayday. This is Interceptor *Zuma's Ghost*. Repeat, Interceptor *Zuma's Ghost*, Zz5. We have lost power. We are going down." Their voice felt raw in their throat as they tried sending the distress call with their own DD. "This is all my fault." Those words slipped out, thankfully lost to the chaos of the bridge.

They pulled harder, fighting against mass and gravity and every other immutable law, and losing, when suddenly Max was there, grabbing the stick and pulling with them.

"Chutes, I need the chutes."

"I've got the stick, Chae," Max gritted out. "Do what you need to."

Chae let go of the stick and kicked at the panel by their left knee. It opened and they reached in. "Deploying chute!" They slammed the levers for the chute releases into position. *Zuma* jerked again as the rear one deployed, yet the ground didn't seem to slow in its rush to meet them. They hit the second set of levers, deploying the airbags.

"Brace! Brace! Brace!" Chae yelled.

Max grabbed them and dragged them from their seat, covering them with her body as *Zuma* came down hard into the red dirt of Trappist-1d.

EIGHTEEN

A jumble of voices filtered back into his brain through the heavy layer of pain and confusion.

"Nika!"

That was Jenks, and the fear in her voice snapped him back to full consciousness. "Are you hurt?"

"Am *I* hurt? You're the one who wasn't responding." She poked him.

"I'm okay," he managed, catching her hand.

"Oh thank fuck. I thought you were dead. Can you move? Your elbow is digging into my spleen."

"Don't make me laugh, brat." He pushed himself up, blinking the dirt out of his eyes, and looked down at her. The rush of events hit him like a rail shot. "We crashed."

"Looks like. Still alive, though. Come on, get off me."

"Are you injured, Jenks?"

She forced out a smile. "Head's still buzzing from that sideswipe of a shock and everything hurts, but I'm all right."

Nika squeezed her hand and let her go.

"Commander Vagin!"

"Over here." Nika managed to get his other arm under him

and rolled off his sister as Petty Officer Diego Cano from ST-1 reached them.

"Easy, Chief." Diego caught Jenks by the arm when she stumbled to her feet.

"Where's everyone else? Is Sapphi okay? Shit, where's my dog?"

"Everyone's outside already, Doge included." Diego looked at Nika. "Are you injured, Commander?"

"I'm all right, Diego. Go with the chief, I'm right behind you."

Nika looked around the bridge. The front window had broken despite the best efforts of the airbags and the place was littered with dirt and debris from what he assumed was their long slide through the earth before coming to a stop.

"Nika, are you there?" Stephan's voice was strained in his head.

"Yeah." He picked his way across the bridge and down the stairs.

"We've got a med shuttle almost at your location. Tivo said your ensign is stable but she took a bad shock. What happened?"

"I have no idea. Let me take care of my crew. We'll figure it out later."

"Nika—"

"No, Stephan. I'm seeing to my crew. The other shit can wait." He disconnected, the memory of Tamago pleading with Sapphi to come back replaying itself in his head. He had to get to them.

The scene outside the ship was organized chaos. He spotted Scott tending to Max. Chae was nearby, slumped against a rock but apparently unharmed; Spacer Emery Montauk was sitting with them. His sister was protesting as Diego tried to herd her over to Chae.

"Jenks, don't argue with Diego. Let him check you," he said as he passed them.

Jenks flipped him a rude gesture, but then grimaced, and for once, Nika won an argument with his sister.

Tamago and Tivo were bent over Sapphi's stretcher, the pair of them calling out readings to each other with easy efficiency.

Nika crossed to them and went to a knee next to Tamago. "How is she?"

"Awake." Tamago's face was smeared with red dirt. "She's not tracking great, though."

"Hey, Nika. When did you get back?"

"Never left." He reached out and took Sapphi's hand. "Gave us a scare there, Sapphi."

"Feels like that time I did a four-day *Space Treachery* tournament. Did I ever tell you about that? I won. Kicked so much nerd ass." She smiled at him, her eyes fluttering closed. "There are squids in my arms."

"She keeps going in and out," Tivo murmured.

"Stephan's got a med shuttle headed—" He looked up as the craft arrived. "Here it is."

"Good. She's stable, but I don't like the readings we're getting and I'll feel better when she's at the hospital." Tamago winced as they got to their feet and went to meet the medical personnel coming off the shuttle.

"You going with them?"

Tivo nodded. "Yeah."

"Make sure Tamago gets checked out." Nika squeezed Sapphi's hand once more and then let go.

"We didn't see an outside shot beyond what hit the trucks," Tivo said in a low voice. "What happened?"

"I don't know. Some kind of short. Maybe entirely coincidental—our ships aren't necessarily top of the line."

"You don't think that."

"I don't. But I can't rule it out." Nika glanced in Chae's direction. "The alternative is unpleasant." He didn't think Chae would have put themself at risk like this, but desperation made people do stupid things. "We'll see you at the hospital." Nika headed back across the open area, stopping next to his sister. "You okay?"

"Yeah, just cracked my head when the ship bit me. Can I go with Sapphi?"

He nodded. "Take Chae with you." He glanced up as several other shuttles came in for landings nearby. It was going to take a hauler to get *Zuma* back in the air and on its way to the yard so they could figure out what went wrong and start repairs.

Nika turned, and as his eyes adjusted to the darkness beyond the lights from the ships, he could see the massive line *Zuma* had dug into the ground during its landing.

Things could have been so much worse.

"Put pressure on that," Scott ordered as Nika joined them.

Max looked away from her brother to Nika as she pressed a patch to her hairline. Blood was streaked down the left side of her face and there was a dark stain on her shirt. "Are you hurt?" she asked.

"I'm all right."

"You sure about that? She said she was all right, too," Scott said, and an exasperated look flickered across Max's face.

"I *am* all right," she said.

"I don't think I'm obviously bleeding anywhere." Nika sat down, linking his fingers through Max's when she reached for him and trying to ignore the rush of relief that followed. "But you're welcome to verify. I sent everyone else on the med shuttle with Sapphi. Do you need to go, too?"

"It's just a scratch. I'm fine otherwise. I can stay and help here."

"There's not much to do." Nika exhaled. "I'm assuming Stephan's already got a call in to figure out how we're going to get *Zuma* back to Jupiter Station."

"The *Laika* will be back in a week," Scott said.

"We're not going anywhere until Sapphi's ready to travel

anyway," Max said. "Stephan better have an answer for me when I ask him who shot at those trucks and what happened to our ship." She let his hand go to rub at her face and Nika shared a grim look with Scott.

He had a feeling the truth was about to come out whether Stephan wanted it to or not.

IT WAS SURPRISINGLY EASY TO PRETEND LIKE THE WORLD wasn't collapsing down on you when everyone else was caught up in worries of their own. Chae sat to Jenks's left in the uncomfortable hospital waiting room chair and bit the inside of their cheek to hold back the tears. They'd both been checked out and cleared by the medical staff and now waited to hear how Sapphi was doing.

Chae wanted to scream. They wanted to cry. But that would mean explaining it all to the chief and they were already in deep as it was.

It'll mean telling her I've been lying all this time. That I was responsible for Sapphi nearly dying, for all of us nearly dying. And it could mean next time, it's my fathers caught in an "accident."

Chae couldn't have found the words even if they'd wanted to. "Dai."

Jenks was out of her seat like an asteroid sucked into a gravity well when Luis appeared in the doorway. She hit him dead center, wrapping her arms around his waist. The big man folded her into an embrace and bent his head, whispering in Jenks's ear.

It reminded Chae, stupidly, of Julia, and how it had felt when she hugged them. Back when they thought the hug had meant something.

They looked away from the painfully private moment, their own emotions joining the symphony of hurt already singing through their body.

"Nika and Max just arrived. They're headed in to see Sapphi. Max figured you two would want to see her also before we go back to base."

Chae realized the words were directed at both of them and looked back as Jenks turned in Luis's embrace. She was smiling and holding her hand out.

"Come on, Chae." She looked back at Luis. "Did anyone tell you Chae landed us? No fucking power, screaming in hot, and they brought us down in one piece. I was unconscious for most of it, but I heard it was impressive."

"No," Chae whispered.

Please, don't . . .

"Listen to them. So modest. Don't believe it for a second." Jenks leaned forward and grabbed Chae's hand. "Come on, let's go give Sapphi grief for lying around while the rest of us are going to have to piece *Zuma* back together."

There was a strange sympathy in Luis's amber eyes as they passed him that only made Chae feel even worse.

In Sapphi's room, Max was bent over the bed, her arms wrapped around Sapphi in a hug. She let the ensign go and stood; those brown eyes locked on Chae and for a second they considered running back out the door.

Except Luis was right behind them.

Jenks crossed the room quickly, but she didn't say anything, simply pressed her forehead to Sapphi's and closed her eyes tight. A soft smile appeared on the ensign's face and she patted the back of Jenks's head, murmuring something too low for Chae to hear.

Then she looked up. "I hear you saved our butts," she said, reaching for Chae's hand, and they somehow got their feet moving. Even as their heart was twisting itself into a hot, painful knot. All they could do was shake their head.

"Seriously, Chae, thank you."

Chae swallowed. "Of course," they whispered. Thankfully Tamago intervened with the doctor and Chae was able to fade into the back of the room.

They had a moment to collect themself before Max appeared. "Come with me." The grip on their arm wasn't painful, but Chae knew there was no escaping it as she propelled them out the door and down the hallway away from Sapphi's room. "You want to tell me what's going on?"

"I don't know what you mean, Lieutenant." Even as the lie slipped out, Chae regretted it.

Max's expression darkened with a fury they'd never seen from her before. She let them go and leaned down until they were nose to nose. "I. Heard. You. On the bridge. You said this was all your fault. Why?"

Chae's mind wiped itself clean.

And this time they bolted.

SHE'D BEEN WAITING FOR IT, SO MAX WASN'T SURPRISED when Chae turned and tried to run down the hallway. She caught the Neo around the waist. In retrospect, she should have spun them away from Luis, who'd followed them from the room.

A cat trapped in a corner is going to try to claw its way out.

Chae kicked Luis in the stomach before he could move out of range and the man staggered into the nurse's desk behind him.

"Chae, damn it, don't." It was a futile plea, she already knew it. The spacer was in a full-blown panic, wriggling like a goddamned eel, trying to escape her grip.

Max braced herself and took the flung elbow to her cheek, riding out the stars that blurred her vision. She wrapped one arm up under Chae's, locking her other around their waist and free arm and lifting them off their feet. "Come on, Chae. You've got no leverage here. I'm not going to hurt you. I just want to know who's pulling your strings. I don't believe for a second you're capable of hurting people on your own. But you have, and it has to stop. Who's making you do this?"

She was angry at Chae, she couldn't deny it, but that voice in the back of her head was equally certain the kid hadn't had any choice but survival. The betrayal stung, even more so because Max knew it was her failure to push her suspicions that had led them to this point in the first place.

"It's going to be okay, Chae," Max whispered. "I promise I'll help you however I can."

Chae abruptly slumped in her grip and their sobbing echoed loud in the silence of the hallway.

"You can't. You can't fix this. No one can. They killed my best friend. They're going to kill everyone I care about, even all of you."

"Who, Chae? Who's doing this?"

"Max," Stephan said from behind her. "Put your Neo down."

NINETEEN

Max leaned against the wall back at base, arms crossed over her chest. The feeling she'd been fighting with for the last few months was about to boil over. Jenks was on her right, D'Arcy on her left. Tamago had stayed at the hospital with Sapphi and three members of ST-1.

Nika was across the conference room, talking to Stephan and Scott in a low voice. Luis and Tivo were sitting at the table in the center of the room. Chae sat on the opposite side, head buried in their cuffed hands.

"All right, fuck this," Jenks muttered. She pushed off the wall, grabbed a chair, and sat down next to Chae. All other conversation stopped.

"Look at me, Neo," Jenks ordered, and Chae's head snapped up. "You've got one chance at this so I suggest you don't fuck it up. I owe you, because even if you were saving your own ass, you kept us all from dying. So I promise I will do whatever I can to help you out of this mess. You have to tell me the truth and do it now."

The story spilled out of Chae in a rush. Jenks listened without a word, her jaw tightening when Chae sobbed out the news of their best friend's death, the beating on the *Laika,* and how they'd sabotaged *Zuma.*

"I'm sorry, Chief. I'm so sorry." They buried their head in their hands again.

"I checked the ship again after you did your inspection and I still missed it," Jenks muttered, dragging a hand through her hair, the guilt and frustration etched onto her face. "You know what I didn't mention about crossing those cables, Chae? That the charge could have killed any of us. It could have killed you. Did you think about that for one second? No. You thought you'd just slap a few wires together and it would stop my damn ship from running?"

"I wanted to keep us on the ground without hurting anyone. I didn't think we'd even lift off."

"You obviously didn't think it through at all." Jenks huffed. "Learn how to sabotage things better."

Stephan rubbed a hand over his face. "Jenks."

"I'm serious. If they're going to do shit like that, at least do it right. Who's making you do this, Chae?"

"I don't know."

"Bullshit. I want names."

"They're telling the truth, Jenks."

Max watched as Jenks curled her right hand into a fist at Stephan's words. "And you know this because you knew the whole time that someone had Chae under their thumb."

Stephan nodded.

"You son of a—"

"Chief." Max's command wasn't loud, but Jenks snapped her mouth shut and shoved to her feet.

She paused and laid a hand on the back of Chae's head. "We all fuck up, kid. I get it, I really do," she murmured in a surprisingly gentle whisper. "I forgive you."

Max waited for Jenks to cross back to her before she spoke. "You all knew." Her words were the equivalent of dropping a grenade in the middle of the room, but she couldn't keep them in any longer. "Nika; my own brother; you, Stephan." The truth of it was suddenly, painfully clear to her. "The smuggling story you fed us is bullshit. What is going on?"

"It's not bullshit, Max. It's just bigger than I told you," Stephan replied.

"Wait, what?" Jenks demanded. "You *knew* that Chae had fucked with the ship? Did you seriously let us go up knowing we could come down in a pile of rubble?"

Jenks was looking at Stephan when she asked the question, and she missed the way Luis flinched and closed his eyes. Tivo looked at the tabletop, his jaw tight. Max could feel D'Arcy coiled like a spring next to her and reached a hand out, laying it gently on his forearm.

"Chief, that's enough." She very deliberately used Jenks's rank a second time, and even though it earned her a dirty look, it was enough to get the woman to cross her arms and lean back against the wall.

Max looked at Stephan. "Tell me what is going on or I'm putting a com in to Admiral Chen right now."

It wasn't bad as bluffs went and would at least serve to distract Jenks from putting all the pieces of this together. Her exploding on Luis and Tivo when she realized they'd been working together was the last thing they needed.

And Max knew the admiral would likely take her call, not only because the woman had shown more than a little interest in her career but also because the Carmichael name did mean something. As much as she hated it, Max wasn't above trading in on the influence.

But she was still only a lieutenant demanding access to information they all knew she damn well didn't have clearance for—injured ensign or not.

Chen would, in the end, shut her down. But the entire thing would be on record and Max suspected that was something Stephan didn't want happening.

Stephan stared at her, silently assessing, and Max stared

right back, waiting for him to call her bluff. She should have confronted him sooner, shouldn't have let Nika convince her she was wrong. Stephan would have told them the whole truth or moved them out of the task force.

Either way, her crew would have been safe.

Except you know that's not true. Chae would still be in danger.

"Don't try to threaten me, Lieutenant. Not only am I your superior officer, but my purview is also complete right now. If I ordered something, then I ordered it, and if you don't believe Admiral Chen is going to back my decisions here, then you don't know her as well as you think."

The Intel commander looked down for a moment and then up at the assembled group. "But maybe you don't know me as well as you think, either, Max," he said, using her name instead of rank now. "That's all right—if anything, that's one of my biggest mistakes. You want in all the way, so that's what we'll do.

"What I'm about to tell you is highly classified. This room is shielded from all outgoing and incoming transmissions, and recording is impossible. If you share any of this information outside of this room without my express permission you will be court-martialed. Is that understood?"

There were murmurs of assent.

"Sir?"

Stephan looked over to Chae, whose eyes were down. "Yes?"

"Should . . . should I be here for this?"

"Are you part of the Interceptor crew of *Zuma's Ghost*?"

"Yes. At least, I want to be. But am I not in trouble for what I did?"

Max was surprised Stephan looked her way again and even more so that she felt herself shaking her head. She wasn't angry at Chae. Much like Jenks, she understood the trap they'd been in.

Her mind flipped back to how determined Chae had been

trying to keep *Zuma* in the air. Someone more cynical might have insisted that it was simple self-preservation, but whatever else had happened, Max still trusted herself enough when it came to reading people.

Most of the time, anyway.

She couldn't stop herself from looking at Nika. His face was blank, but he couldn't keep the pain out of his blue eyes.

"You're part of our crew, Chae," she said. "Unless you want out."

"No." Chae sat up straighter. "No, I want to help. I want to make this right."

"Then you stay," Stephan said.

NIKA EXHALED QUIETLY AS STEPHAN CROSSED THE ROOM and took the cuffs off Chae.

"Welcome to Project Tartarus, people," Stephan said, moving to the front of the room. He gestured at the wall behind him and the images of Senator Tieg and a man named Vincent Grant came up, along with a blacked-out silhouette.

"The data you'll be looking at soon is from a two-year investigation into a smuggling operation that has been targeting the Trappist habitats for the better part of a decade. We believe the corruption extends all the way to the higher levels of the Coalition of Human Nations government." Stephan clasped his hands behind his back. "Senator Rubio Tieg has been our major suspect since the beginning. Pictured next to him is Vincent Grant, who we believe is responsible for any wet work Tieg wants done. There's a third individual we haven't been able to identify, but we believe they're involved in the transportation end of things."

"You said this was bigger than the smuggling. What are they doing?" Max asked.

"At its most basic, this group has been stealing supplies for the habitats and then reselling them to those same habitats on the black market for an outrageous markup," Stephan replied. "But the reality is far more dangerous, especially recently. We believe they're responsible for the resurgence of tensions between Earth and Mars and would be happy if the conflict exploded to distract the CHN from what's going on with Trappist. This is a joint-service operation with the TLF and the Navy. Commodore Carmichael's team was brought on to assist."

Nika was watching his sister and could pinpoint the exact moment the information clicked in Jenks's head. She hadn't quite figured it out that when Max had said, "You all knew," she'd really meant everyone and not just Intel. And Nika suspected that Max's confrontation with Stephan had been as much to distract Jenks as it had been to get the Intel officer to read them into the operation.

"You—" Jenks looked from Tivo to Luis, her mouth open in shock, and both Max and D'Arcy tensed as they waited for her to throw a punch.

Then she did something surprising. She snapped her mouth closed and didn't say a word, but her walls went up. Impenetrable barriers he hadn't seen since the early days of their relationship, when a street kid still didn't believe her life had changed. Didn't trust anyone around her.

His heart suddenly ached for his sister.

"The TLF willingly involved themselves in this?" D'Arcy asked, and Stephan nodded.

"Yes. Chae's fathers were the ones who contacted us. They were concerned by some newcomers to the TLF who'd brought with them a lot of weapons. They were also concerned about the safety of their newly arrested child."

"My fathers knew?"

"Not who was threatening you," Stephan replied to Chae's question. "They didn't trust the government to hold up its end of the deal, and then someone—likely Grant—contacted them with a warning." Stephan pointed to the photo next to Senator

Tieg's. "Cooperate with the newcomers or their kid would suffer the consequences."

D'Arcy's curse was loud in the silence. "There were half a dozen ways you could have handled this better, Stephan."

For the first time Nika saw a crack in Stephan's normally unshakable composure.

"I told Max, and I'll tell you: I don't need you critiquing my op on the back end."

"Well, I'm fucking doing it anyway. You put our lives in danger. You put this kid's life in danger. Now we've got people from the habitat dead, we're down two Interceptors, and we are no fucking closer to catching these people than we were three months ago when you PR'd this bullshit task force scenario!" D'Arcy pushed away from the wall and threw his hands up in the air. "This is the same shit that caused the situation on Mars to spiral out of control—"

"Do not bring up Mars, D'Arcy, not now." Stephan's jaw was tight, and judging from the confused looks around the room Nika guessed everyone else was just as much in the dark about whatever had happened there between the two men as he was.

D'Arcy's dark eyes glittered with anger. "Why not? It's obvious you haven't learned a goddamned thing since then. But hey, it's only habitat population—what does it fucking matter?"

"You bast—"

"All right, that's enough." Scott stepped up between the men. "It's been a long day, and it's pretty obvious no one is going to listen with a clear head. I'm calling this done. Let's get some sleep and we'll regroup tomorrow."

For a moment Nika thought D'Arcy was going to ignore the order and take a swing at Stephan, but he nodded sharply, turned on his heel, and left the room.

"Well, my head hurts so I'm on board with this plan. Chae, come on," Jenks said, patting Doge on the head and following D'Arcy without looking at either Luis or Tivo. The two men remained slumped in their chairs and Nika thought it was for the best they didn't try to go after his sister right now.

Max stayed where she was, staring at the images on the far wall with a hand on her lips. "You don't know who's handling the shipping," she said suddenly.

Stephan looked away from the door. "We don't. Max—"

She waved a hand, cutting him off, and Nika saw Scott mouth *I told you so* in Stephan's direction. "What was in the shipment? Something that would implicate Tieg? Or something that would reveal his accomplice?" She circled the table and touched a hand to the swirling data, picking through the photos until she found what she was looking for. It was a surveillance photo from the drainage project and Nika frowned at the choice.

"Most likely both."

"But you were really interested in whatever could point you at the shipping contact, weren't you?" Max tapped a finger on the photo. "What was it?"

"Less about the item," Stephan replied. "More about who would come after it."

"Were you expecting them to hit the trucks? Did you sacrifice those drivers the same way you did us?"

"I was expecting them to take the trucks, not destroy them. They were automated, Max, I'm not a monster."

Nika couldn't stop the instinctive step backward when Max swung around and faced Stephan, fury in her brown eyes. "Given that Sapphi almost died. That Chae's friend Bean is dead. That Jeanie might be dead because I put her in harm's way. I am not entirely sure the term 'monster' even comes close, Stephan." Grief broke through her cold anger. "All of this was preventable if you'd stopped trying to control everything and put some trust in us to do the job. Both of you." She turned that wounded gaze on Nika and he forced himself to meet it. "*You* treated us like assets instead of your crew."

She spun back to Stephan. "You sent us into this without backup. Worse, you sent us in with deliberately bad intel. You already knew Chae was feeding them information, but you missed the sabotage. Why? Because you don't realize what lengths people will go to when they're desperate to keep their loved ones safe. You don't understand how love works, Stephan, but rather than admit it you just discarded it as unimportant.

"And I'll tell you right now, if this is your idea of how Intel is going to work on Trappist, you can find yourself new personnel. Interceptor crews work because we trust each other with our lives. I'm not putting my people at risk without being able to tell them exactly why."

"You're not in charge of the Interceptor crews, Lieutenant. Or of *Zuma*, for that matter."

"No, I am," Nika said. "And she's right, Stephan. We put Neos in danger when we could have been working together. I let you do it, but I won't anymore."

It was easier than he'd imagined, taking a stand. Finally deciding to be an Interceptor commander rather than an Intel officer. The surprise Max couldn't hide hit Nika hard and he knew he was a long way from making up for this mess, but he hoped it was a start.

Max lifted her chin and tapped the photo one more time. "I realized who this was on the way to the mission. I didn't say anything because I let all of you convince me that my gut wasn't worth listening to. If you want to know who your mystery person is," Max continued as she turned and headed for the door, "I suggest you start with Julia Draven and follow the trail back. Someone hired her, someone who specifically wanted to keep an eye on Chae and on what the NeoG was up to. It's not a coincidence that she was there at that drainage project two years ago. Right around the same time Chae got the idea to try to rob a NeoG warehouse for medical supplies." Max stopped at the doorway and shrugged. "But what do I know, I'm just a lieutenant."

Stephan muttered a curse and shoved a hand in his hair.

"Don't look at me," Scott said. "I told you that you should have brought her on from the beginning."

Nika didn't hear Stephan's reply as he slipped out the door. "Max?"

She stopped in the hallway, but didn't turn around. "I don't want to talk to you right now, Nika."

"I know. I just—I'm sorry."

"You're sorry?" She turned then, unshed tears in her eyes. "Do you realize how you made me doubt myself? That all the work I've done to get clear of my parents' influence got buried again when someone I cared about dismissed what I was capable of doing? When you manipulated me into feeling guilty for not respecting our downtime?"

"I was under orders not to tell you, but you wouldn't let it go." He knew he shouldn't have said it the moment the words hit the air, hit Max, and she recoiled like she'd been punched, but Nika pressed on. "I did what was necessary to get the job done."

She looked away and he thought for a moment she was just going to walk, but then she shook her head and looked back at him.

"This isn't about me, no matter how much you try to make it so. Whatever Stephan's orders were, when we were out there in the black you should have been in charge and the safety of our crew should have been your priority.

"You decided to be Intel rather than an Interceptor, Nika. I don't know why you bothered coming back at all." Her words were such a perfect echo of his earlier thoughts that they took his breath away. "I thought we were going to be a team. I thought you respected me—as a person and as your lieutenant—but that's not the case, is it?"

"Max—"

"You know what hurts the most? You could have just told me that you couldn't tell me. That I didn't have clearance. It would have been understandable. But you didn't." Max lifted her head and the look in her eyes cut Nika down to the core. "You lied to me. You told me I was wrong. That I was imagining things. That I was failing at our relationship." She laughed bitterly. "So no," she said. "I don't want an apology from you. I'll let you know if that changes."

He let her go, his heart breaking as she walked away.

"It's done," Grant said.

"Good." Melanie nodded. "The freighter crew didn't know about the tech they were hauling, did they?"

"No. They thought it was a usual shipment. We've already taken the normal precautions against anyone talking out of turn."

"My lawyers are working on getting them out of custody; they'll be headed back to Earth before the week's out. The freighter will have to be written off, penalty for their screwup."

"Captain Yui won't be happy about that."

"She can come talk to me about it when she gets back," Melanie replied.

"What do you want me to do about the spacer? They told us about the shipment getting moved and whatever they did has put *Zuma* down for the count."

"They'll fix the ship and the investigation into why it crashed may draw more attention than we want. But we'll keep an eye on Chae for now, and maybe we can head things off with a message."

"The usual kind of message?" Grant asked.

"Don't kill anyone, but find one of *Zuma*'s crew and tell them the NeoG needs to back off or more people will get hurt."

"That's not really my style."

"You'll have to live with the disappointment. We need less heat on Trappist, not more, Grant."

"Given what you have planned I find it strange you're

concerned about how much attention we're getting in the first place."

Melanie's smile was slow and deadly. "Trust me, no one will be looking our way after you get done with our little present to Jupiter Station."

Grant's smile echoed hers. "I'm looking forward to it."

TWENTY

The punch caught Chae right in the cheek, pain exploding through their face, and the force of it sent them crashing into the wall.

"You piece of shit." Tamago's eyes were rimmed with red like they'd spent the night crying.

Chae could have blocked the next fist they threw, but instead just took the punch to their stomach. They'd sparred with Tamago a time or two, but obviously the petty officer wasn't holding back the way they all did in the gym.

Chae's breath left them and they went to a knee, retching, more than a little grateful there wasn't anything for them to throw up this early in the morning.

"Get up and fight me, you treacherous shit."

"What the—Tamago!"

Chae lifted their head in time to see Jenks emerge from her room and catch Tamago around the waist, pulling the petty officer away.

"Let me go! They deserve to have their ass kicked for what they did."

"This is not what I meant when I said we'd deal with it

in the morning, Tama!" Jenks grunted as she dragged them back, spinning slightly so that she was in between Chae and Tamago. Only then did she let the petty officer go. Tamago surged forward again. Jenks barely moved, seemed to just settle lower, but her right palm connected with Tamago's shoulder and knocked them back into the opposite wall.

"We'll talk about this, Tama," Jenks said calmly. "You be as mad as you want, but you're not going to beat on them."

"How can you stand there and defend them?" The pain, the betrayal, was clear on Tamago's face, and it made Chae feel like they'd been punched all over again.

"I deserve it, Chief," they said.

"You shut up." Jenks didn't even look behind her when she issued the order to Chae. "You, take a seat."

Tamago didn't move.

"That's an order, Petty Officer. Put your ass in a chair now."

Tamago stalked to the table and dropped into a chair, crossing their arms over their chest and glaring in Jenks's direction.

"I'm gonna have to send Ma a fruit basket. I never realized how much shit he put up with from us," Jenks muttered, scrubbing at the back of her head with one hand while she reached for Chae with the other and pulled them to their feet. "Go sit down, Chae."

Chae sat opposite Tamago and forced themself to meet Tamago's glare.

"Let's start with the basics," Jenks said, leaning both hands on the end of the table. "Everyone is alive."

"No thanks to them." Tamago subsided back to sullen silence at Jenks's warning look.

"*Everyone is alive,*" she repeated. "And while yes, Chae is responsible in part for putting us in that situation, they are also responsible for us not being splattered all over the surface of this planet."

Chae swallowed. "I'm sorry."

"You're *sorry*?" Tamago scoffed. "What good is that? When your best friend dies right in front of you, come try that line again and see how it feels."

Chae flinched and squeezed their eyes shut as the misery surged up into their throat, blocking off all their air.

"Tamago—"

"I'm serious, Jenks. Just because you decided everything was forgiven doesn't mean the rest of us have to do the same."

"Their best friend *is* dead."

The words were like a hydrogen explosion, sucking the air out of the room. Chae kept their eyes squeezed shut and clenched their hands in their lap, but it wasn't enough to keep the sob from escaping.

"These people have been holding the lives of everyone Chae cares about over their head, Tama," Jenks continued softly. "They killed Chae's best friend because we caught that freighter. They threatened their fathers. What would you have done?"

"Told someone! Told you or Max. I—"

"Because you trust us, right? Who was Chae supposed to trust? Their girlfriend was working for these bastards. They already knew others on the station were keeping watch on them. What do you do when you have no one left to trust?"

Jenks pulled out a chair from the table, the legs scraping on the floor, and she sat with a sigh. "I understand the anger, Tama, I do. I also understand what it's like to have no choice at all and still try to keep the people you love alive."

"Permission to be dismissed, Chief?" Tamago's question was properly formal and void of any feeling.

There was a pause before Jenks answered. "Granted."

Chae dropped their head onto the table as Tamago left, burying their face in their hands. Hot tears stung their eyes and dripped down between their fingers. "I'm sorry, Chief. I'm so sorry."

"You don't have to apologize to me anymore," Jenks said,

resting her hand on the back of their head. "Sapphi will likely forgive you with an ease that will surprise you because that's just who she is. Tamago will come around, though I'd avoid them for a while unless you want another bruise. Look at me."

Chae lifted their head and met the chief's mismatched gaze. There was sympathy and an echo of the sorrow that was wrapped around their own heart.

"You had our backs when it really came down to the wire, Chae. I know some of that was self-preservation kicking in, but you could have chosen to let us crash and you didn't. The big question is, what are you going to do from here?"

"Chief?"

"Are you going to be a member of this team? Apologize for your colossal fuckup and make it right with your actions rather than just your words?"

Chae took a deep breath and nodded. "I'm an Interceptor, Chief. *Zuma's Ghost*. I've got your back." They tapped their fist to their heart.

"And I've got yours." Jenks grinned as she finished the handshake. "That's my Neo."

JENKS WANDERED THROUGH THE STREETS OF AMANAVE, hands shoved into the pockets of her cargo pants and music blaring in her head. She was mostly out of uniform, dressed only in a black T-shirt and her boots, but with Doge trundling by her side—and the look on her face—the locals were giving her a wide berth in the afternoon sun.

Amanave was a huge, sprawling habitat, well established and better equipped than most of the smaller outlying ones. Named for a Samoan village lost to the rising waters of climate change and as an homage to the explorers who'd once sailed those same seas of Earth, it was one of the first habitats set down on One-d in 2339.

After the ruckus with Tamago and Chae, Jenks had visited

Sapphi in the hospital and Max had given her permission to catch a ride back out to *Zuma* on the hauler. She hadn't bothered to ask Nika, and she still wasn't sure what to say to her brother about all this.

Instead she'd lost herself in the mundane task of facilitating the ship's transfer to the dockyards in orbit above the planet. Whatever her opinions about the naval yard and their polite refusal of her help, they'd be able to get the bridge cleaned and the window and airbags replaced by the time the *Laika* returned, and the rest of the work could easily be done at Jupiter Station.

That had taken the better part of the day and now, instead of heading back to the NeoG base, she was on the street, studiously ignoring the chat messages pinging her DD.

"You are not answering Luis or Tivo."

She turned the music down and looked at Doge. "Sorry, I forgot to shut down the notices on your end."

"I don't mind. You are angry with them."

"That's a word for it." She rubbed at her chest. "It hurts, Doge. Even if there were reasons, it hurts when people you care about lie to you. I don't really want to talk about it, though, okay?"

"I understand."

Jenks wasn't sure he could, but as long as Doge was quiet right now, she wasn't going to question it. She rubbed at the back of her head as she walked across the street to a somewhat dilapidated hangar. The big doors were closed, but the smaller door at the corner was open and she stuck her head in, turning her music all the way off with a thought. "Anyone in here?"

"Can I help you?" A person with black hair and bright green eyes came around the side of an older-model Winslow shuttle with a bolt gun in their hand.

"I'm Jenks," she said. "I was—"

"Not what your handshake says, Chief Petty Officer Altandai Khan of the Near-Earth Orbital Guard," they cut her off, eyes narrowed as they looked her over, but then those green eyes widened in surprise. "Wait, is that an original ROVER?"

"'Jenks' is the short version." Jenks grinned and kept her hands visible. "And besides—you don't have a handshake at all."

"Ah shit, that's rude. Sorry. The Winslows get weird feed-back going on the internals and I turned it off. Blythe Hup. She/her." The woman's handshake flashed in Jenks's vision as she spoke. "Hup's Repair Shop."

"It's nice to meet you. To answer your other question, this is Doge. Yes, he's an original ROVER. Say hi, Doge."

"It is nice to meet you. You're not going to shoot at us with that bolt gun?"

Blythe laughed and put her hands behind her back. "God no, it can barely get bolts into place as it is. You're a smart one, aren't you? So, Jenks. What can I help you with?"

She swallowed. All she really wanted was to bury her head in machine parts for a few hours and stop thinking about the shit rolling around in her brain.

"This might sound odd but . . . you got anything I can work on?"

Blythe blinked in surprise. "I've got a fussy fuel pump I just pulled out of this beast. You any good with older mechanics?"

"Not bad," Jenks replied, lifting a shoulder and crossing to the woman. "I've worked on a Winslow or two in my time."

"I'll be honest, you don't look old enough to know what a Winslow is, let alone have worked on them. But I've never been one to turn down offered help. I can't pay you, mind—" she said, wary.

"Just want to get my hands dirty."

"Okay, come on, then. Make yourself useful."

An hour later Jenks had the pump disassembled and was bent over the table with all the parts laid out in front of them. "There it is," she said to Blythe, holding up the broken part in triumph. "Those little valves have such a habit of breaking, it's good to keep a few spares on hand. You got a welder? I can make you a new one if you don't have them."

"I'm impressed, Jenks from the NeoG." Blythe grinned at her. "Let me go dig through the pile and see what we have." She disappeared into the back of the hangar.

Jenks returned her focus to the table, humming to herself as she sorted through the pieces in search of anything else that was worn or about to break.

"Jenks?" She stiffened at the sound of Luis's voice and multiple footsteps, turning her head just enough to see two men duck under the Winslow.

She heard Doge growl and Luis's quiet "Jesus, Doge, come on." The growl didn't abate and both men stopped, hands spread wide in surrender. Luis glanced her way. "That was fast, buddy. She put me on the enemy list?"

"You hurt Jenks. You are both currently untrustworthy."

Jenks was glad she'd turned her head back to the table, keeping her surprise concealed. She hadn't done anything with Doge's parameters, but she wasn't about to tell Luis that.

"How'd you find me?" She didn't turn around from the pump parts. It was safer—for everyone—if she kept her hands busy.

"I know you. Once I figured out you weren't up working on *Zuma*, it was a matter of searching around here for your chip."

"My chip's off." Jenks glared over her shoulder.

"Yeah, I know, but Doge's isn't." Luis offered up a smile she didn't return.

"According to the Navy, I'm not *qualified* to work on repairs unless it is absolutely necessary." Jenks changed the subject and looked away again.

If they were back on Jupiter Station the yardheads would let her do whatever she wanted, but they all knew her. Here, she was a stranger.

Which was exactly how she felt with Luis and Tivo right now.

Jenks picked up the rotor and held it to the light. "Go away. Both of you. I'm busy."

"Dai, you've been avoiding us all day." Luis sighed. "Can we talk about this?"

"I've been *working* all day. Trying to keep my crew together. Dealing with my busted ship. And I don't think there's anything to say to either of you. You've been lying to me about this thing from the beginning." She put the rotor down. "Which, fine. Opsec and all that. I get it." She couldn't stop the bitter snort.

"Dai, are you mad that I didn't tell you we knew each other?" Luis asked.

"I'm assuming if something had been going on in the relationship area between you two last year we would have had a conversation about it like adults."

"You assume correctly," he replied.

She forced herself to let go of the wrench she'd picked up without even noticing and stepped away from the table, spotting the way Luis's shoulders relaxed just a fraction.

Of course they expect me to lose my shit. Can't trust Jenks to think things through. I'm just the weapon you point at whatever you want destroyed.

"No," she said. "I get it. That was need-to-know and I didn't need to know. I do have more than two brain cells to rub together. I understand the need for secrecy on something like this, as hard as that may be for you to believe."

"Dai, don't do that."

"Do what?"

Frustration made the muscle tic in Luis's jaw as he closed his eyes briefly. Tivo frowned in confusion, not understanding this argument that had been going on long before he'd met them.

"Don't make this out like I think you're not smart enough to get my work," Luis said. "I meant what I said on Earth:

you are amazingly talented when it comes to piecing things together. Stephan should have—"

"Found it!" Blythe emerged triumphant, took one look at the three of them, and whistled. "Awkward interruption. Gentlemen." She glanced at the two men and then back at Jenks. "Is there a problem?"

Jenks sighed. "No, sorry, Blythe. They just came by for a talk."

"I'll leave you alone, then. My office is in the back. The door isn't too thick, so holler if you need something."

Before Jenks could protest, the woman was gone. She looked from one man to the other. "Putting aside that actions speak louder than words, Luis, you want to know what I'm mad about? Max already told you. You read us into this op in the most half-assed manner I've ever seen. You were just using us as fucking bait. Again. No warning, no way to protect ourselves."

"Jenks—"

"Sapphi died!" She sliced a hand through the air, cutting Tivo off. "If it hadn't been for Tamago she would have stayed dead. If it hadn't been for Chae landing *Zuma* we'd all have died."

"You seem a hell of a lot more willing to forgive them for betraying you than us for doing our jobs," Tivo snapped at her.

Luis winced, then sighed. "Damn it, Tiv, don't—"

"I had my talk with Chae and I know where they stand. I forgive them because I've been there," Jenks hissed. "Trapped between the choice of betraying your friends or watching them die. No one to trust, no one to help. I've lived through the threats and the beatdowns and my friends dying because of choices I made. I knew there was something wrong with that supposed accident with the cargo on your ship." She pointed a finger at Tivo. "I should have pursued it, not let you talk me down.

"I know how Chae felt and why they did what they did.

That's why I forgive them. Because they didn't have a choice, but you did. You chose the mission over the people. And that's your decision. But that means you don't get to be around people, especially me. So fuck you both for this." She shoved a cart near her, the sudden noise and violence putting both men back on guard. "Do you understand that I could have talked Chae through it, coached them on what to do and say to put those bastards at ease? Of course you don't. You didn't stop to consider that angle for a second, did you?"

Luis rubbed at his chin and sighed again. "You're right. We didn't."

His easy agreement only made her angrier.

"You put *my crew* in danger. I get we're just pawns in your game and don't matter to the great minds at Intel, but I'm their chief. I'm responsible for them. This is the only family I've ever had and I would rather die than let them get hurt. I've been tearing myself apart trying to live up to what Ma did for this team and you just fucking pissed on it all."

The men shared a guilty look and Tivo reached a hand out. "Jenks, that's not fair. With what's on the line here—"

"Oh, fuck you and your greater-good speech," she snapped. "We go out into the black every day knowing we may not come back because of the oath we swore. We'd have gladly put our lives on the line for this if you'd done us the courtesy of telling us what we were up against. But you didn't, you just fucking—"

Luis put his hands up. "All right, Jenks, you've made your point. Maybe we should have been up front about it, but that's not how this went down. What do you want?"

"I already told you: for you both to leave me alone." She crossed her arms over her chest and looked away.

"Okay," Luis said softly. "We'll talk about this later."

"No, we won't." The words slipped out before she could stop them, fueled by pain and a history of picking the safer, closed-off road where emotions were concerned. "I mean it, I don't want to see either of you again outside of work. I can be an adult about that, but everything else is done. I can't—I can't be with people I don't trust."

There was a moment of painful silence and then Luis sighed. "Come on, Tiv."

"You're just going to let her—"

"Yes, because that's what she wants right now and I respect her enough to pay attention to the boundaries. Let's go."

As soon as they were gone Jenks slid down to the floor with her arms wrapped around her waist, the unshed tears burning in her eyes. Doge crept closer and pressed his head to hers.

"I am sorry."

"For what, silly dog?"

"You are hurt."

"Yeah, I am." She cupped his head and pressed her lips to the metal. "I've still got you, though, right?"

"For as long as you keep fixing me."

"I will always fix you, I promise." She buried her face against him.

"They also hurt."

"Good."

"No, not good. Hurt is not good, you said so. I liked them. They made you happy, more than the others. Until they suddenly didn't. I don't understand you humans sometimes."

"Me either, buddy." Jenks sighed and got to her feet. "Come on, we should put this pump back together like we said we would."

"You okay?"

She smiled at Blythe as the woman approached. "Yeah. I'll get this fixed back up and get out of your hair. You got that part?"

"Right here."

It was easy to fall back into the rhythm of repairing something, watching it come together under her hands. She handed the completed pump over to Blythe with a little flourish. "There you go. I got sort of interrupted inspecting everything else, but it seemed like that valve was the only issue."

"I'll send you the bill if it still doesn't work." Blythe grinned. "I appreciate the assist, Jenks of the NeoG. You want some free advice?"

No. "Sure."

"I'm not great with people. Machines were always easier. You can usually trust them not to let you down as long as you put the work into them, like this good boy here. But they still break. So do people. Difference is, it's not your job to fix people. It's their job to fix themselves."

"Not sure I'm following this advice, to be honest."

"I said it was free, I didn't say it was good."

Jenks let out a laugh, even though it was weak, and nearly dissolved into tears. Blythe reached out and took Jenks's hand. "From what I heard you have every right to be angry at them. You sit with that for as long as you need. Maybe they'll fix it, maybe they won't. It's not your job, though. Understand?"

"Yeah, I think I do."

"Good. Come on back to my shop anytime."

Jenks nodded and slipped out the door, nearly running into Tamago in the process. "What are you doing here?"

"Came looking for you." Tamago lifted a slender shoulder.

Jenks arched an eyebrow at them.

"Luis maybe told me to."

"He tell you why?" she asked with a sigh.

"Only that you were upset." They looked around. "No one is bleeding, though, so I'm not sure what to think." They heaved a sigh and looked at her through their black lashes. "I'm sorry for this morning. I was out of line."

"Maybe for punching Chae, but even then you're entitled to be angry, Tama. I'm the last person who could tell you otherwise." She pulled her friend into a hug.

Tamago clung to her. "I liked Chae," they whispered. "I want to forgive them, but I don't know if I can trust them again."

"You don't have to figure it out right now, you know?" Jenks pressed a kiss to the side of Tamago's head and released them. "Let them earn it. They know they fucked up and they want to be a part of this team, which means they need to make amends."

"You say that to Luis and Tivo, too?"

"No, I told them to fuck off."

Tamago gave her a look of pure disbelief. "You know you'll forgive them eventually."

"Brat." Jenks slipped her arm through Tamago's and headed back across the street. "Chae wouldn't have been in this position in the first place if they'd told us what was going on. I'm mad at them for putting you all at risk."

"They put you at risk, too. Don't shrug your shoulders at me, Khan. I'm as mad at them as you are, I just hide it better. They were so wrapped up in the end result that they didn't stop to think about the road right in front of them. Stephan treated us all like NPCs to be thrown at the final boss rather than actual members of the party."

"You are such a nerd, I love you."

"I love you, too," Tamago replied. "And I know you're hurting but trying to hide it because big, bad Jenks, the girl from the mean streets, doesn't get hurt."

That hit a little too close to home and Jenks knew her laugh rang false. "It's fine, Tamago."

"No, it's not," Tamago said, coming to a stop. "And it doesn't have to be. This is yucky." They cupped Jenks's face. "And it's okay to say so."

For a moment Jenks allowed herself the weakness of dreaming she could throw herself into her friend's arms and cry, but her survival instinct was stronger, overriding everything else. "Hey, you know me. I'll be all right."

"Sometimes I want to bite your stubborn ass."

"Don't flirt with me if you're not going to follow through." Jenks grinned up at them and Tamago rolled their eyes with a laugh.

"Jenks." Doge only said her name, but the inflection was strange. She turned her head slightly, suddenly realizing the darkened street she and Tamago were on was deserted.

Except for the gang of half a dozen people headed their way.

"Tama, when I say go I want you to run for base as fast as you can. Doge, you go with them and keep them safe. You have permission to shoot to kill."

Doge whimpered.

"Don't whine at me, dog."

"Jenks, no," Tamago whispered.

"You don't whine, either, Petty Officer," she said. "This is an order.

"Go."

TWENTY-ONE

Max stood in the conference room, staring at the shifting data on the wall in front of her, occasionally reaching out to stop the flow of information and read something more closely.

"When I saw it yesterday I thought, 'That's a face I haven't seen in a while,'" D'Arcy said as he joined her. "Tea?" He passed over one of the steaming mugs in his hands.

"Thanks." Max tipped her head at the screen. "Who are you talking about?"

"Vincent Grant." He tapped the image of the hard-eyed man in the news article Max had been reading and then pointed up at the photo next to Senator Tieg's.

"You knew him?"

D'Arcy's laugh was humorless. "Thankfully by reputation only. He's an ex–Mars PeaceKeeper and was heavily involved in the suppression of the protests in '09."

"Stephan was there, too, right?" Max glanced across the room to where the Intel commander was talking with her brother and Nika.

"He was a baby, a shiny lieutenant on his first Intel assignment off-world." D'Arcy grinned at her, but it faded quickly and he sighed. "We were on opposite sides, Max. Most of the time I let it stay in the past. I lost my temper yesterday and I shouldn't have. He and I have both done things we regret."

Max nodded, but it was hard to process that the man next to her had once been part of an organization she'd been brought up to believe was wrong. Ironically, it was less difficult to realize her parents' black-and-white view of the situation wasn't the reality. Everything about the Mars riots was more complex than the news and the CHN wanted people to believe.

What she knew was D'Arcy. Trusted him with her life. He'd wanted his home safe and free, and she couldn't fault him for that. "Why did you join, D'Arcy? Why come to the NeoG when we were basically your enemy?"

"I didn't have much of a choice, though it wasn't the NeoG I was mad at. And for the most part they were actually trying to keep the peace. When everything went down I ended up in custody and was given two options. This seemed like the better path, one where I could make a difference," he said after a moment of silent contemplation. "There are people I left behind who feel like I betrayed everything we fought for just to keep from going to rehab, but it's more complicated than that."

"Most things are." She pointed at Grant. "Tell me about him."

"He's dangerous, Max. Like I said, we never tangled personally, but I lost friends to him and his squad. People were yanked off the street and turned up dead later. The end of it all involved a member of the NeoG killing a protestor—a friend of mine, Hadi Shevreaux."

"I remember reading about that. The captain in question was arrested and charged with excessive force. Discharged from the NeoG and sent to rehab. It was a big reason why the CHN finally came to the table with Mars."

"Still didn't quite work out like we'd hoped, but things are a little better." D'Arcy nodded. "Melanie Karenina. She was a captain who worked with Grant pretty closely, I think—you'd have to ask Stephan. He's the one who investigated her and brought her in." Max raised an eyebrow in surprise, while D'Arcy continued. "Have you talked to your sister? How's Bosco doing?"

"This morning." Max nodded. "And she's stable." The burst of relief she'd felt when talking to Ria reappeared in her chest.

"It wasn't your fault, Max. You didn't know."

"Yeah. I keep feeling like I should have, though. She sent me the information she'd gathered about Julia Draven, including an Off-Earth employee roster with a photo showing a very different woman from the one I met." She glanced at the door as Chae slipped through and a moment later Luis and Tivo came in, wearing identical expressions of frustration and hurt. "I suppose it's a good sign they're still alive?"

"Who? Oh." D'Arcy chuckled. "They tried to talk to Jenks?"

"I told them to leave her be." Max shrugged. "She took this promotion more seriously than people expected her to, and having Sapphi get injured because they all chose not to read us in really did not sit well with her."

"She wasn't the only one. You still mad at Nika?"

"Mad? Not really." Max caught Chae's eye and waved the spacer over. "'Hurt' is a better word. That ache that comes three days after you take a kick to the stomach, you know?"

"Oh, I know."

"LT?"

Max smiled at Chae, and though the worried look in their eyes didn't diminish, they at least smiled back. "Tell me how you met Julia, from the beginning."

"She was working on a drainage project near our habitat. I used to go up and watch on my off days. We struck up a conversation and—" Chae sighed and lifted a shoulder. "I thought she cared, LT. But I was a target from the beginning, wasn't I?"

"I think so. They knew who your fathers were. They were looking for someone to slip into the NeoG."

"Why a newbie?" D'Arcy asked. "Seems like a better idea to find someone with more pull."

"That's a good question. I think, though, they were looking long term," Max replied. "Owning someone from the ground up is a good idea if you're planning for decades. These people aren't amateurs—they had enough power to convince people on a naval ship to beat Chae up. You don't do all this for a get-rich-quick scheme. They clearly see something in Chae to not just kill them then."

"The people who beat me on the *Laika* said it was nothing personal," Chae whispered. "That they did what they were told."

Max nodded. "Chae's smart—and a brilliant pilot. It wouldn't be hard to predict they'd work their way up the ranks while Tieg and whoever else is responsible had the threat of their fathers' lives to hold over them, not to mention all the things they'd done since."

D'Arcy whistled low. "I already didn't like Grant, but the rest of these bastards are working their way up my list."

"Me too, I—" Whatever Max had been about to say vanished when Tamago's panicked call came over the team com.

"LT! Jenks is in trouble!"

Max saw Nika jerk as the message rang in his ear, too, and he looked her way before sprinting for the door.

"It's Jenks," Max said out loud to D'Arcy before following. "Tamago, breathe and give me a sitrep."

"I'm at the east gate with Doge. We were headed back. Six or so people converged on us in the street. Jenks ordered me to take Doge and go."

"Jenks, do you copy?" Nika said.

"Little busy" came her breathless reply, and then a grunt. "I have no fucking clue where I am, so don't ask."

JENKS TOOK IN THE FACES OF THE PEOPLE CLOSING IN ON her. None of them had handshakes, but she recognized one from the wall in Stephan's conference room. "Vincent Grant," she said. "Am I supposed to be impressed I warranted a personal appearance?"

"You should be impressed I didn't just drop you here and now."

Jenks had to admit she was at least curious about that. "To what do I owe the honor of still being alive?"

"You're really a mouthy one, aren't you?" Grant shook his head. "I've got a message for the NeoG: back the fuck off or things are going to get ugly." He grinned. "Uglier."

Jenks kept an eye on the two people circling behind her. This was a fight she didn't want to have. It didn't matter how good she was, six-on-one odds was bullshit beatdown territory.

I've done my time in that arena, no thank you.

But she wanted to keep them distracted and not give them a reason to go after Tamago.

"When you say 'uglier,' can I get a reference point? Like uglier than shorty over there? Or uglier than you?"

Grant's hard stare didn't waver and one of the toughs cracked their knuckles.

That told her everything she wanted to know—they might not kill her today, but they had no compunctions about beating the shit out of her.

"Okay, fine. You're all under arrest." Jenks ducked under the swing from one of the people behind her, grabbing them and bringing her knee up hard between their legs. "Worth a try," she said, dropping them to the ground.

Grant had his fists up and was advancing on her with enough composure to make part of her want to test herself against him.

But this wasn't the time for a contest, so while she rushed at Grant, she actually elbowed the person next to him in the head instead, hard enough to send them staggering into Grant. The move worked in her favor and Jenks sprinted around the corner, away from the base. Maybe two down, but she wasn't trusting her luck, especially with the sounds of pursuit already loud behind her.

Let them thin out, take them out one by one if you can. Watch your step, don't get cornered.

All those lessons she'd learned on the streets of Krasnodar rose back up without any effort. She'd stayed alive, not always by being tougher but by being smarter than everyone else. Jenks ducked into the shadows of an alley.

"Jenks, do you copy?" Nika's voice was a welcome sound in her ear, but it almost distracted her from clotheslining the person who'd been right behind her.

She dropped them hard, knocking the wind from their lungs, and kicked them in the head with enough force that their neck snapped.

Take them out as fast as possible and get clear. Never get caught, never get surrounded.

"Little busy," she managed to reply to Nika, dodging the fist of the next tough who came around the corner. She kicked them, knocking them back a step, and took off running again. "I have no fucking clue where I am, so don't ask."

"Turn your locator back on."

She swore. "Right, sorry."

"There, I've got her," Sapphi said. "Jenks, take the next right."

Jenks did what she was told, suppressing the urge to ask why Sapphi was on coms when she was in the hospital.

"Grant's here," Jenks managed. "Said he wanted to send the NeoG a message to back the fuck off or else."

"Did he hurt you?" Nika's question was issued in a startling snarl.

"Not yet, but he'll give it a go if he catches me."

"GRANT'S GOT SOME HEAVIES WITH HIM," JENKS SAID. "I clotheslined a guy and made him a corpse. I think the others are still on my ass." Her voice was even and Nika knew without a doubt his sister had slipped back into the survival mode of her youth.

This wasn't going to end well, even if she got clear.

"You keep running, okay? Don't engage unless you have to," he replied. "Sapphi's getting us a path to you."

"Nika, can you get Jenks to switch to the main coms?" Stephan asked.

They'd split when the group had hit the east gate. Max and Chae had peeled off with Luis to the north. Tamago and Doge were with Nika. D'Arcy and Tivo headed back the way Tamago had come while Stephan and Scott had stayed behind to gather up more spacers in the hopes they could trap Grant and his people.

"I don't want to distract her with too many voices in her head," he replied.

"I need to know what's going on."

"And I'm keeping my sister safe, so deal with the updates," Nika snapped. *It sucks not having all the info, doesn't it, Stephan?*

"I can relay information, Commander," Sapphi said, and the offer seemed to mollify Stephan. "Nika, take the next left and then an immediate right. You'll have to hop the wall."

Doge hadn't slowed and the ROVER cleared the three-meter-high wall with ease.

"I see that. Tamago, you need a boost?"

"I got it." They ran at the nearby building, tic-tacking off it and grabbing the top edge, pulling themself up to the top. Nika ran at it straight on; catching Tamago's outstretched hand with his left and the top of the wall with his right, he scrambled up.

They dropped to the other side.

"Jenks, you still with me?"

"Mostly. Just took down number—what am I on? Found myself a piece of pipe. Tell Stephan I'm not sorry for leaving a trail of bodies for him to pick up."

Nika could hear the sorrow lurking beneath the thin veneer of glee and it broke his heart a little more. These bastards didn't have to beat on Jenks to hurt her. For all her talk and occasional violence, Jenks didn't like killing; it reminded her too much of the near-feral person she'd once been.

"Just keep moving," he said. "I'm headed your way."

JENKS WILLED HER FEET TO PICK UP THE PACE AND IGNORED the pain in her side. It was hard to tell if that kick her last opponent had landed had cracked a rib or if she was just entirely shit at running.

Probably a little of both.

She forced herself to relax her grip on the pipe she'd found and the ache in her hand subsided somewhat.

Grant was still out there along with at least three others, though she was surprised they hadn't broken off the chase. They had to know she'd get in touch with the NeoG base the first opportunity she had.

Maybe I shouldn't be running so fast.

"Jenks, why are you slowing down?"

"Everyone's circling around to me, right Sapphi? If Grant's still chasing, this is the perfect opportunity to catch him. If I'm going to be used as bait, at least I can do it on my terms. There's a dead end up ahead, let's see if he follows me."

"No, you keep going and turn right, you're almost to Max and Chae."

She went left instead.

CHAE HEARD SAPPHI'S CURSE LOUD AND CLEAR OVER THE coms. It mingled with the one Max let loose into the air.

"What is it?" Luis demanded.

"She's going to try to lure Grant into a fight in the hopes

we can trap him." Max looked back at Chae. "We'll likely leave you behind, so just catch up, okay?"

"Don't need to sprint, LT," they said, and pointed at a gate ahead of them. "We can cut through here, get in front of the chief. The gate's unlocked, or should be unless they've changed something in the last few years."

"How do you know this?"

"Home court advantage, sorta? I used to come into Amanave with my friends in the summer. We spent a lot of time around here."

"Okay," Max said, waving a hand at Luis's protest. "I trust you. Jenks, we're almost there."

"Good to hear," Jenks replied. "Because four-on-one is my idea of a party only under specific exceptions."

Chae choked back a laugh as they pulled the gate open and sprinted through. The back lot of Ouroboros Engineering was often left open by the night guard who had a soft spot for the habitat kids looking for a quiet place to hang. The kids, in turn, kept the place clean and safe and allowed the guard to catch up on his sleep for most of the night.

It was a relief to see that nothing had changed. Chae held up a finger to their lips at the first group they encountered. "We're just passing through," they whispered. "It's okay."

The teens watched them with wide eyes as Chae led Max and Luis through the maze of crates and across to the other side of the lot. They grabbed for the corner of the fence and frowned.

"They moved it over there," a voice whispered from the shadows. "Management found that one and replaced the whole section so we used the darker corner behind that wall over there for the new exit."

"Thanks."

"Hey, are you NeoG?"

Chae froze. "Yes?"

"Cool."

"Chae, we need to move."

Chae threw a quick salute toward the shadows and continued forward until they found the cutaway in the corner and slipped through. They took off running, following Sapphi's map, knowing Max and Luis would close the distance quickly.

Chae rounded a corner and leaped over the body in their way, skidding to a halt just in time to see Jenks take a punch to the face. Her opponent wrapped their other arm around her neck, but before they could take her to the ground, Jenks reached up and grabbed for their elbow with her right hand.

She locked the hand and wrist with her left as she twisted away, pushing upward until the sharp crack of wrist and elbow bones breaking in tandem echoed in the night air.

The tough cried out and staggered away. The only remaining opponent hesitated and Chae kicked them in the back of the knee before they could finish making the choice to attack the chief.

"Hey, Chae," Jenks said, wiping blood from her mouth with a sharp grin as the others clattered into the street. "Thanks for the assist."

TWENTY-TWO

Nika arrived just in time to see his sister drop to a knee. Luis rushed forward, and he was too far away for Nika to call out a warning.

"Don't fucking touch me!" Jenks swung on him, spitting the words with a guttural snarl.

Doge cleared the distance with a snarl of his own that shocked everyone. Luis stumbled back and Nika rushed forward, slipping between the startled man and his sister. "Back up, Luis. It's not you. Give her space. Doge, stand down. Max, don't touch her."

Max frowned, but stopped where she was. "What is it?"

"Flashback, most likely." Nika went to a knee next to Jenks, just inside her reach. Her fists were clenched and her chest heaved with her rapid breathing. "Altandai, look at me."

She lifted her head, but her mismatched eyes were unfocused.

"Tell me what you see." He could hear the buzz and conversations behind him as Stephan's reinforcements arrived on the scene.

"Lotta dead bodies."

"No. Everyone here is alive. Refocus. Tell me what you see."

She blinked and his heart ached at the pain on her face. "You."

Nika exhaled. "Better, give me details. Five things you can see."

"You. Max." She hesitated. "Luis. Pipe on the ground. One of them had a gun, it's over there."

"Good, give me the next one." Nika patiently walked his sister through the grounding process he'd learned would help her.

"Blood, unfortunately," Jenks replied to his final question of what she could taste, and she spit to the side. "Missed a block."

"You're getting slow in your old age." He grinned when she looked sharply at him. "You back?"

"Yeah." She shuddered, rubbed both hands over her face and then swore at the tears she just managed to choke back down. "Sorry."

"You didn't do anything wrong." He got to his feet and offered her a hand. She took it and Nika pulled her up and into an embrace.

She wrapped her arms around his waist and squeezed almost to the point of pain as she buried her face against his chest. "Been a while since that happened," Jenks muttered as the shaking started. "Thanks."

"Always got your back."

Jenks managed to muffle the sob and Nika only heard it because he'd been waiting for it. He hugged her closer, bending his head and kissing Jenks on the top of hers. "I'm sorry, sis, for everything."

"I don't need your apology. I told you before, you're my brother and I'll love you to the heat death of the universe. I've always got your back, too." She looked up at him. "You hurt Max, though, Nik. She's the one you need to talk to."

He'd forgotten how even more unfiltered his sister's mouth

was after an episode and winced at her honest words. "I tried. She didn't want to hear it."

"Then don't use your words. Do the right thing."

"Nika, can I check her?" Tamago asked softly before Nika could reply.

"You good with Tamago touching you?" he asked.

"Yeah."

He passed her off to Tamago and nodded to Max's silent question if she could join them, but he took Luis's arm and tugged the big man in the opposite direction, toward Stephan. "I know you're worried, but you need to give her space."

"She's had a few bad dreams over the years, but nothing like that." Luis clenched a fist. "What happened to her, Nika?"

"I don't know," Nika replied. "She talks to her therapist about it, and she's told me bits and pieces. What it amounts to is she spent most of her childhood on the street, Luis, fighting to survive. That leaves scars. She had a few pretty bad flashbacks right after we met. Baba had been good at helping her manage them. I didn't know how, so I got help from a local clinic."

He glanced over at his sister. Jenks was leaning against Max while Tamago examined her split lip, Doge hovering nearby.

"I told myself I'd never hurt her," Luis said softly. He swallowed and because Nika could see the man's heart in his eyes when he looked at Jenks, he reached out and put a hand on the man's arm.

"She cares about you or she wouldn't be mad. We messed up here, Luis. You saw how easily, how willingly, she put herself on the line. Jenks would die for this crew—in her mind, it's all she has."

"And we put them at risk, yeah." Luis sighed. "She said as much, along with not wanting to see us again. That she couldn't trust us."

"I'm not going to bullshit you, Luis: she might mean it,"

Nika said. "You love her enough to give her the space she needs, no matter how this ends?"

"Yeah, I do."

"Good." Nika patted his arm. "I'd hate to have to kick your ass." He ignored Luis's snort and said, "Let's go see what we can get out of these people."

MAX ESCORTED JENKS, TAMAGO, AND CHAE BACK TO BASE, leaving the others to deal with the cleanup. Grant had vanished, but they had two in custody and it was going to be a long night for Stephan trying to get information out of them.

She'd sent them all ahead to their quarters once back on base and slipped out to the shops right outside the gate. When she returned, Chae was curled up on the corner of the couch while Tamago cleaned up Jenks's split knuckles at the bar.

Jenks had messaged her about the fight between the two enlisted Neos this morning, but it seemed at least for the moment as if tempers had been put aside.

"Here, brought you a present." Max handed the bottle of synth-whiskey over to Jenks.

"Did you steal that?"

"Yes."

"Max!"

She laughed. "Of course I didn't steal it. I bought it."

"It would have tasted better if you stole it," Jenks muttered, but she unscrewed the cap and took a drink. Her shaky exhale didn't go unnoticed.

"Are you okay?" Max asked.

Jenks sat still while Tamago smoothed a heal patch over her knuckles, but her eyes stayed on Max. "Yeah. I think the shock has mostly worn off. Or maybe it's the whiskey." She wiggled the bottle in her hand and Max reached for it. "I'll apologize now if I'm snappish for the next few days—those flashbacks fuck me up."

"It's understandable. We're here for you, whatever you need."

"*You* could have been killed," Tamago whispered.

Jenks pulled them into a hug with her free arm. "They'd have to bring more guys than that," she said. "Besides, they weren't there to kill me, just to send a message."

Max took a quick drink, wincing at the unfamiliar burn. "I'd like to not tempt fate, but Jenks is right. They're going to have to bring more than that if they're going up against us."

"Well, this is serious if LT is *drinking*." Jenks dragged out the last word.

Max grinned and sat down next to Chae, handing them the bottle. "Just the one. Would you like to hear the uncensored version of how *Zuma's Ghost* took down an illegal LifeEx manufacturing operation?"

"A what?"

Max smiled at the spacer's obvious confusion and held the bottle out until they took it. "I'd just joined *Zuma's Ghost* and—"

"By 'uncensored' she means the story that none of us really get to tell because of how fast the CHN and LifeEx Industries locked it down in NDA limbo."

"To be fair," Tamago said, packing their med kit back up, "they weren't wrong about the whole 'eroding public confidence' line."

"People get worked up about fake LifeEx that could potentially kill you. For good reason." It surprised Max a little that she could joke about it now. A number of people had been hurt by the dupe, and her sister was still hard at work trying to find a way to undo the damage from the product that had been slipped into the supply chain.

"A disclaimer, kid," Jenks announced as she hopped off the stool. "You can't talk about this to anyone. It really will cause a bit of a panic."

"Then why tell me?"

"Because you're family," Jenks said, looking at Chae with an amused expression.

"Oh."

"So anyway, it started when we found an old system jumper out by the belt . . ."

THE NEXT MORNING JENKS STOOD IN THE BACK OF THE CON-ference room and watched as the others discussed the information they'd gotten from Grant's people. Grant himself was gone like a hastily chugged pint of beer at closing time. Jenks knew part of her restlessness was due to the fact that she hadn't gotten to face him down after all.

We're not done, you and me.

She didn't engage in the conversation, just cradled the mug of subpar coffee Tamago had pressed into her hands when she'd come into the room, and listened.

It had been so long since her last episode that she'd almost forgotten the aftermath and how much she hated this sharp-edged feeling gnawing on her nerves.

Even worse was that she couldn't just lean into Luis and let his solid warmth ground her. He'd looked away from his work, nodded once with sadness in his eyes, and left her alone.

"You want company?"

Jenks smiled up at D'Arcy. "You got some?"

"I might know a guy." He grinned and leaned on the wall next to her. "Sounds like they got at least one of your attackers to talk, though there's no sign of Grant. Fucking ghost."

"Max mentioned you tangled with him on Mars?" she asked.

D'Arcy shook his head. "Not personally. But I knew of him. He's dangerous, Jenks. Don't get some wild idea to go after him yourself."

"You my dad now?"

"Not even remotely." His grin widened and he shifted,

bending slightly to press a kiss to the side of her head. "I'm your friend. I don't like seeing you get hurt."

"Part of the job, isn't it?"

"Wasn't talking about that."

Jenks hummed and let herself lean into D'Arcy because she knew he wouldn't mind. D'Arcy wrapped his arm around her shoulder.

"Sigund—the guy whose arm you broke—apparently had some recordings he was keeping as insurance in case something like this happened." D'Arcy pointed over at Stephan. "They're cuing one of them up now."

Jenks listened as an unfamiliar feminine voice issued from the speaker.

"They'll fix the ship and the investigation into why it crashed may draw more attention than we want. But we'll keep an eye on Chae for now, and maybe we can head things off with a message."

"The usual kind of message?" Grant's voice was still fresh in Jenks's memory and she recognized it immediately.

"Don't kill anyone, but find one of Zuma's *crew and tell them the NeoG needs to back off or more people will get hurt."*

D'Arcy stiffened and Jenks looked up at him. "What is it?"

"I know that voice," he said, and the room fell into silence.

He slipped away from her. Jenks set her mug on the table and followed. Stephan was frowning. D'Arcy pulled up a news article and threw it onto the screen.

Nika took a step forward and frowned. "Captain Melanie Karenina."

"It can't be," Stephan said. "Fuck. I went over every inch of Trappist Express and couldn't find a single thing to indicate they were involved."

"We were just talking about her." Max looked at D'Arcy. "Are you sure?"

"I won't ever forget her voice," D'Arcy replied, and Jenks moved a little closer, wrapping her hand around his closed fist. He looked down at her and some of the tension bled out of his shoulders.

"Can someone clue the rest of us in on who this is?"

Stephan looked up at the ceiling and exhaled, but before he could answer Jenks's question, Max spoke up.

"She's the CEO of Trappist Express. The company the CHN uses to ship most of the supplies from Earth to Trappist-1."

TWENTY-THREE

Max read through the debrief of Stephan's interrogation as the argument raged in the conference room around her. Sapphi was by her side, the hacker having been released from the hospital that afternoon. She was a little wobbly, but mostly back to normal.

The only physical signs of her brush with death were a pair of Lichtenberg figures decorating the backs of her hands and forearms, the white scars standing out in stark relief against her tan skin. She also now had a tendency to forget she was talking in midsentence, or continue with a stream of consciousness that no one could follow.

"Why don't we push them back harder? Shit, we've got Trappist Express pinned as the source of the shitty goods, right?" Jenks pointed at the wall. "We can hit a few of their ships after Chae feeds them some false info."

"And then what?" Luis asked. "All those freighter captains work on contract, not directly for Trappist Express. We hit them without something to tie it straight to the shipping company, it does us no good. And the captains either end up dead or refuse to talk. And *then* the people we're chasing will know Chae's turned on them, which puts their family at risk."

"You could do your jobs and keep Chae's family safe."

Luis sighed and dragged both hands through his hair. "Dai, I swear, can you think for two seconds rather than just throwing a fist at a problem—"

"You go fuck yourself."

Max stopped reading and looked up, calculating whether she could make it over the table before Jenks threw the first punch. But her friend surprised her and backed off with her hands up. "I'm going for a walk." She slammed the door open and left the room, Doge trailing behind.

"Tamago," Nika said. "Go with her."

Tamago got to their feet. "Yup." They gave Luis a withering look on the way by and the big man rubbed a hand over his face.

"Of all the shitty things you could have said,"—Max stood—"that was a pretty impressive choice. Jenks thinks things through, she just does it faster than most people realize. Plus she's got her priorities straight." She gestured at the men on the other side of the room. "She's thinking about her crew, the way you all should have been. What she's proposing will put the bullseye right where it's supposed to be—on us, instead of civilians. And this time we'll actually be prepared."

Luis's jaw tightened but he didn't say a word.

"They *want* us to back off. Are we really going to do that? Are we going to let these criminals dictate how the NeoG runs their investigations? Or are we going to come at them full force with all the power we have?"

"The problem is we're not full force," Stephan noted. He put a hand up when she turned on him. "I hear what you're saying, Max, and I don't disagree. However, both of your crews are without ships right now, and while I have testimony on Melanie's involvement in this, it's from a man with a lengthy criminal background. I need more evidence to bring the whole thing down, because if I arrest Grant or Melanie right now, that just puts their operation on pause until Tieg finds new partners or gets them freed from custody."

"Whose fault is it we don't have ships? No, don't answer that," Max said. "Answer me this instead: You don't think they'd turn on Tieg with their asses on the line?"

"They might, but do we really want to put all this on a maybe?" Stephan met her glare with a sympathetic expression. "I think you know as well as I do how dangerous powerful people are, especially when they think they're untouchable."

Max knew he was right on that front, but she wasn't willing to let go of the rest. "What do you have planned?"

"I'm sending you all back to Jupiter Station. The prelims are six weeks out, and it's going to take about that long to get the ships fixed. You'll be stuck on station until *Zuma* is back up to spec, and you can spend most of your time training for the prelims—which has the added benefit of making Tieg and the rest think you're done with them. But during that time you can also—quietly—follow up on the leads I have on the station itself. Someone, or several someones, are helping with transport and schedules. I know it wasn't all coming from Chae."

Max had seen the files labeled *Jupiter Station* but hadn't yet looked through them. She nodded tentatively. "It could work. What will you do?"

"We'll go back to Earth and see what we can dig up on that end. Scott and his team can keep patrolling as part of the task force, just to give us an idea of how many ships they're pushing through. But we'll pull the other two task force crews to make them think we took the warning about backing off seriously."

"That's not a bad plan," she conceded. "You think that up all by yourself?"

"I'm Stephan Yevchenko, Intelligence. Have we met?"

She couldn't stop herself from laughing. "I'm still mad at you, don't forget it."

"Duly noted. I messed up, Max, and I'm sorry. You and Jenks are right. This mission is important, but thinking of our people first is more important and I should have done a better job of that. I *will* do a better job."

"It's all I can hope for."

"No, you can always expect better of the people you work with, Lieutenant." A rare grin slid across his face. "Go get packed and train your asses off in between work. I'd rather *Zuma's Ghost* was in fighting shape when we show you how winners actually get the job done."

"You're just begging to get beat now, aren't you?" Nika countered, and Max found herself grinning along with him.

"The bravado is impressive," Stephan replied. "Misplaced, but that's fine."

"Actually, the numbers look pretty good," Sapphi said with a thoughtful look. "And if we have a few weeks to really practice . . ."

Stephan's grin faded. "See, that worries me." He pointed in Sapphi's direction, but then he laughed. "Get out of here, all of you. The *Laika* will be coming in today and we'll get you headed back to Jupiter Station."

Max nodded and headed for the door, then stopped and turned back to him. "Stephan, I'm sorry for what I said earlier about you not understanding love. It was cruel and unnecessary."

"Apology accepted." He dipped his head.

"LifeEx uses Trappist Express for a lot of their shipping," Max said. "Would it be helpful for me to come up with a reason to convince Ria to start shifting their contracts with LifeEx to Portsmith or some of the smaller companies?"

"To what end?"

"It'll make them more desperate when we start hitting their illegal activities." Max shrugged. "I can do it so that Ria's got a legitimate reason why, I just need a little time to figure out what that might be. So before I dig in, I want to make sure it's worth it for us."

Stephan ran his tongue over his teeth as he considered it and then finally nodded. "It's got merit. Run your idea about how they make the change through me before you do it, though, okay? I want to make sure we're not spooking them too much. We want to have as much control of that desperation as we can."

"Noted." Max tapped her hand on the tabletop. "We'll see you at the prelims, then."

"I'm looking forward to it." He pointed past her. "Nika and I get to go for real."

"Should be fun," Nika said, heading for the door.

"Max." Luis followed her to the doorway. "Did Dai head for your quarters?"

"I don't know." Max watched the tangle of emotions race over Luis's face—pain and worry at the forefront—and she softened a bit. "Do you want me to ask her where she is? You can walk with us."

"No. I—it's fine." He sighed. "I'll let her cool off and decide when to get in touch. Have a good trip, Max."

She reached out, touching his arm before he turned away. "She knows you love her, you just went about it wrong."

"By trying to protect her?"

"Exactly."

"*Max.*"

"I'm serious. Has Jenks ever asked for your protection?"

"Does she ever ask for anything?"

"Again: exactly. Because she usually has an answer already . . . since she doesn't make a move without thinking of the angles," she said, pointed. "That's not the only issue, though. She's trying to find her feet—living up to what she thinks Ma brought to the team. It's hard for her to ask for what she doesn't know she needs."

He looked abashed as her words sank in and Max couldn't stop herself from smiling. "Do you need a hug?"

He laughed. "You know, I kinda do. Thanks for asking."

Max wrapped her arms around him and hugged him tight. "Take care of yourself, okay? You two will be all right. Just give her a little time." She let him go and patted him twice on the chest. "And then maybe listen a little more instead of thinking you know the answers to questions she hasn't even asked."

NIKA EXHALED IN RELIEF AS HE STEPPED OFF THE *LAIKA* ONTO Jupiter Station. It hadn't been a long trip, thankfully, but Jenks on a Navy vessel without the refuge of her ship was just asking for trouble.

Especially with the mood she was in.

That mood seemed to dissipate the moment she put her boots on the station deck, though. She slipped an arm around Chae's shoulders. "You doing okay, kid?" she asked as they headed out of the docking bay and down the corridor toward their quarters.

"I am—" Chae took a deep breath, let it out. "Relieved."

"So what did you learn?"

"Learn?"

"Yeah. I'll help you out this time: when you're in a jam, you tell me straight up. Okay? I promise you, I'll back you no matter what it is. You fuck up, we'll fix it. You need help, we're here. You did what you did to protect your family, right?"

"Yes."

"Well, remember this: *We're* family now. I'll protect you. You'll protect me. We'll protect your fathers. We'll protect each other. Got it?"

"Yes, Chief."

Jenks yanked Chae down into a headlock and ground her knuckle into their head until they yelped and laughed.

"Jenks, stop abusing your Neo."

"Tell them to stop with the Chief thing," she called back to Nika as she let Chae go.

"This is the same as the shoelace, isn't it?" he asked Max.

Max smiled as she watched Jenks and Chae continue down the corridor in front of them, and the sight of it made his chest ache. "It is. Though in this case it's Jenks wrestling with feeling like she's not good enough and needing us to remind her that she *is* a chief."

"Confidence issues is the last thing I'd expect from my sister."

"That's because you weren't paying attention to a word I said to Luis." There was a snap in her reply that reminded him he was nowhere close to being in her good graces again, even though she'd been pleasant enough on the ride back to Jupiter. "She's desperately afraid of not living up to Ma's example, and we didn't make things very easy for her."

"You mean I didn't." He held up a hand at her flat look. "I'm not being combative, Max. I'm trying to take ownership of this. You were trying. I wasn't. I'm sorry." Nika stopped and waved Sapphi and Tamago ahead of them. He knew it wasn't only Jenks's confidence that had taken a beating over the last few months. "I've thought of five thousand things I should have done or said. The truth is you were right about all of it. I came into this whole thing thinking like an intelligence agent rather than the commander of an Interceptor crew. I let you all down and for that I am deeply sorry." He took a deep breath. "But I am more sorry for how I hurt you."

Max closed her eyes for a moment. "I didn't want to have this conversation in the middle of everything."

"It can wait. I can wait."

"No." She shook her head, opened her eyes, and looked right at him. "I don't know how we survive this. I trusted you and you used the one thing you knew would hurt me the most against me. That makes me furious."

She took a deep breath and continued down the corridor, leaving Nika to scramble and catch up. "God help me, but I really want to forgive you even in spite of that. Maybe that makes me weak or a fool, but I love you and I'm fairly sure I'd regret it if I walked away from you."

I love you.

The words hurt more than they should have and Nika only just barely managed not to blurt them back at her. He'd messed up more than just his professional relationship with her and that painful truth was only now sinking in. He swallowed down the fear.

"Max, I am so sorry. I know I failed you—as a commander, as someone who wanted to be your partner. I was so wrapped up in how difficult this was for me that I didn't think about how much it hurt you." He stopped and shook his head. "That's not even true. I knew that what I said would hurt you, that it would hurt you even more when you found out the truth; but I did it anyway.

"You're a far better officer of the NeoG than I have been. A better lieutenant than I deserved. I understand if you don't want to continue a relationship on any level, but I did promise you we would be friends no matter what and I need you to know I meant that, if it's something you want. If it isn't, I understand that, too."

She stopped at the entrance to the NeoG quarters and turned before opening the door. Nika held his breath, unsure of what was coming next. "I appreciate that. Truly. Beyond that, I don't have an answer for you, Nika. At least, not right now. I need to think about it."

"I get it and I'm not going to push you. Take whatever time is necessary." He wanted to hold his free hand out but instead shoved it into his pocket. "Whatever happens, Max, from here on out I've got your back."

She smiled then, a soft light of hope in the darkness, and nodded once. "I've got yours."

TWENTY-FOUR

"So, you going to talk to me about this or just sit on it until the universe tears itself apart?" Jenks asked, dodging Max's punch.

"I'm reasonably sure we agreed that I wouldn't talk to you about my relationship with your brother."

"Yeah, well, we've been back a week and you haven't talked to anyone," Jenks singsonged.

Max laughed and avoided the hook kick Jenks attempted. "You're a fine one to give me shit."

"I don't need to talk about anything. I made my decision," Jenks lied. Max didn't need to know about the eighteen letters to Luis and Tivo sitting in her drafts folder.

"Hmm. How many emails have you started?"

Jenks was so shocked she missed the block and only just managed to lean out of the way of the punch Max had thrown, scrambling backward to avoid the follow-up she knew was right on the heels of it.

It wasn't enough. Max had sensed her distraction and the sweep caught Jenks right in the sweet spot. Refocused, she landed hard, but rolled *into* Max, rather than away from the lieutenant.

The squawk of surprise was followed by laughter as Max

wasn't able to get out of the way fast enough and hit the mat herself. Jenks swarmed over the top of her, locking her into a hold before Max could get away.

"I yield. I yield, you brat," Max gasped through her laughter.

Jenks gave her a smacking kiss on the cheek as she let her go and leaned back on her heels. "I love you, Max. I know you're hurting. Nika hurt you. I get that. He didn't have to—he chose to. He knew what he did was wrong and that's hard to find forgiveness for. I also know you want to forgive Nika, and that's okay—in case you need permission. It's easier for you to make peace for the sake of the team, that's just who you are. You don't have to, though."

"I know I'm too soft-hearted," Max whispered.

"That's not a judgment, it's just fact. And honestly, I'm more than a little jealous. They'll have to pry my grudges out of my cold, dead hands."

Max laughed, but the joy in her eyes faded quickly. "I keep asking myself if I have the right to be so mad when they were just doing their jobs."

"Yeah." Jenks scrubbed at the back of her head, trying to ignore the wound in her heart Max's words opened up. "But this isn't about the job here. I'm not willing to put aside the fact that Sapphi died because they chose not to tell us the truth, even if she came back to life and walked away with some cooler-than-shit scars she'll be showing everyone until the end of time."

Max got to her feet and offered her hand, pulling Jenks upright when she took it. "I know. That's what keeps rolling around in my head, too. Because the team means everything to us. I also know Nika's sick over it. That he never would have forgiven himself if Sapphi had died. I'm sure Luis feels the same way."

"Maybe." Jenks shrugged. "It wasn't his team to risk, that's the problem." She sorted through her replies, searching for some way to tell Max to lay off that wasn't cruel and didn't make it totally obvious that she was trying to avoid the subject.

As she slipped her feet into her boots and started lacing them up, she wondered how it was that someone she'd known for barely two years could understand her better than someone she'd been sleeping with for seven.

If we're being fair about it, you should admit that's because you kept Luis at arm's length for more than five years. Plus Max is spooky good at figuring people out and she knows how much this team means to you.

Jenks glanced down at her neatly tied boot and then shot Max a look. "Did you—?"

"What?"

"Nothing." Jenks shook her head, the fleeting thought vanishing as they hit the gym exit. "I appreciate your concern, Max, but I'd also appreciate it if you'd just let me handle it in my own way."

"Okay."

Jenks blinked, not expecting the easy agreement, and equally surprised that part of her had hoped Max would push, dig just a little bit.

You could just ask her for advice on how to forgive someone. She seems to have it figured out, as far as Nika's concerned anyway.

But the moment was lost as they hit the zero-g tube, and Jenks stuffed the words back into the corner of her heart, where they couldn't come back to haunt her.

"THIS IS MUCH BETTER," MAX MURMURED TO JENKS SEVERAL days later as they crouched behind a console in the derelict freighter.

"We're pinned down, weirdo," Jenks replied.

"Yeah, but we're both alive . . ." She did some mental calculations in her head. "And give it fifteen more seconds."

The shooting stopped abruptly, replaced by the frustrated groans of the remainder of *Dread Treasure*'s crew.

Then Sapphi's voice came over the coms. "That's it.

Dread's all down. Time from start: nine minutes and forty-two seconds."

Max popped up, laughing at the sight of *Dread*'s petty officers—Ito Akane and Aki Murphy—lying on the floor with Chae and Tamago standing over them, swords in hand.

"Well, this is a difference, isn't it?" D'Arcy asked as he joined them. "I'd be mad except I'm too impressed. No . . . just mad."

"Come on—you can't be mad at us. Look how well our plan came together," Max replied, bumping shoulders with the big man.

"Not just a plan," he replied with a laugh. "Your whole crew has come together. Good job." That was directed at Nika as he joined them, and Max hid her pleasure when he nodded in acknowledgment of the praise.

Everything really had come together over the last week back at Jupiter. They'd done almost nothing but train for the prelims and investigate leads for potential hostiles on the station.

More, Stephan had surprised Max and had them read the rest of the task force teams in on a plan for hitting the smugglers where it would hurt the most. That level of trust on Intel's side had gone a long way toward peace of mind for the crew of *Zuma's Ghost*.

Sapphi had swept their quarters for bugs and promised it was clean after Nika had produced the one Chae had planted near his room, but also dedicated herself to the task of constantly checking for anything out of the ordinary.

With the mission coming together, Nika had been in the sword ring more often than out of it, with Max offering herself up as a sacrifice when D'Arcy had to take care of the repairs on *Dread*.

It gave her time to spend with Nika, and though they hadn't talked a lot, the conversations in the ring had gone a long way toward easing the ache in her heart. It had also been good for her, even though she wasn't competing, to brush up on her sword abilities. And now she could help Tamago with their training.

It was all going well . . . except for Jenks. The chief was—Max muffled a sigh—not herself, but sort of managing. Potentially with the help of too much alcohol. Max hated to see her friend like this, but she wanted to let her have the space to figure out her own feelings on the matter.

Yet she was also worried Jenks was just going to ignore it in the hopes it would go away.

"I don't mind saying this break has been nice. All this intensive training is going to make for exciting prelims," D'Arcy said. "I like the thought of *Dread* at the top of the scoreboard."

"You and Stephan have some grandiose ideas about your place in the NeoG pecking order. You're going to have to get better at more than just the Boarding Action if you want that to be a reality," Max said with a straight face.

"I'm sure you didn't just throw down a challenge at me, Carmichael."

"I'm only speaking truth. And I prefer to be referred to as 'two-time champion Carmichael,' if you don't mind."

"Nika, you want to get your lieutenant under control?"

"Why? I'm on her side," Nika said, slapping him on the back, and Max couldn't stop the laugh as D'Arcy turned his glare on Nika. "I mean, you're stuck with Locke and Huang, and I have Jenks and Max. It's not your fault I got the better end of the deal."

"Meet me in the sword ring this afternoon, and we'll see whose fault it is," D'Arcy said, and went to join the others.

"I'm in for it now."

"You'll kick his ass." Max raised an eyebrow at his surprised look. "What?"

"I don't deserve you."

It was her turn to be surprised. "Why do you say that?"

"You are effortlessly supportive and so confident that all the rest of us will perform at our best." He glanced at his hands and then smiled at her. "Sometimes I think we'd be better off if you were the commander."

"I don't know that I agree with you. I've made mistakes, too, Nika. I'm still learning how to lead."

"I know, but the fact that you're aware of your inexperience is just one more reason you're good at this job. I'm just—I'm constantly in awe of you. I don't think I've told you enough how competent you are and how grateful I am that you're on my crew." He held out his hand and she took it. "I say this as your commander . . . and I hope as your friend."

"I'd like to try again." Max squeezed her eyes shut and pressed her free hand to the space between them.

"What?"

"I'm sorry, that slipped out." She dropped her hand, forced herself to meet his gaze. "No—I'm not sorry. And now that it's out there, I do mean it. I just hadn't found a way to say it to you yet. I'd like for us to try again. If you want to."

"Of course." Nika's blue eyes lit up. "I do, Max. Absolutely."

The way the weight came off her reminded Max of stepping off a mining platform on Jupiter back into the Earth-gravity standard of the Interceptor ships, and she took a step forward without thinking. But Nika had already opened his arms and folded her into a hug.

Max hugged him back, laughing when Jenks's groan echoed through the bay.

"Get a room, you two!"

Nika muttered a curse in too fond a tone for Max to think he meant it in the slightest. "This is sort of an abrupt subject change, but have you talked to Jenks about Luis?"

"A week ago." Max sighed. "Rather, I tried, but her response was a pretty definitive door in my face. Tamago said she still hasn't spoken to either of them and she's been drinking more at the bar in the evenings. The good news is at least she hasn't gotten into a fight yet."

"Yet."

"Exactly."

"Should I talk to her? I try to stay out of her relationships, such as they've been, but it's obvious she's hurting."

"Let me try again," Max said after a moment. "It might go over a little better." She made a face. "If I get punched, though, you owe me a freebie sword hit."

"Duly noted."

Max gave him a quick touch on the arm, then ran to catch up with Jenks as the group of two crews broke up and went their separate ways.

"Hey, I was going to get changed and go to the yard to work on *Zuma,* but do you want to spar later today?" Jenks asked.

"Maybe, I've got a call with Ria this afternoon. Jeanie's awake and the doctors thought it would help for her to see familiar faces. I don't know how long it's going to take."

"Eh, no worries. You can always just hit me up on chat when you're done if I'm not in quarters."

"Sounds good." Max rolled her words over in her mouth until she found the ones least likely to get her hit. "Jenks, have you talked to Luis?"

There was the slightest hitch in Jenks's stride and then she blew out a breath. "I thought we agreed to leave it. Did Tamago ask you to talk to me? They've been on my ass about it for a week."

"No. This is just me. And you asked, but I don't remember saying I would." Max attempted a smile, but it didn't soften the look on Jenks's face. "You haven't been yourself since we got back and as your friend, I'm concerned."

"Max—"

"You know I'm bullshit at relationships," Max said. "But I'm here if you want to talk about it."

Jenks stopped walking and rubbed at the back of her neck before she turned to face Max. "The truth of it is I thought this would—I gave it a go and it didn't work. I should have known. I'm shit at relationships, too, and I'm realizing they're not worth the work. That's fine. I'm fine."

The words would have hurt coming from anyone, but from Jenks it was like someone had reached into Max's chest and pulled her heart out. She reached for her friend, but Jenks danced away from the contact.

"Jenks, you are worth it—how many times do we have to tell you that? Luis cares about you. If you gave him the opportunity to apologize—"

"No." Jenks shook her head. "Look, LT, I meant what I said about it earlier. And I do appreciate your concern, but this isn't something you can help me with." She sighed and then forced an expression of calm Max knew all too well. "I know what needs to be done here. I just have to do it."

"Jenks. That's not—"

"It's fine," she said as she headed down the corridor away from Max with a wave of her hand. "Nothing lasts forever."

"Fuck," Max muttered in the silence of the empty hallway. "Nice going, Carmichael. You handled that really well."

"GOOD JOB OUT THERE."

Chae looked up at Commander Montaglione with a smile. "I appreciate the fact that you're serious about that."

"I can be impressed and still determined to find a way to keep you from sneaking up on me like a damned shadow." D'Arcy leaned against the hull of the freighter and crossed one ankle over the other. "How are your parents?"

Chae couldn't stop themself from looking around, but they and D'Arcy were the only ones left near the derelict freighter. "Okay, I guess? I haven't talked to my dads for two years."

"At *all*?"

"It was part of the plea deal. Lieutenant Carmichael offered to pass a message to them on the sly, but I didn't want to risk it." They wondered if it would be worth it now, and if the offer was still open.

"She would do that." D'Arcy laughed. "That one knows how

to use her name as a force for good. If you decide to take her up on it, tell them I said hi." He tapped Chae on the shoulder. "For real, though—you did good today. However, one of these times I'm going to catch you, so be careful."

Chae watched him walk away, pride blooming in their chest from the praise.

"Hey, Chae."

They froze. Julia's voice had once been enough to make their heart stutter. Now it was like someone pouring liquid nitrogen down their spine.

Stephan had warned them that they weren't going to interfere with Julia's movement on the station. That it was better for Tieg's people not to suspect anything until it was too late.

She threw her arm around their neck in a seemingly friendly gesture, but her green eyes were hard and the next words out of her mouth made them want to throw up. "We are so proud of you for the work you did on Trappist. Crashing your own ship wasn't something I thought you had in you."

"Thanks?"

"Now, about those listening devices . . ."

"They found them on a routine sweep. I did my best. I can put more up if you want?" Chae hoped their fake stammer was convincing.

"No, it's not worth it."

Chae pulled their racing thoughts together enough to use the tips the chief had been giving them about how to handle Julia. They'd planned for the chance that she would approach them again, but Chae hadn't wanted to believe it would happen. Now it had, though, and they knew they had to step up.

I won't screw this up, too.

"Hey, are there more of us on the station?"

"Us?" Julia laughed. "You think you're one of the team now? Want to have a beer after work like your Interceptor buddies?"

"I—I just thought it would be good if I knew who else to

pass information on to. Like if it should get to you in a hurry, email isn't really the best option, is it?"

Her grip tightened and Chae had to walk along with her or get dragged. For a moment they considered it, wondered what her reaction would be if they dug in their heels and punched her right in her throat like Jenks had taught them to do. She was alone, no bruisers to beat them down while she bled . . .

But they didn't. Instead, the thought that Max would want them to get whatever information they could filled their head and kept their hands loose at their sides.

Suddenly Julia laughed. "I do like you, Chae. You're smart. My boss appreciates smart. She has big plans. It's good for you to be more involved with things."

The words felt strange in Chae's mouth, too obvious, but Jenks had insisted if they suddenly started acting at ease with Julia now it would only tip her off. "I'd like to do more. I think I could help." They gestured back at the bay. "We're training so much for the prelims because the commander is in trouble for what happened on Trappist with the ship. The lieutenant is really mad at him." They were careful not to say anyone's name, trying to give the impression of someone who wasn't attached to the members of their crew.

"Really?"

Chae could almost see the wheels turning in her head as Julia tried to figure out if Chae just didn't know about the attempted attack on Jenks, or if they were lying to her.

"I spent most of the time after the crash in my room. Everyone was in an uproar because Ensign Zika got hurt. They don't tell me anything, I'm just a fucking newbie as far as they're concerned." Chae injected as much annoyance into their voice as they could and hoped Julia would buy it.

"You said Carmichael was mad?"

"Yeah."

"About what?"

"Commander Vagin and Lieutenant Carmichael had a huge

fight while we were on Trappist. I didn't catch all of it, but she was mad about how he's handled things. He told her he wasn't going to be in for much longer, so what did it matter."

The commander is going to kill me, Chae thought. This wasn't quite what they'd planned, but it was too late to take back the lie, and Julia seemed really interested.

"'In for much longer'?" Julia's grip loosened. "He's *leaving* the NeoG?"

"I don't know? Something about losing his arm and his sister being in danger and he was tired of the NeoG not keeping them safe. I didn't hear the rest of it, I was in my room and they left the quarters." Chae managed to wriggle free and held their hands up. "I swear, I'm doing everything you've all asked. I just don't have as much access as you seem to think."

"You'd better get some, Chae, if you want your fathers to stay safe."

"I did have an idea. What if you all approached Commander Vagin?"

"Approached him?"

"Yeah, like to work for you. He's got way better access than I do. You could talk him into staying."

Julia stared at them, her tongue tucked into her cheek, and for a terrifying series of heartbeats Chae thought she was going to call them on their lies. Finally, though, she nodded. "It's not a bad idea. I'll run it by the boss." She smiled, her face transforming into something they used to love looking at. Now it only brought a second wave of nausea and fear. "You're super cute, Chae. I hope I don't have to kill you. Go on."

They ran.

NIKA HELD HIS PRACTICE SWORD LOOSELY IN HIS HAND AND replayed the interaction he'd had with D'Arcy during the Boarding Action as he passed through the door of their quarters. He could hear Sapphi and Tamago as they trailed him down the hall. Max and Jenks had lagged behind, presumably to talk, and he hoped Max had luck convincing his sister to open up some.

"Hey, Nika. You got a minute?" Sapphi asked, holding up her right hand to show him the signal jammer in it as she followed him through the door.

"Yeah." Nika stopped in the middle of their quarters. "What's up?"

"I'm testing out a new jammer. I'm reasonably sure about the security in our quarters, but I'd rather be better than sure, plus we can use this for the conference room meetings if it works out. I've got Tamago down the hall with a listener I built to see how well it works."

"Good, how's the data collection going?" Nika would have put Sapphi onto analyzing all the information they'd been looking at since their return to Jupiter even if the doctors hadn't said that challenging her skills would help her recovery. As it stood it was an added bonus, and did seem to help. She was much more coherent than she had been on the ride back home.

After Sapphi had set up secure communications for them, she'd turned her sights to cataloging everything Stephan had given them on potential suspects here on the station.

"I don't like spying on my friends, Nika." She dropped into the chair and he sat next to her. "Did you feel this bad the whole time you were lying to us? How did you stand it?"

Nika managed to suppress most of his flinch. Sapphi didn't mean for the question to be cruel, but what few filters she'd had seemed to have been burned up by the electrical surge. He'd done his rounds with the members of his crew after Max had forgiven him—would have done the same even if she hadn't, but it felt right to sit down with them each individually and apologize. Still, it was a lot easier to forgive than to forget.

"I did feel that bad." He smiled. "I thought it had to be done."

Sapphi made a face and reached out. Nika took her hand, rubbing a thumb over the scars on the back. Grief choked him, made his next words come out barely above a whisper. "I almost got you killed, Sapphi. I'm so sorry."

"You already apologized. So did Chae." She patted her other hand over the top of his. "I'll tell you the same thing I told them: The people responsible are the ones who are running this thing. They're the ones who have to pay. So stop blaming yourself, okay? Before I get annoyed and zap you."

"Did you get the ability to shoot electricity from your fingertips from this adventure?"

"Sadly no, but I can rig up something on your seat in *Zuma* if you don't watch it." Sapphi grinned. "I am working on a dedicated team chat program. It's maybe not regulation, but I'll feel better if I know for sure we're encrypted above and beyond CHN protocols."

"I'll take the heat on that if something goes sideways." He nodded. "You do whatever you need to. Thanks for always looking out for us, Sapphi."

"It's my job," she protested, but the pleased look on her face told him the compliment had made her happy. "Anyway"—she flipped the jammer off with her thumb—"the projections for the Boarding Action went up thanks to that session. I'm feeling pretty confident about our chances, to be honest."

"As hard as we've been training, I'd hope so," Nika replied, glancing past Sapphi as Tamago and Chae came into the quarters. "Turn that back on, Saph," he ordered in a low voice as he got to his feet.

Tamago was gripping Chae's arm and the spacer looked not quite panicked, but damn close as Tamago ushered them to a chair.

"What happened?" Nika demanded.

"Julia," Chae whispered, looking around the room as if they expected her to pop up at any second.

"We're safe here," Nika said, and pointed at Sapphi, who held up the jammer. "We were expecting this. Take a few breaths, Chae, and tell me what she said." He tamped down on his own fear in an effort to calm Chae down. The fact that they were unharmed was a good sign.

They visibly relaxed, at least a little. "She wanted to congratulate me for crashing the ship. I tried to do like the chief coached me and asked if there were other people like me on the station."

"Did she tell you?"

"No, but she seemed impressed? She didn't care about the bugs being discovered. I said I wanted to help more." Chae suddenly covered their face with their hand as if they'd just remembered something. "I'm so sorry, Commander. I think I screwed up. I told her you and the LT had a fight and you were thinking about getting out of the NeoG. I suggested it would be a good idea for them to see if they could recruit you."

Nika blinked at Chae. "You *what*?"

"I'm sorry! I know it wasn't the plan. I thought if they had other people watching they'd know you and Max had been fighting and maybe if they believed it they'd rather have a commander than just a new spacer and they wouldn't know that you were working for Intel already."

Nika couldn't stop a laugh and Chae flinched.

"I'm sorry, sir. I screwed up."

"No. It's all right, Chae." Nika waved a hand in the air. "I wasn't laughing at you. You did good. Great, actually. Did she buy it?"

"I don't know? Maybe? She said she'd run it by her boss. What should I do?"

"Nothing." Nika patted Chae on the shoulder, his mind already running through the options, and he liked the plan that was forming. "I'm going to tell Stephan and see what he thinks."

"But sir—"

"You may have gotten us an even better line into their operation than we were hoping for when we came back here. If Julia's boss decides to get in touch, I'll be able to tell her exactly what she wants to hear."

Dai—

All right, I gave you two weeks. Are you going to talk
to me face-to-face now? Or at least answer my chat
request? Or just respond to this email?

I know I deserve this silence and I know I said I'd give
you space. I just . . . it's killing me, Dai.

I miss you.

I'm sorry I didn't get this right. I wish I could find the
words to show you how much you mean to me. I think
you'd understand if I said I love you like I love my boys.
It would rip my heart out if something happened to
them and it would rip my heart out the same for you.

I was trying to do my job, but I forgot that part of
my job is keeping all of you safe. Then I made it worse.
I didn't think about the fact that *your* job is also about
keeping your people safe. Max said I should listen
better instead of being so sure I know the answers. All I
want is the chance to actually do that.

I'm sorry. Please call me. Write me.

Anything.

Luis

TWENTY-FIVE

Jenks looked around the empty quarters on Jupiter Station and took a deep breath as she messaged Coms on her tablet. "Hey, Sully."

"Hey, Jenks. Just caught me before I go off duty. What do you need?"

"Can you put a call in to Luis for me?"

"Sure thing," they replied, and she felt a burst of relief when they didn't tease her.

The writhing mass of snakes in her stomach didn't need any encouragement. The screen resolved just as Jenks swallowed.

"Dai," Luis said, smiling at her as if she hadn't been ignoring him for two weeks.

Or maybe exactly because of that.

"Hey." She scrubbed a hand through her now silver-and-black hair and attempted a smile of her own.

"It's nice to see your face."

"I don't think this is going to work."

The words that had been rolling around her head for two weeks flew out and Jenks regretted them as soon as she said them at the look they put on Luis's face. "I—fuck me." She squeezed her eyes shut. "This was a bad idea. I should just go."

"Dai, you hang up on me and I'll be on the next transport out there."

"I can't do this," she whispered, feeling the tears start and scrambling to hold them at bay even as the words spilled out of her like a ship venting air into space. "I tried. You deserve better. I'm no good at relationships. Not like this. I'm not worth it."

"I knew I shouldn't have given you that much space," he muttered.

She opened her eyes. "What?"

His smile was gentle, if blurred by her tears. "All the 'I'm not worth it' dialogues have been going full-blast in your head, haven't they, Dai? That things have to end and people leave you and nothing lasts forever?" His words were an echo of what she'd said to Max yesterday and she couldn't stop from rubbing a hand over her heart.

"Maybe. Okay, yeah, but that doesn't mean they're not true."

"They're one hundred percent not true, and I'm the one who fucked up here. I'm the one who needs to apologize. Who's been trying to apologize. This is about you trusting me and me blowing it; don't try to gaslight yourself into making it about how you don't deserve to be loved."

She stared at him, more than a little surprised at how neatly he'd called her out. Her own therapist had said almost the same thing but Jenks had blown her off, so sure in her own brain that she'd done something to deserve it.

I'm not telling Ilka she was right, damn it. I'll never hear the end of it.

"You don't have to close yourself off, Dai. It's okay to open ourselves up to people we love. It's not easy, and sometimes it's damn hard—especially when an idiot opens his mouth and says something stupid—but it's all part of love. It's going to burn you up, Dai, staying closed off like this. You need to let people in.

"Besides, you promised me tomorrow."

"Tomorrow's been and gone."

"Nope, it's just around the corner." He smiled again, this time with that wicked spark in his eye when he knew he'd won the argument. She'd just tried to throw it away, but now she couldn't imagine never seeing that again.

"Did you sucker me into some never-ending contract?"

"Maybe. In my defense, I knew you'd try to dodge it, though. But I meant what I said, Dai. You deserve to be loved. You deserve to have someone listen to you and help you figure out how to be the kind of NCO you want to be. I want to be that person if you'll let me. If you're willing, I'd very much like to keep having the chance to show you that you are everything to me."

"Why are you so stubborn?"

"Why are you?"

She laughed, but pressed a hand over her eyes as the tears finally escaped her at the same time. "Why won't you just let me end this? Wouldn't it be easier for you not to have to put up with my bullshit?"

"Dai, look at me."

Jenks sniffled and wiped the tears away but made herself look him in the eye. "Seriously, why do you—"

"Hey, hush for a second and listen. If you really want to end this, okay. I just don't want you to do it because you think I'm going to leave first. If you recall, again, I'm the one who fucked up, not you."

"I don't know what I want," she whispered, knowing it was at least partially a lie. She wanted him.

"Love isn't a series of favors to be paid back. It's just loving someone—all of them. You deserve to be loved because everyone deserves to be loved. You just happened to get stuck with my ass."

"I like your ass. God. Sorry, I'm not trying to deflect all this, I swear."

"It's all right." Luis grinned. "I'd like the rest of my life to show you how grateful I am for you promising me tomorrow."

"I guess." Jenks heaved a theatrical sigh, knowing even as she did that Luis would see it for the relief it truly was. "I'm sorry I didn't kiss you goodbye."

"I'll see you in four weeks. You can make it up to me then. Let me win a fight . . ."

"Not on your damned life."

"Are you going to let Tivo apologize, too?"

"Maybe. Will he grovel like you did?"

"Altandai Khan, he's been miserable."

She laughed and glanced at the clock in the corner of her vision. Along with the flashing notification of her upcoming meeting there was a message from Tivo. "I'll talk to him later, I promise. I've got to go meet with Hoboins about how Chae's doing—I'd better get out of here. I'll call you later?"

"Tomorrow. I'm working late tonight. Moms have the boys for the weekend anyway. I love you, Dai."

"Love you, too." She blew him a kiss and then the tablet went black. She flopped back onto her bunk and rubbed both hands over her face one more time, surprised by the feelings rushing through her and the ridiculously strong urge she had to laugh, or cry, or possibly both.

Jenks cranked up the music on her DD chip and gave Doge a nudge as she slipped off her bunk and headed for the door.

"Your serotonin levels are up."

She smiled down at the robot dog and patted him on the head. "Yup."

"Why did you attempt to end things if it made you so sad?"

Jenks skidded to a halt. Doge frequently surprised her. The AI wasn't particularly complex, nor was it top of the line, though it had been at the time of its creation. Rather, it was simply a good twenty-year-old program that had a whole lot more freedoms than its descendants.

Sometimes it seemed like Doge was still learning, which was something she hadn't shared with anyone else. In part because she wasn't sure what it meant, but also because she didn't want to risk him getting taken away.

She paused the music and went to a knee by his side. "How do I explain it? Humans can be really weird, Doge. We think we want something and then get scared when we get it."

"Why, though?"

Jenks laughed and scratched at her face. "This is complicated, buddy. You want me to explain shit I can't even say to my therapist yet." She laid her cheek on his head. "I'm afraid of losing him. I don't trust that anything good in my life is going to last. So my brain insists it's better to push him away than wait for that to happen."

"Because you want to control it?"

"Yeah, I guess."

"You can't control people like machines, Jenks."

She blew out a breath at the echo of Blythe's words. "Tell me about it, buddy. To be honest, I can barely control machines most days. Come on. I'm not going to be doing anything except getting my ass chewed by Hoboins if we're late for this meeting."

"THIS IS WILD," MAX SAID OVER THE COM AFTER THE NEW HEL-met was sealed into her suit. She reached up and patted at the now-solid surface. Even though the engineers at Off-Earth had explained to her exactly how the new polymer worked, it was still hard to wrap her brain around.

"That is one word for it."

Max turned around to face Nika and tried not to laugh at the anxious expression on his face. "We'll be okay," she said. "They've been tested eight million times already, right, Antilles?"

The pilot of their shuttle was also one of the head engineers for Off-Earth's liquid helmet project and she turned around in her seat with a grin. "Absolutely. If anything goes wrong, Jun's right there and they'll pull you back in before you can even get frostbite."

"I am not worried about frostbite," Nika replied, and Max choked down a second laugh. "You know Jenks would have jumped at the chance to do this, so explain to me why I'm here again?"

"Because she has a meeting with Hoboins that starts in two minutes and Antilles has to catch the transport back to Earth this afternoon." She reached out and patted his shoulder. "And because she'd think this was so cool she couldn't be critical of it. Whereas I trust you to treat it with all the seriousness of someone who's aware of their own mortality."

"I hate you."

"No you don't."

Max looked over at Jun. The other Off-Earth engineer was dressed in an old-fashioned helmet and EMU. Their job was to monitor all the vitals and, as Antilles had just noted, haul Max and Nika into the shuttle should something go wrong. "We're good to go here."

"All right, closing my doors," Antilles replied, and the doors between the cockpit and the rest of the shuttle slid closed and sealed.

"The film is reactive, though we're far enough away from the sun out here it likely won't trip the filters," Jun said. "Let me know if you feel light-headed or out of breath at any point." They paused. "If you hear a whistling sound, you want to close your eyes tight and pull your head down as far as possible into the suit. I'll bring you back in, but the helmet might explode."

"Oh, holy Saint Ivan, why did I agree to this?" Nika muttered.

Even Max took a deep breath at the word "explode," but breathed out as the back of the shuttle slid open, revealing

Jupiter Station and the massive gas giant hanging in the black behind it. They were on the side of the station away from the traffic pattern, and close enough that she immediately felt dwarfed by the sheer size of the station itself.

The pair of mushroom-shaped structures were connected by several tubes that varied from five to thirty meters in diameter. The smaller tower was for H3nergy personnel and civilians, while the larger housed CHN military.

For just a moment she was back to two years ago, watching the station from the bridge of the freighter *G's Panic*. That overwhelming sense of home hadn't gone away.

"Commander, Lieutenant? How are you doing?" Jun's voice dragged Max back to the present and she turned so she could get a look at Nika. She gave him a questioning thumbs-up that he returned and Max wished that there was some way they could talk privately. But even out here in the black they had to route everything through the suit coms, and there was no way to know who was listening.

"We're doing good so far."

Which meant Max couldn't ask Nika just what his plan was as far as Melanie Karenina went and how he was going to win the woman's approval without getting both himself and Chae killed.

She'd tried to offer herself up instead, but Nika had refused. Though his primary reason had been that no one would believe for a second Maxine Carmichael would break the law, he also insisted that as the commander, he bore the responsibility.

She'd had to concede he was right on both points.

She hit the thruster on her EMU, keeping an eye on the tether as they sailed farther away from the shuttle and toward the station. "You think Hoboins would be surprised if we knocked on his window?"

Nika laughed and it was only a little strained. "He might. I doubt we could get that close with the shuttle before the warning sensors went off, though."

"Looks like someone is doing maintenance over there, which means the sensors would be off, but we are technically working." Max reached up and tapped on her helmet and swore she could hear Nika's wince over the coms. "Let's run these tests, Jun."

"All right. First one is the full thruster burn, increments of fifteen, thirty, and forty-five seconds . . ."

JENKS HAD TURNED HER MUSIC BACK ON AND SHE DANCED as she made her way into Hoboins's office with Doge at her side. "Lou!"

Commander Lou Seve, Hoboins's chief of staff, looked up from her desk and sighed. "Jenks, why did you bring the dog? You know how he feels about them. I love you, Doge, but the admiral has issues."

"No offense taken, Commander," Doge said, and Jenks grinned.

"I brought him because I figured you needed the break. How's his mood today?"

"It's good, so don't fuck that up."

"What?"

"You heard me." Lou pointed a finger. "Just get in there and talk about how Chae's doing and get your ass out. Do not mention his birthday or so help me I will find a way to put you on kitchen duty for a month."

"You won't. There'd be a revolt and we both know it." Jenks pointed at the side of Lou's desk. "Doge, sit."

The ROVER sat and Jenks went through the door into Hoboins's office.

"What did I tell you about bringing that robot into my office, Chief?"

"He is technically not in your office, sir."

Lee Hoboins looked up from his tablet. "Sit your ass down, Jenks," he said with a smile that always reminded her of what a grandfather should look like. A grumpy, somewhat curmudgeonly grandfather, but one who slipped you old-fashioned candies when your parents weren't looking.

"My *baba* would have liked you, sir." She hadn't meant to say that out loud, and judging from the look on the admiral's face he was as shocked as she was.

"That's good to know, Chief Khan. I like to think your and Vagin's grandmother was a good judge of character. How's Chae doing?"

Straight to business, then. "Settling in." Jenks leaned back in her chair. "They're a hell of a pilot, even better than Ma. They're smart—possibly smarter than the LT, if that's a thing."

Hoboins laughed. "I'm reasonably sure Max would point out there are a lot of people smarter than her."

"Yeah, maybe." Jenks shrugged. "I doubt it, though. Chae's a demon in the Boarding Action, which is where it counts, and I'm still working with them as far as up-close combat goes." She picked her next words carefully. Hoboins knew about the operation on Trappist, but everyone had been cautioned to keep quiet about it unless they were somewhere with an active jammer. "Chae's fitting in a lot better since we came home, if that makes sense."

"It does." Hoboins nodded in approval. "And that's great news. You're doing a good job."

She couldn't stop from squirming in her seat. "I'm not doing anything, sir. It's all Chae."

"Take the praise, Jenks. You're a good chief and we both know it. Ma's proud of you. I'm damn proud of you." He smiled and arched an eyebrow as he tapped at his tablet. "Now, you want to tell me why the mess hall got fifteen hundred gallons of ice cream delivered on the last freighter?"

Busted.

"No idea. Why?" She affected the most innocent expression she could manage as she stood, which only made Hoboins's eyes narrow further.

"It seems suspiciously like something someone would do if they were trying to plan a surprise birthday party."

She lifted her hands. "You know me, Admiral. I made up my birthday, I'm not big on them. Maybe the Navy's planning a 'we found another asteroid' party?"

"You'd better hope so."

"I don't know what you mean by that." She bit the inside of her cheek to keep the laughter at bay.

"I mean I think you ordered all that ice cream and did it behind my back."

"What a thing to accuse me of, Admiral! Is my name on the request form? Why would I do such a thing when I know how much you supposedly hate your birthday?"

"I will bust you all the way back down to spacer, Altandai, do not test me." Hoboins was pointing at her now and this time Jenks didn't bother to hide the grin.

"You know you love me, sir."

"Get the hell out of my office." Hoboins was laughing and he waved a hand at the door. "I've got actual work to do."

Jenks threw a sloppy salute his direction and skipped for the door.

"Lou!" Hoboins shouted toward his chief of staff. "Do not let them throw me a birthday party. I will demote everyone on this station, including you!"

"Damn it, Jenks." Lou groaned. "I told you—"

"In my defense, I did not bring it up. He did. Also in my defense, I have no idea what he's talking about. Come on, Doge. Have a good day, Lou!" Jenks laughed to herself as she escaped into the hallway and headed for the tube.

"Explosive detected."

"What?" She stopped in her tracks, looking down at the ROVER. "What are you on about, goofy dog?"

"You are in the blast radius." He jumped, front legs hitting her in the shoulders, and Jenks staggered back several steps, spitting curses even as flame exploded from the doorway of Hoboins's office and rushed at her.

TWENTY-SIX

There was no sound, only the shocking bloom of red-orange from Jupiter Station too bright against the backdrop of the planet. It was the alarm warning of the deadly spray of debris headed toward them that was loud in Nika's ears.

"Max!" Nika grabbed for her, throwing up his shield as his hand connected with her arm. He pulled her in against his chest and could hear her over the com, voice smooth as glass.

"Antilles, get your shields up now."

"I see it," she replied. "They're up, but they're not going to help, that stuff's moving too slow. What the fuck just happened?"

"Clips. Gotta get the clips undone." Max twisted in his grip and Nika swore.

"What? No."

"Antilles can't get clear with us still attached, Nika. There's mine." He felt her patting at his waist until she found his tether. "Antilles, we're loose. Go!"

"Too late. Shit. Brace!"

Shit.

The debris hit them like a hammer and Nika tightened his

arms around Max as the breath left him in a rush and they spun out of control.

"Hang on, I've got you."

"I've never doubted that for a second." The emotion in her voice bled over the com as Nika managed to stabilize them with his EMU. "I guess we are field testing these new helmets today after all."

His laugh choked off when he caught sight of the shuttle. A larger piece of debris had miraculously missed them but ripped its way through the ship. "Antilles?"

"We're still fucking alive, but I've got nothing. Power's down. Trying to raise the station . . . I'm not getting any response. If I can get out of this cockpit we'll join you, otherwise I'm stuck here until someone tows what's left of us in."

"Do what you can," Nika ordered, then switched the channel. "This is Commander Nika Vagin, can anyone hear me?" he asked, trying the station directly from his DD chip. They were close enough for the DD chips to work, though it was a bit of a stretch, and all he got was static.

"Oh god." Max's exhalation was clear on the coms. "You won't get them. I can see what's left of Coms from here, it's gone and—" She broke off with a pained gasp. "Nika, that's Hoboins's office."

His stomach twisted before Max could even start her next sentence. His first thought was of his sister and the prayer slipped out without a thought. "Most holy God, do not turn your eyes from those who need you in this moment."

"Jenks," Max whispered. "Nonono, please no." She pushed out of his grasp and it took Nika a moment to realize she wasn't just mindlessly flying toward the station but toward something floating through the black, lights blinking.

Doge.

Saint Ivan, please don't do this to us.

Max hit the dog head on, wrapping her arms around him. "Doge, where's Jenks?"

The ROVERs were designed for vacuum, but there was a heart-rending moment when Nika wondered if the AI would respond to Max's question.

"She is on station. Alive, but vitals are dropping."

He pushed through the relief trying to swamp everything else, finding refuge in procedure. "Doge, report. What happened?"

"I detected an explosive device at 15:23 when we were three point three meters from Admiral Hoboins's office. As we were still within the estimated blast radius, I pushed Jenks the rest of the way into the safe zone. I do not know what happened after, as I was pulled into space by the loss of structural integrity and lost contact. She is likely injured by debris or possibly burned by the explo—"

"Doge, enough." Nika couldn't keep his voice even and the dog's head swiveled toward him.

"I have upset you. I am sorry. She is alive right now." There was a fascinating note of sympathy in the ROVER's voice.

"It's fine." He reached out and patted the dog. "You did good, buddy. What's the best way for us to get onto the station from here?"

"I will need a minute to calculate something."

"If we get closer, we may be able to get a hold of Sapphi or someone on the team channel," Max said, and Nika nodded.

"Antilles, how are you looking on getting free?" he asked.

"Eh, not good at the moment, but we are safe. You two go on. Just send someone back for us," Antilles replied.

"We will." Nika locked his hand on Doge's collar next to Max's and shared a look with her. "Doge, let me know when you have something. We're headed in."

"NO, IF YOU SWAP OUT THIS BOARD, WE'LL STILL BE ONE short," Chae said. They heaved a frustrated sigh as they stared up at the guts of *Dread Treasure*'s flight systems. "I'm sorry. We're going to have to wait for—"

The concussive wave rolled through the Interceptor bay just moments before the explosion followed it with the fury of a coronal mass ejection. Chae was mostly shielded by the open panel on *Dread*'s underside, but Lieutenant Commander Locke was thrown a meter away, crashing into a tool cart and sliding to the floor, stunned.

Alarms screamed through the smoke-filled air, echoed by the screams of people. Chae scrambled forward on their hands and knees.

"Locke?" The man groaned and Chae looked around, finally grabbing a spacer who wandered dazedly up with blood streaking down her face. Recognizing her, they said, "Hey, Cora, sit down. Are you hurt anywhere else?"

"I don't . . . I don't think so? What happened?"

"I don't know. You sit here with Locke. Don't move. I'm going to get help."

They sprinted toward Flight Control. The fire suppression system had kicked in, as had the emergency field, and the room at the back of the bay was now split down the middle by the blackness of space, held off only by a shimmering blue curtain.

Chae caught a burned Neo as they stumbled, but the big man was barely able to stand and there was no way they could support his weight. Chae looked around, spotted Kelly Evans from *Burden of Proof*. "Captain, come help me!"

Captain Evans rushed over, slipping under the big man's arm. "Hey, Lane, easy big guy, I've got you."

Chae slipped free. "I've got a few people by *Dread*; it's far enough away from this that it's probably a good spot for the medics to set up."

"Sounds good." Evans looked grim, her face streaked with soot. "There's more injured back there."

"I'll go." Chae continued on. The air filters were working to pull the smoke out, but the acrid stench was choking them, so they covered their mouth with their shirt as they rounded people up, grabbing injured Neos and civilians and sending them in twos and threes back toward the center of the bay.

They turned at the edge of the emergency field and their breath stopped at the sight of a familiar face. Akane, one of *Dread Treasure*'s petty officers, was half-buried under the wreckage of what looked like *Orbital Jam*'s bulkhead.

"Oh no." Chae dropped to their knees at the petty officer's side and felt for a pulse.

There was nothing under their fingertips and Chae choked back the tears as they leaned in around the wreckage and realized why. Akane had been thrown clear of the destroyed part of the bay, but she'd hit the hull of *Flux Capacitor* hard enough to break her neck.

"Chae!"

They almost sobbed with relief at the sight of D'Arcy. "Commander. She's—"

D'Arcy put his hand over Ito's unseeing eyes and the muscle in his jaw twitched. "There were explosions in Coms and Admiral Hoboins's office, too. Where's the rest of your team?"

"Nika and Max were testing helmets outside. Jenks was—oh god." Chae pressed a hand to their mouth, willing the nausea down with nothing but sheer force. "She was in Hoboins's office."

"Fuck." D'Arcy spit the word so viciously Chae couldn't stop from flinching. "Sorry, Chae. Come on. We'll have to leave her here for now."

"Who did this?"

"I don't know," D'Arcy growled. "But we're going to find out . . . and we're going to make them pay."

JENKS'S EARS WERE RINGING AND WHEN SHE MOVED, A HOT spike of pain shot through her side. "Fuck." She rolled onto her back and stared up at the ceiling. "What the fuck?"

She said it out loud but could barely hear herself. She wasn't sure if that was because of her ears, or because her brain felt like it was front and center at a stomp fest.

Her memory refused to dredge up anything past last night in the bar, but the blinking time stamp in her vision clearly said it was the following afternoon. "Maybe Max is right and I need to stop drinking quite so much, I do not—"

"Hey, we got a live one over here!" The unfamiliar voice echoed in her ears, competing with the ringing.

"Oh thank God." That voice seemed familiar, but she couldn't focus.

"You know her, Lieutenant?"

"Yeah, Chief Altandai Khan."

"Got her name in the system as an Interceptor crew—I'll mark her as alive and injured. Everything is fucked right now, even the handshakes aren't showing up properly. I don't know what they hit us with, but it is not good."

Jenks felt like there was something important she needed to remember, but she couldn't make it come to the front of her brain. "Someone tell me what is going on." At least, she was reasonably sure that's what she said. She tried to push herself upright, but a hand landed in the middle of her chest and pushed her back to the floor.

"Stay down, Jenks." She blinked again and Parsikov's face finally resolved itself.

"Tivo, what the fuck are you doing here?" She tried to shake the confusion off, but even that tiny motion made the room spin and Jenks had to squeeze her eyes shut as the nausea overtook her.

"We just got in an hour ago." He smiled down at her. It was gentle, a poor attempt to hide the fear in his blue-gray eyes. "I messaged you, but you were flagged as busy. I guess this counts as busy. Don't move for me, okay? Can you wiggle your fingers?"

"You said don't move."

"Jenks, wiggle your fingers."

She complied.

"How about your toes on your right foot?" There was pressure on the toe of her boot as Tivo reached down. "Good, left?"

Jenks sighed and curled her left toes. "What's the point of this, bright eyes?" The bits of Tivo's words poked at her memory and she tried to sit up again, hissing at the pain. "Wait, I'm mad at you. I wouldn't have answered you anyway, but I was busy."

Busy doing what, she couldn't seem to remember.

"I had my dog with me," she murmured, looking around. "We were—where am I?" There was nothing but debris in what should have been a pristine hallway, and less than two meters from her feet was the empty blackness of space held at bay by a shimmering emergency field. There was— "Why is there space right there?"

"Jenks, I really need you to hold still," Tivo ordered, his voice a fascinating mixture of frustration and fear that broke through her distraction. "There was an explosion and you've got a rather large piece of metal in your gut that I don't want to disturb. So, for once in your life, listen to someone else and stop moving."

"I listen to people." Jenks looked down and whistled at the shard of bulkhead stuck in her side. "That does look bad. Explains the pain, too."

"How bad?"

"Tolerable." She looked around. "What the fuck happened?"

"An explosion."

"I heard you the first time, Tiv. Don't—" Jenks broke off as *Wandering Hunter*'s medic slid to a stop next to them. "Hey, Master Guns."

"You go and get yourself hurt again, Chief?" The levity was forced and Jenks tilted her head at him in confusion.

"Unintentionally. What's going on?" She smacked his hand away before he could shoot her up with pain meds. "No. I don't wanna be all loopy. I want someone to explain to me what the fuck happened."

"Jenks." Tivo swallowed whatever else he'd been about to say when she gave him a deadly look.

"Why do you have to be so holy about doing things your way, Jenks?"

"Because it *is* holy, Quickdraw. So stop infringing on my religious freedom and tell me what the hell is going on."

"Someone hit us, Jenks," Josh replied. "Explosions in the Interceptor bay, Coms, and here at Hoboins's office. More pressing, you've got a forty-centimeter spike of bulkhead going through the left side of your stomach and your kidney. Only reason you haven't bled out is that the damn thing was hot going in. We need to get you to medical for surgery and that means you're going under." He jammed the shot against her arm before she could protest again and everything came flooding back to her, hitting like a second explosion.

Hoboins's office was on the other side of that black chasm. Was.

She couldn't process the thought without screaming and shut the door on that section of her brain as hard as she could. "Where the fuck is my dog?" she managed before unconsciousness slammed down around her.

AS MAX AND NIKA GOT CLOSER TO THE WRECKAGE OF THE station the damage became more evident. They wove through the debris at Doge's direction and though Max tried to keep her breathing even, her sob was loud over the com when they found the first body.

She'd reached out instinctively, but Nika stopped her with a hand on her arm. "We don't have anything to tow them back in with right now, and they'll throw off your momentum. You have to let them go."

"Who did this? Who could have done this?"

"You and I both know who."

The realization hit with the same power as the debris. "Oh god."

"Nika! Max! Can anyone copy me?" Sapphi's voice came over the team channel, startling both of them.

"We read you, Sapphi," Nika replied. "It's good to hear your voice."

"Oh thank the gods. Tamago and Chae are in the Interceptor bay helping with wounded. Where are you two?"

"Just hanging outside in the black."

"*What?*"

"The shuttle got hit with debris," Nika said. "Antilles and Jun are alive. We need someone to send a ship to fetch them."

Max was about to comment when Doge said, "Jenks's vitals have dipped again."

"Sapphi," Nika asked, "do you know where Jenks is?"

"Tivo just sent me a chat message, which in addition to the Babels are two things that are actually working, thank Hera. Can you imagine the shitstorm if we all couldn't understand each other? He's with Jenks and they're taking her to medical. She caught a piece of debris in the side and needs surgery."

"What's Tivo doing back here?" Max asked. "Where's my brother?"

"Search me. I can't get anything else to cooperate right now, LT. Whoever did this didn't only set off bombs but some kind of weirdness that's hammered the shit out of our coms, on top of the Coms *office* being a smoking crater. DD chips are sort of working, and I've managed to get our team channel stabilized. But handshakes and locators are fucked. We're—"

"Sapphi, we need you to focus—"

"I *am* fucking focused, Nika. I'm also pissed. Our friends are dead. Admiral Hoboins is dead. Jenks could have been—" Sapphi's sudden sobs filled the coms.

"Sapphi, breathe in and out for me," Max said gently. "This is awful, and we need to get inside so we can help.

Doge is telling us we can get in through airlock six-six-seven, but that's inside access only. Will you meet us there and let us in?"

"Yeah. I'm only a floor up from you, LT. I'll be there in a few," she replied. Max heard the connection cut off.

"There's a maintenance ladder up and over the other side." Nika pointed and Max reached out to link her gloved hand with his.

"We'll be okay, Nika."

"Sapphi's right," he whispered over the com, but he squeezed her hand back. "They wanted to hurt us."

"Yes. So we need to do what you just told Sapphi to do: focus. First we have to get inside. Then we need to get in touch with Stephan. If the *Laika* is back in port, we'll talk to Scott and get a secure com through the ship if we can. At the very least I can try to get a hold of Ria and route something encrypted through her." Max let her brain focus on the problem, drowning out the worry for her friends with an anger and determination to find the people responsible for this and make them pay.

You picked a fight with the NeoG, Senator. I hope you're ready for the wrath that's going to follow.

TWENTY-SEVEN

Nika stared, disbelieving, at the soot-streaked face of Captain Davi Kilini. "What did you just say?"

"I'm sorry, Nika." The Intel officer blinked rapidly but her tears slipped free anyway and slid down her cheeks. "The explosion was targeted. It leveled their offices. Stephan and Luis were working late. We got a positive ID off what we could find, but I—I don't have anything more right now." She glanced over her shoulder. "And I'm sorry to drop this on you and go, but I have to get back to this."

"No, I understand. We've got troubles of our own here."

"I know. Before I go, though, you're not alone up there, okay? Admiral Chen is sending emergency equipment your direction and the Navy's scrambling more ships. If he's alive, D'Arcy is the senior Interceptor commander there and currently the senior NeoG officer on board. And Admiral Christin from the CHNN is in overall command of the station until we can get a new NeoG staff sent your direction."

"I'll let D'Arcy know." Nika nodded. "Thanks, Davi. I appreciate it."

"I'll talk to you again soon, Nika. I'm so sorry."

The screen in Captain Troika's ready room on the *Laika* went dark. Nika pressed his fingers to his mouth, struggling to keep everything in before giving up and letting his own frustration pour out. He could hear Max crying behind him and her brother's attempt at whispered comfort.

"Fuck."

He shoved both hands into his hair and folded over, the anguished curses spilling out into the air around him. How had this all gone so wrong? Had Senator Tieg's people planned this all along or was it because of what had happened on Trappist?

Please, God, don't let us have been responsible.

But he was fairly sure that wasn't the case. This was too well-thought-out to have been a spur-of-the-moment response. This was terrorism without the fear of consequences— terrorism with no list of demands.

It was violence because it could be, and that's what scared him more than anything.

But that just made him—for maybe the first time in a year—more resolved to get into the thick of it.

To kick some ass.

He struggled to take a breath through the pain and started going over the next steps, trying to tamp down the angry voice in his head saying they should just fly to Earth and arrest Senator Tieg.

You know it won't bring him down. Stephan said as much. You'll have to be careful, Nika, smarter than them.

"Nika." Max laid a hand on his back. He looked up, and she was composed. Whatever grief she was feeling was packed away behind a calm facade. He worked to mirror her. "Tivo just messaged me. Jenks is out of surgery. We should go."

"Yeah." He straightened. "Commodore, can you tell Captain Troika thank you for the use of their coms?"

"I will. And I just got a message that the Off-Earth engineers have been retrieved and they're fine."

"Good. Thank you."

"Anything you need, Nika, just let me know. We've already got our people in the medical bay helping out, and we're going to put our maintenance folx to work cleaning wreckage out of the Interceptor bay as soon as we get the go-ahead." Scott held his hand out, gripping Nika's tightly when he took it. "The Navy is not going to stand idly by. An attack on the NeoG is an attack on all of us."

"We appreciate that."

Scott nodded grimly and touched Max on the back as he walked them out onto the bridge. They were greeted with solemn looks and soft words that continued as Nika and Max headed off the ship.

Words of sympathy, of support, of shared anger and determination.

He wanted to soak it in.

He wanted to scream that thoughts and prayers weren't enough.

But he just kept walking. Because he was a commander, and that's what he was supposed to do.

Max exhaled and rubbed a hand over her face as they came off the ship onto the dock and headed into the station, Doge still following at her side. "Nika, what are we going to do?"

"I don't know yet," he replied. "What I want to do is go to Earth and—"

"Me too," she said before he could finish the sentence. "And I also know we can't."

He dragged in another breath, fighting for the same well of calm he pulled from during sword matches. "Navy has station security covered. Right now our focus is our people. We'll tend to the wounded. Send our dead to their rest. Then we'll figure out what to do next."

"Do you think this was because of us? We spooked them on Trappist; was it bad enough to cause this kind of reaction?"

It was just like Max to have already thought of the question he'd asked himself. "I don't know. I don't think so. Julia's interaction with Chae didn't seem like someone who was spooked. This isn't the kind of thing you pull off on a whim. They had to have planned it." The warning Grant had given Jenks replayed in his brain and Nika swallowed hard. "They told us they were going to do something. I didn't even think they would—"

"Commander Vagin." The Neo at the door of the medical bay greeted them and pointed to her left. "We've got your sister in the room just down the hall. She's not quite awake yet, but I think the doctor is still in there with her, and so is Lieutenant Parsikov."

"Thanks, Mahira."

"Nika." Tivo looked up as they came into the room and got to his feet. Dr. Shaylan was bent over the bed, talking softly to a slowly waking Jenks. "She's okay. She'll be fine."

"What happened?" Max asked, then shook her head and clarified. "What are her injuries?"

"She was in the corridor outside Hoboins's office when the explosives detonated. I don't know how she survived."

"Doge," Max murmured, reaching a hand out to touch the ROVER's head.

Tivo took a deep breath, letting it out on a shaky exhale. "I owe you, dog, big time. A piece of shrapnel hit her in the left side, punctured her stomach and kidney. They pulled it and cleaned it out, but Dr. Shaylan wants to wait a few days before sealing her up for good just in case there's an issue." He looked down at Doge with a soft smile. "She was worried about you, buddy. Where'd you find him?" he asked Max.

"Outside."

"In the corridor?"

"In the black. We were testing helmets and . . ."

Nika crossed to the bed as Max and Tivo debriefed and their conversation faded into the background. "Doctor."

"Commander. Hey, Chief, your brother's here. You want to wake the rest of the way up for me?"

"No." Her grumpy mumble was accompanied by a flutter of eyelids and Nika smiled as he reached down for her hand.

"I brought your dog," he said. Doge nudged up against his leg and rested his head on the edge of the bed.

Her mismatched eyes were still clouded with confusion, but Jenks rolled her head to the side and smiled a lopsided smile at Doge. Nika let her hand go so she could pat the ROVER on the head. "Good boy. You saved my life."

"You are my friend," Doge replied.

Nika put his hand over hers. "How are you feeling?"

Jenks heaved a big sigh. "High." Then, like a switch had been flipped, she blinked and stared at him. "There was a bomb."

"Yeah, we know," Nika said at the same time the doctor said, "Easy, Chief." Shaylan put her hand on Jenks's shoulder and pushed her back down against the bed.

"One day I'm going to remember to not move when I'm injured."

"Not likely," Shaylan muttered, and moved away to check a monitor.

"Nika, what happened?"

"Explosions in the Interceptor bay, Coms, and where you were." He shook his head, making a deliberate choice not to tell his sister the rest of the news right now. "I'm sorry. Both Admiral Hoboins and Commander Seve were killed in the explosion. Our crew is okay, but there are other deaths, and we don't have a total yet."

Her expression didn't change, but he felt her hand flex where it was pressed between his fingers and Doge's head. "You all probably have work to do. You don't need to babysit me. Can Doge stay?"

Dr. Shaylan nodded from across the room.

Jenks groaned. "God, Nika. No one tell Luis, he'll freak

out. Just tell him I'm fine if he asks, I'm sure Intel will be all over this. I'll message him tomorrow."

Nika swallowed, the words stuck in his throat, and nodded. "Okay. Get some rest, and we'll see you in the morning." He leaned in and pressed a quick kiss to her head, turning away before she could see the tears.

Tivo and the doctor followed him out into the hallway as Max said her goodbyes to Jenks in private.

"What is going on?" Tivo demanded.

"There was a bomb—"

"No. There's something else. Something you didn't want Jenks to know."

Nika stared up at the big man with the awful realization that the news was going to hit him just as hard as it would hit Jenks. There was no easy way to do this.

"We talked to Earth before we came here," he replied, keeping his voice low and his words formal. "They hit the Intel building where Commander Yevchenko and Senior Chief Armstrong were working. Captain Kilini confirmed their deaths. They're gone." He grabbed for the lieutenant's arm as Tivo rocked backward, shock on his face. "I'm so sorry."

"What the—no, that's not—he can't—*fuck*." There was sadness and anger in the man's blue-gray eyes as he repeated the curse like a prayer and then his knees gave out.

Nika caught him around the waist, holding Tivo up with no small amount of effort.

"Chair. There's a chair over here." Dr. Shaylan took Tivo's other arm and ushered him into the seat, putting a hand on the back of his neck and pushing his head between his knees.

"Breathe, Tivo." Nika crouched next to him. "I'm sorry. I'm so sorry." He looked up and caught Max's eye as she came out of the room. "I'd stay, but I need to go find D'Arcy and tell him he's in command of the NeoG on the station for the moment . . . ," he said. But he couldn't make himself stand up. Knowing what to do wasn't the same as wanting to do it.

Max nodded. "I'll stay here. You go."

Nika got to his feet, the sound of Max trying to help Tivo with his grief following him down the hallway.

CHAE WAS FILTHY, EXHAUSTED, AND TIRED OF FINDING THE broken bodies of friends. Even as they despaired, crawling under a pile of rubble close to the emergency field, they knew it could have been so much worse.

The explosion had happened in the early afternoon, when most of the Interceptor crews were still in meetings or back in their quarters. A handful of ships were out on patrol and wouldn't be back for at least eighteen hours.

If the explosion had happened now, several hours later, the bay would have been packed with people. Two whole crews would have been in the Boarding Action freighter. The pieces of it that were left were currently being hauled away from the space outside the station by a pair of Navy ships. It had been blown out into the black when Flight Control went up in flames.

Chae dragged in a breath and held it, listening, praying they'd hear signs of life. Nothing but silence echoed back. They rolled onto their back with a sigh and started to scoot toward the opening at their feet.

Something protruded from the burned and twisted wreckage above them and Chae reached a tentative hand up to the mass of wires. They tilted their head, suddenly realizing that this was the edge of what was once Flight Control's massive window looking out over the bay.

And you are touching an explosive charge.

Chae yanked their hand back and then rolled their eyes. "It's so obviously been detonated." They fumbled in their cargo pocket for the pliers that had found their way into it during the chaos and reached up, prying off the evidence as carefully as possible.

They started to compose a message on the team chat that Sapphi had gotten up and working, but stopped just as abruptly. They had no way of knowing what was being monitored. Stuffing the evidence into their right cargo pocket, they slid free of the wreckage and scrambled to their feet.

"Whatcha looking for, Chae?"

Julia's voice raked over their spine and Chae tightened their grip on the pliers as they turned.

"Survivors."

She smiled. "Find anyone? Such a tragedy."

"How can you smile?" Realization dawned on them. "You did this."

Julia clucked her tongue at them. "We warned you, didn't we? Higher-ups decided that there was entirely too much sniffing around and it was time to put a stop to it."

"You were trying to kill us?" Chae tensed.

"Such a high opinion of yourself." Julia snorted a delicate laugh. "No, Chae. We hit the people we meant to hit." She gestured around the bay. "This was mostly to set the stage correctly for what's to come."

"And the problems with the coms? It's not only because you dropped a bomb in there, is it?"

Her smile spread. "You're so smart. That was just a little added test. A new EMP designed for coms only. Seems to be working quite well, doesn't it? A nice layer of chaos on the whole thing."

Chae's horror grew and Julia's smirk only served to destroy their tenuous hold on their temper.

"Fuck you!" They put all their fury and grief behind the punch and it snapped Julia's head back. She staggered away, holding her face, but Chae followed, hitting her again just like Jenks had taught them.

And this time they used the pliers.

Be relentless. Always press forward. When you're as short as we are you can't afford to let up on your opponent.

"Whoa! Whoa!" Hard arms locked around Chae and dragged them back. They struggled, but whoever it was didn't let go. "Chae, it's D'Arcy. Stand the fuck down, Neo."

"They've lost it!" Julia exclaimed, and Chae spit at her.

"She's responsible for this." They felt D'Arcy's grip loosen as the commander tried to process their words, and managed to slip free. Chae launched themself at Julia, hitting her around the middle and taking her to the deck.

"God damn it, Chae!"

"It's Julia!" they shouted, trying to get a grip on her as she screamed and thrashed underneath them. They heard the pounding of footsteps as their fight drew attention across the bay.

Someone grabbed Chae and pulled them up, but before they could protest again D'Arcy moved forward and put a boot in the middle of Julia's stomach. "You stay down," he ordered, the violence in his voice putting a jagged edge on each word.

"Chae, are you hurt?"

They blinked at Nika. He was dressed in an unfamiliar space suit—it was white, not covered in smoke or blood except for the smudges on his arms where he'd grabbed them. That threw Chae for a moment until they remembered Nika and Max had been outside testing helmets.

"Sir, it's Julia. I couldn't—she did this."

Nika's blue eyes went hard as he looked past Chae at the woman on the floor. He reached down, and Chae heard D'Arcy's indrawn breath and then the muffled clang as Julia stabbed at him and he blocked the knife with his right hand.

"Wrong move," he said with a sharp laugh as he disarmed her. "Ian, get her up and cuff her."

The lieutenant commander of ST-1, who'd arrived with Nika, nodded sharply and with D'Arcy's help hoisted Julia to her feet. "Where do you want me to take her?"

"To the *Laika*. Get with Scott. Quickly and quietly. And I want one of your team on guard at all times, no one else."

"You can't do this! I'm a civilian!" Julia protested.

Chae swallowed as Nika took two steps forward and got in her face. "You are under arrest."

"On what charges?"

"Terrorism." Nika fisted his right hand but kept it at his side. "And murder. And I'm sure many other things.

"Get her out of here."

Ian dragged Julia off and Chae sagged a little in relief.

"Did she hurt you?" Nika's demand was met with laughter from D'Arcy.

"She didn't have a chance, Chae was kicking the shit out of her. They whacked her with pliers."

"I wasn't really thinking," Chae whispered. "She was cruel. Delighted."

"It's all right." Nika reached out and touched Chae's face. "Still would like an answer, Neo. Are you hurt?"

"No." *Just my heart, sir.*

"Good." Nika smiled, and then it faded. "I talked to Earth," Nika said. "HQ got hit also. Stephan and Luis are dead—I don't know how many others."

We hit the people we meant to hit.

Julia's words slammed into Chae a second after Nika's, drowning out D'Arcy's whispered curse.

"Admiral Christin is in charge of the station for the moment. D'Arcy, you're the senior Interceptor commander and Neo on board. Admiral Chen says you're in charge of us until they get some staff headed our way."

Chae watched in stunned silence as D'Arcy somehow packed his grief away. The big man straightened immediately, shoulders pulling back, and he took a deep breath.

"All right. I'm going to need a roster list—not just Interceptor crews, but who was working in the bay and Coms and everywhere else. Since we don't have solid DD access at the moment, we'll have to do this old-school to make sure everyone is accounted for." D'Arcy rubbed a hand over his head. "Akane's dead. Someone should probably tell Sapphi."

"I can do it," Nika replied. "She went to Coms to see what she could do to help Sully after she let me and Max in. We checked on Jenks, by the way. She came through surgery fine."

"That's something, at least," D'Arcy murmured, putting a hand on Nika's shoulder.

Chae suddenly remembered the lump in their pocket. "Nika, I found something I think was part of a detonator in the wreckage."

"A detonator?" D'Arcy started to hold his hand out and then shook his head. "We need to take care of this first. There's still wounded in the wreckage. I'm going to go help."

Chae rubbed a hand over their face.

Nika looked at D'Arcy's retreating back, his mouth pulled into a tight line. "Julia wasn't working alone, Chae. We need to find out who else was involved. Hold on to whatever you found for now. We need to focus on our people—the answers can wait."

"I can go tell Sapphi about Akane," Chae offered, and Nika looked at them in surprise, then he nodded.

"Thanks, Chae. I'm going to stay here and help D'Arcy. You stick with Sapphi for now. I don't want you going anywhere alone. Hey, Lupe." He flagged down Spacer Lupe Garcia from *Dread Treasure*. "What are you doing right now?"

"Helping with wounded, sir."

"Go with Chae to Coms. Sapphi's up there and she could use your help."

Lupe nodded and held a hand out to Chae. They took it, finding some relief and solace in the feel of another hand in theirs.

When the world is ending, look to those who will hold out their hands.

Their father's words filled their head as they made their way out of the bay.

TWENTY-EIGHT

Two days later Max sat in the corner of ST-1's quarters as she cross-referenced the list of Jupiter Station suspects with the list of the dead and injured they'd pieced together. She recognized the irony that the only places she felt safe right now were in her own quarters or on a Navy ship.

"Hey, Max, do you read me?"

"Yeah, Sapphi."

"Oh, I can see you on the grid now! You're on the *Laika*, right?"

"I am. What's going on, Sapphi?"

"It's about fu—sorry, LT—it's about time, we finally have coms and everything else back up." The relief in Sapphi's voice was evident. She'd been working in Secondary Coms nonstop since the explosion to fix the damage caused by both the specialized EMP and the destruction of the station's main operations center. "There will be an incoming stationwide announcement shortly."

"Thanks for the preview, Sapphi. Good job."

Max went back to her work, barely acknowledging the announcement that came over her DD five minutes later. With the system back up, Max could now see the location of several of their suspects.

But three were missing.

"Did you get caught in the blasts you set?" she murmured. "Or did you have a way off the station before it happened?"

They'd locked down all traffic—military and civilian—for the last two days, but Max knew that wasn't a foolproof plan. Someone with a shuttle could have escaped in the chaos and been picked up outside of Jupiter Station. Especially since all their sensors had been down.

The news was already screaming about the attack, rumors and worse swirling both on the station and out of it that Free Mars had been responsible. The first time she'd heard it, Max's heart had dropped into the pit of her stomach.

It was what Tieg had planned all along. Pit the NeoG—no, not just the NeoG but the whole CHN military—against the people on Mars as a way to distract from what was happening on Trappist. Sow chaos and reap the unjust rewards. Yet something still seemed off.

"What is your real aim here?" Max wondered. "Is it just about the money, or are you after something bigger?"

"Lieutenant Carmichael?"

Max snapped back to the present, blinking at the petty officer standing in the doorway with a tray in her hands. The handshake over her head was active again and said *Petty Officer Allison Mayon, she/her.* "Yes?"

"The commodore said you hadn't eaten. I brought food in case you were hungry." The young woman had wide dark eyes set in a round face, and looked barely old enough to be in uniform.

"Of course he did." Max smiled and waved the woman in, getting to her feet to take the tray. "Thank you, Petty Officer Mayon, I appreciate it."

"Of course, ma'am." She turned back to the door, hesitated, and looked over her shoulder. "I know the Navy and the NeoG don't always get along, but I want you to know we're all very sorry about what has happened."

Max nodded, the sudden lump in her throat making words impossible. They still had to tell Jenks about Luis and she wasn't sure she could hold it together. The tray clattered loudly in the stillness as she set it on the table and pressed a hand to her eyes, trying to will the tears back down beneath the layer of duty she'd buried them under.

"Hey, Scott? Oh. Max."

Max dropped her hand and turned around to face Commander Laron Chau with a forced smile. "My brother is on the station."

"Sorry, just saw Carmichael on the locator and didn't think about the fact that you'd be here." He lapsed into silence for a moment. "You have my condolences, Max."

The sympathy surprised her. Max's first run-in with the combined SEAL teams at the Games two years ago had been full of veiled insults and thrown punches—plus one bar fight she was still getting teased about. Their interactions had mellowed out some since Max's reunion with her brother, but there was genuine sympathy in Chau's dark eyes.

Because, at the end of the day, we're about the mission, and not petty rivalries.

"We appreciate it," she said.

There was a moment of awkward silence, then Chau cleared his throat. "I'll leave you to eat, and then maybe get some rest? You look terrible."

He was gone before she could think of something to say in response. Max sighed and sat down to eat.

She was just finishing up when Nika came through the door. "Good, you got some food."

"Everyone's suddenly concerned with my eating habits?"

He smiled and sat. "You've been going for fifty-three hours straight with a short nap in the middle of it. I know you well enough to know that you've only eaten when someone has handed food to you."

"Maybe. What about you?"

"An hour ago," he replied with a soft smile. "I know I'm tired of being asked, but how are you holding up?"

"Teetering between wishing this was a dream and burying myself in the data because it at least makes sense. Except then I inevitably come across a name I recognize and start crying." Her stomach flopped in protest at the food in it when Nika glanced at the doorway and laid one of Sapphi's jammers on the table.

"I get it—I do. But . . . we need to talk about something else," he said in a low voice.

"What?"

"D'Arcy and Tivo were both on the station when the explosions happened, but I don't know where."

"There's a lot of people we don't know the location of, Nika, I don't—"

"Not with explosives experience. Not who knew about what we'd come back here to do."

"Oh, Nika, no." Max wondered if everything she'd just eaten was about to come up.

"I don't like it, either. The idea that our friends would do this cuts me to the quick. But we have to consider it, if for no other reason than to clear their names."

Max nodded slowly and traced a finger over the tabletop. "I know one person who may be able to tell us. I just don't know if you'll let me talk to her."

"Who?"

She looked up at him. "Julia. I can get her to talk, if you'll let me handle it."

Nika considered the suggestion, really considered it, and Max felt some of her painful tension release when he nodded. "I trust you," he said. "We need to go talk to Jenks first and then we'll go see what we can get out of Julia."

Max reached out and put her hand over his. "We'll get through this, somehow."

Nika blinked back the tears gathering in his eyes. "I hope so, Max. This is going to destroy her and I wish I didn't have to tell her."

JENKS KNEW SOMETHING WAS WRONG, SOMETHING BEYOND the numerous dead and the massive holes dotting Jupiter Station, but she couldn't get anyone to tell her what it was.

It didn't help that she still couldn't remember the last few hours before the attack, and that gaping hole hurt the same as the one in her side. It felt like there was something important she was missing.

Tivo hadn't come back to see her since he'd found her on the floor, and she'd only just kept herself from messaging him. She wanted to talk to Luis first. She'd found the email from him—the date was the same day as the explosion—but there hadn't been a reply from her.

Did I talk to him? The vague memory of a conversation with Max filtered into her brain, but Jenks didn't let herself chase it. She was afraid. Afraid that she hadn't talked to Luis and also afraid that she *had* and had carried through with breaking things off permanently.

Though chat and the coms were supposedly up and working, she couldn't get Luis to answer her. And for some reason no one would give her access to a tablet to call him directly.

JENKS: Hey, I'm sure someone has told you by now what happened. I'm fine, though. Just bored out of my mind because they won't let me get up. Please message me. I need entertainment.

JENKS: I guess I should have started that with "I accept your apology email and I want to talk about it." Maybe this

isn't going through. Sapphi claims coms are fixed but I
can't get anything on my DD.

JENKS: I know you're not ignoring me, but now I feel like
an asshole for ignoring you. Because not getting a reply
really sucks.

JENKS: I love you. I hope we can talk soon.

"Hey, Jenks."

She looked up and smiled at Max. "Hey, LT. Have you come
to spring me from this prison?"

"You're not cleared yet," Max replied with a tight smile,
stepping aside so Nika could follow her into the room. Jenks
frowned.

"I feel fine, though. Everything's healing up good, doc
said so this morning when she put the patch on." She looked
around, frowned again as her heart rate kicked up a notch.
"What is it?"

"Jenks." Nika cleared his throat as he crossed the room to
the bed. "I want you to know the only reason we waited was because the doctor thought it would be better for your recovery."

She let him take her hand even though her first instinct
was to pull away.

You don't have to close yourself off, Dai.

She didn't know where those words came from or why
they were in Luis's voice in her memory.

"I mean, this whole thing has sucked." She squeezed Nika's
hand and attempted a smile. "Whatever it is, we'll get through it."

Max made a noise like she'd been punched in the gut, but
Jenks kept her eyes on Nika.

He looked down at their joined hands and when he lifted
his head there were tears in his eyes. "Jenks. When the explosions happened here . . . Earth also got hit. Luis is dead."

All the air left her lungs.

"No."

"I'm sorry, sis. I'm so sorry."

You promised me tomorrow.

Max had covered her mouth with her hand, but Jenks met her anguished gaze past Nika's shoulder. There were unshed tears in Max's brown eyes and a depth of sadness she could feel in her own heart.

But she kept the tears in, slipping easily back into the protective mode that had served her well for so many years.

Everyone leaves. Always.

Jenks packed it all back into the box in the corner of her heart and looked at Nika. "Do we know who's responsible for this?"

Nika fumbled at the pointed question. "It doesn't matter right now, Jenks. How can we support you?"

"The fuck it doesn't matter." She didn't raise her voice but he flinched anyway. "Who did this?"

"They're saying it was Free Mars, but there hasn't been an official statement," Max replied.

That was a lie, and looking into Max's eyes she knew the LT didn't believe Free Mars was responsible, either. She knew it as well as the beating of her broken heart. Free Mars had no reason to attack the NeoG like this. No reason to restart a conflict that had hurt both sides so badly after nearly three decades of peace.

"Was it *them*?" she whispered.

"We think so," Nika replied.

"Okay." She nodded. "Well, if you need me, you know where to find me." She gestured at the bed with a bitter smile and saw the confusion flash across their faces.

"Jenks—"

"I'm fine. I'm sure you all have things to do." She squeezed Nika's hand and then let it go, leaning back and closing her eyes.

They left and as soon as she was alone, Jenks pressed both

hands to her face, curling into a ball and letting the silent tears come.

A cold metal nose poked her and she wrapped her arms around Doge's neck, ignoring the pain of her wound. "Am I awake, Doge?"

"Of course you are. Why?"

"I'm hoping for a nightmare."

"You are sad."

"Very. Luis is dead."

"I don't understand."

"Switched off, for good." She pressed her forehead to Doge's as a fresh wave of tears started. "Oh god, Riz and Elliot. His mothers. How am I going to tell them?"

"This does not make sense. He is not off."

"I know, Doge." She squeezed her eyes shut. "It's so much worse than that."

"OH, I RATED THE FAMOUS LIEUTENANT CARMICHAEL," JULIA said, sitting up in her bunk as Max and Nika approached her cell. "Savior of LifeEx, darling of the NeoG."

"Diego, open it up," Nika said. The petty officer nodded and hit unlock, disabling the field. "Get up, Julia, we're going to have a conversation." He watched her green eyes narrow, but she got to her feet and sauntered forward.

"Chae said you were thinking about getting out, but looking at you now I'm quite sure they were trying to play me. How long have you known they were working for us?"

"You mean, how long have we known you were blackmailing them with threats against their family?" Nika replied, leading her to the interrogation room on the other side of the brig. "Long enough. Sit down." He pointed at the chair.

"This is a waste of your time. I'm out as soon as my boss hears of it." Julia sat. She crossed her legs, hooking one arm over the back of the chair and smiling at him.

Nika felt his anger swell, but before he could snap a reply, Max stepped in.

"Bold of you to assume she will hear of it. Is Julia your real name? Or did you steal that along with the job from the Off-Earth woman you killed?" She sat in one of the chairs on the opposite side of the table.

"It is my name. I didn't kill anybody." She shrugged. "And my boss hears about everything. People get chatty when they're comfortable, when they think they're alone." She smiled at Max. "How's your friend Jeanie?"

"Still alive. She said you're all welcome to try again."

"Oh, my boss will. If you don't let me go, you're painting a big target on the backs of everyone you care about."

Nika's stomach twisted at the easy threat, but Max seemed unmoved.

"Here's my offer: you answer my questions, help us take your boss down, and *maybe* I'll turn you over to the CHN for trial with a recommendation for a reduced sentence. If you choose not to cooperate, well, we did just have a terrible attack on the station."

"So?"

"All sorts of people were killed."

Julia looked from Max to Nika. "Nothing to say, Commander? I guess we know who's in charge around here."

She was scrambling and Nika made his voice as emotionless as he could. "Answer the question, Julia. Are you going to cooperate with us?"

"Why should I? You wouldn't dare. People saw me in the bay. Someone will talk."

"You hurt *my family*."

Nika had never heard that snarled tone from Max, not even when she'd been so angry at him on *Zuma*'s bridge. The lieutenant hadn't moved a muscle and Julia's expression grew more desperate.

"My boss will come looking for me."

"No. Your boss will find your name among the dead of Jupiter Station and move on." A cold smile touched the corner of Max's mouth. "And no one here will lose any sleep over you."

"You won't kill me. You don't have it in you."

"I'm not going to kill you, Julia." Max stood with a second smile. "I'm going to put you in a hole so forgotten that no one will ever find you, and I'll let you stay there until you rot. Not CHN. Not NeoG. The black is a *big* place." She tapped on the table twice and headed for the door. "You're not the only one with powerful friends."

"You're bluffing."

"And you're just a pawn that's about to be taken off the board."

"Wait!"

Max turned back around, a single eyebrow raised in question.

Julia hesitated. "I have proof that Melanie Karenina of Trappist Express is involved in all of this, but she will kill me if I give it to you."

"You're already dead. If you tell us now, though, they won't know otherwise until it's too late. We'll keep you safe." Max lifted a hand. "Understand, this isn't because I care what happens to you. It's because I want the people you work for and you can give them to me."

Nika held his breath as Julia's shoulders dropped. "All right, I'll do it."

Max crossed back to Julia and sat down. "You understand I will be recording this conversation and any and all parts of it may be treated as evidence against either you or others. Do you agree to this in exchange for a possible reduced sentence for any crimes you have committed?"

"I do."

"Then start talking. Tell me everything."

TWENTY-NINE

Max stood at Nika's side, the rest of the crew behind them. The other Interceptor teams were clustered around like the broken family they were. There were holes, gaps where the missing should have stood. Akane, Shay, Boris, Sui, Yang, and Winnie.

So many more. It hurt to even try to list them all.

Four whole teams down. Eight ships damaged or destroyed. *Zuma* would have been right in the blast zone if the ship hadn't still been in the repair yard on the other side of the station. Too many other people killed or injured. People she'd worked with, laughed with.

People whose families would mourn them.

Max wanted to scream her fury into the black.

She'd cried on the coms with Rosa and Ma once they'd gotten everything back up. The former *Zuma* members had offered to come to the station, but Max told them to stay put and stay safe. The warning had been intentionally vague, but she could tell it had gotten through.

"Admiral Hoboins used to tease me that the way I talked would make a poet cry." Admiral Kassandra Christin didn't bother to hide the tears tracking down her dark face. "He wasn't wrong. I've never been one for flowery words or useless phrases, and truth be told neither was he.

"We're here today to grieve the loss of a man who knew the meaning of service and the goodness of humanity. We're here to remember him and all the others who were taken from us in this terrible act. People who were our friends. Our family."

The Navy admiral looked around the room. "I know we are hurting and I know we are angry. But I want you all to re-member that you were Lee's family. He devoted his life to the NeoG and believed in its mission to protect humanity no mat-ter where they live. I also know he was deeply, deeply proud of every last one of you."

Max knew without looking that the noise from behind her had come from Jenks. That inarticulate sound turned into a barely audible whisper. "I can't. I can't do this."

There was murmuring and Max turned to see D'Arcy step back and pull Jenks into his arms. Jenks didn't fight him, burying her face against his chest. The big man whispered to her as she sagged against him, and when he lifted his head the anguish in his eyes took Max's breath away.

Could a person really fake that kind of emotion?

She hadn't been able to get confirmation from Julia about who exactly on the station was involved. According to the woman, her boss kept things fluid and gave Grant a lot of leeway to do whatever was needed to recruit people.

In this moment, Max couldn't bring herself to even con-sider that D'Arcy had been responsible, not without losing her tenuous grip on the calm facade she'd built around herself.

But she hadn't argued with Nika about the need to double-check the decisions D'Arcy was making about the station or that it was better for her to do it than anyone else.

Admiral Christin kept talking, but Max didn't really hear the words. Her mind focused on the quiet sobs, the rustling sound of Neos embracing one another, the words of comfort being whispered back and forth.

You really would have been proud of us, Admiral, she thought. *Coming together like this.*

The crowd broke up as Admiral Christin ended the memorial and a chat notification popped up in the corner of Max's vision.

SCOTT: Max, we're in the back. Come find me when you're done.

MAX: Headed your way now.

She looked behind her, but D'Arcy and Jenks had already vanished into the mass of people so she turned back to Nika. "Scott's in the back with Tivo—we should go talk to them. D'Arcy's got your sister, he'll look after her."

Nika sighed and rubbed his thumb over the back of her hand. "I hate this, Max."

"Me too. Let's go get it over with. Tivo will have an alibi. He wouldn't have helped with this." Even as she said the words she thought of Chae, sabotaging the ship and nearly killing them all in the process because they were so desperate to keep their family safe. Would Tivo have done the same?

Would you have done it, Max? If you were the one who had to keep people safe?

The sounds of raised voices broke into her thoughts and a sudden shift swept through the energy of the crowd, grief changing to anger. Max shared a look with Nika before they both started pushing their way through the assembled people to the source of the shouting.

Commander Alice Trine of *Avenging Heroes* was facing off with Commander Janelle Pham of *Sol Rising*. The tiny trans woman was barely taller than Jenks, but Max already knew she hit like an asteroid and right now she stared up at Alice with her hands open but fury in her eyes.

"Free Mars was responsible, Janelle. So how do we know he wasn't involved? He used to be one of them." Alice flung a hand in D'Arcy's direction. Jenks stood in front of him, one hand pressed to her side, the other clenched in a fist.

Janelle took a step closer, ignoring *Heroes'* master chief, Paula Sox, who was trying to keep them apart. "My best goddamned friend died in this attack and you want me to believe one of our own was responsible? Past is past, Trine. D'Arcy wouldn't have done this and you shouldn't be parroting rumors about Free Mars as if they're facts."

"I don't want to go up against you, Janelle, but you need to get out of my way. He has to answer for this!"

"Fuck you." Janelle laughed. "You think you can make it through me, you're welcome to try. And I'll tell you now, you won't get through Jenks, wounded or not."

Alice's gaze flicked over Janelle's shoulder to Jenks. "How can you stand there and defend him when Luis is dead?" she demanded.

The sudden hush that fell on the crowd was what Max imagined getting sucked into the black without a suit felt like. She tensed, waiting for Jenks to launch herself at the commander, but her friend just stared.

There was a long moment of quiet where no one even seemed to breathe.

"Shame on you." Jenks lifted her chin. She looked from Alice to the others in the crowd. "Luis would have been the first to tell you that D'Arcy is one of us. He also would have said: How dare you do this now. When we are grieving. When we are hurt. When we should be living up to what Admiral Hoboins saw in all of us, what he was so proud of having helped create here."

Max watched as some of the Neos on the other side of the

divide shifted uncomfortably. Jenks hadn't even raised her voice, but her words were clear and struck with calm precision to the heart of the matter.

"Shame on all of you," she said again, turning her back on the crowd. D'Arcy put an arm around her shoulders and helped her out of the Interceptor bay.

Max met Paula's gaze and stepped forward. "We're done here, people. Go grieve with your friends." She put her hand on Janelle's shoulder. "Come on."

"Back it up, Commander," Paula said to Alice, and only then did Alice tear her gaze away from Janelle and walk away. "I'm sorry, Janelle," Paula said. "For that and for Shay."

The commander waited until Paula had also walked away before pressing a trembling hand to her lips and turning into Max's embrace.

"I know, I'm so sorry," Max murmured, pressing her cheek against the top of her head.

"Lieutenant, I can take her," Inaya Gorelik said, and Max nodded, allowing Janelle's ensign to lead her away.

She felt Nika's fingers wrap around hers and fought to keep her own emotions in check when all she wanted to do was turn around and let him convince her that this was a terrible dream.

NIKA WATCHED MAX PACK ALL HER GRIEF BACK DOWN INTO some safe place inside her before she headed for the door and wondered how long it was going to be before she allowed herself the space to feel anything.

He hated that he couldn't give it to her.

"Max?"

She turned at the sound of Scott's voice, offering up a poor shadow of a smile at her brother and Tivo.

"We've got almost everyone accounted for now that coms are back up. I'm having the shuttles do a second sweep to look for bodies." Scott reached out and took Max's arm in a gentle grip when she stumbled. "When did you sleep last?"

"When everything wasn't on fire? I don't remember," she whispered, and Nika mouthed, "Yesterday," when Scott shot him a look.

"As soon as we're done here you're going to lie down."

"You're not the boss of me."

Nika swallowed his amusement at how much Max sounded like his sister in that moment. "He's right, Max. You need some rest. And a reminder that I am actually the boss of you, so I'll make it an order if I have to."

She grumbled but didn't protest and they walked the rest of the way to the conference room in silence.

Nika pulled his sword off his belt as he hit the doorway. They'd all been armed for the last week, unsure whether another attack was coming. Max and Scott had agreed they probably should stay armed for this confrontation with Tivo, just in case.

Scott put his hand on the hilt of his sword. "Lieutenant, take a seat."

"What's going on?" Tivo looked away from Max as Nika laid his sword down on the table and leaned both hands on the top.

"Sit down," Nika repeated. "I'd like you to tell us where you were when the explosion happened."

Tivo stared at him and then looked to Scott. Nika watched as the realization dawned in Tivo's eyes. There wasn't any anger on the heels of it, just grief as the man sank into the nearest chair. "You think I was involved?"

"I think I want you to tell me otherwise," Nika replied. *Please, for my sister's sake at the very least.*

"You took off as soon as the ship hit the docks, Tivo," Scott said. "Why?"

Tivo rubbed the back of a hand against his jaw. "I was looking for Jenks," he whispered. "Luis had sent me a message that he'd apologized to her and they'd talked. He said she'd promised to at least hear me out. I went straight from the ship to the Interceptor quarters, but missed her." He looked up at Nika. "I ran into Tamago, who said she was with Admiral Ho-boins, so I thought I'd just head up there and wait. I was in the low-g tube when the explosion happened. At that point I just started gathering up injured. I met up with a few others who were doing the same thing and we worked our way toward the admiral's office, where we found Jenks.

"I've never been so relieved in my life," he whispered, drop-ping his head into his hands. He lifted it, looking at Nika. "I swear to you I wasn't involved in this. Whatever you need from me to prove it, just tell me."

"Tamago confirms seeing him," Max said. "I'm having Sapphi pull the surveillance for the quarters and the transfer tubes."

Nika nodded. "You saw what happened in the Interceptor bay with some of the crews, Lieutenant. You're a demolition expert who knew about our operation. You understand we have to investigate every possible avenue here."

"I get it." Tivo glanced Scott's way. "I don't like thinking that my friends don't trust me, but I get it. This is why you didn't put me on rotation for guarding the prisoner, isn't it, Commodore?"

"At Commander Vagin's insistence, yes." Scott nodded.

"If it makes you feel better, he argued with me," Nika said. "He trusts you."

"You still don't." Tivo's declaration was flat and Nika couldn't argue with him. "I cared about Luis. I care about your sister. I wouldn't ever do anything to hurt them."

"I don't doubt that," Nika replied, but he didn't have time for Tivo's indignation. "Chae also cared about us and they still put us in danger to keep other people they loved safe. These people we are chasing are ruthless. I won't apologize for being cautious about who I trust." He held his hand out. "For what it's worth, I want you to be telling me the truth."

Tivo took his hand. "Just tell me what I need to do to get you to believe me."

JENKS LAY IN HER BUNK IN THE DARK, THE SOUNDS OF HER crew sleeping around her. She'd been awake for an hour, her mind insisting on replaying the fight she'd had with Luis and Tivo back on Trappist-1d in a loop.

She slipped out of bed, wincing at the movement. Her temporary release the day of the memorial had turned into a permanent one, but the doctor had warned her to take it easy.

She'd managed it for a day, but lying around seeing Luis's face in her head was killing her.

Messages of condolence were piling up in her DD. There'd even been one from Asabi Han, though Jenks had shuffled it off with all the others into a folder marked *No* without even opening it.

"Where are you going?" Doge's question was over their personal com so no one else could hear them, but Jenks still froze, almost laughing at the instinctual feeling of being in trouble.

"Out. You stay there and be quiet."

"You should not be up."

"I'll be fine. I'm going for a walk. Don't argue with me." Jenks finished pulling a hoodie on over her tank top and pointed. "Do what I say, you damn dog." The ROVER dropped his head back down onto his bed and she ignored the guilt clawing at her as she slipped out of the Interceptor quarters.

Jenks took a deep breath and continued through the mostly deserted corridors, making her way toward Corbin's as she tried to stay afloat through the endless waves of memories washing over her.

She stopped at the door. The place wasn't crowded and there was a hushed, almost churchlike quality she'd never in her life seen there before. Jenks rolled her shoulders and stalked to the bar, shoving aside the Navy captain who had the bad luck to be in her way.

"Hey! You—" His protest cut off, his eyes widened, and he took a step back.

"Did you have a problem, Captain?" She felt her blood sing at the prospect of a fight, drowning out the grief in her chest.

But he shook his head and took a step back with his hands raised. "No, Chief, not at all."

"Chief, should you be up?" Tussin asked with a frown.

"I'm going to be sitting down right now. I'm here for a drink," Jenks replied, slapping her hand on the bar, wincing as pain shot through her at the motion. "Vodka. Right here."

The owner of Corbin's studied her for so long Jenks contemplated climbing over the bar to get it herself, even though she knew it would probably rip open the heal patch on her side. Then the man nodded and grabbed for a bottle, pouring out a shot and sliding it across the bar to her.

Jenks held it up with a bitter smile. "To the honored dead and all that." She knocked it back, closed her eyes against the burn of it, and set the glass down. She gestured to Tussin and was surprised when he poured her a second without protest.

"Life fucking sucks, doesn't it?" She drank it and held out the glass.

"Hey, Chief, that's probably enough. Let's get you back to quarters."

Jenks spun on Petty Officer Piper just before he could put his hand on her shoulder, and she would have laughed at the collective indrawn breath of everyone in the bar if she hadn't been trying to keep from screaming. "I like you, Piper, but unless you want to fight, don't touch me right now."

"Chief, don't do this. I know how you feel."

"How I feel? I feel like I want another drink." She raised her voice. "And then I want at least one of you to find some fucking courage and take a swing at me."

THIRTY

"Max, Jenks left."

Max rolled over and blinked groggily, jerking in surprise when she realized Doge's muzzle was right in her face.

"I disobeyed," the ROVER said. "She told me to stay and be quiet. But she needs you."

"Where did she go?"

"I don't know. She turned off her locator again. I hate it when she does that; it makes me feel alone."

"Me too. Good job, Doge."

Max was out of her bunk and tugging on a sweatshirt when the emergency call came in from Petty Officer Piper. "Carmichael," she answered.

"Hey, LT, sorry to wake you—"

"I'm up. Is it Jenks?"

"Uh, yeah. How'd you know? We're in the bar. She's trying to get someone to fight her."

"I'm on my way." She didn't waste time waiting for Nika, but sent him a priority message as she ran out the door, Doge on her heels.

Max made it through the station in record time, skidding to a stop outside the bar and then slipping through the crowd. Jenks was in the middle of the room, one hand pressed to her side and the other raised as she desperately tried to get someone to fight her.

But everyone in the bar, even the Navy personnel, were well out of reach, their hands up or at their sides.

"Damn it, Jenks," Max muttered. She knew exactly what was going on: her friend was looking for something, anything, to take the place of the pain that was choking her.

"Hey, LT, how do you need us to help?" Piper asked when she found him.

Max took a deep breath. "First, nobody intervene. Even if she throws a punch at me. She's looking for a fight; don't give her one."

"Nobody wants to, LT," replied a burly naval warrant officer by the name of Seaux. "But we don't want her to hurt herself or you, either."

"I know, but let me handle this. Doge, you sit and stay." She stepped into the empty space. "Jenks."

The whole bar held its breath as Jenks turned.

"What do you want, Max?"

"Come with me, please." Max held her hand out.

"I don't want to."

"I know, but you need to."

Max knew that belligerent set to her friend's jaw all too well, but the wobble was something new and it nearly destroyed her own carefully crafted composure. "You going to throw a punch at me if I won't, LT?"

"No." Max shook her head, attempted a smile.

"Fuck." Jenks blew out a breath and winced as she shoved both hands into her hair. "Why won't anyone fight me?"

"Because we all know you're hurting enough." Max took another step closer. "This won't make it better, honey."

"I don't want better. I want this feeling gone." Jenks

slammed a fist into the space above her heart. "Make it go away, Max. Please."

"You know I would walk through fire for you." Max shook her head once, tears in her own eyes. "But this? I can't fix this. All I can do is sit with you while you grieve."

"I don't want to grieve," Jenks whispered, the rage washing out of her face. "Grieving means he's gone." She stumbled forward, crumpling into Max's arms with a wail that broke the heart of every person in the room.

"He can't be dead, Max! He can't have died thinking I was still mad at him."

"I know, honey. I'm so sorry." Max sank to the floor, rocking Jenks in her arms, oblivious to the rest of the bar.

Nika was suddenly there, wrapping his arms around them both. He pressed his cheek to Jenks's, murmuring words of comfort.

"Let's get her back to quarters," he whispered after a moment, and between the two of them they got Jenks back on her feet, ushering her through the silent crowd. Doge followed behind.

"I'm sorry." Jenks's whispered apology was barely audible. Max could only watch as Nika closed his eyes, the pain overwhelming him.

"I know, my sister, I know." He pressed a kiss to the side of her head. "Come on."

They got Jenks back into her bed and Tamago crawled into the bunk with her, wrapping their arms around Jenks and crooning softly until she fell asleep. Doge lay down on the floor next to her bunk, his head between his metal paws.

Max didn't argue with Nika when he ushered her into his room and closed the door. "You're about two seconds from cracking," he said, sitting next to her on the edge of the bed and rubbing her hands between his.

"I can't fix this," Max whispered. "I want so desperately to fix it and I can't."

"I know, none of us can. All we can do is be there for each other."

Max let out a shuddering breath and leaned into him. "Do you mind if I stay?"

"Not at all." Nika stood and pulled the covers back, lying down, and Max crawled into bed next to him, curling against his side. She closed her eyes as Nika turned off the light and lay there, listening to the thumping of his heart in her ear. The steady rhythm had almost lulled her to sleep when he spoke.

"How did you know what was going on with Jenks?"

"Doge woke me up, said she'd left. He was worried." A curious thought about the ROVER's emotions wandered through her head, but it lost the battle with her exhaustion and Max dropped into oblivion before she could say any more.

CHAE RUBBED BOTH HANDS OVER THEIR EYES AS THEY SAT AT the table in the common room of their quarters. The last few days had bled together, a haze of grief and pain they still couldn't quite believe was real. You couldn't go anywhere on the station without stumbling upon someone in tears.

Jenks was a ghost, drifting through the crew quarters with Doge at her heels, spending most of her time working on the ship in the repair yard. All her laughter and jokes crushed into dust under the weight of her grief.

They rotated who was with her by some unspoken agreement, trying not to leave her alone. If she realized it, she didn't protest, which was worrisome in itself.

Cascade failure, been and gone. Can't fix anything now.

"Chae," Tamago said, and they froze as their crewmate put a hand on their shoulder. "How are you?"

"Not great." The truth came surprisingly easily, as did the apology that spilled out after. "I'm so sorry. I didn't—"

"I know." Tamago squeezed their shoulder and sat down. "I know you weren't involved in this. Whatever happened before, you wouldn't do something so terrible. I'd been thinking a lot about what happened, Chae, and then this . . ." There were tears in their eyes. "I *saw* you helping our injured. I saw you finding our dead. You didn't stop, even with the grief and exhaustion pressing you down.

"I'm no Buddha," Tamago continued with a sad smile. "It's going to take me a while to trust you the way I did when you first joined us, but I'll try."

"I want to earn your trust," Chae whispered. "You had every reason to be angry with me. I deserved it. There's a voice in my head telling me this could have been avoided if I'd told someone what kind of trouble I was in when I first got here."

"I think you should realize you weren't responsible for this. Really let it sink in. This was part of their plan from the beginning," Nika said from the doorway. He crossed the room and laid the jammer on the table. "Max and D'Arcy are on their way. Do you have the detonator?"

Chae caught their breath, their heart rate skyrocketing as their adrenaline spiked in anticipation. "It's in my trunk." They hopped up and crossed the room to retrieve it, noting that at the same time Tamago got up and took their sword off the rack by the beds.

D'Arcy and Max came into their quarters, the LT closing the door behind her. Nika got up and took the detonator from Chae, holding the bag up for D'Arcy to look at.

The big man frowned when Nika didn't hand it over and glanced at Chae. "You found this in the bay? Where?"

"Edge of what was left of Flight Control's big window." Chae shook their head. "I don't know which edge."

"Bottom left, most likely. It would have been out of sight. They couldn't have put it there more than an hour before the explosion, though. Hiding the explosives themselves would have been slightly easier, but an inspection sweep would have caught this."

"Unless someone on the inspection team was convinced to look the other way."

He looked up at Nika. "There was supposed to be an inspection that morning."

"We know, I have the list," Max replied. "I remembered yesterday that I'd said something to Nika about maintenance just before we saw Hoboins's office explode and I narrowed my search. Petty Officer Uileg was out sick." She took a breath. "Paul took over for her, D'Arcy. We didn't tell you, but he's on the list of suspects Stephan gave me."

Chae held their breath. Warrant Officer Paul Huang had always been nice to them, and the thought that he was involved was a kick to the stomach.

"That's why Stephan sent the rest of my crew back to Jupiter." D'Arcy looked at the ceiling. "And you didn't tell me because . . ."

"We weren't entirely sure you weren't involved," Nika finished.

"I see." D'Arcy laughed bitterly. "Was Jenks defending me after the memorial just for show?"

"You think she would do that?" Max replied. "Jenks didn't know about our suspicions."

"You're right," D'Arcy said, dropping into a chair. "She would have just kicked my ass. Is that why you've been like a shadow the last few days, Max?"

She nodded and D'Arcy sighed. "So, what's changed?"

"What changed," Nika said, sitting next to D'Arcy, "is we got a partial fingerprint match back this morning on the guts of this detonator. I have your schedule, D'Arcy, and surveillance puts you across the station that morning when Paul was setting these detonators in the bay during his inspection walk."

D'Arcy surged to his feet, making Chae jump. Max and Nika had been expecting it and neither reacted as the commander headed for the door.

"Get out of my way, Lieutenant," D'Arcy said when Max didn't move from in front of the door.

She smiled and shook her head. "When you're calm, we'll go get him. I've got station security on standby. But this door doesn't open until I know you're not going to do something rash."

"He killed Akane. He killed *Hoboins*."

Chae's eyes filled with tears at the pain in D'Arcy's voice.

"I know. He killed a lot of our family, and I'll be damned if I let him take you down, too." Max held her hand out. "You do what you need to right here to get it out of your system, and then we go."

IT HAD TAKEN D'ARCY LESS TIME TO CALM DOWN THAN NIKA had expected, and the four of them headed through the station toward the Interceptor bay where the locator said Warrant Officer Huang was working on *Dread* with Lieutenant Commander Locke.

Max was talking quietly with station security and with her brother, the force they'd assembled a combination of people Max had personally cleared.

Nika was on edge. The anonymous message he'd received this morning had simply said: *Your sister is in danger.* Nika had wanted to put an armed guard with her, but they were too shorthanded as it was. He had to go with D'Arcy, so he'd sent Tivo to the repair yards where Jenks was working on *Zuma*.

Surveillance records had shown that Tivo was exactly where he'd claimed to be in the aftermath of the explosion, and Max hadn't found anything else that would implicate him. Even with that intel, though, Nika had to hope he wasn't making a mistake.

Sapphi was also with Jenks—neither of them knew about Paul or what was about to go down. Max had agreed with him that it was for the best, and thought having Tivo there as well would make things easier all the way around.

"She needs him," she said with a sad smile. "Even if she won't admit it to herself."

Nika agreed. His next concern was in front of him. "Are we going to be able to get Paul back out of here without a riot?" he murmured as they hit the far door to the bay. Cleanup was well under way, and the area was teeming with Neos.

"Maybe," Max replied. "Scott's got people on all the doors. D'Arcy, you may want to walk a little less like you're ready to kick someone's ass."

"Hard to do."

"Try harder."

D'Arcy slowed down and shifted the snarl on his face into a more neutral expression.

"Hey, D'Arcy," Locke said as they approached. "We got the rest of the components in on yesterday's freighter. Ship should be up and running in a few days." He spotted Chae. "Especially if the spacer there can help me out again. Lupe's been busy putting the station back together and I just sent her to quarters to sleep for at least twenty-four hours."

"Sounds good," D'Arcy replied without slowing, and Nika couldn't stop him from grabbing Huang by the shirt front and propelling him hard into the side of *Dread Treasure*. It was a little surprising there wasn't a dent left behind. "You son of a bitch."

"Damn it, D'Arcy," Nika muttered.

"I expected it," Max said, shrugging at his exasperated look. Locke was staring at them in shock, but Nika was more interested in Paul's reaction.

The warrant officer was smiling.

"Five years," D'Arcy said, fists tightening in the man's shirt. "We've been friends for five years."

"We were friends for two years," Paul countered. "Then I found out the man I admired was nothing more than a fucking habitat terrorist and the Guard I respected had allowed him into their ranks like he belonged there."

"What the fuck is going on?" Locke demanded.

"Take a step back, Steve," Max replied.

"You murdered our people," D'Arcy snarled. "For what?"

"The greater good."

Nika heard Max ordering security to move in even as Locke put everything together and launched himself at Paul. D'Arcy was faster, letting go of Paul to catch his lieutenant commander and propel him away.

"You stay right there," Nika said to Paul. A crowd was gathering, but Nika leaned in as the security forces cuffed the warrant officer. "I want you to know, the people who convinced you to help—they lied. This wasn't for some lofty purpose. You betrayed your friends. You betrayed the ideals of the NeoG for a bunch of criminals looking to get rich. That's all."

He stepped back, watching the confusion and horror flash through Huang's eyes. "Get him out of here."

Luis—

I know you're dead and you're not reading this, but fuck it I'll keep sending these emails for as long as I can because otherwise I will completely lose it.

I almost walked out an airlock yesterday. I ditched Max, everyone's been following me around worse than Doge, and stood there for a solid two minutes staring at the panel. It was so fucking tempting. Just me and the black and some peace. Over and done. You know I'm not a believer. There's no afterlife where I get to see you again. You're just gone.

Obviously I didn't do it, but I wanted to. I should probably tell Nika about it, or Max. Or my therapist, who's pissed I keep skipping my sessions. Someone. I just don't want to put this on them on top of everything else.

Damn it, I know I fucked it up breaking my promise. I know I've got a terrible temper and I should have let you apologize. Why does this shit world not allow for happy endings?

I'm trying, but it's hard to find reasons to keep going.

Your Dai, always.

THIRTY-ONE

Jenks felt, rather than saw, someone stop at the engine room door, but she didn't react and instead kept fighting with the bolt that refused to screw down correctly.

"How much of this work have you done yourself?"

It was Tivo. She slid out from under the pipe and looked up at him. "You haven't been paying attention, have you? This is the NeoG. We don't have people to do our work for us, Lieutenant."

Tivo smiled and leaned against the doorway. "Fair enough."

Jenks eyed him. "Are you here as my bodyguard or to keep an eye on me?" She gestured with the wrench. "I haven't had a minute to myself, except for yesterday, since the fucking explosion, but Sapphi's on the bridge and so is Doge. He's still mad at you, so fair warning, you might get shot."

"Do you want me to go?"

I want Luis back. Which even I know is an awful thing to say to you of all people so I'm going to keep my mouth shut. Look at me, growing up and shit.

He was trying to help. They all were. Ma had sent her four messages she hadn't answered and Jenks knew that he would likely fly all the way out here to kick her ass if she didn't reply to him soon. She also knew that Luis would have told her to stop fighting everyone every step of the way, but she couldn't seem to do that, either. She took a deep breath and rubbed at her forehead with the back of her hand.

"No, you can stay. I'd say make yourself useful, but Navy lieutenant and all."

"Ouch. I'll have you know I haven't gotten lost on a ship in at least two years."

"Yeah, but are you any good with your hands?" She hadn't meant it like that, but Tivo's raised eyebrow and wicked grin made her laugh.

It hurt, but it also felt kind of like relief. Jenks choked on the feeling. "Damn it, you asshole. You know that's not what I meant."

"I do, but Luis told me the easiest way to get on your good side was snark and innuendo, so here we are." He approached, carefully, like she was some kind of wounded animal who might bite.

Aren't you?

"You two talking about me, then?" She refused to speak in the past tense. Couldn't make the words leave her mouth even though she knew she should accept it.

"At the risk of inflating your ego, we did, a bit." He reached out, paused. "Can I touch you?"

"No." She shifted away, tried to ignore the pain in both her heart and her side. Touch was comfort and she didn't want comfort. She wanted to hold this fury close.

It's going to burn you up, Dai, staying closed off like this. You need to let people in.

Jenks flinched from Luis's voice in her head. Words she didn't remember hearing kept flashing through her brain. She'd woken up that morning with Hoboins's voice telling her he was proud of her, a strange echo of the words Admiral Christin had said at the memorial.

"Jenks, how can I help?" Tivo whispered.

"By leaving me the fuck alone. I don't need help." *I need Luis to be alive and for this whole thing to have been a terrible nightmare.* She shoved to her feet and slammed the wrench into the bulkhead. "I don't need anyone!"

Metal clanged against metal, the reverb a shock to her hands, but she kept at it—again and again—and every swing dragged pain up past the grief. "It wasn't supposed to be like this. I didn't get to say goodbye, I didn't get to tell him I loved him." She collapsed against the bulkhead and slid, sobbing, toward the floor.

Tivo caught her before she hit and this time Jenks clung to him. "Shh. I'm sorry, Pocket. I'm so sorry."

"If I tell you I thought about walking out an airlock, will you report me?" The words hurt coming out of her throat, but she made herself say them. She couldn't have Luis back, but she could follow the orders she kept hearing in her head, no matter how hard it was.

Tivo made a pained noise and tightened his arms around her, pressing a kiss to the side of her head. "I'll have to, Pocket, you know that."

"I want to make this all go away. I want to be gone so I don't have to feel anything. Then I think about how it'll hurt everyone who's already hurting and I don't." She buried her face against his chest. "I just don't think I can keep going like this."

"I appreciate you telling me and I'm here for you, whatever you need. Luis wouldn't want this for you. He was so relieved you two had talked and—"

"We didn't talk," Jenks whispered. "I didn't get to say good-bye. I was too busy being angry."

"Jenks, how much of the day of the explosion do you remember?" He leaned back and cupped her face. It hurt to meet his gaze but she made herself.

"Not much," she admitted.

"I have something I'd like you to read."

The notification popped into her vision. Jenks opened the email and all the air left her lungs.

Tiv—

Just got off the com with Dai. She let me apologize, after trying to break it off, because I fell in love with the most stubborn woman in the entire universe. One of these days I'll get her to realize how amazing she is and that she's worth every drop of love I can squeeze into the time we have together.

I know you're set to hit the station again. See if she'll talk to you. I can't guarantee she won't take a swing first, but she did promise to listen and she might accept your apology. Just don't fuck it up.

Give her a kiss for me, if she'll let you.

I miss you both.

Luis

The world went gray around her.

"Hey, hey, breathe for me."

Jenks dragged air into her uncooperative lungs and blinked until Tivo's face refocused in front of her. "I don't—I don't remember talking to him."

"I know. I know. It happens." He touched his forehead to hers. "But you *did* talk to him. I don't know what was said, but from his message it seemed like good news. I was on my way to find you when the explosion went off." She saw the composure finally crack and his own grief spilled through. "I came so close to losing both of you."

"I keep hearing his voice in my head. Words I don't remember him saying, but maybe . . ." Jenks closed her eyes for a moment and then forced herself to meet Tivo's gaze again. "Luis has always been on me about being more vulnerable, about letting people in. Especially the people I care about. All I want to do is shut everything down, but I can hear him in my head telling me not to and maybe those are the last words he ever said to me." She swallowed and whispered, "I'm lying about not needing anyone.

"I need you," she said. "I need my brother and Max and Tamago and everyone else. I can't do this on my own, but I don't know how to ask for help. I'm no good at it. So please be patient with me?"

"It's okay." Tivo shifted and pressed a kiss to her forehead. "I'm here and I'll help you however you need. Starting with finding someone for you to talk to."

"She's got a damn therapist if she'd just talk to her."

Jenks choked on a laugh when Sapphi's voice echoed from behind them.

"I didn't mean to eavesdrop—okay, maybe a little. But Doge wanted to zap the lieutenant and I thought maybe that was a bad idea, so I promised him I'd come check and make sure everything was okay." Sapphi took a breath, dropping to her knees next to Jenks and wrapping her arms around her friend. "I know I'm babbling but I can't help it. I'm sorry. I love you, how can I help?"

Jenks pulled Sapphi into a hug. "I love you, too, and I don't know. But thank you for being here."

"Promise you'll go talk to your therapist."

"I promise, Sapphi."

"SO YOU TRUST ME NOW, RIGHT?"

Nika glanced in D'Arcy's direction as they headed for the low-g tube. "D'Arcy, I trusted you with my life before all this. I just knew other people wouldn't. Why do you ask?"

"I don't like the feeling rolling in my gut, Nika. This was too easy. They hit us without even a hint of what was going down. What happens when they do it again?"

"I don't know," Nika replied, keeping his voice low even though they were alone in the corridor. "Max is working on something, but she doesn't have enough of a plan put together yet."

"Do you think this operation is why Stephan wanted us all to go to Trappist?"

"I know it is—he told me that before I left Earth. It all goes back to Trappist, D'Arcy, and they're trying to start this war with Free Mars purely to distract from it."

"Sacrificing hundreds of thousands of people just to make money." D'Arcy muttered a second curse. "At least the Free Mars leadership denied responsibility."

"We just have to hope that cooler heads in the CHN will prevail on that front, while we work as fast as we can to bring Tieg down."

They walked along in silence until they hit the tube and Nika followed D'Arcy down to the gym. D'Arcy grabbed the practice swords off the wall and tossed one in Nika's direction.

"There's something else I wanted to talk to you about," D'Arcy said.

Nika looked around. The gym was empty for the most part. There were a few smaller groups of Neos talking quietly, some seeking the solace of the weights or the treadmills to ease their pain.

D'Arcy saluted with his sword. "I know what I'm about to say doesn't seem important now, but it is."

"What's that?" Nika saluted back.

"This." D'Arcy struck and Nika brought his sword up to parry. "*Dread*'s out of the running, Nika. Even if I wanted to bring in someone to replace Akane, and . . . Paul. It's too close to the prelims."

"The prelims?" Nika spun sideways, his sword arm moving automatically, slipping under D'Arcy's guard and scoring a touch with a midtoned buzz from the sword. "That's the last thing on our minds at this point."

"It should be the first. Listen to me, and then when you're out in the station, look around. This hurt us, Nika, and it was meant to."

They fought in silence for a few minutes, the only sounds their breathing, the slide of feet across the mat, and the dull chime of swords.

"You and *Flux* have the best chance of winning the prelims now, and you're the recognizable teams," D'Arcy said, lowering his weapon. "They're not going to add five teams from the waitlist, not with this short a notice and this grief hanging over everything. So the field will be smaller. If you all are at the top of your game, you'll do fine."

"We're not at the top of our game, though. Jenks isn't in any shape to fight. I'm not sure she will be in a little over two weeks."

"I suspect you won't be able to keep her out of the cage if she wants to go." D'Arcy stepped back and dropped his sword. "I also wouldn't put it past her and Max to fudge how badly she's hurt, just as a heads-up."

"That does sound like them." Nika rubbed his free hand over the back of his neck. "Recommendations on how to handle it? I don't want to put her at risk."

"Again, I don't think you can stop her. I just don't know if she wants to fight."

Nika thought of the hour he'd spent before this in the medical bay with Jenks, listening to his sister's quiet confession that she'd been considering killing herself and the relentless ache that was causing in his chest.

She was back in their quarters now, the doctor having agreed to release her provided someone was with her at all times. They didn't have the room for her in the med bay with all the wounded still recovering from the attack, and whatever answers Jenks had given Dr. Shaylan and her therapist had seemed to weigh the balance in her favor.

"I don't know, either," he finally said to D'Arcy. "I don't

know what losing Luis will do to her love of the Games. It doesn't seem worth it."

"I know, but it is." D'Arcy exhaled. "This is as much a political fight as it is just a game. If you've got a better way to show these bastards we're not beaten, I'd love to hear it. But in my mind, getting out there and competing in the preliminaries is the best 'fuck you' we have."

MAX STARED AT THE IMAGES HANGING IN THE AIR IN FRONT OF her eyes. It was one thing to help Stephan with his investigation and quite another for her team to have to take it on themselves. She felt like she was starting from scratch and trying to piece together a broken mirror.

Even with the information she'd gotten from Julia, Max wasn't sure how to close that last gap and work up charges against the three people at the top that would stick.

"I wish I'd thought to ask you what you'd already tried and discarded, Stephan," she murmured to herself, reaching out to flick the photo of Melanie Karenina into the foreground.

Sapphi had added to the bios on all the suspects over the last week, mercilessly exploiting her hacker contacts in (and, more accurately, *out of*) the system to build out fairly robust profiles. And the more Max learned about the woman, the more she disliked her.

She'd had it all. A two-time winner of the sword competition in the Games, an excellent career with the NeoG, and none of it had meant anything to her.

The problem, Max knew, wasn't trying to figure out who was responsible. Stephan had put together a solid case on that front. It was figuring out how to make these very powerful people pay for what they'd done.

"That's a look I'm glad I'm not on the receiving end of," Nika said, sitting down next to her. "What are you thinking about?"

"Trying to remind myself why flying to Earth and stabbing

a CHN senator and the CEO of Trappist Express would be ill-advised."

Nika lifted an eyebrow, seemingly unsurprised by the vitriol in her voice. "Probably a bad idea, yes."

"My name might keep me from getting killed," Max said with a bitter smile. "The irony of it finally being worth something doesn't escape me. God, I can hear my mother's disappointed voice now."

"I'd rather you stick around here. We need you."

She ran a finger over the back of his hand with a soft smile. "Jenks is in one of the spare rooms with Tivo. I think she's finally sleeping."

"Good."

"I feel like I let her down," Max whispered. "I should have pushed harder, paid more attention. I didn't even realize she'd wandered away from me to that airlock. When I think about what almost happened, Nika, I—"

"Max, you were not only grieving like the rest of us but trying to figure out how to bring these people down. Don't blame yourself for not managing to be everything to everyone. That's why we're a team." He looked a bit rueful. "One day, we're all going to remember we can't do everything for everyone at once."

Max laughed, the sound a surprise to her ears, and she rested her head against Nika's shoulder for a moment as the feelings overwhelmed her.

"You okay?" he murmured against her hair.

"Yeah, it's been a hell of a week."

"Tell me about it."

She lifted her head. "I'm proud of us, though, coming together when we could have splintered apart."

The moment the words left her mouth she realized how true they were and saw that knowledge reflected in Nika's blue gaze. The members of their team had, in the face of this fire, pulled together even more than any of them expected to.

Chae and Tamago had their heads together in Chae's bunk and Max was relieved that Tamago seemed to have forgiven the younger Neo. Sapphi was sleeping in the other private room after Max had threatened her with a trip to medical if she didn't stop and rest.

They were working together and talking to one another, even with all the chaos of reconstruction and a new NeoG admiral thrown into the mix. Max knew Jenks would be struggling for a while, but she was trying and that was enough.

"There's something else, too. D'Arcy thinks we should make a push for the prelims. Show these people they haven't beaten us."

"*Dread*'s out," Max said, and Nika nodded.

"Yeah, he told Admiral Chen. *Green Machine* lost three members. *Sol Rising* lost Shay, and *Orbital Jam* lost Commander Roussel."

"I liked Shay," Max said, swallowing back the tears. "I'm going to miss sparring with her. It scares me how much I want to make them hurt for what they've done, Nika."

"I know." He took her hand and squeezed it. "And we will, but not by flying to Earth and stabbing them, okay?"

"Can we keep it as a backup plan?"

He wondered if Max knew how much she sounded like Jenks at times. "Yeah, we can keep it as a backup plan. Now, I know you, so tell me what you've been working on."

Max shared out her DD view with him. "I was thinking about what Chae said to Julia about you. According to her she passed that message on before the explosion. How do you feel about using yourself as bait to get Melanie to come to Trappist?"

"Welcome, everyone, to TSN—The Sports Network— where we are starting the second day of the preliminaries for the NeoG. The fight to decide which two teams will go on to compete in the Boarding Games is already in full swing here. I'm Pace McClellan, and with me as always is Barnes Overton."

"Hey folx, as you all know we're dealing with a decidedly different tone this year, as the attacks on the NeoG that happened just a few short weeks ago have made things very subdued."

"That's true, Barnes. Our hearts go out to the families of those who were hurt and killed in the attacks. There was a lot of discussion over the last few weeks about whether these games were even going to happen given that multiple NeoG teams were effectively knocked out of the prelims."

"A lot of discussion, yes. But what we've heard repeatedly from the Neos themselves is that they wanted to compete to honor their fallen comrades, and I can't say I blame them. Though what a rough thing to do, to put aside your grief and focus on the Games instead."

"It's a hard choice to make."

"It is and it isn't, Pace. I served in the Navy, and I have to say that if we'd been hit like the Neos, I'd like to think I'd be raring to go, too."

"From a former Boarding Games champion to your ears, everyone. So let's take a look at where the action has gotten us so far. As we get things started here on the second day of competition, *Zuma's Ghost* seems to be leading the field. In fact, if you're joining us to watch Chief Altandai Khan step into the cage, that's what's coming up next."

"It's interesting, because even prior to the attacks, there were a lot of rumors about whether *Zuma* would suit up given the major personnel turnover they had with the departure of Commander Rosa Martín Rivas and Master Chief Ma Lěi. However, so far it looks like the whole team is focused on taking the number one slot, and I'm here for it."

"Playing favorites?"

"Hard not to like back-to-back champs. I think they can at least defend their NeoG title for a third time."

"It's not an unrealistic goal, Barnes, no matter how new this crew is. We're seeing Chief Khan come out onto the floor now. Jenks, as I'm sure most of you know her, is a crowd favorite, and normally easy to spot even when she's not competing. But she has been less visible for these preliminaries than previous ones. Why do you think that is?"

"Well, we know she was injured in the attack on Jupiter Station, but the details on how are pretty sparse. I'm guessing she's been trying to downplay any injuries to avoid giving her opponents an advantage. More than that, though, she's undoubtedly mourning the loss of her friends."

"Undoubtedly. Jenks is stepping into the ring now—let's see how she handles her first fight . . ."

THIRTY-TWO

"That's match! Winner on points, Chief Khan."

Jenks grimaced at *Avenging Heroes'* fighter, Petty Officer Daly Hunter. "Good fight, Hunter." She meant it to be a smile, but wasn't sure her mouth knew how to do that anymore. Daly didn't seem to need it; he just nodded in return.

She exhaled, touched her index and middle fingers to her mouth for a moment, and pointed them up. The cheers of the crowd fell silent at the tribute and Jenks headed out of the cage.

News cameras were flying around, thicker than usual, but Jenks didn't pay them much attention. At least until the sight of Asabi Han stopped her in her tracks.

"That was quite the fight," she said with a smile. The star was dressed in impeccably tailored pants and a deep blue shirt.

"I'm sorry I didn't answer your email." Jenks closed her eyes briefly with a muttered curse at the ridiculous words coming out of her mouth.

"Oh no, don't apologize. It's perfectly understandable. I just wanted to let you know I was thinking of you." Asabi glanced around. "Do you have a moment? Somewhere more private we could talk?"

"Locker rooms are this way." Jenks couldn't quite believe it as Asabi fell into step beside her, bodyguards trailing behind, and soon the sounds of the academy gym faded into nothing more than a muted roar.

Asabi's bodyguards had stopped at the entrance of the locker rooms and Jenks grabbed for a towel, scrubbing at her head as she tried to think of something to say in the silence.

"I am so terribly sorry, my friend."

Jenks looked up and Asabi was holding out a hand. She didn't think as she took it, but the act of grabbing on to someone seemed like a natural thing to do lately.

Even if the trans woman was still practically a stranger.

They'd exchanged a few emails before the explosion, indulged in some harmless flirting over SocMed that drove their fans wild, but never in a million years would Jenks have considered that someone like Asabi thought of her as a friend.

"I am lost without him," Jenks whispered, trying and failing to offer up a smile.

"I cannot imagine how you feel." Asabi squeezed her hand. "I wish the world were a kinder place where good people didn't get hurt so often."

"We fought before the explosion," she said. She couldn't tell Asabi the whole story, but Jenks could tell her that much. "I was so mad. I apparently talked to him just before, but I don't remember."

"Would you forgive him again if you had the chance?"

"In a heartbeat."

Asabi touched the fingers of her free hand to her lips and gestured upward. "He knows, then. Trust in that small comfort."

Jenks stepped into the offered circle of Asabi's arms. Her chest was a confusing mass of feelings, but for a moment it all slipped away. "I appreciate you coming to watch a fight."

"I wouldn't have missed it. I wish I could stay longer." Asabi smiled as they separated. "I know you're busy and I've taken up enough of your time. Please stay in touch? I'm here if you need anything at all."

"I will. I promise." She waited until she was alone in the locker room to press her hand to her side.

"I just exchanged hellos with Asabi Han," Max announced, looking somewhat dazed as she came in. "She said she was very excited about my piloting competition. Was that your doing?"

"We're apparently friends." Jenks grinned and then winced.

"You hurting?"

"Fuck yeah." She didn't look at Max, but there wasn't any point in denying it. On a good day she should have finished a match against Hunter with either a knockout or a lot more points. "This might not go very well, LT."

"Not if you're dragging ass."

Jenks looked at Max in shock until her friend laughed.

"Seriously, Jenks—you won. You keep doing what you can until you can't. You know Nika's going to be pissed when he realizes we weren't entirely truthful about how well you've recovered?"

"I know, and I'll take the heat for it, but I had to do this." She offered up a half-hearted smile at Max and the other woman crossed the locker room to wrap her arms around her. Jenks leaned into the embrace. "He'd want me to keep fighting, right? I'm not just fooling myself about that to justify getting in the cage?"

"You're not. We all feel like that, Jenks, to varying degrees. But we need to keep doing this—"

"Until we can't."

"Yeah. This is so much more important than just the Games."

"You don't have to tell me. Or the rest of the crew. Sapphi's still not sleeping well. Tamago's doing a good job holding it together for all of us, but I think they're going to burst any second. Chae's maybe doing the best of us all." Jenks sighed and turned to look at Max. "How are you?"

The question seemed to surprise her and Max stared at the bank of lockers for a moment before she found the answer she was looking for. "Scared," she whispered. "Scared of how angry I am all the time now. Scared for the NeoG, scared for everyone I care about. I know how these people operate, Jenks, and they think they're untouchable."

"I'm going to do a lot more than touch them."

That got the smile Jenks was aiming for and Max pressed their foreheads together with a sigh. "There hasn't been a good time to tell you this until now, but when I saw Doge out there in the black and thought you'd—"

"You're gonna make us both cry, LT, and you've got a piloting semifinal that you need dry eyes for." Jenks squeezed Max tight. "I know," she mumbled. "I know how you feel and I love you, too. Go on. Tell Chae to soar like an eagle."

"Get some rest."

"I'll try to pass that message on to my head."

Max snorted.

Jenks stretched experimentally, wincing at the sharp pain, and headed for the showers.

Normally this time would be filled with watching endless footage of her opponents for the prelims, but Jenks cued up a different set of files on her DD chip as she showered, dried off, and changed into clean clothes.

The files were on the only opponents who mattered. All the faces and names from Project Tartarus were slowly resolving out of this blurry mess of pain. She knew the others were doing the same thing—they'd talked about it before leaving Jupiter Station, when Sapphi had told them she'd managed to find a way to lock down their team server so that no one would be able to get into it.

Nika had gone for it and surprised Jenks by ordering

Sapphi to load all the information they had on the operation into the team server. From there they could all access it, and Jenks had taken the opportunity to download every bio they had on potential suspects.

"Hey, kiddo."

She looked up at the familiar voice, an indescribable feeling of love flooding her chest. "Ma."

The retired master chief crossed the locker room and scooped Jenks into a hug. She clung to him like he was the only solid thing in the world.

Ma held her just as tightly, until gently setting her down. As usual there were no useless platitudes from him. He just touched his forehead to hers and looked her in the eye. "You didn't message me back."

"I know. I'm sorry."

"I get it. Max told me." He paused, studied her. "Where are you?"

"Still here, Master Chief."

He smiled and patted her face as he straightened. "You were dropping your left elbow a lot in the fight. That where you got hurt?"

"Yeah. Piece of shrapnel right in my side, nearly took out my kidney."

Ma reached in and touched her where the wound was, applying just enough pressure to make her wince. "Still sore?"

"Still healing," she admitted. "Plus Hunter got a good punch in." She'd never lied to Ma and she wasn't about to start now. From the minute she'd set foot in *Zuma's Ghost* the man had been like a father to her.

You know, the last time that thought crossed your mind Hoboins died.

Jenks cleared her throat, dancing away from the pain with practiced ease. "You bring the girls?"

"Nope, just me and Rosa."

"Rosa's here, too?"

"She went to watch Nika."

"That's good. I was about to head that way myself. Now I have company." She looped her arm through his and rested her head against his shoulder. "It's good to see you."

"Likewise, Chief."

Jenks didn't even bother to hide the smile that put on her face.

NIKA TOOK A DEEP BREATH AS HE SALUTED SENIOR CHIEF JEN Davis with his sword. The fighter from *Super Nova* met him in the middle of the ring and gave a little nod as they tapped each other over the heart with the points of their swords. Their suits lit up in the flashing notice of a mortal wound.

The crowd stayed quiet as the fighters backed off and the referee reset the match. They'd repeated this ritual with every sword fight. Nika hadn't been sure of the reaction when he'd suggested it, but all twenty members of the NeoG competing in the sword had responded yes without hesitation.

Now the fight was on for real. Jen was Nika's height, but he remembered her being fast and he realized as she moved in that she'd gotten faster over the last two years.

The whistle was loud in his ear. "Point to the senior chief!"

The red mark on his suit pulsed just above his left hip and Nika smothered a curse.

Get out of your head, Vagin. You know what you need to do. Just let your body do it and stop fighting it.

Stephan's orders were firm and as Nika took a second deep breath, he spotted Rosa off to the side. She had her arm around Jenks's shoulders and was whispering something to his sister.

The vibration of feet hitting the mat dragged his attention back to the fight, but Nika didn't panic. He lasered in on the action, and as he ducked under Jen's swing, he grabbed her front leg and pulled. Her footing slipped and she went down.

His sword arm had started the motion before he'd even touched her leg, and the tip hit the same spot he'd tapped before the match, lighting up her suit.

"That's a kill shot. Match, Commander Vagin!"

He held a hand out and she took it with a rueful grin. Nika pulled her to her feet. "Good fight, Jen."

"Was it? Over a lot quicker than I wanted. Should have known those stories about you losing your edge were just stories." She hugged him. "It's good to have you back in the ring."

"Good to be back."

Nika slipped under the ropes and into Jenks's arms. "Smooth," she said.

One of the things that really hurt about all this was how subdued she was. This was Jenks's second-favorite time of the year, but it was shadowed by so much pain.

"How was your fight?" he asked.

"Easy peasy." She shrugged. "Won on points."

"Against Hunter?"

"Yeah." She moved out of the way before he could push, but that alone was enough to tell him D'Arcy had been right in his guess that Jenks would fight even if she wasn't fully healed. She should have destroyed Hunter, and Nika wondered if it wasn't just an injury that took their fight to the limit.

He wondered if his sister had gone the full three rounds for the punishment.

Before he could say something that would certainly get him punched, a friendly voice said, "Nika," and Rosa wrapped him in a hug. He hugged her back, somehow translating all the unspoken things he needed to say into the embrace. When she pulled away, there was sadness in her eyes. More important, though, there was love. "There are no words," she whispered. "So we let God pull our prayers from our hearts and our tears."

"From your mouth to Saint Ivan's ears." He managed a smile. "Hey, Ma."

"Nika." Ma hugged him so tight Nika felt a rib pop. "It's good to see you."

"Likewise, although my ribs might disagree. How are your kids and grandkids?"

"Doing well."

"We've missed you both. How are things down here?"

"Tense," Rosa replied, slipping her arm through his as they followed Ma and Jenks back through the crowd to the locker room. "The explosion was close enough to the academy to make all of us wonder if we're next."

"You won't be." Nika shook his head and Rosa lifted an eyebrow at him.

"You going to tell us what's going on?"

"I can't. I can tell you it wasn't Free Mars, but that's all for now." Even that was technically forbidden, but this was Rosa. Yet apparently that magnanimity wasn't received in the way he hoped. He knew he was in for a fight because of the way Rosa's lips drew into a thin line. "Listen—I'm not putting the two of you and your families at risk, and telling you would put you at risk. Please, don't argue with me."

"Hoboins, Lou, everyone else." She shook her head. "They were our family, too, Nika."

"I know," he replied. "Believe me, I do. But the people responsible are dangerous, they've proven that already. I've let too many friends die. So you have to trust me on this and stay out of it."

Rosa opened her mouth to protest, but Jenks's quiet "Please" rocked through the room.

"All right," Rosa said, sharing a quick look with Ma. "We'll keep our noses out of it—*for now*. But if you need us, you call us."

"I'll always need you, Rosa."

She laughed.

"Seriously—we will."

Rosa seemed to be able to accept that, nodding at him.

"We're going to head for the hangar and catch the rest of the semifinals," Ma said. "I hear your new pilot is better than me."

"It's a possibility. Paired with Max, I think they could eventually set all the records."

"That good?"

"It helps that they have young eyes, I'm told."

"Did you go through asshole training when you got your promotion?" Ma asked.

"I'm told I come by it naturally. Ma, I make fun because I miss you," Nika said, and it had the bonus of being the truth. "Look, I'm going to clean up. How about you two go ahead and Jenks and I will meet you there?"

"Sounds good."

"You know they're not going to keep their noses out of it," Jenks murmured as the pair walked away.

Nika sighed. "Yeah, I rather expect not. But hopefully we can keep them at enough of a distance that they won't get caught up in the real serious shit."

"I know." She bumped her shoulder into his. "You should do that kind of quick-and-dirty fight more often."

He glanced down at her. "To be perfectly honest I got distracted by you and Rosa and just reacted."

She reached up and tapped his head. "You always seem to do better when you stop using this, which is ironic, I know."

"That sounds very much like something Stephan told me. That I needed to stop fighting myself so much and just let my body do its thing."

Hoboins had said the same thing to him, Nika realized.

It was going to take a long time before these memories didn't feel like someone was pouring ice into his heart.

"He wasn't wrong." She smiled sadly. "I know I have a reputation for being impulsive. Like sister, like brother?"

"Except you're not," he replied. "You're always watching vids and practicing. You go in more prepared than anyone."

"Sure. But I've got the disadvantage, yeah?" she asked, gesturing at herself. "Too short for the cage in theory, but I make up for it by using what I do have."

"Which is what?" Nika asked the question even though he already knew what she was going to say. He'd listen to her for an hour if it meant there was some life back in his sister.

"I can hit hard and get hit hard. Now this"—she grabbed for his right hand—"this isn't a liability, Nika, it's an advantage. Did you know you can catch a sword with it? Like in the ring? It's not against the rules."

It took him a minute to understand what she was saying. "Grab a sword with my hand?"

"Exactly. I got to thinking about it after Max told me Julia stabbed you on the station. She said you said it didn't hurt, not like if you'd actually gotten stabbed. So I went looking through the comp rules and can't find a single thing that would disqualify you if you pulled something like that in the ring." She grinned up at him. "Someone comes in on you, rather than blocking with your sword, you catch with this hand and boop—poke 'em in the heart."

"Poke?" He didn't hide the grin and she rolled her eyes.

"You know what I mean."

He did, and now that the idea was in his head he could already tell it was going to put down roots and grow. "It'll be most effective the first time. I probably don't want to waste it."

"Yes. But once you do it, they'll still have to consider it as part of your repertoire. How many of them are going to be able to adjust to an idea they've never encountered before? To try to ignore all their muscle memory? So don't overthink it. If you have an opportunity to use it, use it." She shrugged and he saw the wince even though she tried to hide it.

"How are you?"

"I'm fin—" She stopped and took a breath, wincing again as she muttered a curse. "I hurt. Everything hurts, Nika."

He carefully wrapped his arms around her shoulders,

pressing a kiss to the top of her head. "I wish I could make it go away for you."

"I know. We don't get to do that, though." Her voice was muffled against his chest. "This sucks. I'm supposed to be having fun, but how can I when our friends are gone?"

"You don't think they'd want you to?"

Jenks pulled away and tossed her hands up in the air, and Nika muffled the urge to tell her to stop moving so much. "I think that the world was fucking ending and people still went about their lives as if it weren't. Shit, Nik. If I've learned anything from all those memes and jokes in the early days of the Collapse, it's that some people were screaming and the rest of them? They just went about their day. 'The Collapse will be televised,'" she muttered spitefully.

Nika wasn't sure where she was going with her off-topic rant, but he knew enough to just let her get it out. She'd eventually hit on what was really bothering her.

"Did you know that in 2019 and 2020 there were fires in what used to be Australia where more than a billion animals died and still they didn't do anything?" Jenks shook her head. "They called it Black Summer. It was the beginning of the end, but it was forgotten about so fucking quickly by the rest of the world. Shit, in part because of the pandemic that followed, but that didn't even faze them, either!" She hooked her hands behind her head, grimacing at the pain. "I kind of understand it. It was too much to deal with. Part of me wants to just forget and go have fun like I always have."

"Oh, Jenks." Nika closed his eyes as the pain in her voice spiked against his.

"I think humans are hardwired against our own self-interest. It's a goddamned wonder we are still alive. There were kids who tried to speak up about the looming climate crisis. Know what they got for it? Death threats and mocking. Told to shut up and sit down.

"And the adults in the room? They argued over the colors

in reports and who would pay for what. It was always about the money, but in the end no one could eat that, could they? They made people go to work while they were dying. And here we are, right back where we left off with these fuckers doing the same goddamned thing. It's all about money, and fuck everything—and everyone—else."

There it was.

"I'm supposed to go out there and smile and fight and pretend like I'm not dying inside. And I get it, I really do. This is important, to show them we're not beaten. But I'd rather be out there in the black hunting them down."

"Me too." She rounded on him with an incredulous look. "I know I argued for this, and I still do think it's important, Jenks, but I get it. I really do. I also think that this is the best possible diversion. Let them think we're backing away from the investigation. That we're just here to play games. When we get done and go to Trappist, we'll be ready for them and they'll see we're definitely not playing."

Jenks smiled slowly. "I see Max's sneakiness is rubbing off on you."

"I was sneaky before both of you were even alive, you know."

"Sure, big brother. But you're lucky she's not mad at you anymore."

"Why's that?"

"Because you'd never see her coming."

THIRTY-THREE

Jenks pulled up her hoodie as she stepped out into the night air of London and shoved her hands into her pocket. She didn't turn her music on, a concession to Nika, who'd been reluctant to let her go out by herself at all.

But she'd needed to go and do this even as she'd been dreading it. So she'd promised to be careful and Doge was at her side.

The walk to NeoG HQ and the Intel buildings wasn't far from the academy, the streets quiet this late at night. It almost got very loud, though, because as she came around the corner she had to bite her lip to hold in the sob.

The gaping hole in the side of the building where Luis's and Stephan's offices had been located was cordoned off with light tapes that flashed a yellow warning message to passersby. If a tape was crossed, that light would shift to red and the alarms would start.

The alarms were already going off in her head. Over and over, saying, *You shouldn't be here you shouldn't be here you shouldn't be here—*

Not that she was going to cross the tapes. Or go anywhere

near them. At the moment Jenks couldn't even make her legs move, and she fisted her hands in her hoodie pocket as the memories overwhelmed her.

She wanted to scream at the night sky, but there were enough people around to make that awkward. And while it had never really stopped her before—she usually took pride in being an outsize personality—it didn't really fit with the image they were trying to put on for the enemy.

The enemy. Their work was there, right in front of her. "I don't know what you expected out of this, Jenks, but there it is. The fucking ashes of your life," she whispered.

She turned to go.

The person who'd snuck up on her grabbed her and dragged her into the nearby alley. Jenks twisted in their grip, hearing the satisfying sound of air being expelled when she jammed her elbow into their gut.

She wriggled free, knew she should turn and run, but instead put her hands up. "I've been spoiling for a fucking fight, you bastards, bring it." She threw the punch right after the words, but her attacker avoided the strike like they'd been expecting it.

And then they put their hands up.

"Dai, it's me."

The words slipped past her guard in a blow that almost put her on her knees.

Broad shoulders, built like a brawler, anticipating her moves.

I know this fighter.

Her heart stuttered, stopped. Doge hadn't reacted at all and there was only one reason the ROVER wouldn't have come to her defense. Only one reason for him to be standing there with his eyes a friendly blue.

"Luis?"

It was barely audible, as if she was afraid the specter in front of her would vanish if she said his name too loud.

"It's me," he repeated, and she caught a flash of his face in the streetlight as he reached for her.

Jenks threw her arms around his neck, ignoring the pain. There were too many things colliding in her head for her to sort them out and turn them into words, so she just hugged him.

Here was the second chance she'd been begging the universe for. She wasn't going to waste it.

"I'm so sorry, Dai," he murmured against her ear. "There wasn't any way to tell you, we couldn't risk it." He tightened his arms around her until the pain was too much and she gasped. He immediately let go. "I'm sorry, I forgot you're hurt."

She reached up and touched his face. "So are you." A scar arced down the left side all the way from temple to chin. It was healed, but still red. "What happened?"

"Which part?"

"All of it. But start with how are you here? How are you alive? How are you—" Her hands were all over him, touching his arm, his chest, his face. Like she was double-, triple-checking her work to make sure she had the right answer.

Luis just stood there and let her, and it was—for the moment—the most perfect thing in the world.

Finally, she looked back into his amber eyes. "Well? How did I get you back?"

"Grant sent men after us at the same time they hit the station. Stephan and I were able to kill them, but we knew they'd keep coming so we blew up our offices."

"*You* did that?" she said, gesturing out of the alley. "You *faked* your goddamned death?"

"It seemed the easiest way to get them off our tail. Captain Kilini was already on her way. We sent her a quick message and she took charge, gave the false ID on the bodies as us."

"You utter bastard, I should skin you." The perfect moment was over as fury went to war with the joy. "I—three weeks of hell."

"I know." He cupped her face and pressed his forehead

to hers. "I'm so sorry. Forgive me. You don't know how many times I wanted to answer your messages. I was terrified you were going to kill yourself and I couldn't stop you. I messaged Nika anonymously, it was all I could think to do." He kissed her and she could taste the salt of both their tears.

"Oh." She closed her eyes, his words finally sinking in. "You saw my messages?" She thought about it some more. "Nika didn't say anything."

But then Jenks remembered how she couldn't get a moment to herself in the days after the explosion and realized that while Nika hadn't spoken, he'd acted to keep her safe in the best way he knew. The conversation with Asabi came back to her in a rush.

Would you forgive him again if you had the chance?

"I'm giving you a pass on this lie," she murmured. The relief was bigger than any anger she could summon as she touched his face again.

"Stephan's going to kill me for this as it is." He sighed against her fingers. "I saw you, though, and I couldn't let you walk away—god, Dai, I'm sorry."

"I can't believe you're both alive."

He kissed her, his lips gentle on hers, but this time Jenks ignored the pain as she fisted her hands in his hair and kissed him back. They separated as quickly as they'd come together and she dragged in a breath, feeling the tears track down her face, and then pulled him in again.

Finally, her side couldn't overcome the endorphins, and she withdrew once more.

"I heard how close it was for you, too." He reached down and patted Doge. "I owe you, buddy. Whatever you want."

"I am just glad you are not off. I tried to tell her," Doge replied, and Jenks choked on a disbelieving laugh.

"You damn dog, how did you know? I was—" Her breath caught. "Luis, Tivo doesn't know, does he?"

"No." He looked at her with a resigned smile. "And I know

I shouldn't even try to tell you not to say a word, so just be careful."

"No more lies," she said firmly.

"No more lies."

"What about your boys?"

"They know. It's all right. We've got them and Moms in a safehouse a long way from here."

"That explains why I couldn't get in touch with them."

Luis grinned sheepishly. "Mom Gina had some thoughts about the fact that she couldn't talk to you and tell you I was okay. It did include the phrase 'you galaxy-sized asshole,' if you're wondering."

"Have I mentioned lately that I love your mothers?" She stepped into his embrace again, lightly this time, pressing her face to his chest and inhaling. It was him, the familiar smell of coffee and spice. He was here and whole and the world was bearable again.

"Are you smelling me?"

"Shut up."

"I love you, Dai. But . . . I've got to go."

"No. Not when I just got you—"

"It's okay. I'm still here. Death can't keep us apart, Dai. We just proved that."

"You bastard."

"That's what Mom Monica called me. I reminded her that was her fault for not marrying Mom Gina first."

Jenks snorted.

"I know you're going to do what you want as far as telling people, so just be careful. We're headed to Trappist tomorrow to follow up on a lead."

He turned to go, but she didn't want this moment to be over, and so a thought occurred to her to prolong this just a little longer. "Wait—we need to figure out a way to get some info to you. We've been doing our own investigation. Max has a plan." She felt his jolt of surprise. "What, did you think we'd just let it go?"

"I should have known better."

"Well, it's not like we knew you were alive, and we would have been damned if we'd let them get away with it."

"True. Interceptor." He grinned at her.

"Intel," she swore back. "Wait—"

"Dai, I have to go."

"One more thing."

"Okay."

"You really got all those messages from me?"

His laugh was the single best thing she'd ever heard. "Every last one. Even the one about the ducks."

A warmth spread through her, a feeling she hadn't had in weeks. Luis was here. Luis had seen her heart, exposed in those messages. And Luis loved her enough to defy Stephan.

He said, gently, "Tell Nika to talk to Admiral Chen. She'll be able to send you all straight to Trappist-1d after the prelims. We'll meet you at the West Ridge habitat and go from there."

"I'll tell him. But first, I need to tell you one more thing."

"What?"

"I love you." She lifted onto her tiptoes and kissed him again. "I don't remember all of the last conversation we had, but I think I was remembering bits of it because you were in my head. I was trying to do what you told me. Trying to be open about how I felt and letting people in. Trying to live my life without you," she whispered the last bit against his mouth. "I'm really fucking glad I don't have to."

"Same, Dai. I love you, too. So much. Watch your back." He let her go and gave her a little push toward the street.

Jenks went, and her steps were so light it felt like she was walking on the moon, whispering, "I've got yours."

NIKA LOOKED UP AS JENKS SLIPPED BACK INTO THEIR QUARTERS, Doge trailing behind her. The anxious band loosened from around his chest until he saw the tears on her face and it snapped tight again.

"Is everyone here?" she demanded. "Where's Sapphi?"

He frowned at the abrupt question. "Yes and she's in her room."

Jenks disappeared into the room Sapphi was sharing with Chae, emerging a moment later with both of them. As she disappeared into her own room, Nika glanced over his shoulder.

"Hey, Max?"

"Yeah?"

"Come in here."

"One second." She emerged a moment later, a tablet in her hand as Jenks and Tamago came out of their room. "What's going on?"

"Sit," Jenks said. "Sapphi, jammer." She waited for the nod from the ensign and then looked at Nika. "Luis and Stephan are alive."

Nika's own *"What?"* was lost among the exclamations of the rest of the team. The clamoring got to the point that he was afraid that even the jammer wouldn't be enough. "Everyone be quiet," he ordered, and the room fell into silence once more. "Jenks?"

"Not a joke and I'm not losing my mind. I went down to the Intel building to see the wreckage for myself." She shrugged a shoulder in apology, but Nika waved her off. He'd known that was where she was going even if she hadn't said it outright.

"Luis was there. We talked. He said Grant sent men after him and Stephan to kill them but they failed, and rather than continue to be targets they blew up their offices."

"How did they fake the bodies?"

"They didn't," Jenks replied. "The killers were dead. Davi was already on her way because of the alarm and she just took over and told everyone the bodies were Luis and Stephan."

"One of them must have been pretty big," Sapphi said.

"What?" Jenks asked.

"I'm just saying—if you're going to pass off a body as Luis's, they'd have to be pretty big."

"That's what you're worried about?" Tamago asked.

"I am going to kill both of them." Max's muttered promise somehow cut through the chatter.

"Jenks—" Nika hated to even ask, but he had to know if there was any chance it hadn't been Luis.

However, his sister seemed to anticipate the question. An embarrassed look slid across her face and she lifted a shoulder. "He smelled like Luis, Nik, and kissed like him. It was him. You got an anonymous message about me after the explosion, didn't you?"

"How did you know—"

"It was Luis." Jenks looked at the floor. "I emailed him about how I'd almost walked out the airlock when I ditched Max. He got in touch the only way he could without blowing their cover."

"Explains why I couldn't track the sender," Sapphi said. "Luis was always good at covering his tracks. Is good. He *is* good. Hades, I'm glad he's not dead."

Jenks smiled at Sapphi's babbled correction and then tapped Doge on the head. "Plus, this damn dog apparently knew he wasn't dead, don't fucking ask me how, though."

"What are you talking about?"

"He was not off," Doge answered. "I couldn't talk to him but I knew he was still there."

Nika frowned at Doge, then decided to file that information away for later. "Did Luis tell you anything else?"

"Just that they were going to Trappist-1d and you need to talk to Admiral Chen so we can follow them after the preliminaries. He said to meet them at West Ridge."

"We'll still want to come up with something for Admiral Chen to use as a reason besides 'I'm in charge,'" Nika said. "The new admiral on Jupiter station, Kira Oshi, is by the book and we don't have a good reason to leave Jupiter for Trappist."

"I'll come up with something to do with the task force," Max said softly, and Nika looked at her. "Even with *Dread* down two members it shouldn't be hard to have Admiral Chen put in orders to move us like was originally planned."

"Okay." He nodded once, gestured at Sapphi to turn off the jammer. "We've got a day left, people. Let's finish these games strong."

There was a chorus of agreement and Nika pushed to his feet, catching Jenks before she could walk off. He pulled her in close.

"You okay?" He whispered the question against her ear.

"So much better now," she replied, wrapping her arms around his waist, her breath hitching just a bit. "Will you pinch me? I want to make sure this isn't a dream."

He complied, smiling when she yelped and jumped away. Jenks shook her head at him as she headed for her room and he turned to find Max smiling at both of them.

"Do you—" She stopped, hesitating, and Nika waited while she sorted out whatever she wanted to say in her head. "I don't want to sleep alone tonight."

"Me either." He held out his hand.

"Well, Barnes, we are well into the fourth day of the preliminaries and so far it's been a relatively predictable Games, all things considered. *Zuma's Ghost* and *Flux Capacitor* are leading the pack to the point where there's little question that these are the two teams the NeoG will be sending on to the Boarding Games."

"You're right, Pace. Although, if you could have predicted they'd be here, we both could have made a lot of money. It's quite the about-face for *Flux*, especially, their performances in the Games have usually been less than stellar."

"Ha ha, I guess you're right. But we shouldn't have doubted."

"No. It's probably made these prelims all the more exciting for it. And speaking of exciting, we're about to watch *Zuma* and *Flux* go head to head in the Boarding Action championship. And after that we've got Jenks versus Till in the cage match we've all been waiting for."

"Commander Till took Carmichael down earlier this morning, revenge for last year when Carmichael swept her with one of her famous kicks and took her out in the second round with a killing blow. This time, she played Carmichael's game, slow and steady, and let the young lieutenant make an anxious mistake."

"I wonder if Carmichael was just trying for a bold move, or if she simply decided she didn't want to have to face Jenks."

"Can understand why she'd want to stay out of the ring with Khan! Jenks disposed of *Burden of Proof*'s Captain

Evans with a little more vigor than we've seen from the *Zuma* fighter so far in the preliminaries."

"Jenks does seem to be mostly back to her old self, Pace."

"At this point, you almost have to feel bad for Till."

"True enough. But she's a warrior, too, so don't think she's just going to let Jenks walk all over her."

"Definitely not. That's what Jenks is so good at, though—rising to meet her opponent."

"Totally. And that's not all we have going on today, is it, Pace? The fight that everyone seems excited about is going to happen this afternoon between Commander Nika Vagin and Senior Chief Dao Mai Tien of *Flux*. Vagin is performing like his old self, despite his absence from the sword ring for two years."

"It's been a beautiful thing to watch, Barnes. With Ensign Zika easily winning her fifth straight hacking competition and new Neo Spacer Chae Ho-ki taking the pilot slot by storm, I'm starting to think that this NeoG team may actually put up a real fight at the Boarding Games rather than being the underdog we were all expecting. In fact, I'd go out on a limb and say they might be even better than last year's team."

"They're definitely coming into their own. And it's clear they're going to be competing for something more than just that trophy. The honor of the NeoG is on the line here, and these games are proving there are people more than willing to fight for it."

THIRTY-FOUR

"Sector four clear!"

"Sectors five and six clear!"

Chae stayed where they were as the members of *Flux Capacitor* swept through the ship, coming ever closer to their position. As Ensign Rahal and PO Nash passed, they slipped into the open space behind the pair.

Thirty seconds until Commander Till and ZZ come around the corner; move now.

They moved, and stabbed Nash in the back, lighting up their suit, then had Saad down before either man could react.

"Damn you, Chae, did you just materialize out of thin air or what?"

They grinned into the dark at Nash's whisper, moving into the safety of the darkened corridor across from the pair. "Two down, LT. Till and ZZ are up next."

"Be careful, Chae," Max replied. "We're headed for the others. Sapphi's almost got the ship locked down."

The final Boarding Action was a simple enough scenario. *Flux Capacitor* were playing pirates who'd taken over an Interceptor ship. It was the job of *Zuma's Ghost* to escape and take down their captors.

Tamago and Nika were down the stairs and at the back of the ship in the brig, still being held captive by the pirates.

Chae wasn't even sure how Max and Jenks had gotten loose; they knew only that by the time Sapphi had broken Chae out of their locked room, the pair of Neos were coming up the hallway of the replica Interceptor.

Once they'd met up, the plan had come together in a matter of minutes. Make enough noise for the pirates to realize they'd escaped, and then draw them into a hunt. Sapphi had gotten control of the lights from a console and Jenks and Max had played the part of bait perfectly.

Leaving Chae to work their magic and pick off the members of *Flux* one by one.

They melted farther back into the shadows when they heard Till and ZZ approach. The footsteps slowed as Chae had hoped they would when they spotted Nash's and Rahal's bodies.

Two more steps forward, come on.

"Shit," Till said. "Nash and Rahal are down. Why isn't that showing on our DD?"

Whatever answer she got from either Xin or Tien didn't make Till happy and she muttered a second curse. But instead of going forward to check the bodies of her crew like Chae expected, she backed up a step.

"You're lurking in the shadows, aren't you, Chae?" she called, her voice a singsong. "Come out before I have Tien start cutting pieces off your commander."

She's baiting you; just stay quiet.

Chae eased onto the balls of their feet, calculating the distance from where they were to where Till was. She was the more dangerous of the pair. They were fairly sure ZZ would freeze, or at least hesitate, if Chae struck Till first.

"Come on, Chae. Don't make this hard on yourself. Your crew isn't going to survive this encounter, but we could make a deal with you."

Knowing it was a game didn't make the anger in Chae's chest any less real. They'd betrayed this team once already. Never again.

If she won't come to you, you go to her.

Three steps. Chae took a deep breath and launched themself out of the shadows at Till. They hit the *Flux* commander hard enough to knock her into ZZ and all three of them went down in a heap.

Till's suit lit up as Chae's knife found its target and they rolled to the side, taking the blow from ZZ's wild swing in the shoulder.

Knife versus sword wasn't a good look and Chae stumbled backward, ZZ's second strike knocking the knife from their hand. As ZZ lunged in for the kill, the spacer's suit suddenly lit up and she froze.

"You all right, Chae?" Jenks called, and Chae was surprised by the laugh that erupted from their throat.

"Yes, Chief."

"God damn, I should have let her stab you. Stop calling me Chief."

More laughter rang out over the deck as the lights came back on.

"All combatants down for *Flux Capacitor*. That's a win for *Zuma's Ghost*."

Chae took ZZ's offered hand and let her pull them to their feet as Jenks helped Till up.

"Holy crap, Jenks, you taught that kid to hit like you," she said with a groan.

"You tried to get them to flip sides, you deserved it." Jenks winked at Chae and then at Till. "Tien was lying to you, by the way. We'd already taken the brig ourselves when you called. I figured I'd come back here and lend a hand."

"Why didn't you tell me?" Chae asked.

"Didn't want to distract you." Jenks threw her arm around Chae's shoulder. "Plus I was sprinting; you probably wouldn't have been able to understand me anyway. Good job, kid."

NIKA WATCHED TIEN PACE THE RING DURING THE BREAK. *Flux*'s senior chief was a powerhouse of a fighter whose technique had improved dramatically in the last two years. His upper arm was aching from the number and force of her swings that he'd had to parry in the first two rounds of the fight.

The crowd's energy was electric and Nika exchanged a smile with Tamago as another wave of chants filled the air.

"You've got her," Tamago said. "She's pushing because she's frustrated with your defense and your lead. If you get a few more strikes on her she'll get reckless, so watch for her to come straight at you and not stop."

Nika nodded.

"Fighters, you've got thirty seconds left!" the referee announced, and Nika lifted his hand in acknowledgment.

"Anything else before we finish this, Tama?"

They smiled. "You are the best sword fighter I've ever known, hands down. Get out there and be that person." They tapped their fist to their heart. "Got your back."

"I've got yours," he replied, echoing the gesture, then gripping their forearm and touching his forehead to theirs.

Tamago ducked out of the ring, joining the rest of *Zuma's Ghost* clustered just outside of the combat area. Nika saluted them with his sword and moved to the middle of the ring, where the referee waited. Tien joined them a moment later.

"One more go?" he asked, and she bared her teeth at him.

"See if you can keep up, Vagin."

He saluted her, a plan already forming in his head with an ease that surprised him. Tien rushed forward the moment the referee blew the whistle and Nika spun to the side, blocking her strike and kicking her in the hip hard enough to stall her movement.

Tien's eyes narrowed and Nika grinned, spinning his sword briefly in his right hand, to the delight of the crowd. She rushed in again and they fought in silence for several minutes until Nika saw his opening.

Tien pressed him, raining down blow after blow that Nika parried as he backed toward the ropes. He dropped his sword into his left hand, knowing that Tien would think it was a fumble. She did and so did the crowd, if the collective indrawn breath was any indication. Nika dropped his head slightly, his eyes never leaving her sword as Tien moved in for the kill.

Nika caught her sword with his right hand, his glove lighting up with the expected injury, but he'd done it before she started the downswing, so that even if his hand had been flesh and blood the damage would've been minimal because he'd grabbed at the unsharpened part closer to the hilt.

He straightened and pushed, bringing his own sword up to her suit just under her rib cage. Had this been a real fight his sword would have gone straight up through her lung and heart. Her suit recognized the hit and lit up.

"You son of a bitch," Tien swore at him. "You cheating son of a bitch."

"I didn't—that's legal." But he saw she was grinning.

"I thought I had you."

"Guess I kept up," he deadpanned. "It was a good fight, though, Tien. You're a force to be reckoned with."

"Kill shot recognized! Winner, Commander Vagin!"

Nika let go of Tien's sword and she wrapped her right arm around his neck with a laugh. The crowd was on its feet and he saw Max and Jenks and the rest of the team celebrating. Squeezing Tien once more, he let her go and went to join them.

In that moment, he found it almost unthinkable that he had ever doubted his ability to do this job.

"ADMIRAL." MAX SALUTED ADMIRAL CHEN AS THEY CAME INTO the head of the NeoG's office. She saw Nika echo the gesture out of the corner of her eye and Chen smiled, returning the salute.

"Congratulations on your win, *Zuma*. Sit down, you two."

Max glanced Captain Kilini's way and the woman offered up an apologetic smile that spoke volumes.

"This room is shielded," Chen said as she wheeled around the side of her desk, stopping near Max. "But we don't have a lot of time before you all need to leave, so I'll make this quick. I know Senior Chief Armstrong made contact with Chief Khan—against orders, by the way—but given the circumstances it's hard to be too angry at him. Or rather, I'll be angry at him when we finish this mission. Still, I am sorry for the grief this has caused all of you. We had little choice and this seemed the safest option in the moment."

"We understand, Admiral," Nika said.

"Good. The time is running out on this operation. We need to move before they get truly spooked and shut everything down. I do not want to spend another five years building a case against Senator Tieg. To be blunt, I am fucking tired of seeing his face on the news." Admiral Chen sighed and tapped on the desk. "I know Stephan read you all into this after your crew was injured, but we can't officially put you with Intel on the off chance it'll trigger something with Tieg's people.

"So what I'm doing is following Max's suggestion and officially moving the task force to Trappist-1d as we planned. Ostensibly we're doing this ahead of schedule because of the damage to the station. You and the other three crews will head directly for Trappist aboard the *Laika* and the *Normandy*. I

know Commander Montaglione doesn't have a full crew—
we'll get that taken care of after this is over."

Admiral Chen looked down at her hands. "We should have
moved on Warrant Officer Huang sooner. Stephan wanted to
and I overruled him. That was my mistake. I'm sorry. Everyone else has been checked and checked again since the explosion, but if you are concerned about anyone on these crews,
I'm willing to listen."

"No," Max replied without hesitation, and Nika knew she'd
put the work in to make sure that answer was right. "I trust
them all."

"Good. This has been a dangerous and deadly operation,
Max. I know you're upset, but I need you to go into this with a
clear head. I don't want to lose any more people I care about,
understood?"

Max nodded. "I do, ma'am."

"Good. I also hope you understand I expect things like
you threatening to make a prisoner disappear don't happen
again." The admiral raised an eyebrow and Max swallowed.
"Given Julia's unique position and the fact that it's best her
bosses don't find out we've apprehended her, I understand
your actions. I just don't want to see you make a habit of it.
That's not what the NeoG is."

"I understand, Admiral. It won't happen again."

Chen looked at Nika. "Commander, you'll attach to the
Laika for the ride to Trappist in the morning along with *Dread*.
Stephan and Luis will meet you at the West Ridge habitat. I
understand you have an idea for drawing our targets out into
the open."

"We do, Admiral."

"Good luck to both of you." Admiral Chen held her hand
out to Max. "I can't tell you how proud I am to see you grow
into your role, Max. Be careful at Trappist."

"I will." Max pushed her chair back as she rose. Nika was
already on his feet and taking Chen's offered hand.

"You're a credit to the NeoG, Commander. Hoboins always spoke very highly of you. He was happy to have you back where he felt you belonged."

"Thank you, Admiral. That means a great deal to me."

They headed away from the admiral's office, and Captain Kilini walked with them out of HQ into the bright sunshine.

"Watch your backs, *Zuma*," she said with a short nod.

"We will," Nika replied.

"HERE, KIDDO."

Chae looked up at the beer Jenks was waggling in their direction. They took it and she handed out two more to Sapphi and Tamago.

"Jenks, did you smuggle beer onto the ship?" Nika asked from the doorway to the galley.

"No," Jenks replied, handing him a beer with a grin. "I just walked it on. Figured we deserved a round since we aren't partying like normal. Besides, we're hitching a ride, no one needs to be sober enough to fly. LT, I got you one, but I'll drink it if you don't—"

"Don't you dare drink my beer," Max said, grabbing it, and Chae looked at her in surprise.

Jenks hooted a laugh, then lifted her own. "To Admiral Hoboins, Lou, and all the others we lost."

Chae lifted their beer, murmuring their assent and taking a drink. "Chief?"

Jenks shot them a look with her mismatched eyes that could have melted paint off the hull, but then she chuckled. "I'd throw this beer at your head, but I don't want to waste it. What?"

"I just wanted to say thanks," Chae said, lifting their beer again. "To all of you. Thanks for taking me in and making me part of this crew."

"To *Zuma's Ghost*," Max said.

"To family." Tamago lifted their beer.

"To payback," Sapphi said quietly, and everyone nodded in agreement.

"To the NeoG." Nika saluted the room.

Jenks didn't say anything in reply, but the wink she sent Chae warmed their heart.

Dear Ms. Karenina,

It is my hope your associate passed on my request about a potential job with Trappist Express before her unfortunate passing in the attack on Jupiter. My initial offer has changed. I have something I think you'd rather the NeoG not get and I'm willing to discuss terms to keep my sister and myself safe. Meet me on Trappist-1d to discuss further. You can contact me when you are on the planet.

Sincerely,

NV

Melanie read the email again, tapping a finger against her lower lip as she idly spun the sword in her hand.

"It's a trap," Grant said.

"Maybe," she admitted, dismissing the email and returning her focus to their fight. Grant was barely adequate with a sword, but his brute force made her have to adapt her own style and Melanie had found it to be good practice. "But Julia did say that he might work as our eyes on the command level, and with her dead and Paul under arrest for the attack on Jupiter, I may have to take the chance." She smiled at him as she easily deflected his clumsy thrust. "Besides, you'll keep me safe."

"You know I will."

"The NeoG is scrambling and it sounds like Vagin is scared. I like people who are scared; they're easy to manipulate." She nodded and came in with an attack of her own, pressing him back until she stripped the sword from his hand and tapped the point of her own against his chest. "We'll go to Trappist and see what Commander Nika Vagin can offer us."

"And if it's a trap?"

"We kill him and leave his body out for the coyotes to eat."

THIRTY-FIVE

Chae eased the Interceptor out of the *Laika*'s bay. "We are clear. Thanks, Control."

"Anytime, *Zuma*. See you on the flip side."

"*Zuma*, we are on your low five o'clock. *Dread* is at seven. We have clearance from Trappist-1d traffic control to breach atmo and head for the West Ridge habitat. You have the lead." Lieutenant Commander Ian Sebastian's accent was straight Oribo City, the largest habitat on the other side of Trappist-1d.

"Roger that, ST-One."

"Oh, and Chae? Welcome home for real this time," they said, and Chae felt a little blossom of heat in their chest.

All that fell away as the ship broke through the atmosphere and flew down over the beautiful canyons that circled the West Ridge habitat. The rock was multiple shades of red and orange fading down to the palest cream and then back the other direction to a brown so dark it was almost black.

Chae could see the fields beyond and the structures of the habitat clustered in little circular patterns reminiscent of the crop circle phenomenon that happened on Earth in the late twentieth century. On Trappist, they were both artistic homage and the best answer to the sometimes strange weather events that resulted from terraforming.

West Ridge wasn't as massive and sprawling as Oribo City, nor as cosmopolitan as nearby Amanave, but it also wasn't a three-structure 'tat, and Chae felt a rush of emotion as they brought the Interceptor down to the landing pad on the eastern side of the habitat.

"We're down," Chae announced. They started the postflight checklist as the others got up.

"I'll grab your bag for you," Sapphi said, patting them on the shoulder.

"Thanks." There hadn't been much point in unpacking anything; they'd been on the ship for only about ten hours total between the transit time away from Earth and then into the Trappist system.

The other navy ship, the *Normandy,* and its two Interceptor passengers had arrived at Trappist an hour earlier. Unlike *Dread* and *Zuma,* they'd gone to the NeoG base outside Amanave.

"You doing okay, Chae?" Jenks asked when they came down from the bridge a few moments later.

"Nervous," they admitted.

"Everything's going to be fine. Come on." She slung her bag over her shoulder and hopped down the stairs.

Chae followed, taking a deep breath and closing their eyes as they stepped off the ship. Amanave hadn't really counted as being back. They'd visited the big habitat a lot, but this was truly home.

The dry air of this southern part of one of three massive continents brought tears to their eyes and when Chae opened them, they had to blink several times to get the figure standing by a transport to resolve.

Their heart thumped painfully in their chest. "Dad?"

"Go on," Jenks said, nudging them forward.

Chae sprinted across the landing pad and launched themself into their father's arms. "Dad!"

"Ho-ki." Michael swung them in a tight circle, laughing in delight. "Look at you! You went and grew up on me," he said, setting Chae back down and cupping their face.

"I did." Chae couldn't stop the sob and threw themself into their dad's arms again.

"It is so good to see you. We've missed you and were so worried until Lieutenant Carmichael started emailing us with updates."

"She what?" Chae lifted their head and found Max in the approaching crowd. She extended her hand.

"It's a pleasure to finally meet you, Mr. Chae."

"Just Michael, but likewise, Lieutenant. Thank you."

The introductions went quickly. Chae knew they should probably let their father go, but they didn't want to, and no one—least of all their dad—seemed to mind.

"I've got the transport ready for you. The outpost is a little ways from the habitat in the wide spot of Yara's Canyon. The rest of your friends arrived this morning," Michael said.

"Good," Nika replied.

THE YARD OUT IN FRONT OF THE OUTPOST WAS TEEMING WITH people. Chae spotted their other father and leaped from the transport before it had come to a complete stop, hurtling across the packed dirt and into his arms.

Jenks smiled and heard Tivo chuckle. "Softy."

"Hush." She grabbed her bag and Chae's and jumped out of the transport, one eye on the building in front of her.

Jenks heard the noise Tivo tried to suppress when Luis came out of the main house. When she'd told him the news in the safety of the SEAL quarters, she'd known he couldn't quite allow himself to believe it until he could see Luis with his own eyes.

She would have done the same.

Tivo crossed the red dirt yard, grabbing Luis by the face and kissing him hard before he pulled the senior chief into a tight hug.

"Commander." She nodded to Stephan. He had dark circles under his eyes and seemed to be favoring his right arm. "You look terrible."

"It's good to see you, too, Chief." He held out his left hand. "I'm sorry, Jenks, about everything."

"This is not on you." The forgiveness came easy on the heels of everything else as she took his hand and squeezed.

"It's kind of you to say." Stephan smiled and Jenks knew that look. The painful effort it took to keep up appearances and pretend everything was okay.

"Hey, Stephan. You know I'd tell you if I was still mad. We fuck up, we get back up." She spread her arms and was surprised when he stepped into the hug. She patted him, careful of his arm, and whispered, "They started this, we're here to finish it."

"I hope you're right."

She snorted. "I'm always right." That got a laugh out of him and Stephan straightened, giving her a little shove toward Luis and Tivo.

"Go say your hellos and don't vanish, we've got dinner in ten minutes," he ordered as Nika joined them.

"I'd say something, but it would traumatize you both." Jenks dodged Nika's laughing swing and ran across the yard.

NIKA WATCHED HIS SISTER JOIN THE MEN BY THE DOOR, THE pair enfolding her into their hug without so much as a pause, and then looked back at Stephan. "I am both relieved you are alive and furious at you."

"If it helps, this was never part of the plan."

"What happened to your arm?"

"One of Grant's goons broke it. Should be completely healed in a few weeks."

Nika smiled. "Well, you've got all year. There are people around here to do the heavy lifting in the meantime."

"So I've heard. You want to tell me about this plan of yours? All Admiral Chen would say was that I wasn't going to like it."

"You're not, but it's done. I just got a message from Melanie Karenina that she'll be on Trappist-1d tomorrow." Nika met Stephan's suspicious look with a blank expression. "I may have implied that I have proof of her involvement and I'm willing to sell it to her so that Jenks and I can get out of the NeoG."

"You did what?"

Stephan's voice was loud enough to carry across the yard and draw the attention of the half-dozen people in the area. Nika waved Max over, figuring it was only fair she get yelled at also.

"Did I mention it was Max's idea?"

"What was my idea?" she asked as she joined them.

"Using me as bait."

"Ah, yeah." Max grinned. "Did Admiral Chen mention I threatened to make Julia disappear?"

"I left you all alone for *three weeks*." Stephan closed his eyes and shook his head. "Get your asses in the house."

Nika felt Max slip her arm around his waist as they headed for the door of the main house of the outpost. For a few moments, chaos reigned as the SEAL team, *Zuma,* and the four members left of *Dread* were introduced to the TLF contingent led by Chae's parents.

"All right everyone, listen up," Stephan said, raising his voice over the crowd. "Rooms are down that hall, there's plenty of space. Go get your gear stowed, be back here in five minutes."

MAX SETTLED INTO A CHAIR BETWEEN D'ARCY AND NIKA AT the long table located on one side of the massive kitchen.

"How are you holding up?" She rested a hand on D'Arcy's arm. There hadn't been much of a chance to talk with him about Paul during the prelims, but Max knew the warrant officer's betrayal had wounded him deeply.

"Pissed, but better." He smiled at her. "I'm glad you're here. Happy these two assholes are alive." He gestured at Stephan and Luis. "Still angry about what's happened."

Stephan slid a pot of greens onto the table, negotiating for space amid the dishes already there. "We're about to deal with it. Eat up everyone."

They passed food around and chatted as they ate. Max watched everyone. Scott was in a conversation with Stephan, and her brother smiled at her when he looked her way. Jenks was talking to Tamago across the table, but she was leaning against Luis and kept reaching her left hand out to touch Tivo's forearm where it rested next to her.

Chae was eating, eyes on their plate, but Max could tell they were listening to the conversations and she wondered if they could keep track of them all.

After the meal had wound down and the food was cleared from the table, Stephan tapped a hand on the wooden surface and waited until everyone had fallen quiet. "All right, people. I'm running on the assumption that everyone got introduced before dinner—if not, do your intros when we're done here. We're going to be working together in close quarters even after this is over. I don't expect you all to be best friends, but I do expect you to be moderately professional."

"You know that's asking a lot of me, Commander." Jenks snorted and Stephan sighed.

One of the TLF soldiers, a slender trans man by the name of Ro, choked back a laugh at Jenks's grin. "I like you already," he said, pointing a finger across the table.

Jenks winked, but then Max watched the amused expression slide off her face like water off glass. "Get to it, Stephan.

Melanie is on her way here and I want these people in custody before sunset tomorrow."

"That's my cue, then." Nika cleared his throat and stood, detailing out the plan that Max had thought of and they'd refined on their way to Trappist. Jenks had already protested the idea of Nika going alone, and judging from the set of her jaw she was about to do so again.

"I'm coming with you."

"You are not," he said.

"You're not going solo," Jenks replied. "And no one else but me can go without raising suspicion."

"I could, Chief." Chae raised their hand and Max suppressed a smile when the Neo didn't flinch from Jenks's sharp look.

"No. I'm not putting you in danger when I could go myself. It makes sense for me to go with you, Nika, especially if we want Melanie to buy that we both want out."

"At the risk of getting yelled at for interrupting this sibling argument, does someone want to clear up for me how this is actually going to implicate Melanie in Tieg's operation?" Luis asked.

"It's not," Nika admitted, and the disappointment flickered across Stephan's face. "It's just a smokescreen to get her here. She's got too much influence on Earth and we don't want Tieg to be tipped off that we've got her until it's too late. We've already got the proof we need that she's involved."

"What proof is that?"

"Cabbages."

THIRTY-SIX

"What? I'm not following," Stephan said.

"Julia was smart," Max said. "She made herself an insurance policy. Logs and details of the operation, and recordings of conversations she had with Melanie stretching back more than five years. I suspect it's still not enough to convict all our targets, though it would damage Senator Tieg's reputation.

"However, Trappist Express's supply chain program has a flaw. One Melanie Karenina was able to exploit, and it explains why you didn't find anything when you investigated her. Using her master override, she could order the program to siphon off product and assign it to freighters of her choice rather than ones the algorithm assigned it to. They have freight controllers who do the same thing, but this program is meant to be used as an emergency protocol only for when ships are damaged or need to be commandeered for specific purposes. The adjustments don't show up on the main logs."

"I didn't realize they had a separate program." Stephan cursed.

"Precisely." Max looked around the room. "Unfortunately for Melanie, the program keeps logs of the overrides and she never bothered to cover her tracks because she was the only one with access."

"Or so she thought," Nika added.

"Julia was able to copy the logs and Sapphi thinks they're legitimate. Now, the logs themselves are hard to use as proof in our case, but when Sapphi looked at them she found that Melanie had exclusive control over where this product went, including how long it would sit in the warehouses. Because of that, she was able to avoid tripping the spoilage warnings that all the shipping companies are required to have when she was sending bad product out to the habitats and then forcing them to buy the unspoiled stuff she could get cheaply thanks to Tieg."

"And the freighter we tagged for spoiled cabbages was owned by Trappist Express. It wasn't a contract run." Jenks drummed a little tattoo on the table with a pleased grin.

"You found the freighter in the logs," Stephan said, and Max nodded.

"We did and it's not the only one we found. Moreover, we think Nika can get her to admit her involvement when he meets with her."

"When *we* meet with her," Jenks corrected.

Max didn't try to argue and instead shot Nika a quick message.

MAX: I'm going to let you handle that, Commander.

NIKA: Are you at least going to back me if I order her to stay?

She glanced at him, grateful that for the moment Luis was protesting Jenks's insistence that she go with Nika.

MAX: You know you'd be setting her up to disobey a direct order. Is it worth it to you to see her get busted back down again?

NIKA: It's worth it to keep her alive.

MAX: If she goes with you it might keep both of you alive.

NIKA: Do you think if Grant is there, which he likely will be, she won't go after him? This was personal for all of us, but Hoboins was the closest thing to a father she ever knew.

MAX: And you are the only family she has left. Asking her to stay here while you put yourself in danger is asking for trouble.

NIKA: Whose side are you on here?

MAX: I'm saying Jenks is an unstoppable force, and we both know it. Given my choice, I'd keep you both out of harm's way, but I can't do that. So I'll do the next best thing and have you watch each other's backs.

"I'd like to see you make me." Jenks's voice had escalated to the point where it dragged Max's attention back to the room rather than her conversation with Nika.

"I could just sit on you until you see reason," Luis snapped. "This isn't the Games, Jenks. You lose a fight here, it's for good."

"What am I, a newbie spacer? No offense, Chae."

"None taken, Chief."

"That's enough," Nika said, holding up his hand. "Jenks'll come with me."

"Nika, you can't—wait, did you say I could go?" Jenks whipped her gaze to Max, who kept her face expressionless.

"You'll come with me," Nika repeated. "You'll do as I say, understood?"

"Yeah." She leaned back in her chair and shot a smug smile at Luis, who in turn glared at Nika.

CHAE CUPPED THE WARM MUG OF TEA BETWEEN THEIR hands and walked out of the house. The sun was just setting over the western side of the canyon edge and the last streaks of gold were illuminating the burnished walls. Max stood by the edge, one arm wrapped around her waist, the other cradling her own mug.

"I don't mind the company," she murmured over her shoulder. "Did you get caught up with your fathers?"

"I did. Thanks, LT." After the meeting had wrapped up, people had splintered off, some lingering in the kitchen while others—like the Chief—had immediately vanished. Chae's fathers had stayed for several hours before heading back to their own house in West Ridge.

"Is it good to be home?"

Chae was silent for a moment, sipping at their tea. "Yeah," they said finally. "This is weird, but good. You know?"

"I don't," Max admitted. "I guess Earth is sort of my home, but it's not. Not really. I didn't grow up anywhere but on ships, and that whole 'home is where the heart is' thing only works if your family has a heart."

"So that means you've come home, too?" Chae held their mug up in salute and Max laughed.

"I suppose you're right." She tapped her mug to theirs. "This is really good."

"One of the great things One-d puts out," Chae replied with a nod. "The tea, or whatever it is they call tea, on Jupiter Station was so horrible I went looking to see if I could buy some Trappist tea. Do you have any idea how much they sell that for? I was so shocked."

"It's apparently a big deal on Earth," Max said with another laugh.

"I almost asked you to call my dads just to have them send me some. We make ours off the crop remnants, and it's still better than anything off-world. Thanks, by the way, for keeping them updated, LT. I really appreciate it."

Max bumped her hip into them with a smile. "It was the least I could do."

"You do a lot, LT. You know we're all thankful for it?" The question seemed to surprise Max, but any reply she could have made was lost as Jenks slipped out of the house and joined them.

The chief didn't say anything, just stole Max's mug from her hands and took a sip before handing it back. The three of them stood in silence, watching as the sun disappeared under the ridge.

"Wait for it," Chae murmured.

It was almost like magic the way the stars appeared, scattered over the quickly darkening sky, a handful of glittering glass tossed against blackened silk. It was startling to realize how much they'd missed it while on Earth and then on Jupiter Station. Nothing could compare with the night sky on Trappist-1d.

"Look at that," Max whispered.

"In the summertime Bean and I used to sneak out of the house and climb up the canyon. We'd watch the stars and listen to the coyotes."

"I forgot they brought coyotes here as part of the Resurrection Project." Jenks looked up at the sky and whistled in appreciation. "I guess they survived, then?"

"Thrived." Chae nodded, dropping to the dirt and setting their mug down so they could stare up at the sky. "You have to watch out for them at certain times, and occasionally we have a pack go heavy feral and start edging in on the habitats. Otherwise they mind their business and we mind ours."

"I've never seen a coyote," Jenks mused. "Lots of feral dogs in Krasnodar. Best case, they'd only steal your lunch. Worst case, they made you lunch." She crouched down next to Chae, Max following.

"I grew up worrying about explosive decompression more than feral dogs," she said, and Jenks snorted.

"Honestly, the coyotes were the least of our worries," Chae replied. "Buildings collapsing because they were made with substandard materials. Wondering if we were going to have enough food to get through the winters. People getting sick with diseases that Earth never considered an issue because they're specific to Trappist." They reached for their tea, took another drink, and then looked at Max. "This has been going on a lot longer than Tieg, you realize that, right? He just decided to profit off what the CHN has been doing to the habitats for years."

"I am starting to figure that out." Max elbowed Jenks when the chief snorted again. "I may be super-clueless rich, as this one likes to say, but I am learning."

"The thing about the TLF is that most habbies support them because they want to make things right. We're at risk all the time out here and some of it is because of the terrain, but some is because Earth is frequently clueless when it comes to setting policy for us. They don't know what we need. They don't know when we need it. People die because the leadership on Earth can't admit that. I want my people to have the best lives they can. They don't really want to separate from Earth, they want to be treated with equity. Just because we're habbies doesn't mean we don't deserve the same protections and guarantees that Earth dwellers have.

"I know these people. They're scared. But they're angry, too, and willing to fight. We don't need the NeoG to save us. We just want the chance to save ourselves."

Max blinked and then nodded. "I appreciate that perspective, Chae."

"Anytime, LT."

"But I think this time, we should let the NeoGs kick some ass," Jenks said.

"Totally."

NIKA WOKE TO THE PING OF A NEW MESSAGE ON HIS DD. HE read it and rolled out of bed, dressing quickly and heading out of his room in search of Stephan. He found him in the kitchen, looking like he'd been awake for a while despite the early hour, chatting with Scott, Jenks, and D'Arcy.

"Morning." Scott pointed at the counter on the far side. "There's breakfast."

"I just got a message from Melanie," Nika said. "Meeting time and place—this evening in downtown Amanave." He shared it with the others.

"Smart of her," Stephan said, frowning as he read the brief note. "That's an area where the NeoG isn't very welcome and that bar is too small for us to be able to blend in well. You walk in in uniform there's bound to be a fight with the locals."

"I can get with Chae and their fathers, we'll be able to at least put some outfits together for me and Nik that won't out us as NeoG," Jenks said. "And I'm sure there are plenty of out-of-towners in the area."

"I'm more concerned about your backup," Stephan replied. "If we were outside of town we could set things up easily with some air support. Here we'll have to stay on the ground and work around the civilians."

"You're going to have to stay here, Doge," Jenks said to the dog lying behind her. "You'll draw too much attention."

"I don't like it."

Nika raised an eyebrow at the ROVER's flat tone but grabbed his breakfast and joined the others at the table. "We can manage it," he said to Stephan. "Melanie's not going to try anything in public, either."

"Don't put it past her," D'Arcy said. "This is the woman who set explosives on our station, remember."

"Fair point," Nika conceded. He pulled up a map. "Let's take a look at what we're working with."

The answer to that question was "not much," but as more people woke up and wandered into the kitchen, they managed to put a game plan in place that would at least allow the backup teams quick access to the bar in question to move in and arrest Melanie as soon as Nika gave the signal.

The day passed faster than he'd expected it to and as the sun set, Nika found himself alone with Max.

"I wish I could be in there with you," she said, smoothing a hand down the rust-colored jacket he was wearing.

"Who'd be there to watch my back outside if you weren't?"

"I know." Max forced a smile. "Don't trust her for a second, Nika, okay?"

"Of course not. But there's more, right? What is it?"

"I don't know."

"Max, if you think we should call this off, I'll back you." He saw the surprise before she buried it and smiled ruefully. "I know, but I mean it. I trust your gut."

"I'm not sure I do," she whispered. "I want to call this off, but we can't pass up this chance, and I know sometimes I truly need a better reason than my instinct pinging funny. I hate that we're going to cut her a deal to get Tieg, even though I did the same thing with Julia. I just—"

"Want this to be more definitively 'bad guys get their due'?"

"Yeah."

"I hear you." Nika nodded. "Try to remember that she's not getting away with anything. Whatever deals we make, she's responsible for the deaths of a lot of people, and the CHN doesn't take that sort of thing lightly."

Max was silent for a long moment before she nodded.

"You two ready?" Jenks asked from the doorway. Tivo and Luis were behind her, the pair wearing identical grim looks.

Nika took a deep breath. "Let's go."

Jenks looked at Max. "You got my back," she said.

"You got mine." Max leaned in and pressed her forehead to Jenks's after finishing the handshake. "Be careful."

"I will," she replied.

The ride into Amanave with Chae's other father, Gun, was quiet until he pulled the transport to a stop near the downtown area. "Bar's up ahead three streets and to your right."

"Thanks," Nika replied.

Jenks slipped her arm through his as they headed down the street. His sister was dressed in the same rusty coat with a darker brown hat pulled down over her distinctive hair. Sapphi had doctored their handshakes, removing the NeoG designations, so that to the untrained eye they didn't look like anything more than a pair of locals out enjoying the evening.

"Try to smile some, Nik," Jenks murmured before they hit the doorway of the bar. "That expression says you want to murder someone."

"Might be a good idea in this place," he muttered back as they stepped through into the dimly lit bar.

Jenks just laughed and slipped her hand down to take his, pulling him through the crowd to a nearby empty table as though she'd been here a hundred times. "Hey, couple of beers?" she called to the waiter, who responded with a wave of their hand.

As Nika settled at the table, Jenks leaned in. "Two men at the bar talking about us. Don't quote me, but one looks a lot like the guy I dropped with a crotch shot when Grant confronted me and Tamago."

"What did they say?" Sapphi asked over the coms.

"Nothing beyond 'The NeoG is here.' Now, it could just

be locals making us. But I doubt it." She kicked a foot up on a free chair and smiled at the waiter when they returned. "Thank you," she said, taking the beers with a wink that had them blushing.

"Really?" Nika asked with a raised eyebrow. "Can you control yourself for one minute?"

She grinned. "What?" And then reached a hand out, laying it on his arm with a tiny shake of her head before he could take a drink. "I wouldn't, just to be safe."

They sat and watched the crowd, chatting about inconsequential things as Jenks occasionally mentioned over the live coms when she spotted another person who could have been sent by Grant.

"That's eight you've tagged so far," Luis said. "Still no sign of Melanie."

"Grant's here, though," Nika replied as the man appeared from behind a group and headed for their table.

"I didn't see him come in, did anyone else?" Stephan demanded.

"No, shifting for a better position on the back door now," Tivo replied. "Can I—"

The coms cut out with a suddenness that could only indicate interference and Nika noted Jenks's fingers flexing on her beer mug as Grant stopped in front of the table, three men behind him.

"Two behind us, Nik," Jenks murmured, turning slightly in her chair so they were back-to-back.

"Where's Melanie?" Nika asked Grant.

"Waiting for you elsewhere. Come with us."

Without coms Nika wasn't willing to go anywhere, plus he could bet that whatever was interfering with the systems included their locators. "No, I agreed to meet her here. Tell her we'll wait for her to show up or no deal."

"You walk out or we carry you out," Grant replied.

"You do remember what happened last time?" Jenks asked.

The smile that appeared on Grant's face was cold. "Nowhere for you to run now, little rabbit."

"Who's running, asshole?"

Before Grant could respond, one of the men behind them grabbed for Jenks and dragged her out of her seat. She managed to get a booted foot up and kicked the table, sending it slamming into Grant and the other three goons, knocking one of them over. The man staggered back into an innocent bystander, who predictably objected by bringing a massive fist down on his head.

"I want it on record that I did not start this bar fight!" Jenks shouted as she elbowed her attacker in the stomach and wriggled free. She dodged the man's wild punch and countered with a brutal uppercut that dropped him like an asteroid.

"Noted!" Nika hollered back, ducking down and putting his shoulder into the chest of the man who'd rushed him, flipping him over his back. He hit the floor hard, the air leaving him, and Nika gestured at Grant. "Come on then, you want to carry us out you're going to have to work for it."

Come on, Stephan, what is taking so long with that backup?

Grant moved in, and Nika had only a heartbeat to think that the man was almost as fast as Jenks before he blocked the punch and threw one of his own. Grant staggered back, clutching at his face, blood streaming from between his fingers. The next man surged in, but Nika caught him by the arm, locking onto his biceps and digging his thumb into the ulnar nerve, pressing in until the man gasped in pain.

Nika spotted the knife too late, and even though he twisted out of the way the edge bit deep into his side, and he could feel it scrape along a rib. Pain flared and he cursed loud enough to be heard over the chaos.

"Nika!" The distraction cost her. Jenks missed a block and her opponent grabbed her by the throat, flinging her hard across the room. She hit the wall and slid limply to the floor.

Nika started forward but a hard arm around his throat stopped him. "Should have just come with us when we asked," Grant snarled in his ear, and dragged him out the back door.

THIRTY-SEVEN

Jenks woke with a groan, tried to rub her face, and realized her hands were cuffed above her head. She found her footing, wincing as the motion released the tension on her shoulders and the feeling flooded back with painful swiftness. "All I need now is some guy with a bloodstained machete and I could be in the movies," she said, looking up at the cuffs.

She was chained to a pulley of some sort and she didn't want to think about just how far up that ceiling was. A memory of being hoisted so that her feet dangled helplessly tried to assert itself and she pushed it away through sheer force of will.

"Jenks?"

She turned her head to see Nika next to her, similarly bound. "What happened?"

"You got thrown into a wall."

"That explains the headache. Hey, look at me." Nika was too pale and she spotted the bloodstain on the right side of his shirt as the events of the fight came flooding back to her. "Nika, how bad are you hurt?"

The door crashed open before he could reply. All eight

people who came inside had their handshakes turned on, which didn't bode well at all.

Melanie Karenina's blond hair was perfectly done and her attempt to blend in on the surface of a habitat world was a laughable pair of fancy slacks tucked into a pair of obviously borrowed boots. Her white shirt already bore several orange smudges of the dirt of Trappist-1d.

"Goddamned rich people," Jenks muttered loud enough for only Nika to hear.

Grant was at Melanie's side, his hand on the gun at his hip. The other six people were evenly split, three men and three women.

"They're all armed with guns," Nika murmured. "Except for Karenina."

Jenks could see the sword hanging at Melanie's side. "Can you get loose?"

"Unlikely. You?"

"Not at the moment." Jenks shot a bright smile at the group as they approached. "That looks like it hurts, Vince. You go see a doctor about it?" Grant currently bore a pair of angry-looking black eyes and a swollen nose, courtesy of her brother.

"Shut the fuck up."

"Vincent." Melanie lifted her hand and smiled at Jenks. "Commander Vagin. Chief Khan, I am Melanie Karenina. I'm disappointed you didn't just come with my people."

"I don't like it when people change venues on me," Nika replied. "If you wanted to do this exchange under the radar, your people made a mistake starting a fight and kidnapping us."

"Ah yes, this *exchange*. Did you really think I was going to buy into your ruse, Commander?"

"'Ruse'? Who talks like that?" Jenks kept her face blank even as she cursed loudly in her head. No one else could hear it anyway; she couldn't get even a hint of coms on her DD, no chat, no emails. They were being jammed and good.

"It got you here, didn't it?" Nika replied with a smile.

"True, but I figured it was worth the trip. Let's have a conversation."

Jenks rattled her cuffs. "Take these off, we can chat."

"I'm smarter than that, Chief Khan," Melanie replied.

"Couldn't be too smart if you've gotten in bed with that idiot," she said, jutting her chin out at Grant. He moved to strike her, but Melanie put her hand out.

"Enough. This thing has escalated far beyond where it should have. I'm hoping we can settle it like civilized people."

"Sweetheart, I grew up on the streets," Jenks replied with a grin. "And you killed my friends. We're way beyond civilized. So let's try this instead: you take off my cuffs, and I'll shove those fancy boots up your—"

Grant moved from his spot at Melanie's side, hitting Jenks in the stomach with a brutal punch. All the breath rushed out of her, and through her own hacking sobs Jenks could hear Nika spitting curses.

The throbbing pain wasn't anything new, though, and she pushed off and up from the ledge behind her, managing a shot to his face with the crown of her head. There was a satisfying crack as she broke his nose a second time and Grant staggered back, blood streaming down his face.

He surged forward again, grabbing her by the throat. "You fucking bitch, I am going to cut you to pieces."

"No you won't," Jenks gasped. "Because she's in charge and if she wanted us dead, we'd already be dead. So get out of my face before I decide to make *you* stop breathing. The adults are having a conversation."

"Grant, stop." Melanie's order rang out before he could hit Jenks again. She waved a hand. "Leave her alone. Go clean yourself up."

For a second Jenks was sure the man was going to ignore Melanie and crush her throat, but she made herself keep her eyes on his until he let go and backed away.

"Fine." Grant marched off.

Jenks watched him go, then shared a look with Nika. It was a relief that she'd been right about Melanie wanting them alive, but there was no telling how long that luck would last. They needed to buy the others as much time as possible to find and rescue them.

Because Jenks knew they would.

She smiled her warmest smile at Melanie. "I'd say he's charming, but we both know that's a lie."

"He has his uses." Melanie lifted a shoulder. "You know what that's like, Chief Khan. Every good team needs the ones who can hit hard, but don't bother thinking of much else."

"Are you talking about me? Listen, you bougie piece of—"

"Jenks, she's just trying to get under your skin," Nika murmured.

"Oh, I know that. Like I told Grant, this is just two adults talking. At least she knows what she's dealing with. I hate uninformed opponents." Jenks let the smile on her face slide from warm to vicious. "Cut to the fun stuff, Melanie. What do you want from us?"

"You have proof, supposedly, of everything that's gone on in this operation, and you can keep it. However, in exchange, you're going to let me walk away from this. You can have Senator Tieg and anyone else involved in this rapidly collapsing scheme." She gestured behind her. "You'll leave me and these six people out of it."

"Grant's not on the list?" Nika asked.

"No." Melanie smiled, shaking her head, and Jenks caught a glimpse of the cunning the woman had been hiding behind her pleasant demeanor. "Grant is worth something to you, and if I'm crossing him and Tieg, I figure it's better if you take care of him. I don't like the idea of spending the rest of my life looking over my shoulder."

"You seem awfully sanguine about all this."

Jenks glanced at her brother. There were lines of pain etched on Nika's face and it looked like the bloodstain on his shirt was spreading.

"I am a businesswoman, Commander. All good things come to an end eventually and only fools try to stay longer than they should. A lesson I learned on Mars. Senator Tieg is unwilling to listen to reason about the shift in opinion concerning the TLF. And how it will only get worse if we continue to mine these habitats for money."

"Senator Carmichael has managed to convince a number of his key supporters to change their votes on an upcoming bill. If that bill passes, he'll lose his seat on the Habitats Committee."

"And he'll lose his ability to control this operation," Nika said.

"Precisely. I've known men like this my whole life. He's already spooked by that possibility and thought that having Grant attack the NeoG would help turn the tide."

Jenks gritted her teeth against the lie but stayed silent. Julia had told them Melanie ordered the attack and had the recordings to prove it.

"You have to let us go," Nika said.

A smile briefly peeked out at the corner of Melanie's mouth, then disappeared. "I don't think that's quite the case, Commander, but I'll let you contact your team and tell them where to meet us. We'll do the exchange. You two get to live, I get to walk."

"In exchange for keeping the shit ton of money you made off this scheme." Jenks snorted. "Okay, Hans. Try not to fall off a tower."

Melanie frowned at her. "Hicks, shoot them both if they try anything." She moved forward, not toward Jenks but to Nika.

As she reached for the chain holding his cuffed arms above his head, Melanie stopped. Jenks watched as disbelief followed by fury screamed across the woman's face. "You froze my accounts?"

Nika smiled. "Took a little longer than I'd hoped, but Sapphi had a lot to track down, didn't she? She got all of them, I'm guessing? Even the ones you didn't think we knew about."

Melanie snarled and punched Nika twice.

Right in the wound in his side.

"You fucking—" Jenks broke off when Nika's legs gave out and he tried, but failed, to hold in his gasp of pain.

"Still bougie, gutter trash?" Melanie asked, then stepped up onto the ledge behind them and released the tension on the chain holding Nika's cuffs. He collapsed to the ground, his cuffed hands pressed to his side.

The tension on Jenks's arms released a moment later as Melanie hit the same release and Jenks breathed a sigh of relief that the chain was long enough to allow her to scramble over to Nika. "Hold still." She pulled his shirt up to examine the wound and swore.

"It's fine," he whispered with a weak smile.

"Like a fucking dog surrounded by fire fine," she snapped, trying to tamp down the fear crawling up her throat.

"You'll need this." Melanie tossed a med kit at Jenks, who snarled in response. "Look at it this way, Chief Khan, now we're on a time limit. You'll want to tell your people to hurry and get my accounts unfrozen."

"If he dies I'm going to take you apart." Jenks didn't even look up when she said it, all of her focus on bandaging his wound with the grimly archaic supplies she'd been handed. "What the hell? Have you been hoarding these since the Collapse?"

"You're infinitely amusing, but that mouth of yours is going to get someone killed one of these days," Melanie said.

"Let's all hope it's you," Jenks replied as she helped Nika sit up so she could wrap the bandage around his middle. She pressed her forehead to his for a moment and then turned to Melanie. "Let me call my lieutenant or so help me neither this chain nor those goons behind you will be able to stop me from killing you."

MAX SAT IN A CHAIR IN THE KITCHEN AND PATTED DOGE AS the conversation swirled around her. The dog was pressing so hard against her leg it was probably going to bruise, but the sensation was strangely calming.

"Jenks is scared," Doge said over the com.

"How do you know that?"

"Can feel it. Can't find her, but can feel her."

Max frowned, unsure how to respond to the ROVER, who shouldn't be able to feel anything, let alone understand what it meant. "I don't blame you for being scared," she whispered.

"Not me. Jenks. She was angry before. Not scared. Jenks is so rarely scared. Now she is and I do not know why?"

Max looked down at the ROVER. He was talking only to her, not over the team-wide com, and he lifted his metal head to rest it on her knee. "How do you know she's scared, Doge?"

"Does it matter?" The lights in his eyes flickered through a range of colors before settling back to his normal cool blue shade. Then they flashed red. "We need to go help her. I do not want her to be scared."

"I know, but we don't know where she is, buddy."

"Then we should go find her."

"Max, I've got an incoming call for you," Sapphi said from across the room.

"Who is it?" Max asked.

"It's Jenks."

The sound in the room dropped to zero.

"Put it on the main screen, incoming but not outgoing video."

"Got it."

The image resolved and Max felt Doge vibrate at the

sight of Jenks. But she wasn't alone; Melanie Karenina was standing next to her with a gun to her head and there was blood on Jenks's hands when she raised them and rubbed at her cheek.

"Jenks, are you okay?" Max asked.

"She's fine, Lieutenant Carmichael," Melanie replied.

"Where's Nika?" Stephan asked.

"He's fine. Bleeding a little—okay, a lot, but it's not life-threatening. Was that Commander Yevchenko? Back from the dead?"

Stephan gestured at Sapphi and Melanie's smile widened as the picture resolved itself on their end so she could see them.

"Well, I, for one, am glad you're not dead. Is Luis still around?"

"What do you want, Melanie?"

"I'm not injured," Doge said. "N was stabbed in fight. M just punched him and he's bleeding a lot. She knows accounts frozen."

Max didn't look down at Doge when the dog started talking over the com again. Jenks still had her hands up, her index finger restlessly tapping against the side of her throat.

"What are you saying, Doge?" Max murmured, trying to keep her mouth from moving.

"Don't know where we are. G here. Six goons plus M and G."

It was hard to focus on both the ROVER and Stephan's conversation with Melanie, so she let him do his thing and concentrated on what the dog was saying.

When she got it all, she went back to listening to Stephan.

"We'll meet, then. Discuss terms. You can give me my money and I'll give you your people back." Melanie glanced downward and smiled. "I'd hurry. He doesn't look well."

Max gave Jenks a little nod before the screen went black.

Scott's low curse rolled through the room. "What the fuck did she do to Nika?"

"He got stabbed in the bar," Max replied, and Stephan raised an eyebrow at her.

"You know that how?"

"Doge, go to external speaker. Give me the full playback."

The ROVER complied and Stephan frowned as he recited the same thing over again.

"Where did he get that?"

"Jenks," Luis said. He brought his own hands up and tapped on his throat. "She was communicating. Doge is the only one who caught it."

"Sapphi, give me the playback without sound," Stephan ordered. A few moments later he nodded. "It's Morse code. I missed it. I was watching Melanie."

"Correct. That is what I'm here for, Commander Yevchenko. Jenks taught me. She said it was a good thing for me to know."

Tivo laughed. "Trust Jenks to have taught her dog Morse code."

"We need to get moving. That location she gave us is pretty far from the outpost," Scott said.

"I know those coordinates," Chae said. "That's a danger-ous area, lots of washouts and unstable ground."

"They are no doubt already there and will be able to pick their spot," Stephan replied. "The only thing we have going for us is that Melanie wants to make a deal and she wants her money back."

"Why does she only want *Zuma* to show up for this meet-ing if she wants us to take Grant into custody?" Tivo asked, and Max realized she'd missed more than she thought of the conversation.

"Because that means there will only be four of you versus their eight—at minimum. She's hoping you'll be concerned enough about Nika that you'll be more willing to agree to her terms," Stephan replied. "She'll try to pull something; I know her well enough to know that. I don't think she's really inter-

HOLD FAST THROUGH THE FIRE   389

ested in turning Grant over to us, no matter what she said. We'll send you in for the handoff, but the rest of us will be stationed here and here." He brought up a map on the screen and pointed at the location.

It was a large washed-out gulley at the canyon's edge where the landscape flattened out and spread into the flatland in one direction, while on the other side was a sheer drop-off into a deeper part of the canyon. Max made a face. "That's a shit location. There's no cover."

"Yeah, she knows that. It's probably also why she reopened Nika's wound, to keep us from arguing over the meeting place. Melanie wants control of this—it fits with everything else she's done so far."

"I don't like her," Doge announced. "She's made Jenks scared."

The dog's comment dropped a second blanket of silence on the room. Max shared a look with Scott, who got to his feet.

"Well, like it or not, this is what we're doing. Let's get our shit and get out there."

THIRTY-EIGHT

"You all right?"

Chae looked at Max for just a moment and then returned to the task of landing *Zuma* on the edge of the meeting spot. There weren't words for everything rolling around in their head right now, though a strange calm had descended on the whole ship, Chae included.

Luis and Tivo were with them, but the others had come in on ST-1's ship, to be split and stationed at strategic points both above and within the canyon yawning to their left.

Melanie may have picked this spot, but Stephan was determined to make the most of it, and with Chae's help they'd been able to do just that. Chae knew this canyon inside and out, knew where all the hidden tunnels were—and more important, which ones were still probably open even after the heavy spring rains.

The canyon continued to their right, the washed-out portion running only forty meters or so before the walls dropped sharply again.

"Chae?"

"Sorry." They shook their head. "Yeah. I'm fine."

"Dog in a fire fine? Or actually fine?"

"What?"

She laughed weakly. "Sorry, I was trying to—never mind—I don't have Jenks's sense of humor."

Chae reached for her hand. "They'll be okay. We'll make the handoff and get them back."

Max squeezed their fingers once before letting go. "You're right. Melanie won't risk ruining her chance at a deal."

"I still don't want to make a deal with her, LT."

"Me either, but we don't have much choice. Not with Jenks and Nika still in danger."

"Why not just go in force, then? We've got the proof from Julia—everything we need to bring all of them down. She's got to know that. I don't trust her. What if she's planning something else?"

"Again—this is the way we can keep our people safe. But you're right: she most likely is planning something, Chae. Because here's the thing about rich people—pre-Collapse and post—they care more about their money than anything else." Max frowned in thought.

"What is it, LT?"

"Just a—hey, Sapphi? How easy is it to make it look like Melanie's accounts are unfrozen?"

The ensign made a face, tapping her hand on the top of Doge's head. "Not easy. Why?"

"Chae has a very good point: we don't actually *need* Melanie to bring Tieg down. At this point we're negotiating purely for Nika and Jenks's safety. Once we have that, all bets are off, right?"

"I could unfreeze them and then rescind the order. It's risky, though, Max. If it happens while she's still got them, her reaction will not be good."

"I know."

"I feel like they'd both be on board with this plan," Chae whispered. "If it meant Melanie wasn't going to get away."

"Maybe, but it still means putting them at risk and I won't do it without their approval."

"They agreed to the risk."

"Not for this."

MAX WATCHED THE SHAME FLICKER ACROSS CHAE'S FACE.

"LT, I didn't mean—"

"I know you didn't," she cut them off. "It's all right." If anything, the reminder was for herself, that she wouldn't do the very thing she'd been so angry with Nika and Stephan over. Even while her mind was spinning for some way to tell both Nika and Jenks what they had planned and get approval.

Sapphi still didn't have them on coms and there was no way to tell if Melanie had cracked the encryption and could listen in to those or monitor the chats. Whatever Max did would have to be verbal.

The memory of an old TV show Jenks had foisted on her surfaced and Max frowned again as she headed down the stairs of the bridge.

Would it be enough?

"I know that look, LT," Sapphi said. "What is it?"

"I might have an idea." She switched on her com. "Stephan, you copy?"

"Here."

"I have an idea, not sure if it will work, though. Permission to give it a try and we'll just go back to plan A if Jenks doesn't catch my signal?"

There was a moment of silence, then Stephan spoke. "Is it dangerous?"

"More than what we're already doing? No."

"All right, permission granted."

Tamago, Luis, and Tivo met them at the already opened airlock and silently waited for Max and the others to shrug into their harnesses before passing over their swords. Doge was sitting nearby and Max put a hand on his head.

"Doge—"

"Lieutenant Carmichael, please do not ask me to stay behind."

"Doge, you can come," she said. "But if you shoot anyone, make sure it's not lethal, and you cannot shoot until I say so."

"Noted, Lieutenant." Doge jumped from the doorway, landing easily in the shifting red dirt.

Max followed Luis out of the Interceptor, squinting against the late-afternoon light cutting through the canyon.

"Here they come," Luis murmured from her side. "What's this new plan you've got?"

"It's not much different from the current one, just involves not letting Melanie get away. Sapphi thinks she can unfreeze and then refreeze her accounts, we just need to make sure Nika and Jenks are safe before Melanie realizes what we've done."

Max didn't look away from the transport as it dipped down into the washout. Grant was driving, Melanie next to him. Jenks and Nika were in the back surrounded by three guards.

"I see three more targets behind the rocks on your one o'clock," Stephan said over the coms. "Scott and I are in position. The others are in the tunnel, headed your way. They'll take those three out first."

Nika leaned on Jenks as they got out of the transport. He was paler than usual and Max could see the lines of tension on both his face and Jenks's.

"They're both cuffed, hands in front," she murmured, bringing up her gun as the group drew closer. The guards responded by bringing their own weapons up until Melanie lifted her hands with a smile.

"There's no need for such hostility. Luis, how are you?"

He looked past her to Jenks and Nika. "You okay, Dai?" he asked.

"Better when we're done here," she replied.

"Ms. Karenina." Max handed her gun to Tamago and stepped forward. "We're here as requested."

"I recall saying just the members of *Zuma's Ghost*."

Max didn't bat an eyelash. "Well, we were short two so I made a command decision. Couldn't let you have too much leverage." She looked to Jenks as she spoke. "Sapphi's on the coms with Hardison right now. Check your accounts."

Hardison? Jenks mouthed when Melanie and Grant were distracted. Max allowed herself only the slightest of smiles, hoping that her teammate would make the connection on her own. The quick thumbs-up from Jenks seemed to confirm it.

"Well, Carmichael, you came through," Melanie said, gesturing to Grant. "Uncuff them." She backed off with the guards and Max took a few steps forward, catching Jenks when Grant shoved her over and pushing her in Luis's direction without taking her eyes off of Nika.

Grant didn't notice Melanie getting back into the transport as he unlocked Nika's cuffs.

"Mr. Grant, I regret to inform you that I no longer have need of your services."

He whipped around to stare at Melanie. "You b—"

Max jumped forward, putting her shoulder into Grant and knocking him back a step as she grabbed for Nika. She spun him out of the way, covering him with her body as shots rang out.

NIKA LANDED IN THE DIRT HARD, MAX ON TOP OF HIM.

"Sorry," she said in his ear as she rolled off him, dragging him behind the dubious safety of a large rock. "Tamago!" she hollered, and then was gone.

"Right here. Stay down, Nika." Tamago slid to a stop next to him, med kit in hand. "Let me see."

"It's fine. Just slap a patch on it for me so I can get up."

Nika could see Melanie from where he was as she leaped from the transport and ran for the canyon.

"Excuse me? Beyond the gunshots whizzing around, you've been stabbed."

"Tama, come on. Don't make me order you."

"You've lost a lot of blood, Nik, and it's messing with your head," they said, pulling out a heal patch. "But I get it, and this is nasty but not life-threatening or I'd never let you go. Looks like Stephan put a shot into the engine of Melanie's transport and at least one of the goons is down. Jenks and Chae took off after Grant."

"Where's Max?"

"She followed Melanie." Tamago smoothed down the patch. "I put some numbing agent on there, too, but you're not invincible so don't act like it. It's going to hurt cleaning it later and I'm going to have to do a thorough job because you're being pushy." They pulled their sword free and pressed it into his hand. "That way." They pointed into the canyon. "And Sapphi says to tell you that Melanie's accounts have been refrozen."

Sapphi comes through again.

Nika sprinted after Max. Melanie had turned and run for the canyon, dodging behind the cover of the scrub brush. He slid over the top of a rock, Tamago's sword in hand, landing on the balls of his feet and continuing on.

He heard the clash of swords, ducked under a massive boulder that had tumbled from the top of the canyon, and slid to a stop.

Max and Melanie were locked in a fight in the hollowed-out circle of the canyon floor. Their swords rang together, Max's matte black against the shining silver of Melanie's blade, and then separated.

"You're really going to be unsporting about it and go two on one?" Melanie asked as Nika circled around her.

"Trust me," he said. "If I had a gun I'd shoot you right now."

Melanie smiled and lunged at Max, who managed to side-step enough that the tip of the woman's sword hit her on the outside of her shoulder rather than in her heart, where Melanie had aimed.

Max kicked her, knocking Melanie back toward Nika, who rushed forward. The woman spun, as fast as Stephan, and deflected his swing to the side.

"When you first came to Trappist, we were afraid you were after us, you know. But we soon realized you weren't aware of Stephan's investigation and were just on One-e for regular duty. We appreciated the distraction LifeEx provided. It was a pity about your arm." The smile on Melanie's face was ugly and Nika kept his mind cleared of the memories as they circled each other.

"Nika, she's hoping to distract—" Max was whispering over the com, but he had to shut her out. He needed to focus.

Max was putting pressure on her right shoulder, but Nika could see the blood leaking between her long fingers. And if he kept thinking about that, he'd lose.

He was always thinking too much.

"Why'd you hit Jupiter Station?" Nika asked. "That was an unwise move. All it did was get the entire CHN military hunting for your heads."

"Calculated risk." Melanie shrugged as she wove her sword in a figure eight. "We'd hoped to take out all the important players and pin it on Free Mars. Wars are good things—not only to distract certain people as we wrapped up our operations on Trappist, but because they would have opened up all sorts of new business opportunities. Things I could have exploited once Tieg was out of the picture."

"You really thought your warning on Trappist-1d did the trick," Nika said, the realization hitting him. "That we were just going to head back to Jupiter and pretend like nothing was wrong. For someone who was in the NeoG, you don't know us very well."

This time Melanie's smile was tight and Nika knew he'd hit the mark. "Fucking NeoG, always so righteous," she hissed. "I hated every second I was in, with the exception of Mars. Because I actually got to feel like we were doing something down there busting heads."

Nika conceded some ground when Melanie threw out a testing strike and made a mental note to thank D'Arcy for all those practice bouts that involved a lot of conversation. He took a quick step forward, slicing through shirt and flesh with the tip of his sword.

Melanie stumbled back, the look she shot him full of hatred. "I was disappointed that we only just missed your sister with that bomb. Then I thought maybe we'd lucked out and put you all out of play with the news of Luis's and Stephan's deaths. But you just kept at it. Was it because you knew they weren't dead?"

"No, we thought they were dead and we knew you were responsible." Nika parried her expected swing, countering with his own and driving Melanie back several steps with the force of the blow. "Didn't you ever wonder, Melanie, how we knew? Where the proof came from? How we found your accounts?"

She didn't have time to answer as he swung at her with controlled fury. Melanie barely blocked his strike and Nika twisted his wrist so that the hook at the end of his sword locked onto Melanie's blade. He sent it flying with a sharp movement.

"You fucked with the NeoG and we were determined to bring you down. On your knees, and put your hands behind your back."

Nika glanced at Max, who nodded and approached them with her sword in her left hand, reaching for the cuffs in her cargo pocket.

Melanie rolled away from her, spinning and kicking Nika's legs out from underneath him. He hit the ground and couldn't bring his sword up in time before Melanie tackled him, knocking it from his hand. Nika heard Max shout, but he caught the knife that appeared with his right hand and watched the shock flare on her face as he easily bent the blade.

"I swear I will drive this sword through your rotten heart if you don't roll off him," Max said.

Melanie complied. Max nudged her with a foot. "On your face, now."

Nika tossed the twisted knife aside and grabbed Max's cuffs, quickly restraining Melanie and hauling her to her feet.

"Listen, that's a lot of money," Melanie babbled. "Enough for a good life away from all this. You can take it all, just let me go."

Nika looked at Max, who laughed.

"First off, your accounts are frozen again," Max said. "We already *have* your money and it'll be going where it belongs—back to Trappist."

"Second," Nika added, "you know who you're talking to, right? We're the NeoG, and we've already got a good life."

THIRTY-NINE

Jenks sprinted across the open terrain at the edge of the canyon, Chae on her heels. "You running from a little rabbit, Grant?" She should have known the taunt would do exactly what she'd intended, but Grant moved fast, coming to a stop and lining up a shot with the gun still in his hand. "Chae, drop!"

Jenks ducked, rushing forward and putting her shoulder into his diaphragm, lifting him off his feet. He lost his grip on his weapon at the impact, but brought his knee up into her nose as they fell onto the hard-packed dirt. Pain exploded through her head and Jenks rolled to her side, blood streaming down her face.

"Jenks!"

She spit a mouthful of blood out onto the ground. "I've got it," she said to Luis as he and Tivo skidded to a stop. "Doge, you stop. Do not shoot." The ROVER's eyes flashed red and for a second she thought he was going to disobey her.

"Come on, big guy," she said to Grant. "You and me. Let's go." Her nose was throbbing, but it was nothing compared to the rage screaming in her head.

"This isn't your fucking cage." Grant rasped, getting to his feet.

"You're right. I have to follow rules in the cage." She gestured. "Take your shot before I let Luis here put you down."

He rushed her, spinning to the side. Jenks blocked his punch with her left elbow, slapping Grant across the face with her open right hand. She could see the poorly banked fury in his eyes and grinned, knowing it would push him over the edge.

Because whatever barbs Grant wanted to throw about the cage, preparing for a fight was what Jenks was good at, and she'd been studying him since before the explosion that took Hoboins away from her.

Then, he'd been just a target like any other. Killing Hoboins made it personal. She'd found every scrap of footage she could of Grant's days with the Mars PK, every fight he'd been in, every arrest.

Her rage was clarity. The coldness of space. Despite her anger, Jenks treated this like a cage match and she already knew all her opponent's weaknesses.

Left hook is slower than right.

She caught the punch, pressing down on his elbow with hers as she yanked upward. Grant's howl of pain almost drowned out the snapping of bones. She stepped in past his guard, bringing her right elbow up into his chin.

Jenks easily avoided his fumbling grasp as he stumbled back from the blow.

Right knee injury from time in PeaceKeepers.

"You hurt my crew," she said, bringing her boot down on his right knee and slipping away from him as he fell to the ground. "Get up."

Grant staggered to his feet. Jenks had purposefully not broken his knee; she wanted him mobile, and this time when he came at her, she dodged his swing, slamming a fist into his jaw. Grant staggered back and went down again.

"You hurt my family." She kicked him in the chest, knocking him onto his back. She took two steps forward and put her boot on his throat. "It would be so easy to put my full weight on you and end this." She felt her iron control slip as she pressed down and he choked.

"Dai." Luis's quiet voice extinguished her fury and Jenks dragged in a breath, glancing away for just a moment.

Grant grabbed her leg, yanking it out from underneath her. She heard the others yelling as he swarmed over her, somehow getting his good arm across her throat and dragging them both upright.

"You all back the fuck up now," Grant snarled. "Or I'll—" He broke off on a gasp of pain.

"Let the chief go, or so help me I'll shove this sword the rest of the way into your back and sever your spine." There wasn't the slightest tremor in Chae's order and Jenks pulled Grant's arm away from her throat. Tivo and Luis swept in, shouting for Grant to get on the ground as Chae moved out of the way.

Jenks pulled them into a hug.

"Got your back, Chief," Chae murmured in her ear, hugging her tightly with their free arm.

"Damn right you do."

"WELCOME BACK TO EARTH. HOW'S YOUR SIDE?" STEPHAN held a hand out to Nika as he disembarked from the *Laika*, the rest of *Zuma's Ghost* behind him.

The Intel specialist had taken the NeoG's newest transport, the *Gajabahu*, on two short wormhole hops from Trappist back to Jupiter and then to Earth while the rest of them had taken the slower route on the Navy ship.

Everything about the operation had been locked down tight, though the interrogation of Melanie and Grant on their ride back to Earth had proven more than useful as the pair turned on each other and on Senator Tieg with surprising swiftness.

It only added to the evidence and testimony from Julia, who was still safely in custody.

"Tamago says it'll heal fine. After they got done punishing me by cleaning it."

Stephan chuckled. "How's Chae?"

"Still a little dazzled by how Max managed to talk her sister into supplying whatever the habitats on Trappist need as a humanitarian project until the money we confiscated from Melanie's accounts can be assigned by the Habitat Committee." Nika shrugged. "Other than that, they'll settle once we're back on Trappist. It'll be helpful to have someone from the area involved in the work we're going to do there."

"This was by no means the only group exploiting the habitats, but it was the largest. Melanie refuses to elaborate on what she said to you regarding Free Mars and the potential war there, but we'll deal with that another day," Stephan replied, exchanging nods with the other members of the team as they came off the ship. "We've got a transport over here and Senator Carmichael is waiting for us. Ready to take down Tieg?"

Nika looked behind him at the rest of *Zuma's Ghost*, the five Neos nodding in unison. "We're ready."

PEOPLE STUMBLED OVER EACH OTHER IN THEIR HASTE TO GET out of the way of the group of Neos and Navy personnel who marched into the CHN Senate building. Max strode at Nika's side, resolutely ignoring the twinge in her shoulder.

"Sir, I'm sorry, you can't—" The guard who tried to stop them fell silent when Pax appeared.

"These are my guests." Pax gestured for them to follow her down the hallway.

"Senator Carmichael, the Senate is in session." The guard at the next door frowned at Max's sister.

"I know that, Sergeant. This is a matter for the Senate. Open the doors."

"Yes, ma'am."

The doors were pushed open and Max followed her sister into the chamber. The noise level dropped abruptly with their entrance but then rose again as the protests started.

"There will be order!" An older woman whose handshake read *Speaker Quanella Watson, she/her* held up her hands and the room fell silent once again. "Senator Carmichael, we are in the middle of a debate—on your habitat assistance bill, I might add. What is the meaning of this interruption?"

"Madam Speaker, my apologies, but this has to do with my bill. If I could introduce Commander Stephan Yevchenko of the Intelligence Division of the Near-Earth Orbital Guard. He and his team have been investigating charges of corruption, theft, and dereliction of the oath sworn to the Coalition of Human Nations."

"Senator Carmichael, you know you are supposed to put witnesses on the roster."

"I do, this was a matter that required some discretion, so I hope you'll forgive me and listen to what he has to say."

"We're going to have a runner," Max murmured to Jenks, tipping her head back toward the door. Jenks nodded and nudged Luis and Tivo. The pair followed her and Max schooled her expression into one of polite disinterest as Senator Rubio Tieg stopped edging toward the exit.

"Esteemed senators, five years ago we began investigating rumors that funds and the supply chain for the Trappist habitats were being misused." Stephan stepped into the center of the chamber with the same poise as any of the people in this room. "I am happy to tell you that today, almost all of those involved have been apprehended."

"Senator Carmichael," Senator Watson said, "while this is amazing news, I am certain you didn't interrupt your own bill debate just to let us all know this. Could you get to the point?"

"Yes, the point." Pax turned around and looked at Senator Tieg. "The man in charge of all this, who was profiting off the suffering of the very people we all swore an oath to protect, is in this very room. I am here to inform him of his conspirators' arrests. I am also here to ask my colleagues to allow these Intelligence officers to arrest Senator Tieg."

The murmurs grew louder, but Pax was unmoved by her fellow senators' protests. "You can go quietly, Rubio, or they can drag you out of here. It's your choice. I'd remind you, though, that your actions caused the deaths of an admiral of the NeoG, a man many of these people served with and respected a great deal." Pax smiled. "Choose wisely."

The roar of the Boarding Games crowd vibrated the walls and floor around them as the circle of Neos stood with their hands touching. Nika shared a smile with Commander Till of *Flux Capacitor* and then looked at his sister.

Jenks grinned. "We ready to win this?"

"You know it," Chae said with a smile of their own.

"For Admiral Hoboins," Max replied and the team's response echoed back at her.

"For the NeoG."

ACKNOWLEDGMENTS

I'd like to thank David Pomerico and Mireya Chiriboga as well as all the other folx at Harper Voyager whose tireless efforts made this novel come to life.

Many thanks to Reginald Polynice for his gorgeous cover art and the design team for their hard work.

To my agent, Andrew Zack, for all *your* hard work, your sharp eye, and your support.

To Josh McGraw and Kelly Evans for graciously donating to the Australian bushfire relief early in 2020. I hope you enjoy the characters who appeared on the page as a result.

To my family and friends. Thank you all for your support, your love. There's no one else I'd rather go into battle with than you.

To my readers, thank you for your time. I know it's in short supply and your choice to spend some of it reading my stories is never taken for granted.

Read on to enjoy a fun,

thrilling excerpt from

A PALE

LIGHT IN

THE

BLACK

Book One of the NeoG series

available now from Harper Voyager!

SOL YEAR 2435,

ONE DAY POST-BOARDING GAMES

The hardest part was the smiling.

Commander Rosa Martín Rivas pasted another smile onto her face as she wove through the crowds and headed for her ship at the far end of the hangar. She and the rest of the members of *Zuma's Ghost* had weathered the post-Games interviews with as much grace as a losing team could, answering question after question about how it felt to come within three points of beating Commander Carmichael's SEAL team without ever breaking expression.

That wasn't entirely true. Jenks had slipped once, muttering a curse and giving the reporter a flat look. Nika had smoothly stepped in and covered for his adopted sister, giving the volatile petty officer a chance to compose herself.

"Hey, Rosa?"

She stopped, letting Commander Stephan Yevchenko—leader of the NeoG headquarters' team *Honorable Intent*—catch up to her, ignoring the snide smiles from the naval personnel who passed by her. Yevchenko's people had made up the other half of their group for these Games. And though the Neos had all performed admirably, it had been Rosa who'd let everyone down.

The slender, brown-haired Neo stuck out a hand. "Next year, right?"

"We'll see." It was the best response she could come up with, and something of her mask must have slipped because Stephan didn't let go.

"It wasn't your fault," he said in a low voice. "Don't spend a year convincing yourself it was."

"Too late for that." The reply was out before she could stop it. Rosa muffled a curse when he smiled. Stephan was always good at getting people to say too much. "It's all good. See you at the prelims next year."

"Likely sooner," he said. "We've got a case building. I might need your help with it."

Rosa nodded, but didn't press. Stephan's work in Intel meant he'd tell her when he could and not a moment sooner. Instead she once again forced the smile she was really starting to hate and headed for the Interceptor ahead of her. The interior of *Zuma's Ghost* was dead quiet when she boarded, a far cry from the laughter and conversation that usually dominated the ship. Rosa pulled the hatch shut behind her.

"Take us home, Ma," she called up to the bridge.

"Roger that, Commander."

Rosa headed for the common area, taking in the downcast eyes and tight mouths of her crew. "All right, people." She spoke with a firmness she didn't quite feel, but if there was one thing she was good at, it was putting on a brave face for everyone else. "You've got the ride back to Jupiter to get it out of your systems. It's just the Games."

"We lost, Commander." Jenks's mismatched eyes weren't quite filled with tears, but there was a sheen to them and her jaw was set in a determined pout.

"I know. We don't lose out there, though, right? What are we?"

"The NeoG." The automatic reply echoed back from everyone, and this time Rosa's smile was genuine.

"That's right. Don't forget it."

T-MINUS FOUR MONTHS UNTIL
PRELIM BOARDING GAMES

The battered ship drifted in perfect synchronicity with the asteroid as it passed across the face of Sol, for just a moment blotting out the G-type yellow dwarf almost five hundred million kilometers away.

Upon visual inspection, the ship appeared as dead as the asteroid, its gray surface pitted and dulled by years in the black. It was, or at least appeared to be, a shitty early-days system jumper made for long-haul flights from Earth to the Trappist-1 system.

The SJs had been made well before the days of wormhole tech and instantaneous travel. Their names were painfully incorrect, as they didn't jump anywhere but instead took the long, slow path thirty-nine light-years across the galaxy. Their inhabitants trusting that they'd go to sleep before launch and wake up a long way away from Earth on a brand-new planet.

Lieutenant Commander Nika Vagin watched as his little sister, Petty Officer First Class Altandai Khan of the Near-Earth Orbital Guard, put her hands on her hips and stared up at the ship from the asteroid's surface. "That's it. Ship 645v, aka *An Ordinary Star*. Launched on June 17, 2330. Carrying three hundred and fifty-three popsicles—"

"Jenks." He let the threat in her nickname carry over the coms.

"Sorry," she said with a grin, clearly unrepentant even through the dim glare of the star on her helmet. "Three hundred and fifty-three *people*."

She wasn't wrong about them being popsicles, though. These poor bastards froze themselves for nothing. The Voyager Company developed wormhole tech just before the last wave of transport ships left Earth. When they were sure it was going to work, Off-Earth sent in larger freighters via wormhole to scoop up the SJs and take them on to the Trappist system.

Correction: they picked up the ones they could find. Nika shuddered a little at the thought.

Some were destroyed by system failure or space debris and nothing was left but rubble floating in the black. And some had simply vanished into the great nothing—no signal, no trace. All told, there were still a few dozen registered vessels missing, and a double handful more unregistered ships carrying a few desperate families who hadn't realized or hadn't cared that there was one—and only one—company with the legal ability to ship humans off-world.

"I'm getting no life-sign readings at all," Nika said, staring up at the ship. "There had better be someone on that jumper. If there isn't and I hiked my ass halfway across this surface when we could have just called the station and had an Earth Security Cutter tow them in, I'm going to chew out someone's ass."

"Relax, Nik." Commander Rosa Martín's voice was crisp over the com. "There are people. Though the ones on ice are probably freezer burned and the ones who aren't have everything locked down so tight we can't see a single thing from out here."

"I still don't see why we couldn't have just used the EMUs straight from *Zuma's Ghost*."

"Because she's noisy on the radar," Jenks said, "and then I wouldn't get to do this." She took off running with that low-gravity bounce, did a handspring over an outcropping, and launched herself into the starlit blackness beyond.

Nika cursed, his ears ringing from Jenks's whoop and the laughter of the rest of the team as he followed her. His helmet display gave him the necessary trajectory, although he was sure his little sister had done it on nothing but faith.

He launched himself off the asteroid's surface, flying through the vacuum toward the mysterious ship. Jenks soared through space ahead of him, kicking in the thrusters on her EMU to slow her approach at the last second so that she made less noise than a piece of space debris when she hit the hull of the ship. The name was faded and pockmarked from dust impact but still read clearly AN ORDINARY STAR next to the door.

"This is an older model of SJ, Jenks." Ensign Nell Zika's cool voice came over the coms as the readings from Jenks's scan scrolled across her terminal back on their ship. "One of the last waves from 2330. It's registered, though, legal and everything. Huh—that's weird."

"What's weird, Sapphi?" Rosa asked the ensign. "Tamago and I just connected with the back end of this beast."

"We see you, Commander. Did you know that there were twenty-seven missing ships in total? And twenty of them were from the last wave?" Sapphi asked.

"I did *not* know that," Jenks replied. She didn't look up as Nika made contact with the ship next to her. "How many were in the last wave?"

"Only thirty," Sapphi replied. "The wormholes were the big news story and people wanted to wait and see what would happen with them."

"Yeah, I get that, but a sixty-seven percent loss for a single wave seems like a really high failure rate for Off-Earth Enterprises, and it was never in the news?"

"How do you know that?" Nika asked.

"I read the briefing."

Nika reached out and tapped the side of his sister's helmet once, hard enough to push her into the ship.

"Okay, maybe I read more than the briefing," she said. "It was interesting. People were flipping their sh—"

"Focus, Jenks, you had your fun. Time to work," Rosa ordered.

"That's on Sapphi, Commander. We're just hanging out in the middle of a deadly vacuum, waiting. Gotta do something to distract Nika here, or you know his noodle gets in a twist." She grinned at Nika's glare. She knew he hated space work and teased him about it mercilessly every chance she got.

But, in a way, she had a point—what fool pursued a career with an Interceptor crew when they were terrified of being out in space?

You. You're the fool, he thought.

"Give me two hundred seconds and you'll be in." Sapphi's voice was soothing on the com.

The timer in the corner of Nika's vision started ticking down as the ensign turned her brilliance toward the lock on the outside of the ship.

"Nika, if things go sideways in there you grab Jenks and get the fuck out, copy?" Rosa's order came straight to him rather than broadcast on the team channel.

"You expecting trouble?" He turned in toward the ship so Jenks couldn't spot his lips moving. His little sister had an amazing ability to read lips that she exploited mercilessly.

"Something feels off. I know Off-Earth wants any SJs recovered intact and there may be live passengers on board—though you and I know the odds that anyone on ice for as long as these folks have been not having freezer burn is atom small—but why would someone be hanging out in the belt with a derelict ship? I don't like it, and regardless of what Off-Earth wants, I'll blow that ship to pieces before I risk living, breathing people on a piece of space junk."

"I thought you wanted to space Jenks yesterday." He couldn't resist the tease, and Rosa chuckled.

"That's a daily occurrence, but I know you'd miss her, so I let her keep breathing."

"Eh, today you're right." Nika smiled as Jenks continued to worry over the problem of the ratios on a sixty-seven percent failure rate for a launch. "Intel said one, maybe two pirates and no more than five for a boat this size. I think they may actually be right—the ship's not big enough to handle a crew of more than five, and I doubt they'd expend that much personnel on something like this. Jenks and I will handle the front end. But yes, if things go wrong we'll double-time it out. Hand to Saint Ivan."

"From your lips to God's ears. Be careful in there."

"Same to you, Commander."

"Will do."

The airlock opened. Jenks looked at Nika with a smile. "You got my back?" she asked, thumping her chest twice with a gloved fist.

He grinned, swinging his own arm out, tapping the back of his fist against hers before grabbing her forearm and leaning in to bump their helmets together. "You've got mine."

"Let's do this."

The pair slipped into the airlock and pulled it shut behind them. As he watched the numbers cycle, Nika debated whether they should take their helmets off. If they did, leaving them here in the airlock would be safest, but it also meant they'd have to get back to this spot in order to get off the ship.

"We've got air. This can's been refilled," Jenks said. "There's definitely someone walking around in here. Helmets off, Nik?"

The fact that she even asked him meant Jenks was already

in battle mode—focused, unassailable. She'd keep with the jokes, but she'd do what he told her without question.

"Yeah, take it off. We'll stash them here." He hit the release on his own and pulled the dome loose. He shoved it into a spot behind the old suits hanging in the airlock, surprised they didn't crumble to dust when he touched them.

"I wish Off-Earth would hurry it up with those new prototypes. I'm tired of lugging this thing around." Jenks set her helmet next to his and tugged her skullcap off, revealing the bright shock of orange hair running down the center of her head.

"I'm as excited about a helmet that folds into our suits as you are, but I saw those failure tests," Nik replied. "I'd rather they take their time and make sure they figure out what the heck happened with the seals so we don't die out there. Speaking of not dying . . ." He jabbed a finger at the door behind them.

"Come on, Nik, live a little." She winked her blue eye at him and reached over her shoulder. The magnetic clamps released the moment Jenks's palm touched the sensor, the microsheath flowing away from the tip and down into the hilt.

Guns on spaceships were bad news, and no one yet had the lock on a reliable handheld laser weapon, a fact that Jenks regularly bemoaned even though she was more likely to settle something with fists than with her sword anyway.

The matte black blades of the NeoG weapons were ten centimeters at the widest point and thirty-five centimeters long, with the handle making it an even fifty. A wicked-looking hook curved back toward the hilt a handful of centimeters from the end point.

Nika's favorite trick with that during the competition fights was to hook his opponent's sword and send it flying. In real combat, though, it was equally effective in making folks more concerned about keeping their guts in than fighting him.

Jenks preferred to slap people with the flat of her blade,

which Nika felt was an accurate representation of how each of them approached the world. Jenks would kill if there was a need, but she didn't like it and avoided it right up to the line of endangering her own life.

He hoped neither one of them had to put their philosophies to the test today.

"Tamago and I are on board," Rosa said.

"Copy that, we are proceeding forward," Nika replied, and then turned off his com with a thought. "Jenks?"

She paused at his call, hand hovering over the entrance panel. "What's up?"

"Be careful in there."

"You think it's going to turn into a muck?"

Nika shrugged and reached back to pull his own sword. "It might."

"Can do, then." She blinked twice. "Readings inside are showing three life signs in the front section, two more in the back end by the commander." She highlighted their locations on the shared map. "Front two are just off the engine room and one up on the bridge. The ones in the back are with the pop—uh—people."

"I see them, Jenks," Rosa said. "We'll deal with these two, you and Nika take the trio."

Jenks looked at Nika, one eyebrow raised. The question—*How do you want to do this?*—was floating unsaid on the air. Nika gestured at the door and Jenks opened it.

It was a risk either way, because the commander would kill him if they split up. He'd put either of them in a two-on-one fight, but he also knew it was dangerous odds. Anything could go wrong. But if he and Jenks stayed together and went for engineering first, the one on the bridge could vent the ship if they heard a commotion.

Or engineering could blow the ship if they thought something was up.

He hated this. Snap decisions weren't his forte. Too many things to sort through, too many things that could go wrong. It paralyzed him every damn time, no matter how hard he worked on it. *You are a hell of an officer, Vagin,* he thought bitterly.

"You want an opinion?" There was no sympathy in Jenks's question, something he was always grateful for from her. She continued at his nod. "Let's do the bridge first. We'll take whoever it is out, and I can convince them to call one or both up from engineering. We'll just ambush them on the way. The odds that engineering will blow the ship are only slightly greater than zero. Survival instinct is strong no matter what is going on here."

"You really should have gone to the academy, Jenks."

"Pfft." She rolled her eyes. "I'd be trash as an officer and we both know it. You're the smarter one. I just know how to sneak up on people." Jenks tapped the panel and slipped through the door as it opened.

Nika knew it was more than that, but Jenks was right about the sneaking up on people.

That's how he'd met his adopted sister, when he'd been twenty-three, home on leave to deal with the remnants of his grandmother's life. Jenks had been a fifteen-year-old street dweller his dear grandmother had taken in and neglected to tell him about. Which meant their first meeting had been her thinking he'd broken into his late grandmother's house and trying to brain him with a frying pan.

She'd survived the streets of Krasnodar for eight years, and according to the letter written in his grandmother's shaky hand, she'd been living with her for close to three months.

That day, standing in his *baba*'s kitchen staring down into the girl's wide eyes—one blue, one brown—Nika could hear his grandmother's voice. *"We take in the strays, Nika, and there's nothing wrong with it as long as you open your heart to the hurt that will come. Because you can't save them all—but some is better than none. Just don't lose yourself in the process like your mother did, you understand?"*

And that was how a brand-new ensign in the Near-Earth Orbital Guard had offered a fifteen-year-old girl a permanent place in his family and somehow managed to raise her through his first years in the NeoG without killing both of them.

He'd done something right in the end. Jenks could have split at any point, but not only had she decided to stay, she also fell in love with NeoG and enlisted the morning of her seventeenth birthday.

"Hey."

Nika jumped when Jenks tapped him on the chest, blinking dry eyes and swearing under his breath. "Sorry, took a trip."

"And Commander tells me to focus." She grinned at him. "Let's move."

K. B. Wagers is the author of the Indranan and Farian War trilogies with Orbit Books and the new NeoG novels from Harper Voyager. They hold a bachelor's degree in Russian studies and a second-degree black belt in Shaolin kung fu. Born and raised on a farm in Colorado, K. B. lives at the base of the Rocky Mountains with a pile of spoiled cats. In between books, they aimlessly wander the mountains, scribble down new ideas, and die in video games. You can find them on Twitter @kbwagers, ranting about politics, posting cat photos, and occasionally talking books. They are represented by Andrew Zack of The Zack Company.